Other Novels by

water's Edge

Other Novels by
Robert Whitlow Include

water's Edge
ROBERT WHITLOW

THOMAS NELSON
Since 1798

NASHVILLE DALLAS MEXICO CITY RIO DE JANEIRO

Published in Nashville, Tennessee, by Thomas Nelson. Thomas Nelson is a registered trademark of Thomas Nelson, Inc.

Thomas Nelson, Inc., titles may be purchased in bulk for educational, business, fund-raising, or sales promotional use. For information, please e-mail SpecialMarkets@ThomasNelson.com.

Scripture quotations are taken from THE NEW KING JAMES VERSION. © 1982 by Thomas Nelson, Inc. Used by permission. All rights reserved; and the Holy Bible, New International Version®, NIV®. © 1973, 1978, 1984 by International Bible Society. Used by permission of Zondervan. All rights reserved.

Publisher's note: This novel is a work of fiction. Names, characters, places, and incidents are either products of the author's imagination or used fictitiously. All characters are fictional, and any similarity to people, living or dead, is purely coincidental.

Page design by Mark L. Mabry

Library of Congress Cataloging-in-Publication Data

Whitlow, Robert, 1954-
  Water's edge / Robert Whitlow.
    p. cm.
  ISBN 978-1-59554-451-3 (trade pbk.)
  I. Title.
  PS3573.H49837W37 2011
  813'.54—dc22

                                                              2011014866

Printed in the United States of America

11 12 13 14 15 16 RRD 6 5 4 3 2 1

Stand at the crossroads and look; ask for the ancient paths, ask where the good way is, and walk in it, and you will find rest for your souls . . .

—JEREMIAH 6:16 NIV

To those willing to walk in the ancient paths.

Chiseled deep into the rock face of Stone Mountain, Georgia, is a football field–sized carving of Jefferson Davis, Robert E. Lee, and Stonewall Jackson. Young Atlanta lawyer Tom Crane was on the brink of a promotion as important to him as Lee's selection as commander of the Army of Northern Virginia—litigation partner at Barnes, McGraw, and Crowther.

The phone on Tom's desk buzzed. He picked it up.

"Arthur Pelham from Pelham Financial is on line 802," the receptionist said. "Do you want to take the call?"

"Yes, put him through."

"Good afternoon, Tom."

"Good afternoon, Mr. Pelham," Tom replied in his best professional voice.

"It's time you started calling me Arthur," the sixty-year-old investment adviser replied. "I was Mr. Pelham when you and Rick were playing on the same Little League baseball team in Bethel. You've been earning a paycheck long enough to use my first name."

"I'm not sure I can do that," Tom answered, relaxing. "Would it be okay if I called you Sir Arthur?"

"As long as you stay away from King Arthur." The older man laughed. "I heard too much of that when I was in grade school and someone wanted to pick a fight with me. Listen, I know you must be busy, but do you have a few minutes? It goes back to our conversation at the cemetery after your father's funeral."

"Sure."

"We had a board meeting in New York yesterday, and I brought up the possibility of hiring your law firm to handle some of our litigation load. Most of our clients are happy with our services, but there are always a few bad apples who get upset and file lawsuits for all the crazy reasons you're familiar with."

Tom sat up straighter in his chair. Landing a client like Pelham Financial with offices in New York, Boston, Los Angeles, and Washington, DC, would be the most significant event of his legal career. It would cement his rise to partnership status and give him instant influence at the highest levels of the firm.

"That would be outstanding," Tom said, trying to contain his excitement. "Would I be the primary contact person for your firm?"

"Yes, you're the man I trust. Lance Snyder, our general counsel, wasn't at the meeting yesterday, and I want to get his input before making a final decision. Until that happens and I get back to you, I'd ask you to keep this conversation confidential."

"Of course."

"Excellent. I'll be in touch with you by the first of next week." Arthur paused. "How are you doing personally?"

"Okay. I have to make a trip to Bethel soon to shut down my father's practice. Bernice Lawson is contacting his clients, but there are things only I can do. The trick is finding the time to work it into my schedule."

"You're not too busy to take on more business, are you?"

"No, no," Tom answered quickly. "And if I have the opportunity to represent Pelham Financial, it will become my top priority."

"That's what I like to hear. Every client believes his files are the most important matters on his lawyer's desk."

"With you, that will be true."

"Excellent. I hoped this would be a good time to bring this up with you."

"Yes, sir. It couldn't be better."

The call ended. Stunned, Tom sat at his desk and gazed out the window. Stone Mountain never came into focus. Future potential always outshines faded glory.

The following morning Tom and Mark Nelson, another senior associate in the securities litigation group, were in a small conference room down the hall from Tom's office. Spread before them were documents delivered the previous evening from a regional stock brokerage firm that had been sued by a small group of disgruntled investors who lost several million dollars in a corporate bond fund.

"What are we missing?" the dark-haired Mark asked. "Each of the plaintiffs signed comprehensive acknowledgment and disclosure documents. They knew the risks before they invested a dime."

The two lawyers worked in silence for several minutes. Tom laid out a complete set of the disclosure forms so that the signature pages were side by side, then carefully inspected them.

"Take a look at this," Tom said to Mark. "The handwriting for the signatures is similar, even though the names are different."

He slid the documents across the table to Mark, who held them up in front of his face.

"Maybe."

"Particularly the *m, p, t,* and *w*," Tom continued. "And one is from a man, the other a woman."

"So?"

"Yet both are written in a feminine style."

Mark leaned over for a closer look. "The originating broker on both accounts is a woman, Misty Kaiser. If you're claiming she forged both signatures, it doesn't fit the gender and makes you a chauvinist."

"Unless Ms. Kaiser is like the girl you dated last year who took you on a ten-mile hike and had to stop and wait for you to catch up every fifteen minutes."

"It was every thirty minutes, and I've got the right girl now," Mark replied, tossing a crumpled piece of paper at Tom's head. "Megan may not be as flashy as Clarice, but she's not texting me in the middle of important meetings demanding that I pick up her dry cleaning and stop for Chinese takeout on the way home."

"What about the signatures?" Tom persisted.

Mark shrugged. "I have to admit the handwriting is similar. Should we get an expert to take a look at them?"

"Maybe. But first let's find out if Kaiser is still with the company. I don't want to bring up something this inflammatory based on a random suspicion."

"I'll call Sam Robinson, the human resources director," Mark said. "He'll also know whether there are complaints on file from any of her other clients."

Tom looked at his watch. "Why don't we circle back this afternoon? I have a meeting with McGraw in a few minutes."

Mark sat up straighter. "Are you going to talk to him about a partnership?"

"That's for him to bring up, not me," Tom answered evenly.

"You know McGraw. His agenda will be my agenda. I scheduled this meeting to ask for time off so I can close down my father's practice in Bethel."

"Okay, but just to let you know, I'm putting my name in for a promotion," Mark said.

"I wouldn't expect anything else. I'm going to let them know I'm interested too."

"What are you going to say if they ask us to critique each other?"

With the conversation with Arthur Pelham in his pocket, Tom knew the time would soon be right to broach the partnership issue with McGraw; however, he didn't want to hurt Mark.

"Becoming a partner isn't about cutting you down," Tom replied. "I'm going to make my case, not criticize you."

Mark took a deep breath and sighed. "They've been watching both of us for years. Nothing we say now is probably going to make much difference. But you can imagine how stressed out I am. I've been here almost eight years. If I don't make partner soon . . ."

Mark didn't finish the sentence. He didn't have to.

Tom stood in front of the gold-framed mirror in the hallway on the thirty-sixth floor and straightened his tie. Six feet tall with broad shoulders, wavy brown hair, and dark-brown eyes, he was wearing the blue suit he usually reserved for court appearances. Reid McGraw was an old-school lawyer who sneered at business-casual attire. If Tom wanted to become a partner, he'd better start dressing like one.

The trip to the thirty-seventh floor was a journey to another world. Tom's floor was a beehive of activity with lawyers and support staff crammed into every available inch of space. Phone conversations spilled out from scores of cubicles. Humming copy machines spit out reams of paper. People walked fast, talked fast, and worked frantically because every tenth of an hour was billable time. On the floor above them, the senior partners operated from spacious offices with individual secretaries. Millions of dollars were discussed as casually as thousands.

Tom passed the office formerly occupied by his boss, Brett Bollinger. Tom liked Brett's cherry desk. When he moved to the thirty-seventh floor, he'd keep it. The beige carpet, on the other hand, would have to go. Something with a pattern would be nice. Clarice had a good eye for decorating.

McGraw's office was a corner suite with its own reception area. The senior partner's assistant was a very attractive young woman about Tom's age. When she was hired, Tom thought about asking her out; however, the risk was too great. If she didn't like him, it might cause her to make a sour comment to McGraw. His future at the firm couldn't be subject to the whim of a woman.

"Hey, Marie," Tom said when he entered the secretary's office. "Is he available? I know I'm a minute or two early."

The dark-haired secretary removed her headset and leaned forward with a glistening white smile.

"Go in. He's waiting for you. But don't run off when you're finished. I have a question for you."

"Sure," Tom said as he opened the door.

McGraw's desk was positioned where the exterior glass walls came together. The balding, medium-built attorney was turned sideways and staring at his computer screen. Through one glass wall Tom could see the gold-plated dome of the state capitol.

"Come in," McGraw growled in his deep voice.

"Hello, Tom," another man said.

Olson Crowther, the partner in charge of the corporate and real estate division of the firm, was sitting in a leather wing chair to the right of McGraw's desk. Crowther, a former JAG officer, sported a high and tight haircut. He stood and shook Tom's hand. Seeing two of the principal partners in the same room caused a rush of excitement mixed with anxiety to wash over Tom.

"Have a seat," McGraw said, pointing to a leather side chair in front of his desk. "We're waiting on Joe Barnes to join us on a conference call. He just got back from Spain and is working from home today. Marie should have him on the line shortly."

"Okay," Tom said, his mouth dry.

McGraw turned his attention back to his computer.

"Sorry about your father," Crowther said. "Did you receive the card I sent?"

"Yes, sir. Thanks."

"Did the police determine what happened?"

"No one knows for sure. They were fishing from a small boat on a private pond. It wasn't more than fifteen feet deep."

"Life jackets?"

"No. The authorities think the boat capsized. My father was a decent swimmer. Maybe he tried to help the other man and failed."

"Real shame," McGraw grunted.

Tom cleared his throat. "Speaking of my father, I need to spend a week or so in Bethel shutting down his law practice. There isn't much to it. After that's done, I can totally devote myself to my responsibilities here. Now that Brett's gone, I'd like the opportunity to—"

Marie's voice came over the intercom. "Mr. Barnes on line 803."

McGraw pushed a button. "Joe, are you there?"

"Yeah, but I'm still battling jet lag. The older I get, the harder it is to bounce back from these overseas trips. And in two weeks

I'm off again to New Zealand. Do you remember the river where we caught those monster trout?"

"Yes."

"I'm set up with the same guide."

The fact that Joe Barnes, the founder of the firm, was on the phone meant only one thing. Tom's hands began to sweat.

"Wish I were going with you," McGraw said. "Olson and I are here with Tom Crane."

"Have you told him what happened with Crutchfield Financial?"

"No," McGraw answered.

Barnes spoke. "Tom, we've lost Crutchfield to King and Spalding."

Tom raised his eyebrows in surprise. Crutchfield Financial was one of the firm's largest clients. Its senior management didn't hesitate to file lawsuits to enforce their will and rarely settled claims until the eve of trial. Tom racked his brain for any way the litigation group might have contributed to losing the client. Nothing came to mind.

"Uh, that's too bad," he said.

"Aaron Crutchfield would have stayed with us," Barnes replied, "but there's been a power shift on the board of directors since Aaron retired, and the new chairman has strong connections with King and Spalding."

Tom licked his lips. "Are they going to pull all their litigation files?"

"Yes," McGraw answered. "Rumors have been flying for several months. That's one reason Brett took the general counsel job with Fairfield Group. As general counsel, he'll be able to keep Fairfield from bolting."

It was the perfect time for Tom to drop his bombshell about the call from Arthur Pelham. He clenched his teeth. Arthur's specific instructions to keep quiet about hiring the firm kept the news bottled up in Tom's throat.

"Our business from Linden Securities has been picking up," Tom said, bringing up a second-tier source of business. "Mark and I were working on a major lawsuit this morning. That should take care of some of the slack caused—"

"No, it won't," McGraw interrupted. "I talked with Bruce Cathay in Macon yesterday. There's overt fraud in that case. It's going to be a damage-control situation."

"Forged signatures on the disclosure documents?" Tom asked, shocked that his suspicions might be true.

"You talked with him too." McGraw nodded. "They fired the woman involved, and the insurance company on the fidelity bond is going to assume responsibility for defense of the case. They'll have their own counsel. The bottom line is we're going to have to make another cut in my litigation group, and you're it."

Tom's mouth dropped open. "I'm being fired?"

"No, no," Barnes replied from the speakerphone. "It's a staffing consolidation move."

Barnes's euphemism didn't change the result.

"When?" Tom asked numbly.

"Effective the end of the day," Barnes replied. "The firm will give you a good reference and pay a month's severance in addition to your accrued vacation and personal leave time. You've worked hard, and this was a difficult decision. That's why I wanted to be part of the conversation. I hope you appreciate that."

"Yes, sir," Tom mumbled.

"Very well. I'm going to grab a nap to knock back this jet lag," Barnes said. "You gentlemen finish without me."

The phone clicked off. Tom didn't move.

"There's not much else to discuss," McGraw said. "Bring Mark up to speed on any cases you've been handling solo this afternoon. He and I will reassign them."

"Is he going to make partner?" Tom blurted out.

"That wouldn't be appropriate for us to discuss with you, would it?" Crowther replied with a tight smile. "You heard Joe. We appreciate the work you've done, and I'm confident you'll find a good place to land. In the meantime, you can take all the time you need to settle your father's affairs without feeling rushed. My father was a small-town CPA, and it took twice as long to administer his estate than I thought."

"I'll send out a firm-wide memo about the change in your status within an hour," McGraw added. "Nothing negative about you."

Crowther stood and extended his hand to Tom. "Best of luck to you, son. You've been well trained and can take that with you wherever you go."

McGraw turned toward his computer screen. The meeting over, Tom stumbled from the office. He passed Marie's desk, faintly hearing her call his name as he dashed down the hall. Olson Crowther had made Tom's tenure at the firm sound like an advanced class at a canine obedience school. The dog part of the comparison was right. Tom felt like a loyal pet dropped from a car in the middle of the city and left to fend for itself.

The hustle and bustle of activity on the thirty-sixth floor now had a discordant tone. The first person Tom saw was a middle-aged paralegal who spent half her time working on Crutchfield files. His firing wouldn't be the only fallout crashing down from the thirty-seventh floor. He resisted the urge to grab the woman and suggest she clock out early so she could take her ten-year-old son to Chastain Park and play catch with a Frisbee. Tom avoided making eye contact with anyone until he reached his office and shut the door. Plopping down in his chair, he swiveled to the side and looked out the window. Stone Mountain hadn't moved; Tom's world had crumbled like a dried clump of red clay.

chapter
TWO

O n the corner of Tom's desk was a glass paperweight, a gift from his father, shaped like a miniature rainbow trout. Beneath the paperweight were John Crane's last words, a typically cryptic message delivered to Tom's administrative assistant. The phone call came in while Tom was out of town taking depositions. Before Tom could return the call, he'd received the news that John Crane had drowned. Tom removed the paperweight and, for the hundredth time, read the note:

> I've been fishing in a new spot, and the water is too deep for me.
>
> Can you come home for a few days and help me out?

Tom crumpled the note and threw it in the trash. It was time to get rid of the worthless stuff he'd accumulated during his time at the firm. A message from his father that didn't make sense was a good place to start. Tom had emptied two drawers of his desk when the phone buzzed.

"Clarice is on line 750," his assistant said.

Tom's girlfriend worked in the marketing department of a

major soft-drink manufacturer. In her world, success was measured by a half-percent increase in sales to the Brazilian market.

"I'm trying to decide the best colors to include in a pie chart," she said in her slightly shrill voice. "Do you think it's tacky to put magenta next to yellow? The new outfit I bought last week, you know, the one with the magenta top and yellow sweater, looks nice, doesn't it? That's what gave me the idea."

"They go well together. And you look super in the outfit." Tom paused for a second. "I just got fired."

"Fired from what?" The natural tension in Clarice's voice ratcheted up a notch.

"My job. They called it a staffing consolidation, but the end result is the same."

"What did you do wrong?"

"Nothing."

"That doesn't make any sense."

Tom told her about the meeting with the senior partners without revealing the names of the clients involved.

"At first I thought you meant you'd been fired by one of your clients," Clarice said in a more subdued voice when he finished. "Where are you now?"

"In my office."

"They didn't seize your computer and escort you out of the building? That's what happens here when someone gets axed."

"No. McGraw asked me to work to the end of the day."

"Do you think they're letting you down easy? I mean, there had to be something you messed up."

So far, Clarice was failing miserably in the comforting words department.

"No."

"Didn't Brett Bollinger recommend you for his position?"

"Yeah, but I guess his influence ended when he left the firm. I don't have a clue why I became a target."

The phone was silent for a moment.

"Did you miss a statue of limitations? A girl in our legal department did that last month and got canned on the spot."

"It's statute of limitations. And no, I didn't."

"Don't try to make me look dumb," Clarice replied with a snort. "I'm doing my best to help."

"Of course you are. Look, I'm pretty shook up. I'll see you at home."

"I have to work late, so don't forget to pick up dinner. I'm in the mood for Chinese again. You'll feel better after you drink a glass of wine and eat a couple of spring rolls."

Clarice ended the call. Tom placed his phone on the desk. It was going to take more than wine and spring rolls to get him through this crisis.

———

The hour that passed before McGraw's e-mail hit Tom's in-box seemed like a week. When the senior partner's name finally popped up on his screen, Tom counted to five before opening it.

> Tom Crane will be leaving the firm at the end of the day. We wish
> him well in his future legal endeavors.

A couple of minutes later there was a knock on his door.

"Come in," he said, steeling himself for an onslaught of sympathy that might or might not be genuine.

Mark Nelson, his laptop under his right arm, stuck his head

through the doorway. "I got a terse memo from McGraw ordering me to meet with you about your files. A minute later the one about you leaving the firm hit my server. I called McGraw's office to get more details, but he didn't have time to talk to me." Mark ran his hand through his hair. "Did the request for time off to shut down your father's practice have anything to do with it? I had a feeling that wouldn't sit well with McGraw."

"No."

Mark came in and closed the door behind him. "What happened?"

"McGraw didn't send you anything about Crutchfield Financial?"

"No."

Tom broke the news.

"That will be bad for a lot of people," Mark replied. "Did my name come up?"

"Only in connection with reassignment of files."

"I'm sorry, man."

Tom studied Mark for a moment. He didn't sense any phoniness in his colleague. They weren't close friends, but they'd been through many legal wars together. Combat of any type has a way of bonding men together.

"I thought you'd be the one to make partner." Mark shrugged. "I'd even started floating my résumé to other firms a month ago. Last week I had an interview with a medium-sized firm in Sandy Springs."

"But if our firm—" Tom corrected himself: "If Barnes, McGraw, and Crowther lets you stay—"

"I'll hang around. The other job was a pay cut, but at least it was a job. I can't expect Megan to start married life with a husband drawing unemployment benefits." Mark sat down across from Tom and opened his laptop. "I bet Sweet and Becker would offer you a job, maybe even a partnership on the spot. You've hammered them several times, and Nate Becker has a lot of respect for you."

"How do you know that?" Tom asked in surprise.

"He told me. A friend and I signed up to play in a charity golf tournament and ended up in a foursome with Becker and one of his associates. He talked about you the whole round and asked me a bunch of questions."

"Why didn't you tell me about this?"

"Would you have cared?"

"No," Tom admitted. "It would only have fueled my ego."

"And today your ego needs a little fuel. But Becker wasn't asking for social reasons. You're on his radar as a possible hire."

Sweet and Becker was a solid law firm, not nearly as large as Barnes, McGraw, and Crowther but with a good core of clients. On the downside, the smaller firm might not be a suitable match for Pelham Financial.

"Don't start daydreaming about your next job yet," Mark said, interrupting Tom's thoughts. "Turn on your computer, and let's get started on the transition. If the firm is going to fire me, I don't want it to be because I fumbled a handoff from you."

Mark already knew bits and pieces about most of Tom's cases because of biweekly status meetings. When they reached the new Linden Securities case, Tom mentioned what McGraw told him about the fraud committed by their client's broker. Mark raised his eyebrows.

"What did McGraw say when you told him you already suspected that?"

"I didn't get a chance. It came up after he cut me loose. If I'd interrupted him at that point, it would have seemed like a last-ditch effort to save my job."

Personnel decisions by the partners, no matter how capricious or arbitrary, rarely affected bottom-line profit. There was always a fresh pool of top-notch legal talent anxious for the opportunity to work at a place like Barnes, McGraw, and Crowther. Tom felt degraded that his status had changed from "Future Partner" to "Former Associate," a description forever synonymous with failure. As he and Mark worked, Tom struggled to push his disappointment and hurt feelings aside.

"Let me know when you're ready to leave," Mark said when they finished. He closed his laptop. "I'll help you carry your stuff to your car."

All Tom's personal belongings fit neatly into four boxes. He'd decided to leave quietly. At 5:30 p.m. there was a knock on the door and Mark entered.

"I knew you'd try to sneak out. I'm not going to let that happen."

"I can handle it," Tom said. "It will only take a couple of trips."

"Don't argue."

On their way to the elevator they passed the cubicle where Allyson Faschille, the administrative assistant who'd taken the last phone call from John Crane, worked. She glanced up.

"Bye, Tom. I'll miss you. Best of luck. Congratulations, Mark. I'll miss you too."

Tom turned to Mark. "Congratulations?"

"I'll fill you in once we're on the elevator."

The elevator door opened, and they stepped inside.

"Did you accept the job with the firm in Sandy Springs?"

"No."

"But Allyson said she would miss you too."

Mark stared straight ahead. "I had a meeting with McGraw after you and I went over your cases. I'm moving upstairs into Brett's office. Allyson and I won't be working together."

Tom's jaw dropped open. "They made you a partner?"

"Yeah," Mark replied with an apologetic look on his face. "It's as much a shock to me as it is to you."

"Did he tell you why?"

"If you mean why me and not you, the answer is no. He mentioned I was doing a good job, then gave me a big stack of paperwork to read and sign. It was over in less than five minutes."

The elevator reached the ground floor. Tom stumbled into the foyer.

"I wanted you to hear the news from me," Mark said. "If I had the authority, I'd tell you to take that stuff back to your office."

The two men walked in silence to the parking deck and put the boxes in the trunk of Tom's car. It was an awkward moment.

"That's great news for you and Megan," Tom said, hoping his face didn't reveal the struggle inside. "You need the security that comes with a partnership more than I do."

Mark smiled. "Man, you should have heard her scream when I called and told her the news. She's probably online looking for houses right now."

Tom tried to smile, too, but suspected it looked a bit crooked.

"Give me a call as soon as you're back in town so we can grab lunch," Mark said. "And keep me in the loop on your job search. Now that I'm a partner I can write a killer letter of recommendation for you."

"Thanks," Tom managed. "I'll do that."

Tom sat in the driver's seat of his car for a few seconds and wondered if he would have been as gracious as Mark if their situations had been reversed. He watched the excited new partner disappear through the door leading to the office tower. Tom drove out of the parking deck. There were a lot of emotional potholes on the road to unemployment. So far, Tom felt like he'd hit every one.

Tom could get home in less than thirty minutes unless he had to stop off for Chinese, Mexican, Japanese, Indian, Jamaican, or one of the other types of ethnic food craved by Clarice. Tom's girlfriend grew up shuttled between divorced parents, neither of whom cooked. To her, take-home was the same as home cooked.

There were four apartments in the two-story building where Tom lived. It was an older structure with high ceilings, crown molding, chair rails, and dark wood floors. His apartment was on the ground level. He parked in a reserved spot off the street beside a high privacy fence that sealed in a tiny backyard. The smell of the food on the car seat made his stomach growl.

As soon as he opened the door, Tom was greeted by the throaty bark of a large, mostly brown dog that Clarice insisted would easily win the ugliest dog in Atlanta contest. Tom acquired the furry animal when a girlfriend prior to Clarice dragged him to the local humane society one Saturday morning.

While Tom waited at the shelter, he stood in front of a cage that contained a brownish-black animal with long legs, floppy ears, square jaw, furry tail, and black tongue that protruded slightly from the right side of its mouth. The dog looked at Tom with bloodshot eyes that would have shamed a drunk.

"What is it?" he asked a middle-aged woman serving as a volunteer.

"It's your dog," she responded brightly. "See the way he's looking at you? He's been neutered and had all his shots."

Tom shook his head. "Neutering him was a good idea. Puppies that look like that wouldn't be good for the canine gene pool. Is he housebroken?"

"Probably, although we can't guarantee that sort of thing. Dogs respond well to routine. Do you see the nose and ears?"

"They're hard to ignore."

"Based on those features, I suspect he has a significant percentage of bloodhound. The black tongue and furry tail most likely come from a chow. The brindle coat doesn't go with the solid-brown head, so that part is a mystery. I'll bring him out so you can get a closer look."

"No thanks."

"At least let him lick your hand." The woman reached for the latch on the cage. "Dogs in this area are scheduled to be euthanized on Monday."

Tom muttered while the woman opened the door of the cage. The dog ambled over and sniffed Tom's hand, then leaned against his leg. Tom reluctantly rubbed the top of the mutt's head, causing the animal to emit a low moan of pleasure.

"I already have a cat," Tom said to the volunteer.

"Cats are great pets, but a dog like this will be devoted to you forever and ask for nothing except love in return."

Tom's girlfriend returned with a frisky golden retriever on a leash.

"What's that?" she asked when she saw Tom and the ugly dog.

"Ask her." Tom pointed to the volunteer. "She can tell you all about him while I fill out the adoption paperwork."

The first time Tom brought the dog home, the beast put his nose to the floor and began crisscrossing the living room like a four-legged vacuum cleaner. Whiskers, Tom's calico cat, retreated to the top of the sofa with intense suspicion. As he watched the dog's antics, Tom considered naming him Vacuum, but a more suitable name immediately came to mind.

"Rover," he said with a satisfied nod of his head. "If a dog ever deserved that name, you're it."

Rover turned out to be thoroughly housebroken, never jumped on the furniture, ignored Whiskers, and didn't chew Tom's shoes. However, for all his good qualities, Rover had one bad one—he couldn't keep stray drops of drool from leaking out the side of his mouth. Every so often, Tom had to do a quick run through the apartment with a damp mop to remove the residue.

The girlfriend and her golden retriever left Tom's life shortly after Rover entered it. Dragging Tom to the humane society was the best thing she ever did.

Rover sniffed the paper bag in Tom's hand before leading the way into the small kitchen. Whiskers didn't move from her spot on top of the sofa. Tom placed the food in the oven on low to keep it warm, then changed into exercise clothes for a fast thirty minutes on the treadmill. Rover lay in the corner of the spare bedroom with his head on his paws and a look on his face that questioned Tom's sanity for running in place.

When he saw the lights of Clarice's car flash through the windows of the kitchen, Tom took the food out of the oven and lit a candle in the middle of the tiny round table where he and Clarice ate their meals. The front door opened. Rover woofed but didn't leave Tom's side.

"Yum. I can smell dinner out here!" she called out.

Clarice walked into the kitchen and kicked off her shoes. Whiskers followed and brushed against her leg. Tall and shapely, with blond hair and blue eyes, Clarice Charbonneau had attracted Tom's attention at a pro-am golf tournament twelve months earlier. For the past eight months they'd not dated anyone else.

"Magellan was in a horrible mood today," she continued. "Three people were royally chewed out during the planning session. I kept my mouth shut, but it made me wonder why I put up with the stress he stirs up every time he comes into town. If he was based here instead of L.A., it would be unbearable." Clarice paused. "Oh, I went with the magenta next to the yellow and held my breath during the meeting. Magellan didn't comment on it one way or the other. Alice thought it was pretty."

Clarice continued talking while she washed her hands in the kitchen sink, then took a bottle of wine from a small wooden rack. She poured two glasses and held one out to Tom, who took it from her.

"Here's to your future," she said, looking him in the eyes. "Barnes, McGraw, and Crowther lost a brilliant young lawyer today. Their loss will be someone else's gain."

They clinked glasses and took a sip of wine.

"That's what you think?" Tom asked.

"Of course." Clarice sniffed. "After the shock wore off, I was furious. The loyalty-and-hard-work thing you tried doesn't work in the twenty-first century. Law firms are getting to be more and more like big corporations where everyone is as disposable as a plastic water bottle. But don't worry. You'll collect a half-dozen job offers within a month and take your pick. Then, someday you'll get a case with McGraw on the other side and teach him a lesson. Let's eat."

Clarice handled chopsticks like an expert. The two slender pieces of wood frustrated Tom, and he defaulted to a fork. They divided the food, with Tom taking two spring rolls. While they ate, Clarice prattled about her day at work and a phone call with her mother, who lived in Sarasota.

"Mom was completely out of line," Clarice said between bites. "I told her it was none of her business whether Nicholas goes to culinary school in Charleston instead of getting his MBA at Wake Forest. He's paying his own way, and she can't order him around like she did when we were kids. And with a name like Charbonneau, any restaurant would be thrilled to hire him. Of course, she didn't listen. All she wanted to do was vent."

Tom had met Clarice's mother on two occasions. Her venting reminded him of a volcanic eruption.

"You don't think I'm like her, do you?" Clarice asked, stopping to take a sip of wine.

"Not at all."

"Liar," Clarice replied with a smile. "But I like it when you tell me what I want to hear."

"Your mother has unresolved issues."

"You think so?" Clarice responded, rubbing her temples with the tips of her fingers. "Every time she blows up, it scares me that I'll end up the same. It took me an hour to calm down after she called."

"Was that before or after I phoned about losing my job?"

"After, which partly explains how I felt. Like I said, I was already upset."

"Did you mention my situation to your mother?"

"No, that would have made her talk for another thirty minutes, and I couldn't risk that with Magellan on the rampage."

They finished dinner and the bottle of wine. Clarice had been right. The meal and the drinks calmed Tom down. Then they watched a sentimental movie that made Clarice cry. When the movie was over, she yawned.

"I'd better head home," she said. Clarice shared an apartment with another young woman in a modern complex about ten minutes away. "I have to be up early in the morning for a red-eye meeting at work before Magellan flies back to the West Coast. After that I'm going to Savannah and won't be back until midday Saturday."

"Why Savannah?"

"A photo shoot. There's no need for me to be there, but Magellan wants to make sure the photographer knows how to focus the camera." Clarice touched Tom's hand. "We could have a lot of fun."

"No, I'm going to use this time to close out my father's practice in Bethel."

"And you're leaving tomorrow?"

"The sooner I start, the sooner I'll finish." Tom paused. "And I need to get out of the city for a few days to clear my head."

"How long will you be gone?"

"A couple of weeks at the most. Then I can dive into the job market."

Tom told her about Mark's conversation with Nate Becker.

"See, I told you," Clarice said and nodded when he finished. "There will be a bidding war for your services. But it will be lonely without you."

"You could stay here and take care of Whiskers and Rover. They're great company."

Clarice pulled back. "Whiskers is fine, but I'm not babysitting that dog by myself. Can't he go with you?"

Rover, who was lying at Tom's feet, looked up and gave a moan that started as a deep rumble and ended as a high-pitched whine.

"See, that's all he does when you're gone," Clarice said. "Just hearing about you leaving sends him into the pits. When you were in Miami taking depositions last month, he moped around the house the whole time and slobbered twice as much as usual. I couldn't go barefoot and almost slipped and fell in a nasty wet spot he left in the kitchen."

"Okay, okay. I'll take Rover. I just hope Uncle Elias likes him more than you do."

Clarice stood and stretched. "Hanging out with your uncle and the dog should be interesting. My mother isn't the only one with issues. Your relatives have their share too."

"You only met Elias once."

"Which was enough. I'm glad you're not like *him*," Clarice said with emphasis. "While you're there you can collect the inheritance coming from your father. That should tide you over, and if you need help spending any of it, I'm available."

Tom swallowed. He'd kept information about his father's affairs private.

"There isn't much in his estate," he said.

"You're kidding. He was a lawyer for over thirty years."

"Who didn't make a lot of money and did a bad job managing what he earned. I had to put the funeral bill on a credit card. After he sold the house and moved in with Elias, he gave most of his money away."

"Gave it away?"

"He supported a bunch of religious causes, and there's no shortage of them holding out their hands. The worst part is he didn't keep back enough from the sale of the house to pay the federal tax due on his gain. I don't know what he was thinking. Anyway, he worked out a payment plan with the IRS but was only partway through it when he died. There are thousands still owing. Also, he hadn't paid any estimated tax on the income he earned at the law firm for the current fiscal year. I haven't run all the numbers, but after the government is paid, there may not be enough left to justify probating the will."

"That's wrong," Clarice responded emphatically. "Your father should have thought about you first when it came to his money. This makes me madder than you losing your job. At least McGraw was your boss, not your dad."

"It hurt," Tom admitted. "But then I haven't paid a lot of attention to him for the past few years."

"Which is no reason to leave a mess for you to clean up." Clarice waved her finger in the air. "If your father was such a godly man, he would have paid the government its due and left something for you to enjoy, not given his money away to strangers. I can't imagine my parents doing that to me. Why didn't you tell me about this?"

"I was embarrassed," Tom replied with a shrug.

"Yeah, I can see why." Clarice stepped back. "I'd better get going."

"And you'll pick up Whiskers tomorrow?"

"After the meeting with Magellan. Brittany can help out while I'm in Savannah."

After Clarice left, Tom turned on the gas logs in the small fireplace in the living room and sat in a leather recliner watching the flames. The harsh reality that John Crane had left him nothing except the hassle of dealing with the IRS and the responsibility of closing down a law practice hurt more than Tom wanted to admit.

While the fire flickered, Rover lay at Tom's feet. The dog's world was simple. His master's presence was enough to bring him contentment. No such person inhabited Tom's world. He was as isolated as a castaway on a desert island, a man alone in a city of millions.

chapter
THREE

The following morning Tom unpacked the boxes he'd brought home from the office. He took out the photo of his mother taken during a trip to Callaway Gardens when he was five years old. Quiet and reserved, she taught high school English composition and literature for twenty years. Her death from breast cancer when Tom was a junior in high school took away the only ears he knew would listen.

Caught in a web of joint grief, Tom and his father shared space in the same house for a year and a half until Tom left for college. By the time he graduated four years later, Tom had convinced himself that he'd grown stronger through the tragedy because it forced him to be more self-reliant. This became a mantra, and he repeated the theory whenever he told someone about his past. Not everyone was convinced. A girl Tom dated shortly after moving to Atlanta told him it sounded like something a redneck football coach would tell one of his players. They only went out to dinner once after that.

Tom's cell phone buzzed. It was an unfamiliar number.

"Hello," he said.

"Tom, it's Arthur. I called your office, and the receptionist told me you no longer work at the firm. What in the world happened?"

Tom's stomach twisted into a knot.

"I met with the three main partners after you and I talked yesterday. We lost a major client. I was the first of several casualties."

"Did you tell them about our conversation?"

"No. You asked me to keep it confidential until you had a chance to talk with Mr. Snyder. I didn't want to violate your instructions."

"Talking to Lance was a formality. If I'd known your job was in jeopardy, I would have given you permission to bring it up. Who's the real decision maker at the firm? Give me his direct number. I'll call him as soon as we hang up and get this straightened out."

Tom was shocked. It wasn't the response he'd expected.

"Uh, I'm not sure how they operate. But I doubt they'd be willing to change their minds—" Tom stopped.

Joe Barnes, Reid McGraw, and Olson Crowther would do anything to entice Pelham Financial into their fold. They'd reinstate him in a second and might even throw a cocktail party to celebrate his return. But asking Arthur to step in made him feel like a kid on a baseball team begging his father to intervene with the coach. It ran counter to every independent bone in Tom's body.

"Thanks," he said. "But it's time for me to move on. If I can't trust the judgment of the people I'm working with, Barnes, McGraw, and Crowther isn't the place I want to be for the long term."

"I can appreciate that," Arthur replied thoughtfully. "I've had the same conversation with employees over the years. Trust among coworkers is as much a key to our business as it is to yours. But are you sure about this?"

Tom searched his heart one last time. He knew if he turned

down Arthur's offer of help, it was the end of one road. Where the next road might lead was uncertain.

"I've cut the tie," Tom said with finality. "When I find another job, I'll let you know if the new law firm can provide the kind of representation you deserve."

"That will take time to determine."

"Yes, sir, because you deserve the best legal advice available. Do I have your permission to contact you if I end up with another firm that might be a good fit for Pelham?"

"Of course. And with your father gone, you have an open invitation to ask my advice about anything. Do you have my cell and direct phone numbers?"

"No, sir."

The older man gave the numbers to Tom, who entered them into his phone.

"Tom, I'm sorry about the job," Arthur said. "I know it stings, but this isn't a failure. It's a stepping-stone to something better. I've seen it happen over and over."

"I believe that," Tom replied with more confidence than he felt.

"Don't hesitate to call."

"I won't."

"Good-bye, son."

Midmorning, Tom left for a couple of hours to run errands before leaving town. When he returned and walked through the living room on the way to his bedroom, Whiskers wasn't in her usual place on top of the sofa. Tom stuck his head in the kitchen. The cat wasn't in her second-favorite spot in the corner beside the oven.

"Whiskers!"

Going into the bedroom, Tom opened the door to his walk-in closet, the cat's secret hideaway. What he saw stopped him in his tracks.

All his shirts, suits, and pants were neatly lined up in a row. On the left were his casual clothes and the heavy winter coat he wore on the few days in Atlanta when the temperature dipped into the teens. But the section of the closet he'd vacated so Clarice could keep a few outfits available at his apartment was empty. Feeling like he did when his car was once towed from a downtown parking lot, he stared at the empty spot as if the clothes would magically reappear. They didn't. He glanced over his shoulder at the bed and saw an envelope on the bedspread. He took out a heavily scented piece of paper.

Tom,

What's happened the past twenty-four hours has made it clear to me that it's time for both of us to move on. Your trip to Bethel makes the separation easier. If you find anything else that belongs to me at the apartment, let me know. Whiskers is with me. I promised to watch her while you're out of town, but what I'd really like to do is keep her as a positive reminder of the fun times we've had together.

Hugs,
Clarice

Move on. It was the same phrase Tom had used when he told Arthur Pelham that he didn't want help getting his job reinstated at the law firm. Apparently Clarice thought about Tom the same way he did about Reid McGraw. Opportunities to become more self-reliant were coming faster than he could process them. He lowered the note so Rover could sniff it.

"She perfumes a note breaking up with me and wants the cat?" he said to the dog. "I can only hope she and Whiskers will be as happy together as I am with you."

Returning to the kitchen, Tom thought about the girl who'd taken him to the humane society the day he first met Rover. Her fate would be his. In a few years, Tom would be a barely remembered footnote in the book of Clarice's life, Whiskers an entire chapter. He dropped the envelope and note in the trash can and closed the lid.

Tom sat at the small table where he and Clarice had eaten many ethnic meals together. There was no use delaying a response. Tom's fingers raced across the phone keypad.

You're right. Whiskers is yours. Best of luck. Tom.

An hour later Tom's car crawled through Friday afternoon traffic. Rover lay contentedly in the passenger seat of the car, a towel positioned to catch any stray saliva. It was a hundred miles north and a hundred years back in time from Atlanta to Bethel.

Once clear of gridlock, they traveled another hour before leaving the interstate for a cross-country drive through a rolling rural landscape dotted with weathered farmhouses, an occasional cluster of mobile homes, and massive new estates that were surrounded by horses grazing behind long white fences and Angus cattle in herds near small ponds. The owners of the estate properties were akin to eighteenth-century English gentry who made their money in the city and moved to the country to enjoy it.

Bethel was nestled in the northwest corner of the state. Uncle Elias, the family historian, claimed the original member of the Crane family came to America from England in 1825 and migrated to Etowah County shortly after the Cherokees were expelled from the region in 1837. When he was a boy, Tom found bucket loads of Indian artifacts in the fields that surrounded the ancestral home where Elias now lived.

The population of Bethel remained stagnant until 1910 when a railroad spur connected the community to the surrounding region. This led to an economic boom that changed the region—the growth of the textile industry. Words like *creeling, spinning, tufting,* and *doffing* became part of the local vocabulary. Cash wages replaced share-cropping. People moved *to* Bethel, not away from it. Men became supervisors in the mills and built houses in town. Plant managers joined the country club established by the owners of the mills. Then, after two generations of prosperity, the bottom dropped out. Even the low pay in the area's nonunionized mills couldn't compete with the minuscule wages paid to workers in China, Guatemala, Pakistan, and a score of other countries. Mills closed. Those that stayed open became niche manufacturers for the most expensive garments. Then help came from an unexpected source.

Arthur Pelham saved his hometown.

Pelham Financial refurbished a bankrupt textile mill building and hired five hundred people to perform telephone marketing, cus-tomer assistance, data entry, mail processing, bookkeeping, clerical activities, and other support functions that didn't require a high level of formal training or professional licensure.

When he was in Bethel, Arthur lived in a restored home near the center of town. The antebellum Parker-Baldwin house was already the grandest residence in town when Arthur bought it. He then poured a large sum into a major restoration. Now the house appeared in guide-books about places to see in north Georgia.

Tom crossed the shallow creek that marked the eastern boundary of Etowah County. The road gently wound its way through the hills. Shortly before arriving at the city limits, he saw the driveway that led to the house where Derrick "Rick" Pelham, Arthur's son, lived. Tom could barely see Rick's house nestled on top of a hill. A shiny black pickup truck came barreling down the driveway into the road directly in front of Tom, who honked his horn. The driver of the truck slammed on his brakes and got out of the car.

It was Rick Pelham.

"Let's settle this right now!" Rick yelled as he charged toward Tom's car. "I'm ready to pound you worse than I did when we were in the fifth grade."

Tom flipped on the emergency flashers and got out of the car. Rick, a short muscular man with close-cut dark hair, grabbed him in a bear hug.

"I won that fight," Tom replied when Rick released his grip. "You had a black eye."

"Which wasn't nearly as bad as your bloody nose. Mrs. Fletchall thought you were going to have to get a blood transfusion."

"Your left eye still looks a little crooked," Tom observed.

Rick drew back his fist, then pointed up the driveway. "Can you come up to the house?"

"Now? You looked like you were going somewhere in a hurry."

"Nothing as important as seeing you. And you'd already stopped in the middle of the road. When I saw your BMW, I thought you were another northern carpetbagger wanting to buy my place."

"Does that happen?"

"Every so often someone rings the doorbell." Rick grinned. "But there aren't many people who could afford the house and the twenty-two hundred acres that go with it."

"You're up to that much land?"

"Yeah. I'm a bona fide tree farmer. Everything scientific and organized. But enough about me. How are you doing? You seemed okay at the funeral, but I know things like that hit you hard later on."

"I'm fine most of the time." Tom paused. "Have you talked to your father recently?"

"Not since last week."

Tom decided not to mention the loss of his job. "I'm here to wrap up my dad's affairs," he said.

"That can wait an hour or two."

"I'll be in town for a few weeks. And I don't want to surprise Tiffany."

"She's always ready to see you."

Rover stuck his head out the passenger window of Tom's car and barked. Rick leaned to the side to take a look.

"Is that thing yours?"

"Yeah, he's a beauty, isn't he?"

"If you say so. Where are you staying?"

"With Elias."

"Why don't you camp out with us? We have four empty guest rooms. And your dog could hang out in the kennel beside the horse barn. It's heated and air-conditioned. After he eats and naps he could romp with my black Labs."

"No, I need to be with Elias. He's not doing too well with all that's happened."

An older car with a broken muffler and a hood painted a different color than the rest of the vehicle came up beside them. A middle-aged man shut off the engine and rolled down the passenger-side window.

"Need any help, Rick?" the man asked.

"No, Billy. Just talking to an old friend. This is Tom Crane. His father was John Crane, the lawyer."

The man squinted and looked Tom over. "Yeah, I can see that. Your father sued me once. Dragged me in front of Judge Caldwell over a five-hundred-dollar plumbing job I did out of the goodness of my heart for a woman who complained the whole time."

"I didn't know that," Tom said, glancing sideways at Rick.

"Billy, you probably deserved to get sued," Rick cut in. "Give me a call tomorrow. I've got some work for you to do at one of my rental houses on Beaverdale Road."

"Sure thing."

The man started the car and continued on.

"I guess that's one of the disadvantages a lawyer has practicing in a small town," Rick said as the car left in a cloud of oily smoke. "Half the people in town like you; the other half hate you because you sued them."

Two more cars and a pickup truck approached and slowed down so the people in the vehicles could stare at them.

"If we stay here much longer, we'll have our picture in the paper tomorrow with a silly caption underneath it," Rick said. "Give me a call so we can set a date for you to come out for supper. And make it soon."

"Okay," Tom replied. "It's good seeing you."

Rick put his hand on the door handle to his truck, then turned back toward Tom.

"You can run off to Atlanta, but this is the place where you'll find the people who really care about you."

Tom nodded. At that moment in his life he didn't have a reason to disagree.

————

Tom followed Rick for a quarter mile before the truck turned onto a side road. Rick stuck his hand out the window and waved as Tom continued toward town.

Tom and Rick were lifelong friends. Tiffany had come along later. Tom first met her during his sophomore year of high school when Tiffany's father accepted a management position with Pelham Financial and moved to Bethel from Montgomery, Alabama. Tom spotted the cute brunette with brown eyes the first day of school and made a point to sit beside her during lunch. They walked the halls together for a few weeks, but then she met a guy who shared her love for horses. The combination of man and beast was too much for Tom to overcome.

The summer before their senior year Tom and Tiffany's romance rekindled. This time it burned hot. From the start of school they were inseparable, but two weeks before the homecoming game they got into an argument. Tom couldn't remember what it was about, but he was willing to put it behind him and ask Tiffany to the big dance. The day before he popped the question, Rick pulled him aside and told him he had a major crush on Tiffany but had kept quiet because Tom was dating her. If Tom didn't object, Rick wanted to ask Tiffany to the dance. Tom told him to go ahead. His friendship with Rick was stronger than any feelings he had for a girl who'd made him mad.

For Rick and Tiffany the homecoming dance was the beginning of a relationship that culminated in marriage four years later. The couple didn't have any children, but Tiffany had a barn full of champion American Saddlebred horses and a wood-paneled room in her home crammed with blue ribbons and three-foot-high trophies.

Tom reached the city limits of Bethel, a line marked by a simple metal sign that read "Bethel Town Limit—Speed Limit 35 MPH Unless Otherwise Posted." Beyond the sign was another that read "Bird Sanctuary." The residential area on the east side of town contained modest wooden homes built during the heyday of the textile era. The condition of the homes varied greatly. Some were neat and tidy with well-kept yards and carefully trimmed bushes; others looked neglected and rundown with patchy grass and peeling paint.

Near the center of town Tom passed a church whose educational wing was named in memory of Arthur Pelham's mother. Just beyond the church was the Etowah County courthouse, a two-story redbrick building with an entrance framed by a pair of white columns. The courtroom in the Etowah County courthouse was the place where Tom decided to become a lawyer.

As a boy, Tom loved visiting the empty courtroom with its dark wood floors, high ceiling, and ornate judicial bench. Tom would rock back and forth in the jury box chairs and swear himself in using a Bible whose cracked cover looked like it'd never been opened. Then he'd hop down and sit on the smooth wooden bench where prisoners waited to hear their fates. The only place off-limits was the judge's chair. However, his heart pounding in his chest, Tom occasionally slipped into the high-backed black leather chair and surveyed the room. It was a view comparable to that of Zeus from Olympus. And in a town like Bethel, there was no greater power than a superior court judge seated on the bench. His judgments were thunderbolts, his orders sharp-tipped spears.

The lawyers of Etowah County clustered around the courthouse like grapes on a vine. For years Tom's father had rented an office in a one-story brick building a block away. Tom pulled into an empty parking space in front of the glass door with his father's name stenciled on it. The black lettering was chipped around the edges. There were two sheets of paper stuck to the door. One gave the date, time, and place of his father's funeral service. The other announced "All Clients Call the Office on Wednesday or Saturday between 9:00

a.m. and 12:00 p.m." It was signed "Mrs. Bernice Lawson," his father's longtime secretary.

Through the glass door Tom could see the simple reception area with its cracked leather sofa to the left and three mismatched leather side chairs facing it. Bernice's desk divided the room in half. The door to his father's office was directly behind her desk.

Tom had a key to the office, but he didn't go inside. There would be plenty of time later to determine what needed to be done. He'd asked Bernice to contact as many of his father's clients as she could and tell them they needed to hire another lawyer. Many of the files had already been copied and picked up. Rover barked. It had been a long ride for the dog. Tom returned to the car.

"This isn't the place for you to get out," he said. "There are better trees for you to sniff at Elias's house."

chapter
FOUR

E lias Crane lived three miles north of town in a 125-year-old white frame house. Tom passed fields filled with stubby brown stalks left after the year's soybean harvest. It was hard to see Elias's house from the road but easy to tell where it stood. A grove of massive trees surrounded the homeplace. The Crane family farm had shrunk over the years to a few acres around the house and a perpetual easement for the dirt driveway that led to it. Tom turned onto the driveway. A cloud of red dust followed him. It would be impossible to keep his car clean during his time in Bethel. He parked beneath a large oak tree in the front yard. There was a detached garage to the right of the house, but it was filled with an old tractor and boxes of junk.

Tom opened the car door, and Rover bounded out. The dog wouldn't wander far. There was plenty to occupy his nose within a few hundred feet of the house, and he always came when Tom called. Leaving his luggage in the trunk, Tom walked up three broad steps to a wooden front porch that stretched the length of the house. He opened the screen door and knocked. He banged louder. No answer. He turned the knob. It wasn't locked. He entered the front room of the musty old house.

"Elias!" he called out. "It's Tom!"

After a few seconds a door on the opposite side of the room opened and Elias shuffled out. The slender elderly man was the younger brother of Tom's deceased grandfather. He squinted through rimless glasses and ran his fingers through a thick head of white hair.

"Didn't hear you knock," the old man said, gesturing with his hand over his shoulder.

Tom knew the room on the opposite side of the front room was his uncle's study, a place devoted to the preparation of sermons during the years the older man served as a pastor. It was as off-limits to children as the judge's chair in the courtroom.

"You're not preaching anywhere, are you?" Tom asked in surprise.

"No, it's secret work."

Elias could be more obscure in his speech than Tom's father. It was a family trait Tom hoped had skipped his generation. Elias blinked his eyes, then took out a wrinkled handkerchief and wiped away a tear.

"There's no use damming up sorrow," he said. "Seeing him in you set it off. The river of grief has its own course and takes its own pace."

Tom's father had lived with Elias for five years and taken care of the old man after Elias suffered a heart attack. John Crane's untimely death had been a sharp blow. Elias returned the handkerchief to his pocket.

"It's not right that he's gone and I'm still here."

Tom touched the older man on the shoulder. "There's nothing we can do about that."

Elias reached up and grabbed Tom's hand in a surprisingly strong grip. Rover barked. Elias looked toward the open front door.

"Is that the dog you told me about?"

"Yes."

The men stepped onto the porch. Elias held out his hand so Rover could sniff it. A glob of drool dripped from the dog's mouth onto the porch.

"I'll understand if you want him to sleep out here or in the garage," Tom said. "He's housebroken, but as you can see, he slobbers a lot."

"This house has seen worse. You remember Uncle Albert? He'd cram a big wad of tobacco into his cheek but never could get the hang of keeping the spit from dripping down his chin and onto the floor."

Elias held the door open for Rover, who sauntered in, sniffed a few objects in the front room, then headed directly for the study.

"Is that okay?" Tom asked.

The older man nodded. "Sometimes animals can tell the anointing."

"What?" Tom asked before he could catch himself.

"They're not limited in what they see by what they don't believe," Elias replied. "Do you remember the story of Balaam's donkey?"

"No," Tom admitted ruefully.

"The donkey saw what the prophet couldn't. I'll show it to you later. Do you want to stay in your father's room?"

When John Crane lived with Elias he slept in a downstairs bedroom across the hall from the room where Elias slept.

"Will the upstairs blue bedroom be okay?"

"Yes, Amanda Burk's daughter cleaned it the other day. I don't often go up there, but everything you need should be there."

"I'll get my luggage."

Tom unloaded the car and carried his suitcases up a narrow flight of stairs. The floors creaked with each step he took. There were three large bedrooms on the upper level of the house and a spacious bathroom built into a space that once served as a summer sleeping porch. The bathroom had a sloping roof that required Tom to stoop when he took a shower and a bank of windows that offered a nice view of the trees on the west side of the property. Unless someone was walking in the yard, it wasn't necessary to close the curtains. There wasn't another house within two hundred yards.

As a child, Tom always stayed in the blue bedroom when the Crane family gathered for biannual reunions. The boy cousins slept in the high poster bed and spilled over into sleeping bags on the floor. While Tom was unpacking his suitcases, Rover joined him. The dog walked into the bedroom, thoroughly sniffed it from one end to the other, then plopped down in a spot near the foot of the bed.

"Are you sure that's the place you want?" Tom asked him. "That's where my cousin Rudy used to put his sleeping bag. Rudy hated taking baths."

The dog rested his large head on his paws and watched with bloodshot eyes as Tom finished putting away his clothes. Tom glanced at the clock. It was 6:00 p.m. There was no sight or smell of supper when he arrived. He went downstairs to grab a bag of dog food from the car. Rover, an expectant expression on his face, followed. Elias was sitting in his chair in the front room with his eyes closed and didn't stir as they passed through the room.

The large country kitchen was at the rear of the house. Tom poured a generous helping of dog food into a large bowl, then checked the refrigerator. It contained a hodgepodge of leftovers. Elias had served as pastor of three different churches in the northwestern Georgia area, with stints in between as a quality-control supervisor in textile mills when no church was available. Tom recognized the names of former church members on some of the plastic and glass containers.

It was a relief that folks were stepping up to take care of Elias now that Tom's father was gone. Rummaging through the containers, Tom selected meat loaf, mashed potatoes, green beans, and something that looked like a corn soufflé. He stuck his head into the front room. Elias, his eyes open, was reading a book.

"Are you hungry?" he asked.

"Not really, but there's plenty in the refrigerator," Elias answered with a wave of his hand. "Whatever you want is fine with me."

Tom added a wedge of corn bread from a pan on the kitchen counter to each plate and warmed up the food. The kitchen was designed to serve crews of farmworkers, and the long table against the wall could seat twelve people. At reunion time family members ate in the kitchen and spilled over into the front room, where they gathered around makeshift tables made of broad boards set on sawhorses and covered with white sheets. Tonight the two plates at the end of the big table seemed overwhelmed.

"Supper's ready!" Tom called out.

Elias shuffled into the kitchen. "I see you found the meat loaf. Velma Higgins from Rocky River brought that. She made it using grocery-store beef and pork from hogs raised on their place."

"Homegrown pork is hard to find in Atlanta," Tom said. "What do you want to drink?"

"I'll have water, but there's tea in the refrigerator."

Tom poured two glasses of water. The deep well that supplied the house contained just the right touch of iron to make the water sweet. Tom waited for Elias to sit at the head of the table, but the older man moved to the side.

"Don't you want to sit at the head of the table?" Tom asked.

"No. You need to get used to it."

Tom sat down and waited for Elias to pray. The old man kept his hands folded in his lap and did nothing.

"Are you going to say the blessing?" Tom asked.

Elias leveled his gaze at Tom. "You do it."

"No, sir." Tom shook his head. "You're the praying person in this family. This food will get cold before I talk to God about it."

Elias leaned over and inhaled the aroma of the plate in front of him. "Ignoring this corn bread isn't God's will. I'll pray."

Elias closed his eyes and began to pray. Tom kept his eyes open and watched. There was no denying the existence of something special about the old man. Even though there were a few small holes in his flannel shirt, he looked noble.

"Amen," Elias said.

Tom dived into the meal and cleaned his plate. Elias ate the corn bread but picked at the rest of his food.

"If you had food like this as rarely as I do, you'd appreciate it more," Tom said between bites.

"I appreciate it. Fix yourself a second plate."

Tom loaded up and put his plate in the microwave. "Is that a coconut cream pie on the top shelf in the refrigerator?" he asked.

"Yes. Baked by Bobby Joe Hargrove," Elias answered, brightening up. "Do you remember him? He drives a logging truck. Years ago his father spent time in jail for moonshining but got saved before he died."

Elias's memory for remote events was crystal clear. His mention of Mr. Hargrove uncorked a series of stories about the Mount Pisgah Church, a stone building beside one of the main highways west of Bethel, and the people who worshipped there. Finally, Elias stopped. He stared at Tom for a moment, then looked out a window.

"Are we still on daylight savings time?" he asked.

"Yes."

"Do you want to go to the cemetery? It won't be dark for another hour or so."

"No, that can wait for another day."

"What about Austin's Pond? I've not been able to get over there by myself. That's what I really want to do, especially now that you're here."

"I just got here," Tom answered impatiently, "and I'm not sure it's a good idea to go to the pond. There's nothing there but bad memories."

Elias frowned. Tom decided to change the subject.

"I'm not going to be working for the same law firm in Atlanta," he said. "Yesterday was my last day."

"What happened?"

Tom spent the rest of the meal telling Elias about losing his job. The older man kept shaking his head from side to side. Tom didn't mention his conversations with Arthur Pelham.

"I know, it's hard to believe," Tom said as he neared the end of the story. "It was a huge shock. And to top it off, Clarice broke up with me. She's the woman who came up from Atlanta with me to attend the funeral."

"God is good," Elias responded, pushing his chair away from the table. "I'm thankful for all he's doing in your life."

Tom gave the older man a puzzled look. "Are you saying it was God's will for me to get dumped by Clarice and lose my job?"

"I say what I hear." Elias ran his fingers through his hair. "I don't believe God's sovereignty is an excuse for man's mistakes, but I'm confident that he's working all things for your good."

The old man stood and walked slowly to the sink with his plate. Tom wasn't interested in unraveling Elias's theology. Instead, he went to the refrigerator and took out the coconut pie.

"Do you want a piece?" he asked.

"No thanks, but help yourself. Coffee is in the cupboard to the left of the stove if you want it now or in the morning. I'm not drinking it anymore. It's not good for my heart."

Tom cut a generous piece of pie. "I'll be going to the office early, so I may leave before you get up."

"Probably not." Elias put his plate in the dishwasher. "You'd think I'd sleep more soundly the older I get, but it doesn't work that way. It's not often the sun beats me out of bed."

"Then I'll see you in the morning. Thanks for letting me stay with you."

"This place is as much yours as it is mine."

Rover was lying in the corner. On his way out of the kitchen, Elias dropped his hand. The dog lifted his head and licked the old man's knuckles. Tom had never seen Rover do that to anyone else.

"I like your dog," Elias said. "I'll be glad to keep an eye on him while you're in town."

"If you can stand the drool, he won't give you any problems."

Elias left, and Tom turned his attention to the thick slice of coconut pie. He thrust his fork into the meringue and through the creamy filling. The pie was delicious. If eating pie was God's will, Tom was all for it. He swallowed a bite and pointed his fork at Rover.

"You've made a good first impression. Don't ruin it."

Later that evening Tom read for a while in the front room with Rover at his feet. In the city the sound of honking horns and the wail of distant sirens were constant. Urban noise numbs the senses and blurs the mind's ability to think. In the silence of the isolated house, Tom found his senses alert, his mind active. He laid the book on a side table and glanced across at Elias's study. The door was closed. Tom couldn't remember exactly what the room looked like. He peered down the hall toward his uncle's bedroom. If Elias awoke before the sun rose, he probably went to sleep shortly after it set. Tom gingerly walked across the floor. The house was only quiet when he was still. Any movement brought forth creaks and pops that seemed to echo off the walls. Tom approached the closed door and reached out with his right hand to grasp the doorknob. At that moment, Rover let out a loud groan. Tom jumped. The dog, his black tongue hanging out the side of his mouth, rolled over. Tom chuckled and withdrew his hand from the door.

In the middle of the night, Tom had a nightmare that woke him up. He went downstairs to the kitchen to get a drink of water. At the bottom of the stairs he saw a streak of light beneath the study door. After getting a drink, he returned to the front room. There was noise coming from the study. Tom stopped to listen but couldn't make out the sounds. Slipping along the wall, he edged toward the door. It sounded like Elias was wrestling with an intruder. Tom put his ear to the door. The mixture of groans and unintelligible words strung together made the hair on the back of his neck stand up. Elias had to be praying, but the noise bore as much resemblance to the blessing spoken over supper as a summer breeze bore to an autumn hurricane. Two loud thuds against the floor were followed by a sharp cry. Before Tom could jerk the door open, the cry was followed by the sound of singing.

Elias had an excellent baritone voice; however, age had made the old man's vocal cords brittle. Remembering how melodious his uncle sounded in his prime, Tom was saddened by the slightly tremulous voice that came from the study. He recognized the song. It was an old hymn about the blood of Jesus. The message of the song was primitive and barbaric, but Elias seemed to caress the words. The old man sang several verses, stopped for a moment, then started another song Tom didn't recognize. This one focused on the beauty of a God who can't be seen but reveals himself in nature. Tom loved the outdoors. Separation from meadows and mountains was one of the chief drawbacks of living in the city. Then Elias stopped singing and started talking. Tom couldn't be sure, but it sounded like verses from the Bible. Tom suddenly felt like a trespasser. He backed away from the door and returned to bed. He slept soundly through the rest of the night.

_____

Early in the morning Tom took Rover downstairs and let him outside. It was a cool fall morning with a thin layer of mist above the dewy ground. Tom stood on the front porch, the wooden planks cold against his bare feet. The morning was quiet except for the distant crowing of a rooster.

The water from the well made good coffee, and in a few minutes Tom sat at the kitchen table enjoying the first few sips. His father had liked coffee too. It was one trait they had in common.

Tom stretched out his legs under the table. There weren't any deadlines to meet, so he didn't have to gulp the coffee and rush off to the office. He rubbed his hand across the slightly ribbed surface of the table. Elias came in through the kitchen door. He was dressed in blue overalls, a blue work shirt, and white socks.

"Good morning," Tom said with a smile. "Planning on doing some farming today?"

"Only in your heart."

Elias had a book in his hand. He placed it on the table in front of Tom. It was a Bible with a bookmark in it.

"I marked the passage about the donkey. It can be your morning devotional, then we can talk about it later."

Tom didn't touch the black book. "Reading the Bible isn't part of my routine."

"Why not?"

"To use a legal term, I've not found it relevant."

"When was the last time you gave it a try?"

Tom was in a good mood from the coffee and wasn't going to let Elias steal it from him.

"I thought you retired from running a church, but if you still have the itch to lead a congregation, I'm not signing up. I'm your great-nephew, nothing more."

"Which makes you even more precious to me. Read one chapter. If that doesn't interest you, I'll leave you alone"—the old man paused—"for a week."

Tom tapped the Bible with his index finger. "Promise on this?"

Elias held up his right hand and pointed at the Bible with his left. "Deal."

The old man left the kitchen. Rover ambled after him. Tom stared at the Bible. He'd grown up going to Sunday school and absorbed a lot of religious information by osmosis. Elias was the latest in an unbroken line of ministers in the Crane family, dating back four or five generations. However, none of Tom's cousins had shown an interest in church work. Elias was the last of the breed.

Tom started reading. The Old Testament chapter was about a wizard named Balaam and a talking donkey that saw angels. The story had a fairy-tale feel to it. A king wanted to hire Balaam to curse the Israelites, a service that bore an uneasy resemblance to what clients often wanted lawyers to do to the other side in a legal dispute. The ensuing negotiations between king and wizard were similar to modern dickering over the terms of an employment agreement in which money is always the key component. After a deal was struck, the talking-donkey part added spice to Balaam's journey to the job site but wasn't the main point of the story.

Tom reached the end of the chapter without finding out what happened. He glanced toward the front room. Elias and Rover weren't making any noise. He read three more chapters to find out what happened, then closed the Bible. He had to admit the passage contained an interesting mix of narrative, character development, and poetry. When he walked through the front room to go upstairs and get ready to go to town, Elias was sitting in his easy chair with Rover at his feet.

"Did you keep reading?" the old man asked.

Tom had his hand on the stair railing. He stopped. "Yes."

"Was it interesting?"

Tom turned toward Elias. "In a mythical kind of way."

"Mythical?" the old man replied. "You'll have to explain that to me."

"Many ancient cultures produced stories like that," Tom said patiently. "That happened to be a good one."

"I'm glad you liked it." Elias adjusted his glasses.

Tom climbed the stairs. There was no harm in humoring Elias. A tall tale about a talking donkey wasn't a threat to Tom's intellectual integrity.

chapter

FIVE

S aturday morning office hours from 8:00 a.m. to noon in Bethel were a modern accommodation to an old-fashioned custom. For generations rural clients had been coming to town to shop for groceries, pay bills in person, and, if need be, consult an attorney.

Tom lowered the windows of the car so he could enjoy the feel and smell of the fall morning. The highway followed an old cow path and contained a few sharp turns that made driving fun. No cows or tractors slowed him down.

A large number of cars and pickup trucks were clustered in the center of town. A seasonal farmer's market, its stalls piled high with corn, tomatoes, okra, squash, watermelons, and pumpkins, was doing a brisk business. Tom parked in front of his father's office. A little brass bell on the wall next to the door announced his arrival.

Bernice Lawson was sitting behind her desk, her thick fingers pounding the keys of an electric typewriter. In her early sixties with hair dyed a light brown, Bernice peered over half-frame glasses that rested on her thick nose and chubby cheeks.

50

Tom's father hired Bernice when her husband was forced to retire on disability after injuring his back in a textile mill. Bernice's rusty typing wasn't up to professional standards, but the plump woman had one asset that couldn't be taught—she knew everyone in Etowah County, a huge help when it came to deciding whether to accept a new client, sue an unknown defendant, or evaluate the credibility of a witness. If Bernice said someone couldn't be trusted, John Crane knew to proceed with caution. Over the past twenty years, she'd kept the office running even when John's interest in the practice of law waxed and waned.

"Land's sakes," Bernice exclaimed in a voice that made the need for an interoffice intercom unnecessary. "I didn't expect to see you for another hour. Unless he had an early hearing, your daddy rarely came in before nine o'clock."

"I was up early, drank a cup of coffee, and read three chapters in the Bible," Tom replied with a smile.

"That last part was Elias's doing, I bet."

"Yeah, he wanted me to learn about Balaam and his donkey so I read a chapter or two in the book of Numbers."

"Your daddy and Elias were always talking about stuff in the Old Testament. It's all I can do to try to understand what's written in red." Bernice stopped and shook her head. "I still don't have it set in my mind that your daddy is gone. Every time the bell rings I look up and expect him to walk through the door."

"Still no computer?" Tom asked, wanting to avoid a sentimental conversation. "This has to be the last law office in Georgia that doesn't use a word processor."

Bernice patted the old typewriter. "It would just make me sloppy. And there really isn't much to do. I was typing a few envelopes when you came in."

Tom glanced around the office. There had been no noticeable change in the place since he was in high school.

"I'd better get to work," he said.

"Let me show you where to start," Bernice said, pushing herself up from her chair with both hands. "I put the open files in boxes in your father's office."

John Crane's office was directly behind Bernice's desk. The large walnut desk and matching credenza were scratched and scarred. Bookcases filled with aging law books lined the walls. The only volumes kept up-to-date were the black-and-gold set of the Official Code of Georgia Annotated.

"Where are the pictures?" Tom asked when he saw the empty spaces on the credenza reserved for family photos and snapshots of his father's favorite fishing holes.

"In that box." Bernice pointed to a smaller cardboard box in the corner of the room. "I couldn't bear to see them every time I came in here. If you want to get them out, I know exactly how he had them positioned."

"No, that's okay."

Bernice rested her right hand on several large boxes stacked on top of one another. "These contain the files for cases that haven't been picked up. I've tried to contact everyone, but some clients don't have a phone, and others may have called back when I wasn't here."

Tom quickly counted ten boxes. His father had been busier than he thought.

"Did you get an answering machine for the office?" he asked.

"The day after you told me to. I wasn't sure how to set it up, but Betty Sosebee from the Sponcler firm helped me. She recorded a very professional greeting that explains why the office is closing and asks folks to leave a phone number along with the date and time they called. Some of the personal messages are precious. I've saved a few from folks who had such nice things to say about your daddy. One of the best is from Judge Caldwell."

"I'll listen to those later. Is Judge Caldwell still filling in as judge of the probate court?"

"Yes, the county commissioners aren't going to call a special election, so the governor asked him to serve until November. Three or four people are lining up to run for probate judge. Carl and I are supporting Sheri Blevins."

The door opened.

"Good morning, Randall," Bernice called out to a dark-haired, middle-aged man who entered the reception area on crutches. "I've been trying to get in touch with you. This is Mr. Crane's son, Tom."

The man awkwardly propped himself up on one crutch and held out his hand. Tom shook it.

"What happened to your leg?" he asked.

"Car hit me, and I had to have an operation. Sorry to hear about your father."

"Randall's file is in one of the boxes I showed you," Bernice said. "He was standing on the curb at the corner of Poplar and Westover minding his own business when a car ran off the road and knocked him down. The driver was Owen Harrelson, an executive at Pelham, who was down here for a meeting. I think he lives in New York or Boston."

"I never saw him coming until it was too late," Randall added. "Next thing I know, I'm flying through the air."

"Harrelson claims a pothole caused him to swerve," Bernice said. "But I think he'd been drinking. He and some of the other bosses had been playing golf all afternoon at the country club. Everyone knows there's usually a cooler of beer strapped to the backs of the golf carts. It's more about boozing and socializing than hitting the ball into the hole."

"Did the police perform a blood alcohol test?" Tom asked.

"Yeah," Randall replied.

"What did it show?"

"I hadn't had anything to drink. Stopped after I got out of the navy."

"I mean the driver of the car. Was he tested for alcohol?"

"No," Bernice said. "Your daddy was going to interview the people who were at the club to find out if Harrelson had been into the sauce."

"Why wasn't Harrelson tested?"

Bernice rolled her eyes. "He probably showed the policeman his corporate ID."

"You're kidding."

"No."

"I want to see the accident report."

"It's in one of those boxes," Bernice responded. "I'm not sure which one. Do you want me to find it?"

"No, I'll do it. Mr.–" Tom stopped and looked at Randall. "I'm sorry. What's your last name?"

"Freiburger."

"Come into the office and have a seat. I don't want you to be uncomfortable."

Randall sat in a side chair while Tom rummaged through the files. There were a lot of different files in each box. At Barnes, McGraw, and Crowther, a single case would quickly fill a box. His father's practice killed fewer trees.

"Here it is," he said, pulling out a thin folder with "*Freiburger v. Harrelson*" written on the tab in black ink.

Inside, Tom found a medical release form signed by the client, a contingency fee contract, two pages of scribbled notes in his father's difficult-to-decipher handwriting, medical records from the emergency room at the hospital, and an accident report completed by a Bethel police officer named Logan. A diagram on the report showed the position of Harrelson's car, the pothole, and Randall Freiburger.

"This shows you lying in the street," Tom said.

"He knocked me into the street when he hit me. That's where I was at when the police arrived."

"Were you knocked out?"

"No, I was sitting on the asphalt and waiting for an ambulance. My knee wasn't working at all."

"This diagram doesn't show Harrelson's car veering off the roadway."

"It wasn't. After he hit me, he swerved back onto the road."

"Were there any skid marks?"

"I didn't see any."

"Was there a pothole?"

"A little one, but I don't think it would cause someone to lose control of his car. It's been filled in since this happened, but you can go over there and see how small it was."

Tom shook his head. "Based on the police drawing, there's no way to prove the defendant's car actually left the road. You could have stepped in front of him."

"But I didn't."

"Were there any witnesses?"

"Maybe. A guy in a pickup stopped to make sure I was okay. He was right behind the car that hit me."

Tom looked at the bottom of the accident report. It didn't list any witnesses.

"Did the driver of the truck stay and talk to the police?"

"No, once he saw I wasn't dead, I guess he kept on going to town."

"Do you know this man's name?"

"I think it was Junior."

Tom smiled. "Having a name like Junior won't be much help in tracking him down. Any other information about him?"

"He had an older model white truck, maybe a sixties Ford. It all happened so fast. I was kind of woozy."

"I understand." Tom closed the file. "Well, I'm sorry my father wasn't able to see the case through, but since he's gone you'll need to find another lawyer to represent you."

"You're a lawyer, aren't you?"

"Yes."

"Could you help me?"

Tom shook his head. "I'm here to shut down my father's practice, not keep it going. I live in Atlanta and need to wrap things up as soon as I can. There's no problem with the statute of limitations, so you have plenty of time to find someone else to represent you. But hire someone soon. Witnesses tend to forget what they saw and heard."

"Okay." Randall struggled to his feet and leaned on his crutches. "What do I owe you? My insurance at work paid part of the bill for my surgery, and things are going to be tight around my house for a while."

"You don't owe me anything. My father took the case on a contingency basis and because he didn't collect any money, there won't be a fee. The medical records from the hospital only cost a few dollars. I'll take care of that."

"That's nice of you. If you change your mind, let me know. I won't be running out to hire another lawyer until I start feeling better."

"Someone needs to track down those witnesses," Tom reminded him.

"I understand."

Randall slowly left the office. Tom stood in the doorway of his father's office and watched him make his way down the sidewalk. He turned to Bernice.

"Who should he hire to represent him?"

"Reggie Mixon would take the case."

Tom grimaced. Mixon had a reputation for flamboyant incompetence.

"That's not good."

"It's going to be hard to find a decent local attorney," Bernice said. "Lamar Sponcler would do a good job, but he's slowing down. The big firms are tied in with Pelham and would see the case as a conflict of interest."

Bethel's definition of a big law firm started at three lawyers. Based on that criteria there were two large firms, one with five lawyers, another with three. The population of the county bar, including the attorneys in the district attorney's office, was seventeen.

For years the preeminent trial lawyers had been Lamar Sponcler on the plaintiff side and Carnell Waycaster on behalf of insurance companies. When they butted heads in court, a handful of spectators, mostly retired men with nothing better to do, might show up to watch the oratorical fireworks.

Presiding over the local bar was superior court judge Nathan Caldwell. Appointed to the bench when he was barely thirty-two years old by a governor distantly related to his mother's family, Judge Caldwell had been reelected without opposition nine times. Big-city lawyers who came to Bethel thinking they could dominate Judge

Caldwell's courtroom left with wounded pride, damaged egos, and a respect for the country jurist.

Tom began reviewing the other files in the box that contained the Freiburger case. He found a hodgepodge of cases that ran counter to the modern view that an attorney must specialize to be competent. There were real estate files, contract disputes, probate matters, civil lawsuits, traffic ticket cases, and even a few misdemeanor criminal files. Tom set the criminal cases aside for closer scrutiny.

The bell on the front door jangled, and Bernice called out a greeting. Tom didn't have a clear line of sight and got up from his chair so he could see. A group of black men and women, all wearing nice clothes, had come into the office.

"Tom, this is Reverend England," Bernice said, introducing a large man wearing a dark suit, white shirt, and black tie. "He's the pastor of the Ebenezer Church on Highway 201."

The pastor shook Tom's hand with a firm grip. "Please accept our deepest heartfelt condolences."

The other people with the minister nodded in agreement.

"Thank you."

"Brother Crane helped us walk through a difficult situation a few years ago. Now something else has come up. It involves a brother and two sisters arguing over who should pay a bill for repairs to the family homeplace after the death of their parents. I've been told you're a lawyer too."

"Yes, but I'm not accepting new probate cases."

"It's not a lawsuit," the minister replied. "They want to follow 1 Corinthians 6."

Tom stared blankly at the minister.

"The siblings don't want to sue one another," one of the other men continued. "We've shown them what the Bible says about

Christians taking their disputes in front of unbelievers, and they've agreed to obey the Scriptures."

Pastor England spoke: "Several years ago Brother Crane served as a peacemaker in another situation involving members of our church. It worked out so well that the folks were reconciled without anyone having the burden of an unresolved offense weighing down their souls."

Tom was mystified by the preacher's request and the religious lingo wrapped around it. He turned to Bernice for help.

"What are they talking about?"

"Every so often your daddy would serve as a private mediator for Christians who got in a fuss. He'd schedule a couple of meetings to try to help people work through their differences."

"Mediation?"

"Only different, because he tried to get the folks who were at odds to forgive one another first. Once that happened, settling the practical stuff almost always followed. I went with him a few times to take notes. It was all new to me."

"Confession of sin and seeking forgiveness are powerful weapons," Pastor England said, nodding his head. "It's one thing to talk about; another to practice when the old sinful nature cries out for its own way."

"Is there anyone else in Bethel who could help these folks?" Tom asked Bernice.

"We came to you," one of the women spoke up. "The apple doesn't fall far from the tree."

Tom shook his head. "You're wrong about that. I'm not from the same orchard as my father and don't share his beliefs."

The woman who mentioned the apple stared wide-eyed at Tom for a moment, then closed her eyes and raised her left hand high in the air.

"Lord, we praise you for bringing us here today. We thank you for Brother John Crane and pray that every good thing stored up in heaven for his offspring will be revealed in due season. Speak tender words of love to this young man and lead him in the way everlasting."

Two more people took up the prayer, apparently following some kind of unwritten religious protocol. Tom had no choice but to listen.

Finally Pastor England prayed, "Heavenly Father, we thank you for this young man's life and declare that the enemy of his soul will not be able to thwart the purposes of God. In answer to these prayers, deliver Mr. Tom Crane fully into the kingdom of your dear Son, our Lord and Savior, Jesus Christ. Amen."

Everyone else said "Amen." The woman who started the impromptu prayer meeting stepped forward and gave Tom a big hug.

"We came here for one reason, but the Lord had something else in mind!" she exclaimed. "Thank you for letting us pray with you."

"I didn't hear you ask his permission, Sister Tamara," Brother England said drily. "Let me know if we can be of service to you."

"Uh, I'll keep that in mind," Tom replied. "And I hope you find someone to help with the family dispute."

Pastor England turned to the oldest man in the group.

"Brother Stevens, maybe the Lord is telling us to take what we learned from Brother Crane and care for the sheep ourselves."

"I'll speak to the family about it."

As soon as the group left and the door closed, Tom sat down in one of the reception room chairs.

"That was different," he said.

"They turned the office into a church, didn't they?" Bernice said.

"Church? I thought it was rude."

Bernice cleared her throat, adjusted her glasses, and turned her

water's edge

attention back to her typewriter. The rest of the morning passed without interruption. Tom organized half the files in one box, dictated several letters to clients, and prepared three motions to withdraw in pending court cases. Bernice brought him a document to review and sign.

"If I brought in my computer, I could type this stuff myself," he said.

"Are you saying you don't need me?" Bernice asked, a wounded expression on her face.

"No, no. You proved your worth today with Randall Freiburger and the Ebenezer Church crowd. If you'd not been here when the religious folks walked in, I'd still be trying to figure out what they wanted. Don't take it wrong when I bring my laptop. I'll mostly use it to organize the financial records."

"Oh." Bernice winced. "That's the area where your daddy and I struggled the most."

"Did you balance the checkbook?"

"Most months," Bernice said hopefully. "And the bookkeeper reconciled things the best she could when she prepared your father's tax return."

"What about the trust account?"

"Your daddy took care of that himself. It's in the bottom right-hand drawer of the desk."

Shortly before noon, Bernice came to the door of the office. "If it's okay, I'll be on my way."

"Could you stay a few more minutes?" Tom asked. "I have something personal to tell you."

Bernice sat in one of the chairs in front of the desk and listened as Tom told her about losing his job. Partway through the story, she started to cry and grabbed a handful of tissues from a box on one of the bookshelves. She blew her nose. Tom paused. He'd not been trying to stir up emotion.

"Do you want me to stop? I wasn't trying to upset you."

"No, it just breaks my heart to think about you being treated so badly."

Bernice's empathy was an ingrained characteristic. She always saw the people who walked through the front door of the office as hurting people first, clients in need of legal services second.

"Once we're finished shutting down the office, I'll go back to Atlanta and start looking for a job. I have to pay the rent on my apartment, the lease for the BMW parked out front, and a couple of credit cards with balances that have crept up too high."

Bernice wiped her eyes and blew her nose.

"And after I'm gone, you should take a vacation," Tom concluded.

"I've already planned one to North Carolina. We've never been to Kitty Hawk."

"You'll like it. The Outer Banks is a special place, and there's decent surfing near the Hatteras Lighthouse."

"I don't think Carl and I will do much surfing." Bernice managed a smile.

"Thanks for all your help," Tom replied, standing up. "Not just to me but for all the years you served my father. He couldn't have done it without you."

Bernice grabbed another tissue from the box on the desk and left.

chapter
SIX

Tom walked up a slight incline to the tree-lined street that ran in front of the courthouse. Two blocks to the south he stopped in front of the Chickamauga Diner and looked inside a large plateglass window. The restaurant was filled with people sitting in metal chairs around square black-vinyl-topped tables.

The Chickamauga Diner hadn't been around as long as the Civil War battlefield that gave the restaurant its name, but it had occupied the same location for two generations. On weekdays most of the patrons were local businessmen. Today, families with children dominated the lunch crowd. The diner didn't offer plastic toys in bags, but the fried chicken was great.

"Hey, Tom!" called out Alex Giles, the current owner of the diner. "Have a seat at the counter or wait for a table?"

"I'll sit at the counter."

Tom perched on a shiny black stool atop a chrome pole. Waitresses scurried back and forth carrying plates of food and small baskets of corn bread and yeast rolls. Alex's mother refilled glasses with sweet tea. Several people nodded in greeting to Tom when they saw him. A mechanic who'd worked on the Crane family cars for years invited Tom to join his group, but Tom shook his head.

"What'll it be?" asked the unshaven cook, wiping his hands on a white apron.

"I need something to get the taste of cheap Atlanta sushi out of my mouth," Tom replied.

"How about a steak burger on the grill topped off with onions, mushrooms, and American cheese? That's as far from sushi as you can get."

"Sounds good."

The best grills season over time, and the sizzling flattop at the Chickamauga Diner was in prime condition. Tom watched the cook prepare his food. The man placed chopped onion directly on the grill and let it cook for a couple of minutes before adding the mushrooms. Opening the door of a small built-in refrigerator, he took out a large metal bowl filled with bright-red ground round and scooped out a generous portion that he formed into a thick patty. The meat sputtered when he dropped it on the grill. He dusted the top of the meat with salt and pepper.

After turning the burger once, the cook added the onions and mushrooms, topped it off with the cheese, and hid it under an aluminum dome. He dropped both halves of the bun facedown on the flattop. Unveiling the meat, he deposited it on the lower half of the bun. The melted cheese dripped down the side of the sandwich. Crisp lettuce, a thick slice of fresh tomato, and a fat pickle rested beside the burger on a plastic plate.

"Is that American enough for you?" the cook asked.

"More than apple pie."

Tom carefully lifted the assembled product and opened his mouth as wide as possible. The first bite didn't disappoint. The melded flavors caused his taste buds to stand up and cheer.

Halfway through the sandwich Tom felt a tap on his shoulder and turned around. It was Charlie Williams, the local district attorney. In his midfifties, the prosecutor boasted that a felony indictment in Etowah County was a prepaid ticket to the penitentiary. He slid onto a vacant stool beside Tom.

"What brings you back to town?" Williams asked.

Tom wiped his mouth with a thin paper napkin. "Shutting down my father's practice and settling his estate."

Williams, a former college football player, put his beefy hands on the counter, glanced around, and leaned closer to Tom. "I know he was having financial trouble. Was there enough life insurance to take care of everything?"

It was a blatantly inappropriate question.

"I'm working through that," Tom replied carefully.

Williams nodded. "He talked to me about his situation with the IRS. I told him Matt Franklin was the best young CPA in town and could probably cut a deal for him, maybe even get a reduction in the amount he owed. Did he ever contact Matt?"

"I'm not sure."

"You might want to check with him. He could help you too."

"Okay."

Williams slid his right hand across the counter, knocking a bread crumb to the floor. "Pressure from the IRS is tough to handle too. Was that the only problem he had hanging over him?"

"As far as I know. Once he moved in with Elias, his life was simple."

"That's good to hear. I know he liked to fish a lot."

Tom took another bite of his burger.

"Do you know much about his relationship with Harold Addington?"

"We never discussed it."

Williams tapped his finger against the counter. "Addington met Arthur Pelham in London about five years ago. Arthur hired him to develop the overseas market for Pelham's investment products. About a year ago Addington was transferred to Bethel and moved here with his wife. That's a long way from London, isn't it?"

"About six thousand miles, give or take a few."

Williams didn't smile. "Did your father ever represent Addington?"

"I'm not sure since I haven't gone through all his files. Why do you want to know?"

Williams turned his head so that his eyes met Tom's. "Two men died in what everyone says was a tragic boating accident. It's my job to make sure that's all it was."

Tom's mouth felt dry. "Do you have any reason to think differently?"

"My job is to ask questions."

"Have you talked to Addington's widow?"

"Yes." Williams nodded. "Did you know she has multiple sclerosis?"

"No."

"She takes an injection every day that's supposed to help, but the illness is starting to give her more problems, maybe in part due to all the stress she's had."

"What did she tell you about the relationship between her husband and my father?"

"They went fishing a lot. She said the first time a largemouth bass hit her husband's lure he couldn't get enough of it. Of course, your father knew all the fishing holes where big bass like to hang out." Williams paused. "She also says your father represented her husband but she doesn't know why, which seems strange to me. I was hoping you could help me with that."

"I can check the files."

"You should do that. One of Addington's daughters is handling the business affairs. According to the probate records, she's the executrix of the estate. You might want to talk to her too."

"What's the daughter's name?"

"Rose. She was in Serbia at the time her father died and couldn't get a flight out for a couple of days."

"Serbia?"

"Yeah, she works for an international adoption agency."

"You've really been checking this out, haven't you?"

"Noah Keller helped." Williams motioned to a slightly built man with dark, close-cropped hair sitting alone at a table across the room. "He's a detective with the sheriff's department. Like I said, there's no formal investigation, but I'm sure you want us to exercise due diligence."

"Of course."

"When can I expect to hear from you?"

"The beginning of the week if I talk to the Addington family and they waive the attorney-client privilege. Most of the cases I've looked at so far are small stuff. My father never handled any complex litigation or business transactions."

"Right. If he'd ever put his whole heart into it, he could have had a solid practice."

The DA stood and put his hand on Tom's shoulder again. "Any chance you'll stay in Bethel? With your local connections, you could make a name for yourself and build a solid practice."

"No. This is home, but it's not where I want to live."

"Caught the big-city bug?"

"Yeah, I guess so."

"Too bad. Give me a call as soon as you find out anything."

Williams left. The last bite of the hamburger on Tom's plate didn't look nearly as appetizing as the first.

Returning to the office, he placed all the boxes on the floor and began looking for files with the name Addington on them. Toward the back of the fourth box he found a folder with the words "Addington Matter" written on the tab. Tom pulled it out and flipped it open.

It was empty.

He continued searching through all the other boxes, but the empty folder was the only one with the former Pelham employee's name on it. He called Bernice at home, but there was no answer. She didn't own a cell phone.

Tom's father kept older, closed files in a mini-warehouse, but if Addington had lived in Bethel for only a year, it was unlikely any recent cases would be there. To be sure, Tom checked the metal box that contained index cards about closed files for the current and previous year and found nothing about Harold Addington.

While engaging in his fruitless search, Tom stewed about his conversation with Charlie Williams. He didn't appreciate the DA's asking personal questions and casting about vague insinuations without substance. It was bad enough for him to do that to Tom; it was worse to do it with Addington's widow and daughter.

When Tom left the office, the afternoon sun had warmed the mountain air. As he drove, Tom decided it would be fun to take Rover on a hike so the dog's nose could experience sensory overload. When he pulled up to the house, he saw Elias sitting under the large oak tree with Rover at his feet. The old man was wearing an orange camouflage cap. The dog rose up and barked at the approach of the car, then trotted over with his tail wagging.

"Rover seems happy," Tom said.

"I am too," Elias replied. "He's a good dog. I took him to the mailbox and back."

"I had something longer in mind. Maybe take him—"

"To Austin's Pond," Elias interrupted, sitting up straighter in the chair. "If you park at the first dirt road it's a nice flat hike, not more than half a mile. Of course, you can go to the second road and drive to the edge of the water, but I feel up to a short walk. The hay has been cut and stored in the barn."

Elias was like a young child who wouldn't accept "no" or "later" as an answer.

"We should probably get that over with," Tom answered with a sigh. "I'll change clothes."

Tom put on jeans and a short-sleeved shirt and grabbed two bottles of water from the pantry. When he went outside, Elias and Rover were in the garage.

"Here it is," Elias said, triumphantly holding up a camouflage cap identical to the one on his head. "You'll need this."

The hat still had the sales price on the bill.

"Why?"

"You don't want a deer hunter taking a shot at you."

"It's not deer season."

Elias grinned, and Tom put the hat on his head. If Clarice had any second thoughts about ending their relationship, seeing him wearing the cap would make them vanish.

"What's all that?" Tom pointed to rows of boxes stacked four and five high at the rear of the garage.

"Things your father brought over from the house. He never got a chance to go through them."

Sorting through all the boxes would be a hassle. It would be easier to haul everything, sight unseen, to the dump.

"That was over three years ago," he said.

"Anything you don't want, I can give to the Burk family to sell in a yard sale."

Elias opened the passenger door of the car. Rover pushed past the old man and hopped onto the seat.

"It's okay, I can sit in back," Elias said.

"No." Tom came around the car. "He needs to learn to respect his elders."

Tom dragged Rover out of the car, then lifted him into the backseat. He slipped a towel under the front half of Rover's body just in time to catch a large glob of drool. Elias settled into the passenger seat with a walking stick between his legs. The older man seemed more energetic and alert today.

"How are you feeling?" Tom asked, turning the key in the ignition.

"Like I said, it's a good day. Having you and Rover at the house is medicine to me."

Tom started the car.

"And I'm back in the fight," Elias continued. "It's a paradox. The battle wears me out and builds me up at the same time."

Tom didn't want to open the door to a spiritual conversation. His morning encounter with Balaam's donkey followed by the meeting with Pastor England and the members of the Ebenezer Church had been more than enough religion for a month of Saturdays.

It was about four miles to the spring-fed pond where John Crane and Harold Addington drowned. Tom knew the spot well. It was one of his father's favorite fishing holes.

"There it is," Elias said, peering ahead.

Tom slowed and turned to the right. It was less than a quarter mile to the first dirt road. Reaching it, he parked between two pine trees. A rusty "No Trespassing" sign was nailed to one of the trees.

"Bud Austin won't recognize your car," Elias said.

"I'll leave a note. But first, I'd better leash Rover. He usually comes when I call, but I can't completely trust him out in the open."

Tom hooked a retractable leash to the dog's collar. Rover sniffed in the immediate area of the car while Tom scribbled a note on a sheet of paper and stuck it under one of the windshield wipers.

The road was rarely used, but there were two bare tire tracks visible with grass and weeds growing in the middle. Tom opened a metal gate that led to the hayfields.

"You set the pace," Tom said to Elias.

They set off at a slow walk, which suited Rover, who could spend ten minutes exploring the smells offered every hundred feet. Tom walked behind his uncle. Leaning on his stick, Elias looked like one of the Old Testament prophets in the illustrated Bible Tom read as a boy—except for the blue overalls and orange camouflage hat, of course.

The road was mostly flat with a few undulations, but before they reached the pond it crested a slight rise. Elias stopped. He was breathing heavily. Tom wasn't sure letting the old man talk him into a mini-hike was a good idea.

"Are you okay? We're almost there."

"I know. Little hills I wouldn't notice at your age seem like mountains now."

"When we get ready to leave, I can walk back to the car, drive in, and pick you up."

"We don't have to decide that now."

Elias took a long drink of water. Rover's tongue was extended to its full length.

"Not much farther," Tom said to the dog. "There's a pond full of water in your future."

"Go ahead so he can get a drink," Elias said. "I'll catch up in a minute."

"Are you sure?"

"Yes."

Tom and Rover walked rapidly down a short hill. When they reached the pond, Rover put his front paws in the water and began to lap noisily. Except for a few faint ripples, the water was smooth. The pond was oval, about 75 yards across and 150 yards in length. Not far from the spot where Rover enjoyed a cool drink, the surface of the water was disturbed by tiny bubbles produced by an underground spring seeping through the earth. The hidden spring was the water source for the pond and kept it from becoming stagnant.

Water grass and reeds rimmed the edge. Sunfish and smaller bass camped out near the reeds and waited for minnows and aquatic insects to venture far enough from safety to become dinner. The kings of the pond were the largemouth bass. John Crane had caught some of the behemoths in Austin's Pond so many times he recognized them when he lifted them out of the water. The big bass lurked around an invisible mass of fallen trees about thirty yards from shore. It was where the aluminum boat had capsized. Tom imagined the peaceful scene disrupted by two men desperately struggling to stay afloat, then forever sinking beneath the surface. The bodies were found by divers from the sheriff's department. He looked away.

Elias, his breathing still labored, came up beside him.

"Why did you want to come here?" Tom asked.

"Where did they find the boat?" the old man asked, wheezing slightly.

"Why is that important?"

"Please, tell me."

Tom pointed to the spot above the sunken trees. "The report from the sheriff's department contained a diagram showing the boat upside down over there. That's where the big fish hang out. Dad and Harold Addington would have wanted to cast across the top of the logs underneath the water. They threw out a small anchor to keep the boat from drifting."

"Was it still attached to the anchor when the deputies got here?"

"That's what it says in the report. I'm not exactly sure where they found the bodies." Tom clenched his teeth together for a moment. "Look, now that we've come and I've answered your questions, can we go? I'll jog back to the car and drive to the other entrance."

"It was a lot of work getting here," Elias replied. "I'd like to sit quietly for a few minutes."

"Suit yourself," Tom responded abruptly. "I'm going to go for a walk."

Tom jerked Rover's leash. The dog backed out of the water, then shook his head vigorously. Tom followed a faint path around the end of the pond where a tiny stream trickled down a hill. He stepped across the stream and continued along the far side of the water. He could see Elias sitting in a sunny spot with his walking stick across his lap. The old man had his head bowed. Tom continued along the path. On another day, in another place, he would have enjoyed walking with his dog around a peaceful pond.

But not today, not here.

This was the place of his father's death, its watery surface a cemetery monument. Rover wanted to take a leisurely stroll, but Tom pressed on. The sooner he made it back to Elias, the sooner they could leave.

They reached the far end of the pond where years before Bud

Austin had placed a concrete picnic table and two benches in the middle of a small grassy space. An empty cardboard bait container that once held night crawlers rested on the edge of the table. Tom knocked the container to the ground so Rover could sniff it. After a few seconds, Tom pulled on the leash to continue, but Rover protested. He wasn't finished savoring the exotic smells. Yielding to the dog, Tom sat down on a bench. The gentle heat of the sun warmed his face. He closed his eyes.

And he remembered a long-ago day.

It was another Saturday. Tom was about ten years old, and the Crane family had come to the pond to fish and eat a picnic lunch. Tom and his father hurried off to fish while Tom's mother sat at the cement table, which then was smooth and white, and fixed sandwiches. After a few minutes she joined Tom, who was close by. She listened to him explain all he knew about catching fish. In proof of his expertise, Tom hooked several sunfish in rapid succession. Each one violently jerked his rod and dragged a red bobber underwater. Then his father called out from the far end of the pond. He'd hooked a big one.

Tom and his mother ran down the path and arrived in time to see a massive bass angrily churn the water. Compared to the scrappy sunfish, the bass was a great white shark. John Crane fought the fish until it tired and came to his hand like an animal to be petted. Lifting the bass from the water, he let Tom measure it against his body. It stretched from Tom's fingertips to his shoulder. Looking into the fish's gaping mouth, Tom knew why the species was called largemouth bass. After proudly holding the fish high up in the air, his father gently returned it to the water. In that happy moment, no one in the Crane family knew the tragedies that would one day shatter their lives. Tom returned to the present, leaned forward, and put his head in his hands.

And cried.

Tears that should have flowed freely when his mother died seeped from the caverns where they'd been confined. Tom wept like the ten-year-old boy in his memory. Tears seeped through his fingers. His chest heaved. He tried to stop, but the pent-up flow could not be denied. He struggled to catch his breath.

Tom had responded to the loss of his mother by attempting to forge strength from heartbreak, a manly thing to do, but tragically incomplete. His mother's burial closed a coffin lid on his feelings, leaving him entangled in the veil between boyhood and manhood. He grew physically and intellectually, but inside he remained emotionally frozen, like an embryo in suspended animation. Then he laid the death of his father into the same broken paradigm.

In the autumn sun of Austin's Pond, the thawing process began.

Tom wiped his eyes and cheeks on the sleeve of his shirt. Through blurred vision he saw Rover inspecting a clump of reeds at the edge of the water. Elias was still sitting in the spot where he'd left him.

Another wave of emotion hit him. This time he didn't try to fight it. He even blinked his eyes to clear the way for more tears to flow. As each salty drop rolled down his cheeks, he felt a tiny release of pressure lodged deep inside his chest, an inner tension he'd come to accept as his normal state. He'd never considered that tears, even those produced by grief and loss, could be good.

Finally the caverns emptied, leaving his eyes swollen. He wiped his wet cheeks with his already damp sleeve. Rover returned from exploring, stuck his nose in Tom's face, then licked his hand. Tom rubbed the dog's neck. Rover groaned in pleasure.

"This is enough for one day," Tom said. "Let's get Elias."

Tom walked slowly along the path. He didn't want his uncle

to see the signs of grief on his face. When he reached the old man, Elias was standing at the edge of the pond stirring the water with his walking stick. Tom cleared his throat.

"Ready to go?" he asked Elias.

"What happened?" Elias asked without looking up.

"What do you mean?"

"At the old picnic table."

Before Tom could answer another wave of emotion swept over him. His assumption that he had no tears left was wrong.

Elias turned to face Tom. "Don't fight it," the old man said softly.

After a few moments the wave passed.

"I don't think I have what it takes to fight this." Tom sniffled. "When I sat down at the table, I remembered a happy day when I was a boy and came here with my parents. It was like a dam breaking. I've never cried like that."

"You've lost a lot."

"I wasn't wallowing in self-pity. It was–" Tom stopped.

Elias put his hand on Tom's shoulder. "Tears are a gift from God. Sorrow can grieve over a loss and still be grateful for the time you had."

"Yeah."

Elias tapped his stick against the ground.

"Do you want me to hike out and drive the car in on the other road so I can pick you up?"

"No," Tom answered, managing a slight grin. "I'll make it."

Elias smiled broadly, causing his face to wrinkle. "I believe that with all my heart."

They left the pond together.

chapter
SEVEN

Tom matched his steps to those of the older man. Rover, his nose overflowing with new smells, ambled along beside them. When they reached the car, both men took a long drink of water.

"I should take a walk every day," Elias said, wiping his mouth with the back of his hand. "I stay cooped up way too much."

Tom screwed the cap onto his water bottle.

"Rover would like it. Just don't go too far from the house. I don't want you passing out in a field or in the woods. Rover isn't a rescue dog. As far as I know, he doesn't have a drop of Saint Bernard in him."

During the drive home, Tom glanced over at Elias. "Why did you want to go to the pond?"

"I wasn't sure. I just knew from my time praying for you that we should go and the sooner the better."

Tom kept his mouth shut and his eyes on the road.

Rover slowly hopped out of the car and made it to the porch where he collapsed. A few minutes later Elias was stretched out in a recliner with his eyes closed and his mouth slightly open. Tom found a copy of *Huckleberry Finn* in a bookcase upstairs and sat on the porch in a rocker to read. He'd not read for pleasure in years. He was surprised by how much he enjoyed escaping into Mark Twain's imagination. Nineteenth-century life on the Mississippi wasn't that much different from twenty-first-century life in Bethel.

That evening Tom and Elias ate a creamy chicken casserole for supper.

"Where do you want to go to church in the morning?" Elias asked.

"How do you know I want to go at all?"

"I don't, but it seemed like a better way to ask the question."

"Sunday is my day to sleep late and then enjoy the newspaper."

"I don't get the paper."

"And I don't want to be around a lot of people from the past. Except for Rick and Tiffany Pelham, I'm not in town to socialize."

"We could visit Rocky River Church," Elias suggested. "Not many people there know you, and I should thank the folks who've been kind enough to bring food."

"Didn't that church run you off?"

"That was years ago."

Tom hesitated. "I guess I can tag along. But don't expect much from me."

"If you mean asking you to preach an impromptu sermon, you're safe. The church has a good minister. We'd better get there early if you want a good seat."

The church was on the south side of Bethel, and they had to pass through town to get there. Cars filled the parking lots for the large churches near the courthouse. Sunday morning church attendance was still part of the normal weekly routine for most people in Etowah County. Absence from worship on a regular basis carried a social stigma for which there was no polite excuse.

The Rocky River Church was two miles beyond the town limits. Located near the golf course, it was surrounded by new subdivisions. The sanctuary was built of smooth stones harvested a hundred years earlier from the stream that gave the church its name. Tom parked between a black luxury car and a red pickup truck with a bale of hay in the bed.

"That's Kenny Poindexter's truck," Elias said. "His wife is the one who made the chicken casserole we ate last night. They've been coming here for years."

"Did he vote to kick you out when you were the pastor?"

Elias smiled. "Yes, but we decided not to stay in that spot for the rest of our lives."

People greeted Elias as they made their way across the parking lot. The sanctuary was a long room with a sharply pitched ceiling. Elias led the way down the aisle. Stained-glass windows depicting events from Jesus' ministry lined the walls. Brass plates beneath each window identified the name of the family that paid for the window. Elias didn't stop until he reached the first pew.

"Is this your idea of a joke? We're early enough to get a good seat."

"No." Elias looked at Tom with a cherubic smile. "I want to sit up front so I can hear better."

"There's nothing wrong with your hearing."

Elias sat down. Tom joined him. The platform directly in front of them had two pulpits, one on the left and another on the right. A choir with twenty members paraded in and stood in a space in the middle of the platform. The organist hit a loud chord, and the choir began to sing a call to worship. Everyone stood. The minister, wearing a suit and tie, entered from a side door. He was in his midthirties and bore a close resemblance to a lawyer Tom knew in Atlanta who grew up in New Jersey. However, as soon as Rev. Lane Conner opened his mouth, it was clear that the minister wasn't from New Jersey. He spoke with the melodious accent of south Georgia.

"Where's he from?" Tom whispered to Elias.

"Moultrie."

When it came time for Reverend Conner to welcome people to the service, he asked Elias, as a former pastor of the church, to stand. In a slightly tremulous voice, the old man thanked everyone who'd brought food to the house. He then put his hand on Tom's shoulder.

"And I'm glad that John's son, Joshua Thomas Crane, has been here to help me eat it," he said. "He's in town for a few weeks to close down his father's law practice."

When Elias sat down, Tom nudged him sharply with his elbow. "Joshua?"

"It's on your birth certificate," the older man replied, keeping his eyes straight ahead.

The service followed a familiar pattern, and Tom grew bored; however, when Reverend Conner began to speak, he understood why people were coming to the church. The minister delivered the sermon with personal sincerity and self-effacing candor. Tom made a few mental notes of the preacher's techniques that would be effective in jury arguments. Conner's text was from the sixth chapter of Paul's letter to the Romans. Tom wasn't interested in the theology of dying to sin and experiencing resurrection life, but he admired the way Reverend Conner made his points. Time sped by, and when the minister said the message would be continued the following Sunday, Tom found himself wanting to return. After Reverend Conner pronounced the benediction, he stepped down from the platform and shook hands with Elias and Tom.

"Good job," Tom said, not sure if that was the proper way to compliment a sermon.

"Thanks," Conner replied. "Let's get together while you're here. Call me at the church, and we'll set a date."

"I might do that."

After the minister moved on, Elias turned to Tom. "Will you?"

"Probably not."

"You should." Elias looked past Tom's shoulder down the aisle of the church. "There's Esther Addington and her daughter."

Tom had met Harold Addington's widow at the funeral home but not the daughter. Esther was a small, thin woman with gray hair and a slightly pinched face. Her daughter was petite but sturdy looking, with short auburn hair and blue eyes. Esther used a cane for support. The two women had been sitting a few rows behind them. Tom and Elias met them in the aisle.

"Mrs. Addington, how are you doing?" Tom asked.

"It's hard, but I'm getting by," the woman replied. "This is my younger daughter, Rose. She was out of the country when you came to the funeral parlor."

Tom shook Rose's small hand. The young woman had a firm grip.

"Tom Crane," he said.

"Rose Addington," she replied in a crisp British accent.

They walked down the aisle.

"They had to delay the funeral two days waiting for me to arrive," Rose continued. "I'm sorry I couldn't be here for your father's memorial service. Everyone tells me he was a wonderful man."

Tom suddenly felt embarrassed that he'd rushed back to Atlanta and not stayed for the funeral of the man who'd died with his father.

"How long will you be in Bethel?"

"Until we sell the house." Rose gestured toward her mother. "My mum wants to move back to Newcastle so she can be close to my younger brother and older sister. They're both married with children."

Tom remembered the families from the visitation time at the funeral home. They stepped outside into the afternoon sun. Rose took her mother's arm and started to move away.

"Mrs. Addington," Tom called after them. "Could I talk to you for a minute? I have a few questions I need to ask you."

Esther and Rose stopped. Tom came over to them.

"In checking the files at my father's office, I found a folder with the name Addington written on it, but there wasn't anything inside. Do you know why your husband may have consulted with my father as an attorney?"

Esther looked at Rose.

"That's interesting," Rose replied. "We suspected my father may have retained your father's services as a solicitor."

"Why would you suspect that?"

"Based on a few things Harold said," Esther replied slowly.

"What sort of things?"

"That he was going to talk to your father about a situation at work. Harold never mentioned any details to me, and I didn't ask, but I remembered it when the government barrister came by for a chat."

"Charlie Williams?"

"Yes, that's his name."

"It was a very upsetting meeting," Rose added. "He has a way of making everything he says sound accusatory."

"That's why he's called a prosecutor," Tom replied, remembering Williams's tone at the Chickamauga Diner.

"If you find anything, will you let us know?" Rose asked.

"Certainly."

Rose reached into her purse and took out a business card.

"My cell number here in the States is on the back."

Tom looked at the card. It bore the name and address of an adoption agency in London on the front and a handwritten phone number on the back. Rose and her mother stepped away. Tom turned to Elias as soon as the women were out of earshot.

"Did my father ever mention any business dealings with Harold Addington?"

"Not that I remember, but we rarely talked about his cases."

"Did you meet Addington?"

"Several times but just for a few minutes when they stopped by the house on their way fishing." Elias paused. "Your father did ask me one night to pray for him and Harold."

"What about?"

"He didn't say."

"I wish he had," Tom grunted.

At 3:00 p.m. Tom was sitting in the front room of the house reading *Huckleberry Finn* when he received a call on his cell phone. It was Rick Pelham.

"Can you come for supper tonight?" Rick asked. "Tiffany has been bugging me since I saw you on Friday to set something up, and my father came into town last night. He's only going to be here for a few days and wanted to see you too."

"What time?"

"Six thirty."

"I'll be there."

A t 6:28 p.m. Tom turned onto the long driveway that led to Rick and Tiffany's house. No cloud of red clay dust boiled up behind his car. Carefully shaped Bradford pear trees lined the pebbled concrete surface. To the right was an apple orchard. On the left, the rolling hills were covered with trees waiting to be harvested.

The large brick home was perched on top of the hill and featured a massive recreation room where Rick and his buddies could watch football games in theater seats or play the latest combat-themed video game in raucous surround sound. So long as she could hang out with her horses, Tiffany let Rick cater to his inner man-child.

Tom parked beside the white Italian sports car that Arthur Pelham drove when he stayed in Bethel. The vehicle's unique lines and throaty roar instantly announced Arthur's presence around town. Most people in Bethel were proud, not jealous, that one of their own had achieved a level of success that enabled him to buy a car that cost more than most houses. By creating local jobs, Arthur proved his loyalty to his roots.

One of Rick's black Labradors bounded up to Tom's car with a red ball in his mouth.

"Hey, Bosco," Tom said, rubbing the back of the dog's strong neck. "If I bring Rover out to play with you, will you wear him out?"

The dog dropped the ball. Tom picked it up and threw it across the hill toward the apple trees. The dog raced after it. Tom walked up to the front door and rang the doorbell. Instead of a simple chime, the bell played the first few notes of the fight song for the college Rick and Tiffany had attended. Peeking through one of the glass panels, Tom saw Tiffany approaching. Age had been good to Tiffany. Her brunette hair was stylishly cut, and she was wearing a blouse and slacks that flaunted her shapely figure. Flinging open the door, she threw her arms around Tom and gave him a kiss on the right cheek.

"I was so excited when Rick told me the two of you stopped traffic to talk on Friday!"

Tiffany released her grip.

"You look great," Tom said, stepping across the threshold.

"You're not so bad yourself," Tiffany answered with a coy smile. "How are you getting along with that tall blonde who came up from Atlanta for the funeral?"

"It's over. She broke up with me and took my cat with her."

"What?" Tiffany's mouth dropped open.

"It stung, but I don't think I'll miss either of them very much."

Tiffany grabbed Tom's arm and led him across the silk rug that covered the foyer.

"You'll find someone ten times better, and she'll be the luckiest girl in Georgia. The boys are in the cigar room."

"When did you start calling Mr. Pelham a boy?"

"Ten seconds ago."

"The other day he told me to call him Arthur."

"I'm supposed to do the same thing, but it's kind of weird. I mean, my dad still has to call him Mr. Pelham at work."

Tiffany stopped in front of a formal oil portrait of Arthur, Rick, Tiffany, and Arthur's much younger second wife, the dark-haired Larina.

"What do you think?" Tiffany asked.

"Very well done. You could almost be Larina's daughter."

"Shut up. She's only eight years older than I am." Tiffany touched the bottom of the painting. "Rick went nuts having to get all dressed up for the sitting. He's only happy when he's hanging out with his friends downstairs, hunting with the dogs, and chewing tobacco."

"Rick is dipping?"

Tiffany lowered her voice. "Not really. Hal Millsap got him to try it, but it made Rick sick, and he promised me he wouldn't get used to it. I saw enough of that stuff from my uncles when I was growing up. The cigars are okay. I've smoked a few myself."

Tom couldn't tell if Tiffany was joking or not. They reached the cigar room, a small rectangular area adjacent to the main-floor den. Tiffany flung open the door. Whiffs of white smoke curled out.

"Someone called the fire department," she announced. "And look who they sent!"

Arthur and Rick Pelham were sitting across from each other in red leather chairs. Rick jumped up and gave Tom a hug. Arthur carefully put his cigar in a crystal ashtray and rose more slowly. Taller and thinner than his robust son, Arthur Pelham had neatly trimmed gray hair and intense dark eyes. He shook Tom's hand.

"Hello, Tom. Remember what I told you," the older man said.

"Hello, *Arthur.*" Tom forced his lips to form the word. "Good to see you."

"Excellent," Arthur replied, patting Tom on the shoulder. "That makes me feel ten years younger."

"Can I call you Arthur?" Rick asked.

"No, that would make me think you're not going to obey me."

"That's certainly not an option," Rick replied, rolling his eyes at Tom.

Rick took a long puff on his cigar and put it out in an ashtray.

"I thought cigars were for after supper," Tom said.

"This is warm-up. It depends on the leaf," Rick replied.

"Don't get them started on that," Tiffany cut in. "The poor little tobacco plants in Cuba have no idea all the arguments they're going to start about when, where, and how they should be burned up."

Tiffany led the way down a hallway. They passed the formal dining room. Unlike the kitchen table at Elias's house, the table in Tiffany's dining room shone with unblemished beauty. When they entered the kitchen, Arthur's cell phone rang. He slipped it from the pocket of his shirt and answered it.

"Go ahead," he said, waving the others forward. "I've been waiting for this call."

"Since it's just the four of us, I thought we could eat on the veranda," Tiffany said.

A door at one end of the long kitchen opened to a veranda built onto the rear of the house. The glass walls of the veranda could be opened during warm weather to catch the breeze that often blew across the top of the hill, then closed during the winter when a garden fireplace in the middle of the room provided extra heat. The weather was mild, and the windows were cracked open. From the veranda Tom could see the horse barn. Beyond the barn was an outdoor riding ring.

"Did you ride today?" he asked her.

"Every day. The barn is my happy place."

"My four-wheeler is my happy place," Rick said.

Tiffany stepped back into the kitchen. "Mary, we'll eat here."

"You have a cook?" Tom asked.

"And a full-time maid, plus a groom at the barn, and a guy who works three days a week on the yard," Rick responded sheepishly. "I enjoyed cutting the grass with my tractor, but Tiff didn't think I did a good job."

"You have more important things to do, honey," Tiffany answered, patting him on the arm. "And I don't want you turning the tractor over on top of yourself. Besides, Junior needs the work. He has two babies and a third on the way."

"Junior?" Tom asked. "What kind of truck does he drive?"

"Uh, I think it's an old Ford," Rick answered.

"What color?"

"It used to be white, but it's pretty scuffed up. Why?"

"It has to do with one of the files I was reviewing at my dad's office."

"Is Junior in trouble?"

"No, no. My father's client was a pedestrian hit by a car. He thinks a man named Junior may have seen what happened."

"I don't know Junior's real name, but his last name is Jackson," Rick replied. "He'll be here in the morning, and I'll tell him to call you next week."

"Thanks. If he's the right guy, I need to pass the information along to my client so he can give it to his lawyer."

"Why don't you help the man who was hurt?" Tiffany asked.

Tom shook his head. "I'm here to shut down my father's practice, not continue it."

"I wish you'd move back," Tiffany answered with a slight pout.

"Me too," Rick said.

A middle-aged woman with bleached-blond hair entered the veranda with plates and silverware in her hands.

"Thanks, Mary. I'll get the glasses," Tiffany said.

Tiffany left. Mary quickly positioned the plates and silverware on a glass-topped table and left. Tom leaned closer to Rick.

"Did Larina come with your father?"

"She hasn't been to Bethel since Christmas. My father loves the Parker-Baldwin house, but she gets bored here in thirty minutes. It's a sore subject. But I'm always relieved when she doesn't come. Larina makes Tiffany feel uptight about committing some massive social faux pas."

"Faux pas?" Tom responded with raised eyebrows. "Isn't that what Coach Ackerman yelled from the sidelines when you dropped the pass in the fourth quarter of the play-off game against Walker County?"

Rick punched Tom in the arm. "You didn't block the linebacker who was blitzing, and the ball came in too low. No one could have caught that pass. It almost bounced off the ground."

Tiffany and Arthur joined them.

"Rick and I were telling Tom that he should move back to Bethel and continue his father's law practice," Tiffany said to Arthur.

"Forget that," Rick replied. "He won't leave his fancy law firm in Atlanta."

Tom looked at Arthur, who shook his head slightly.

"There's been a recent change," Tom said, clearing his throat. "I'll fill you in over supper."

They ate roasted Cornish game hens with herb dressing, green beans seasoned with almonds, and a stewed squash dish. Tom told them about losing his job and the breakup with Clarice. Arthur added his part about Pelham Financial.

"Couldn't Tom still do some legal work for you while he's looking for a job?" Tiffany asked when Arthur finished.

"It's not that simple," Tom cut in. "Pelham Financial's legal needs are more complex than a sole practitioner can provide. It takes a team of lawyers to service—"

"Don't sell yourself short," Arthur interrupted. "I predict a bull market in Tom Crane stock. And I'm rarely wrong. I believe in investing in the people who've invested in me and my family. No one has done that more than you. I think something will open up for you soon."

Tiffany caught Tom's eye and winked. "Which brings me back to my original question," she said. "Why don't you stay in Bethel?"

"Yeah," Rick said. "There's a decent airport in Chattanooga. And if Elias gets tired of taking care of you, you can stay with us. You can even bring that handsome dog of yours along."

"I'd love having you at the house," Tiffany added. "There's a guest suite that hasn't been used more than a couple of times since we moved in."

Tom was touched by Arthur's encouragement and Rick's and Tiffany's kind words. Every friendship in Atlanta had been an arm's-length transaction. His eyes watered. Rick leaned forward.

"Hey, I'm not trying to make you cry," Rick said.

Tom coughed into his hand. "It's been an emotional couple of days. And not just because of the job and the situation with Clarice. Elias and I went to Austin's Pond yesterday. While I was there a lot of feelings about losing my mom and dad came up, and I cried like a little kid. And when I think about how long we've been friends and your invitation to stay here, it just—"

Tiffany leaned forward and put her hand on his arm.

"Bethel will always be your home," she said.

"That's what Elias says."

"True," Arthur said, "but sentimentality aside, it may not be where your future lies. You need to deal with the past, but don't get stuck there. Most people miss their best opportunities in life because they're looking backward and not forward."

"You like coming here." Rick cut his eyes toward his father. "If you had your way, you'd live most of the time in Bethel."

"I live where I want to live," Arthur responded with an edge to his voice. "And Tom may have outgrown what's here for him. Bethel is a great launching pad, but it's not necessarily the place where a man with ambition should end up."

"What about me?" Rick asked. "Are you saying I don't measure up because I'm not itching to leave? Is that why you've not been inviting me to the board of directors meetings for the company?"

Arthur didn't reply.

"Honey, you can't be a tree farmer in the middle of the city," Tiffany said with a nervous laugh. "Or satisfy my heart's desire to be with the horses every day. I couldn't stand it if I had to drive miles and miles to a stable. And who wants to sit in a stuffy boardroom and read financial reports?"

Rick looked down at his plate. Tom wanted to deflate the tension. He turned to Arthur.

"Arthur, what can you tell me about Harold Addington?"

"What do you want to know?" Arthur's eyes remained steely.

"Uh, anything that might be interesting. All I know is he was from Great Britain and liked to go fishing with my father."

"He worked in the international development branch of the firm," Arthur replied curtly. "Professionally, he was a disappointment to me."

Tom waited for additional information, then realized he'd

reached the limit of the older man's willingness to discuss Harold Addington.

"I saw his widow and daughter Rose at Rocky River Church yesterday," Tom said when the silence became awkward. "Rose works for an overseas adoption agency."

"Bunches of people are going to Rocky River," Tiffany responded brightly. "They say the young preacher, uh, what's his name?"

"Lane Conner."

"Yeah, I heard he's a great speaker. Reverend Moore at our church makes my eyes glaze over three minutes into the sermon. Maybe we could all go to Rocky River next Sunday."

"No way." Rick held up his hand. "I already have plans for a rafting trip with some guys on the Ocoee River, and I was hoping Tom would join us."

The Ocoee River was one of the best white-water rivers east of the Mississippi.

"It's been awhile since I bounced around in a raft," Tom said.

"It's like riding a bicycle," Rick replied. "What will it be? Going to the Rocky River Church to sit on a hard pew or hurtling down a bona fide rocky river in a raft over world-class rapids?"

"Let me think about it."

"That shouldn't take too long."

"I'll call later in the week."

Dessert was a chocolate cream pie that was good but not better than the coconut pie in Elias's refrigerator. After they finished, the men returned to the cigar room. Tiffany curled up in the den with a magazine and didn't join them. Arthur selected a cigar for Tom, who lit it and took a few puffs. The expensive cigar didn't attack his throat like the cheap stogies he'd smoked while playing dorm room poker in college, but it was still just a burning plant. They talked about Rick and Tom growing up together in Bethel. Tom snuffed out the cigar before it got too strong.

"I'd better be going," he said. "I have to be up early in the morning. Elias and my dog will see to that."

"Call me if you need anything," Arthur said. "I'm in town until Wednesday afternoon."

"And we'll be leaving the house about six thirty in the morning next Sunday for the rafting trip," Rick added.

Tom left the two men in the cigar room. Tiffany glanced up from her magazine when he came out.

"Are you part of the brotherhood?" she asked.

"Yeah. What kind of cigar do you prefer?"

"I was joking. The last cigar I had was made of pink bubblegum."

Tiffany led the way from the room. They passed the family portrait with its glued-on smiles and returned to the foyer.

"Thanks for supper," he said.

Tom reached for the door, but Tiffany put her hand on his elbow. "I really, really enjoyed seeing you," she said. "Come back as soon as you can. You're welcome in this house, even if Rick isn't here."

chapter
NINE

Tom drove home troubled. The family dynamics in the Pelham household proved money wasn't a magic poultice for problems.

It was dark when he crossed the front porch and opened the front door of Elias's house. Rover was lying at the old man's feet. He woofed when Tom entered, then carefully sniffed up and down Tom's legs. Elias watched from his chair where he sat with an open book on his lap and a steaming mug of tea on the table beside him.

"That's what a black Lab who loves to chase tennis balls smells like," Tom said. "And secondhand smoke from the fancy cigars we smoked after supper."

When Rover finished, Tom sat on a faded yellow couch. The dog returned to his place at Elias's feet and plopped down.

"You've stolen my dog's affections," Tom said.

Elias nudged the dog with his toe. "His heart is big enough to hold loyalty to two people."

"The Pelham family needs what he has. Tiffany isn't happy, and there's tension between Rick and Arthur. Several times this evening I felt uncomfortable."

"Do you think you're supposed to help them?"

"I'd have no idea where to begin."

Elias took a sip of tea and returned to his book. Tom finished *Huckleberry Finn*, then logged on to his laptop to check e-mail. The invisible signal that brought the Internet into the front room didn't discriminate between a chic coffee shop in New York City and a 125-year-old wooden farmhouse in Etowah County, Georgia. There was at least one difference between Huck's world and his.

———

The next morning Elias was in the kitchen when Tom came downstairs. Bacon sizzled in a skillet on the stove. The coffeepot beeped, signaling the brewing cycle was complete.

"I thought you didn't drink coffee," Tom said.

"It's for you. How do you want your eggs?"

"Uh, scrambled with cheddar cheese if you're taking orders, but you don't have to do that."

Elias cracked an egg and dropped the yolk into a metal bowl.

"Two or three?" the old man asked.

"Two."

Tom poured a cup of coffee and sat at the kitchen table. "How often do you cook breakfast?"

"This is the second time since your father died. Before that he and I took turns several times a week. One day oatmeal, the next pancakes, followed by eggs and grits. We didn't get in a rut."

Tom could imagine the two men working together in the kitchen. John Crane loved a hearty breakfast. He considered it the most important meal of the day.

"I could do it tomorrow," Tom offered. "What would you like?"

"It's cook's choice."

Elias sprinkled shredded cheese on top of the eggs in the skillet. They enjoyed a quiet breakfast. Elias took Tom's plate to the sink as soon as he finished.

"Thanks for letting me serve you," the old man said. "It's something I need to do. I've been getting selfish in my old age."

Tom put down his cup. "If you're selfish, what does that say about the rest of us?"

————

It was a cool morning, and Tom didn't lower the car windows during the drive to Bethel. When he pulled into a parking space in front of the office, Bernice was slowly getting out of her car. When she stood up, Tom saw she was using a cane for support.

"What happened?" Tom asked as he stepped past her to unlock the office door and hold it open for her.

"Got out of bed this morning and twisted my back."

"Then you should have stayed home."

"No." Bernice shook her head. "I know how badly you want to get everything taken care of so you can get on with your life."

"That's ridiculous."

Bernice gave Tom a hurt look.

"I mean, it's ridiculous that I gave you that impression," Tom corrected himself. "I don't want to be that selfish."

Tom took Bernice by the arm and gently turned her around. "Please go home, and do what you should to feel better. There's plenty I can do on my own."

"Okay," Bernice said. "It flared up like this a few weeks ago but felt better the next day."

"If it doesn't feel better tomorrow, stay home or go to the doctor. Is Dr. Frye still practicing?"

"Yes, he's treated Carl's back."

"Go see him if you need to."

"I'll stay near the phone."

"Okay, but I'll try to leave you alone."

Tom walked with Bernice to her car. "Oh, there is one thing I needed to ask you before you leave," Tom said as he held the car door open for her. "What kind of work was my father doing for Harold Addington? I found a file folder with Addington's name on it, but there wasn't anything in it."

"I saw that too," Bernice said as she flopped down in the car seat. "I remember Mr. Addington coming in several times. He always huddled up with your daddy in the office with the door closed."

"What did they discuss?"

"I'm not sure. It could have been their next fishing trip. I didn't type any documents or pleadings, so I figured it was personal, not business."

"I saw Addington's widow at Rocky River Church on Sunday. She believes her husband was a client but didn't seem to know why."

"If your daddy did any legal work for Harold Addington, I'd have known about it."

"Yeah, I'm sure you're right. All right, go home and get off your feet."

Tom waved as Bernice backed her car away from the curb.

After Bernice left, Tom brought his laptop and portable printer in from the car. Setting up in his father's office, he plowed through a box of files, typing letters and motions to withdraw from existing cases. Tom took a break midmorning and phoned some of the clients Bernice hadn't been able to contact. Several asked if he'd be willing to take over representation in their cases. Tom knew the request had nothing to do with him—it was a testament to the high opinion the clients had of his father. He also listened to the messages Bernice had saved on the answering machine.

One file raised an issue of federal law unfamiliar to Tom. He checked the books on his father's shelf and didn't find a resource that could provide an answer. Because his father never subscribed to an online legal search engine, Tom's only recourse would be to use books. The best place to do that would be the county law library.

Locking the office, he walked up the hill to the courthouse. The law library was on the second floor next to the jury room. As he climbed the steps, Tom met an older lawyer on his way down. It was Lamar Sponcler. They stopped and shook hands on the landing.

When the plaintiff's lawyer was younger, he had a thick mane of wavy black hair. Now Sponcler's hair was wavy and completely white, but his eyes retained the fiery spark that made hostile witnesses fear that the next question from his lips would torpedo their testimony.

"If you're going to see Judge Caldwell, he's in his chambers with Charlie Williams and a defense lawyer from Rossville," Sponcler said.

"No, I was going to do some research."

"Research?"

"Yes. My father never subscribed to a legal research service. In fact, he never bought Bernice a computer."

"He had his ways." Sponcler chuckled. "What's your issue?"

Tom told him. The spark in the older lawyer's eyes ignited.

"I had that come up in a case several years ago. It's a tricky procedural point."

"Would you be willing to represent the client?"

"I'd rather we do it together."

"Together? I'm here to shut down my father's practice, not keep it going."

"Why do that? I heard what happened to you in Atlanta. Take it from me, Bethel is a great place to ply your trade. I've made tons more money here than I would have wasting my career working for someone else in a silk-stocking law firm."

Tom's mouth dropped open. "How did you know I lost my job?"

"Charlie Williams mentioned it when I saw him earlier today."

"How did he know?"

"Legal gossip has always been faster than the Internet," Sponcler said, shifting his briefcase to his other hand. "Look, your former firm's mistake can be Bethel's gain. I'm winding down my practice and would be glad to help you get up to speed on plaintiff's work. I can't stand the thought of retiring and all the good cases going to Reggie Mixon. He'll lose the close ones and settle the rest for half what they're worth. Believe me, contingency work beats the daylights out of being tied to the billable hour."

"I don't know."

"Think about it," Sponcler said with a smile. "I'll swing by and take you to lunch one day so we can talk some more. I can be very persuasive when I put my mind to it."

Sponcler continued down the stairs. Tom entered the windowless room that housed the county law library. Musty books lined the walls. It took him forty-five minutes to find what he needed and make notes on a legal pad about the relevant cases. Sponcler was right. It was a tricky point of procedure. Tom was replacing the books he'd stacked on the table when the door opened. It was Judge Caldwell. Tom immediately stood up.

"Have a seat," the judge said with a wave of his hand. "The courtroom is thirty-five feet east of here."

Unlike Lamar Sponcler, Judge Nathan Caldwell's hair had fallen out instead of turning white. His bald head shone as if buffed with a cloth. An angular, bony man, the judge looked best concealed in a black robe. Dark-framed glasses, which had been the style when he was first appointed to the bench and recently returned to vogue, rested on his nose. He sat across the table from Tom.

"How are you doing, son?" the judge asked.

"Okay, I guess. Thanks for the message on the answering machine at the office. I was going to stop by and see you before I left town. My father had a lot of respect for you too."

"He will be missed. Death comes to all of us, but it has a greater sting when it strikes a man or woman who gave more to life than they took."

"Yes, sir."

The judge took off his glasses and rubbed his eyes. "Charlie Williams told me what happened at your law firm in Atlanta. Sorry to hear about that."

"I saw Lamar Sponcler on the stairs, and he mentioned it too. How did Charlie find out?"

"He brought your name up to someone in Atlanta who knew about it."

"Any idea who it was?"

"You'd have to ask him." The judge returned his glasses to his nose. "Both Charlie and Lamar think you ought to consider moving back to Bethel. A small-town law practice has its unique challenges and benefits."

"I've been hearing that from a lot of people, but I'm only in town for a few weeks to close down my father's practice and try to land a job with another firm in Atlanta."

"I understand, but I hate to see good people leave Bethel. The most important thing is to take the good influence your father had on you wherever you go."

Judge Caldwell was treating him like a peer.

"I've not valued what my father had to offer as much as I should."

The judge smiled. "That's the testimony of an honest witness. Just remember that what he gave you is like seeds inside you. Give them water and light and they'll grow." The judge leaned back in his chair and studied Tom for a moment. "Did you know your father occasionally came by my office to chat even when he didn't have a legal matter to bring before me?"

"No."

"It started years ago. As a judge I have to isolate myself from both the public and the lawyers who appear before me. But with your father I could crack that door open without compromising my obligation to neutrality. If I saw him the next day in court, I could listen to his argument and either accept it or reject it without regard to what we'd discussed in private. That's rare."

"What did you talk about?"

"Everything from fishing to the people who were important to us."

Tom looked down at the table for a moment. "We didn't have that kind of communication, especially after my mother died."

The judge leaned forward. "Even though he may not have told you how much he cared about you, I know that he did. Sometimes we have the hardest time telling the people we love the most how much they mean to us."

"Did he ask you to tell me this?" Tom asked in surprise.

"No, but I knew him well enough to believe he'd want me to. That's why I asked you to come see me in the phone message I left at his office."

"Do you think my father would have wanted me to continue his practice?"

"He would have been more interested in you continuing his faith."

Tom pressed his lips together and didn't respond. The judge took out one of his cards and wrote something on the back.

"Here's my cell phone number. You don't have to go through any hoops to talk to me."

After the judge left, Tom remained at the table, staring unseeing at the bookshelf across the room.

chapter
TEN

W hen he returned to the office from the courthouse, Tom dove into the financial records stashed in his father's credenza. His heart sank as he pulled out stacks of handwritten receipts, scribbled entries, and hard-to-decipher notes in the margins of the old-fashioned checkbooks. He cleared everything else from the top of the desk and began placing everything in little piles. Tom couldn't understand why his father hadn't bought a simple computer-software bookkeeping program.

Three hours later, and to his great relief, Tom had determined the general business account contained a few thousand dollars with no significant checks outstanding. A stack of bills, some overdue, would take the account to zero, leaving Tom on the hook to pay Bernice's salary for the days she'd worked since John Crane's death.

Tom's concern about the IRS was confirmed. His father had made three payments of $10,000 each, leaving an amount owed of $167,000. There wasn't that much money in the estate. Fortunately, the IRS couldn't hold Tom personally liable for the remaining balance. He closed the tax file. His inheritance would be limited to the goodwill expressed by people like Judge Caldwell and the folks from the Ebenezer Church.

Finished with the regular account, Tom found the trust account records in a separate drawer. Every lawyer is required to keep money that belongs to clients or third parties in a separate bank account. It was embarrassing that his father owed the government money, but it would be a permanent moral stain on John Crane's good character if Tom uncovered irregularities in the trust account. There hadn't been much activity in the trust account, and Tom was able to quickly verify correct amounts for ten open cases and made notes so he could notify the clients. A slip of paper stuck in the margin of the trust account check register caught his eye.

DTA – SDB – 35-89

The initials didn't make sense, but the numbers were part of John Crane's method of case identification. The first two digits were the length of time his father had been practicing law—thirty-five years at the time of his death. The second set of numbers indicated the order in which a case was opened in a calendar year. Tom moved a few boxes and found the cases that contained files opened since the beginning of the year. He flipped through the folders looking for number 35-89. When he found it, he didn't have to pull it from the box to discover what it contained.

It was the Addington matter.

Tom knew the file folder was empty, but he carefully inspected the manila cover for any writing or notation, no matter how faint. There was nothing except a slightly bent tab on top. He searched both the regular and the trust accounts for any references to money paid by or to Harold Addington. Nothing turned up. Stumped, he knew there was only one person who might be able to help him. Picking up the phone, he called Bernice.

"It's Tom."

"Thanks for checking on me," she said. "I'm alternating between an ice pack and heating pad, and it seems to be helping."

"Keep it up. Listen, I've been going through the bank records—"

"Uh-oh."

"No, no. Everything seems to be okay. But I found a slip of paper in the trust account ledger with 'DTA – SDB – 35-89' written on it. That's the file number for the empty folder with Addington's name on it. Did Harold Addington ever pay him any money?"

"Not that I remember. Did you find any deposits to the trust account in Addington's name?"

"No, and I checked for any fees coming into the operating account since the beginning of the year. Any chance there might be something before that?"

"I doubt it. They didn't start spending time together until late February or early March. Before that, it was too cold to go fishing."

"Okay, get some rest."

"If I wake up in the morning and feel better, I'm going to get in the car and come down for a few—"

"Bernice," Tom interrupted.

"Yes, sir. I'll stay home if I need to."

After Tom hung up the phone, he opened his wallet and took out the business card Rose Addington had given him. He didn't have much to tell Esther and Rose Addington, but he owed them a brief response to their questions. He dialed Rose's number. She answered on the third ring, and Tom identified himself.

"Is your mother available?" he asked.

"She's resting right now. May I take a message and have her ring you later?"

"Uh, I can probably fill you in." Tom quickly summarized what he'd found in the trust account ledger. "I wish I could shed more light on the matter, but I can't. The small amount of money left in the trust account is clearly linked to other clients, and there's no record of a fee paid by your father to the operating account."

"Can you come over now?" Rose responded.

"Excuse me?"

"It's too late for tea, but maybe you could drop by on your way home? Mum lives at 4598 Windermere Lane."

Tom knew the street. He passed the entrance to the subdivision on the way to and from Elias's house.

"Why do you want to see me?"

"So we can have a chat."

The British lass wasn't very chatty.

"Okay. Would thirty minutes be too soon?"

"That will be fine. Do you need directions?"

"No."

Tom turned onto Windermere Lane, a short cul-de-sac at the backside of a subdivision known as Western Heights, a neighborhood of well-built two-story brick homes on large lots in natural settings. As soon as he heard the address, Tom knew that Harold Addington, even if he was a disappointment to Arthur Pelham, must have earned a decent salary. The Addington house was on the right as he entered the cul-de-sac. Tom drove through a buffer of trees and parked in front of the house. The small yard between the natural area and the house was carefully manicured, the bushes neatly trimmed. Twin stone lions crouched on either side of the front door.

Something about the place made Tom uneasy. He looked around. There were multiple cameras on the house and several on trees in the wooded area. Extensive home security systems weren't common in Etowah County. Some residents didn't even lock their doors at night. He walked up the steps and stood between the lions while he pressed the doorbell. The glass sidelights were obscured by intricate ironwork, which doubled as a barrier to forced entry. He heard two dead bolts click before the door opened. Rose Addington, wearing blue slacks and a gray shirt, stood on the threshold.

"Come in," she said with a smile. "Mum is in the kitchen."

Tom followed her from the foyer into a formal living room. The interior of the house was furnished with typical American furniture.

"Did your father work from home?" Tom asked.

"Quite a bit, actually. He had an office upstairs." Rose pointed to a long staircase. "After you called I double-checked the checking account records for the year and didn't find any payments by Papa to your father's office."

"Neither did I."

"But that doesn't answer all our questions."

Tom noticed two more surveillance cameras that monitored activity on the staircase. They passed through a dining room into a long narrow kitchen with a breakfast nook. Esther Addington, looking tired, was sitting at a round table surrounded by four chairs. She extended her hand to Tom.

"I'm not feeling too well today," she said. "Please sit down."

Tom and Rose sat on opposite sides of Esther.

"Tell me what you found," the older woman said.

"Not much," Tom began and then repeated what he'd told Rose. "Does that mean anything to you?"

"Is everything we discuss with you confidential?" Rose asked.

"Not necessarily. We're talking about my father's law practice, not mine, which means I'm not here as a lawyer but as executor of his estate."

"Do you represent Arthur Pelham or his company?"

"No."

"But you might in the future?"

"It's possible."

"If that happened, would you reveal what we discuss with you?"

Tom shifted nervously in his chair. "Not if you consider this conversation as a preliminary step to hiring me. Under the rules, that sort of exchange of information is protected from disclosure by the attorney-client privilege."

"Even if we don't ultimately hire you?"

"Yes. Please get to the point."

Rose ignored him. "And I'm told you're a close friend of the Pelham family."

"That's true." Tom nodded. "Rick Pelham is a lifelong friend, and Mr. Pelham has reached out to me, especially since my father's death."

"Mum," Rose said, glancing at her mother, "I'm not sure this is a good idea."

"Your papa thought differently."

Esther, who had her hands in her lap, placed a folded sheet of paper on the table.

"After Harold's death, I found this in the nightstand on his side of the bed. I believe it may help."

Tom picked up the sheet of paper and opened it. John Crane's name and phone number were written at the top, followed by phrases that included "termination of employment agreement," "disclosure to third parties in UK, US, and Barbados prohibited," "confidential communication applies to financial transactions," and "transfer of funds." At the bottom of the sheet Addington had written "Tom Crane???" Tom looked up.

"Harold was concerned about his position at Pelham, and it's likely he talked to your father about it," Esther said.

"And when we saw your name at the bottom, it made us wonder if your father ever contacted you about Papa's concerns," Rose said.

Tom remembered the phone message he'd thrown away when he cleared out his office in Atlanta, and Arthur Pelham's comment that he was disappointed in Harold Addington's job performance. He handed the paper back to Esther.

"No, my father never mentioned any member of your family to me. But you believe your husband was worried he might lose his job?"

"Yes." Esther nodded. "He was under enormous pressure at work but wouldn't tell me exactly why. He felt it might cause problems for me later if I knew any specific details."

Tom felt himself go cold on the inside. Men in the financial arena who shielded their wives from information occasionally did so to shield them from harm in anticipation of criminal charges.

"That's the way he put it?"

"Yes, he knew I didn't understand the technical aspects of his work."

Tom stood. He wanted to end the conversation as soon as possible.

"I'm sorry I can't shine any light on the situation. If I find out anything else, I'll contact you immediately."

"Thank you." Esther sighed.

"Oh, one more thing," Tom said. "I'm going to tell Charlie Williams, the district attorney, that I've not found any clear evidence of a professional relationship between my father and Mr. Addington."

"From what we've talked about today, I'm not sure there wasn't a 'professional relationship,' as you put it," Rose responded. "You don't know why there is an empty folder with the Addington name on it in your father's office or the reason your father put a note in his financial records with the file number written on it. And we found a sheet of paper with notes apparently made during a conversation between them about business matters. Would I be missing something?"

"No," Tom admitted.

"And why did the government's barrister ask us questions? It really upset Mum when he came by the house with a detective in tow."

"Two men died, and it's his job to do a brief investigation," Tom replied. "I wouldn't read anything more into it than that."

"Just the same, we'd ask you not to tell Mr. Williams anything until we have a bit more clarity," Rose said.

Tom didn't think Rose could legally muzzle him but didn't tell her so. She led him to the door.

"Thanks for stopping by," she said.

When Tom was in his car, he counted five exterior surveillance cameras, with an unknown number throughout the house. Now he had a reasonable suspicion why the district attorney was investigating the dead British man. And it had nothing to do with a boat tipping over at Austin's Pond. If Addington was engaged in some form of criminal activity, the grave wouldn't stop the investigation—especially if it involved fraud or theft committed against Arthur Pelham and Pelham Financial.

ELEVEN

Returning home, Tom found the front room empty and the study door closed. A scratching sound revealed Rover's presence. A moment later both Elias and the dog emerged from the study.

"I thought you didn't like company in there," Tom said, scratching Rover's head as the dog moaned softly.

"That dog is a blessing," Elias replied.

"Huh?" Tom asked as a drop of drool dangled precariously from Rover's mouth.

"Have you already forgotten about Balaam's donkey?"

"No," Tom answered, looking up. "But the day you tell me Rover is talking to you is the day I contact Dr. McMillan to discuss putting you in a place with locks on the doors and strong orderlies who will keep you from wandering off."

"You don't scare me."

Tom looked toward the kitchen. "What's for supper? I'm hungry."

Fifteen minutes later two plates were on the table. While they ate, Elias talked about his day with Rover. Tom was glad the old man

and the dog were doing so well together, but his thoughts kept drifting to his father's federal tax liability.

"Did my father ever talk to you about his financial problems?"
Tom asked during a lull in the conversation.

"I know he owed the government money. Will you have to pay it?"

"No."

"Do you think you should anyway?"

"Is that what the Bible teaches?"

"I'm not sure."

"Don't spend any time trying to find out. I have enough problems in my life without adding to them."

While they rinsed the dishes in the sink, Elias said, "What do
you think about inviting some folks over for supper? I have an old
charcoal grill in the garage. We could cook steaks."

"It's your house."

"Good. I was praying this afternoon and believe we're supposed
to invite Esther and Rose Addington for a meal. We didn't get the
chance to talk much after church on Sunday and—"

"There's no need," Tom interrupted. "I went to their house on
my way home from work and finished the conversation." Tom put
the soap in the dishwasher and closed the door. "God answered your
prayer as soon as it left your lips."

The following morning Tom fixed pancakes and link sausage for
breakfast. He waited until Elias came into the kitchen to drop the
pancake batter on the griddle.

"How did you sleep last night?" Tom asked.

"I was up for a while praying," Elias responded with a yawn.

"If I get to sleep through the night without waking up, I'm going to take advantage of it. You don't have to go anywhere during the day. Why don't you pray then?"

"That's not how it works. Before Jesus selected the twelve apostles, he spent the entire night in prayer."

Tom flipped over a pancake. "Why did he have to pray? He knew everything."

"He was showing how a man can walk with God. The Bible says Jesus only did what he saw his Father do."

When the pancakes were ready, Tom put them on plates and took the sausage from the oven where he'd been keeping it warm. He'd already melted butter and warmed up pure maple syrup. Elias took a bite of pancake.

"Well?" Tom asked as the old man thoughtfully chewed and swallowed.

"As good or better than the ones your father made. He always liked to use a bit of almond extract in the pancake batter."

"I found it in the cupboard. I've watched him make pancakes many times."

"That's good." Elias smiled. "Keep doing what you saw your father do."

Tom was enjoying the short commute from Elias's house to the center of Bethel. Unlike Atlanta, none of the drivers he encountered on the road were struggling with coffee-deprived road rage.

The office was quiet. He checked the answering machine and retrieved a call from Bernice that she was going to spend another day at home recuperating. Instead of immediately getting to work,

Tom thought about Elias's comment at breakfast. What would John Crane do if he arrived early at the office and didn't have to rush off to a court hearing? Tom knew the answer. His father would chat with Bernice for a few minutes, then go into his office and close the door. And commit the day's activities to God.

When he visited the law office as a boy, Tom would sit wide-eyed as his father bowed his head and talked to God. A child who sees an adult pray other than before a meal or in church remembers it. John Crane's prayers from behind his desk always contained a request that he represent his clients with skill and integrity. Tom remembered the specific words: *skill* and *integrity*. Wondering if they might be from a Bible verse, Tom pulled a well-worn Bible from the bookcase and located a concordance in the back. He looked up the word *skill* and found nothing that seemed right. He then checked the word *integrity* and scored a hit. He turned to Psalm 78:72, a passage about King David and the people of Israel. John Crane had underlined the verse with a red pen and drawn a blue star in the margin.

So he shepherded them according to the integrity of his heart,
and guided them by the skillfulness of his hands.

Tom read the verse silently a couple of times. It was quiet in the room, but the stillness wasn't stagnant. He looked up from the Bible for a moment, then softly read the verse out loud. As he spoke, the meaning of each word reverberated in a place inside him that Tom didn't know existed. He read the verse again, and the sensation increased. Tom had studied great books and listened to eloquent speeches, but nothing he'd ever read or heard was more majestic and profound than a single verse of Scripture coming from his own mouth.

"What is going on?" he asked.

The answer to his simple question came to his mind before he had a chance to imagine one. And it didn't come from his intellect. It came from a place not visible to the eye, in a voice that didn't need sound waves to communicate. He intuitively knew what was happening to him.

God was speaking to him.

Tom sat up straight in the chair. He'd always thought conversation with the Almighty would follow a great debate in which God proved his existence by superior logic. No, God's voice proceeded from his presence. Human theories, arguments, opinions, and ideas shrank to insignificance. The awareness of God's reality shot through Tom like a lightning bolt. And if God was real, the most important thing in life was to know him. Tom was stunned.

"I'm sorry," he said, realizing how proud and arrogant and independent he'd been.

Humility opened the door of his heart wider. He read the verse again, not with curious neutrality, but as a thirsty man drinks a cup of cold water: "So he shepherded them according to the integrity of his heart, and guided them by the skillfulness of his hands." God's description of David wasn't limited to an ancient king in a faraway land. The words on the page were for today. Tom suddenly understood why his father prayed as he did. A dormant seed awakened. Desire rose up in him. Tom hesitated. Reason demanded he slow down and let his understanding catch up.

"No," he said emphatically. "I want this to be true about me."

Taking out a legal pad, Tom began to write down everything he was thinking and experiencing. Using the concordance, he flipped through the Bible. The relevance of the words in the book wasn't limited to a single verse in Psalms. He found wisdom and insight wherever he turned. When he finally took a break, he looked up from the notes scribbled on the pages and remembered Judge Caldwell's words from the day before.

Tom was beginning to share his father's faith.

He spent the rest of the morning exploring the new world in the ancient book. The phone didn't ring; no senior partner interrupted his thoughts. The room was as isolated as a monastery cell. He read several chapters in the book of John, who boldly claimed Jesus was the Son of God, the Light of the World, the Savior of mankind, the Way, the Truth, and the Life. For the first time in Tom's existence, the claims made perfect beautiful sense.

He kept reading. Turning to Paul's letters, he read verses he would have considered offensive and arbitrary twenty-four hours earlier. Now they revealed the goodness of God. Amazed at the change in his perspective, Tom discovered an answer in 1 Corinthians 2:14: "But the natural man does not receive the things of the Spirit of God, for they are foolishness to him; nor can he know them, because they are spiritually discerned." That was it. He'd been a natural man. He was becoming a spiritual one. He marked the spot with a sticky note and closed the Bible.

It was lunchtime. Tom had spent the entire morning reading the Bible, making notes, and writing down his thoughts. He was hungry. Going outside, he blinked his eyes in the bright sunlight. He inhaled the fresh air. Walking up the hill to Main Street, he greeted several people he didn't know as he passed by on the sidewalk.

Inside the restaurant, Alex Giles was scurrying around seating customers. Tom saw a solitary stool available at the end of the counter. He moved toward it.

"Hello there," a female voice behind him said.

Tom turned around. It was Rose Addington. She was standing beside a group of four waiting for a table.

"Are you by yourself?" she asked.

"Yeah. And you?"

"Yes, I was in town for a bit and decided to drop in for an authentic American meal."

"This is the perfect place. Enjoy your lunch."

Tom turned away in time to see someone sit down on the counter stool he had his eye on. He faced Rose. She was wearing dark slacks and a light-blue top. Her wavy auburn hair looked like she'd only brushed it once or twice before leaving the house. To ignore her would be rude. He cleared his throat.

"Would you like to join me?" he asked.

"I wasn't meaning to intrude."

"No, it's okay."

Tom motioned to Alex Giles and held up two fingers. The owner pointed to a table wedged into a spot against the rear wall of the diner. Tom followed Rose. There were two menus on the table. Before they had a chance to look them over, a waitress appeared.

"Ready?" she asked with a harried glance over her shoulder.

Tom gestured across the table toward Rose. "I think she needs more time before—"

"No, I've eaten here several times," Rose replied crisply. "I'll have dark-meat fried chicken, collard greens, stewed okra with tomatoes, and sweet tea, please."

Tom's eyes widened. "Uh, hamburger steak with onion gravy, candied yams, broccoli casserole, and sweet tea," he said.

The waitress scurried off toward the kitchen.

"You like collard greens?" Tom asked.

Rose picked up a small bottle of vinegar seasoned with hot peppers that was on their table next to a napkin dispenser.

"Adding a dash of this is what makes the dish."

Tom suspected Rose wasn't the type of woman to complain if the accommodations weren't four-star quality.

"I guess you have to eat different kinds of food as you travel in your work," he said.

"And learn not to ask too many questions about what's put before you. I often pray that what goes in my mouth will stay in my stomach."

The waitress brought their tea. There was a lemon wedge stuck on the rim of each glass. Rose squeezed the juice into the tea.

"The lemon custom struck me as strange," she said, dropping the rind into the glass. "Brew the tea with sugar to make it sweet, then add lemon to make it sour."

They sat in silence for a moment.

"Tell me about your adoption work," Tom said.

While they waited for the meal, Tom learned that Rose had worked the past five years facilitating adoptions from Eastern Europe, mostly from Bosnia and Serbia.

"Ethnic cleansing orphaned thousands of children without any close relatives who could take them in. But it's not just finding the children homes. It's also getting help for the trauma they've gone through. Some of these children have seen horrible things. However, there are sad stories with happy endings."

Rose then told him about a ten-year-old boy whose leg had to be amputated after he was injured when a land mine exploded. He'd recently been adopted by a Swedish family whose little girl had lost a leg to bone cancer.

"Instead of shutting themselves off, the family opened their hearts to receive another child in need. They understood the boy's loss better than anyone else could."

The waitress brought their food. When Tom saw the collard

greens on Rose's plate, he thought about Clarice. She would have never let her fork touch collard greens.

"Do you want to say grace?" Rose asked. "It's one of the things I've enjoyed seeing folk do here in the States. It's rare to see someone praying in a public house at home."

"You go ahead." Tom motioned with his fork.

Rose bowed her head and closed her eyes.

"Lord, thank you for this food and that this restaurant received a sanitation grade of 'A.'" She opened her eyes. "That should take care of it."

Rose reached for the vinegar and dribbled it on the collard greens. Tom ate a bite of meat, then stuck his fork in the broccoli casserole.

"Were you put out that I asked you to pray?" she asked.

"No. I've been praying and reading the Bible all morning."

The words were out of Tom's mouth before he could pull them back. Rose raised her eyebrows.

"The differences between lawyers in America and in Britain are greater than I thought," she said.

"It wasn't my usual morning."

"Are you saying you had an encounter with the Lord this morning?"

It was a moment of decision. Tom could dodge the question or tell the truth.

"For the first time in my life."

Rose's face beamed. "I could see something different in you when we were standing at the doorway. And I thought to myself, *I may be wrong, but I wager he's had a sweet time with Jesus before he came to work today.* That's one reason I invited myself to join you, although I had no idea it was such a momentous day." She leaned forward. "Don't worry. I won't pry. A touch from heaven like that is so personal a stranger like me doesn't have the right to look in on it."

Rose's enthusiasm made him feel safe.

"I don't mind talking about it, but I'm not sure I have the vocabulary to do it justice. It was an amazing time."

"I'd love to hear anything you'd like to share."

Tom glanced around the restaurant before answering. Rose waited with an expectant look on her face. Tom cleared his throat and quoted the verse from Psalm 78. As he described what happened, tears formed in Rose's eyes.

"Is this upsetting you?" Tom asked.

"No," she said as she wiped her eyes with a paper napkin. "It's so wonderful. There are people who have been sitting in churches their whole lives without knowing the goodness of the Lord like that."

As he talked, Tom discovered that telling Rose didn't dilute the experience. It had the opposite effect, increasing his confidence that something profound had occurred.

Rose dabbed her eyes again. "This is better than a mess of collard greens."

Tom laughed.

"All the good bits poured into you by your father, uncle, and others are starting to come together and make sense," Rose said.

"You sound like Judge Caldwell."

Tom felt a tap on his shoulder. It was Charlie Williams.

"Glad I caught the two of you together," the DA said. "What's the update on your father's representation of Mr. Addington?"

Tom glanced at Rose. "I don't have anything to report," he replied.

"That's it?"

"Yes."

The DA rubbed his jaw. "If we were in front of the judge, I'd argue that answer was unresponsive to the question."

"It's the only answer I have."

Williams patted Tom on the back. "Keep digging. There must be something in the old files that will shed light on it. And you might want to check the ethical rules on whether the attorney-client privilege survives the death of both client and lawyer. Give me a call."

Williams left. Rose followed the DA across the restaurant with her eyes.

"What's he trying to do?" she asked, leaning forward. "Why does he keep pestering us with these questions?"

There was nothing but innocence on her face.

"You don't have any idea?" he asked.

"How could I?"

Tom swallowed a bite of food before answering. "Was your father having any financial difficulties?"

"No. Papa had no debts. The house is paid for, and he left my mother with enough money to take care of herself for the rest of her life."

"Why is there such an elaborate security system at your house?"

"Papa was a philatelist."

Tom was about to eat a bite of broccoli casserole. He almost dropped his fork. "A stamp collector?"

"Yes, mostly nineteenth-century British Empire. There are several very rare specimens in his collection. Mum thought he should keep the most valuable stamps in a lockbox at the bank, but he said there was no use having the stamps if he couldn't enjoy looking at them. The reason I came to town this morning was to rent a box to hold the best of the lot until we can arrange a sale in London next year."

Rose's explanation for the expensive security system at the Addington residence made sense as a way to protect a valuable stamp collection, but it did nothing to explain away Arthur Pelham's negative reaction to her father's job performance. And if Harold Addington misappropriated funds from Pelham Financial, Arthur would want to be discrete about an investigation to avoid shaking investor confidence in the firm's security measures. Tom had witnessed that scenario before. Investment advisers charged with safeguarding customers' resources hated admitting a breach of trust, even if the embezzlement of funds was committed by a rogue employee. Rose interrupted his thoughts.

"Was your father having financial troubles?" she asked.

"He owed money for back taxes," Tom said defensively, "but that didn't have any connection to your father."

Rose pressed her lips together.

"And if Charlie Williams had any concrete evidence, he wouldn't be talking to us," Tom added.

"Evidence of what?"

Tom instantly regretted his slipup. "Williams is the district attorney for this circuit," he said slowly. "He's only interested in a situation if there is the possibility a crime occurred."

"Crime? That's crazy."

Tom shrugged. He didn't want to continue the conversation. Rose seemed pensive. They finished the meal in silence.

"It was an honor hearing how the Lord touched your heart," Rose said with a sigh. "I'm sorry the government barrister interrupted our conversation and dragged us from heaven down to earth." She leaned forward and spoke emphatically. "Don't let him or anyone make you doubt what happened to you this morning. I know the sound of truth, and it rang clear from your heart."

They walked together to the cash register.

"Let me buy your lunch," Tom said, holding out his hand for her ticket.

"No, you blessed me much more than the price of a meal."

Tom liked Rose Addington. It was a terrible shame what lay ahead in her future. Charlie Williams wasn't interested in philately. Larceny was more his area of expertise.

ware's edge

They walked together to the cash register.

Let me buy your lunch," Tom said, holding out his hand for
the ticket.

No, you blessed me much more than the price of a meal,"
Tom liked Rose Addington. It wasn't the flattery she'd
paid to him or the genuine interest she'd shown in what he
[illegible]

I never was more his own of experience.

chapter
TWELVE

Tom glanced through his notes from the morning. Rose
Addington was right. The thoughts and prayers he'd
written still stirred his heart. He stared for a moment
at the stack of boxes in the corner of the room. The prospect of
an entire afternoon reviewing old legal files now seemed incred-
ibly boring. He winced. Hopefully, the morning's events hadn't
rendered him so spiritually minded that he was incapable of the
practice of law.

Opening the middle drawer of the desk, he saw a small envelope that contained the key to the safe-deposit box his father rented
at a local bank. Tom didn't have any valuable nineteenth-century
British Empire stamps to safeguard, but as executor of his father's
estate, he needed to inventory the contents of the box. A walk to the
bank would also provide an excuse to ignore the boxes crouched in
the corner.

The Bethel Commercial Bank & Trust, a hundred-year-old
institution, was controlled by a local board of directors who had
rebuffed all takeover attempts by out-of-town megabanks. The
bank's name was engraved in granite across the front of the building.

Tom stepped into the marble-floored lobby. As a boy, Tom loved going to the bank because it had the coldest air-conditioning in town and a never-ending supply of lollipops beside the tellers. The vault was set into the wall beyond the last teller station. An older gentleman sat at a small desk near the massive metal door.

"Hey, Mr. Howell, how are you doing today?" Tom said when he reached the man's workstation.

"Can't complain, Tom," Howell responded, straightening his tie. "What can I do for you?"

Tom handed him the numbered key.

"I need to open the safe-deposit box. My name should be on the card."

The older man flipped open an index card box and thumbed through it. The bank had made the leap into online banking; however, there were still vestiges of the old ways that hadn't been modernized.

"Here it is," Howell said with satisfaction.

When he signed the card, Tom noticed that there were years his father didn't open the box at all; however, John Crane had been to the bank vault twice in the six-month period prior to his death. Mr. Howell led Tom into the vault and inserted his key in box number 429. Tom did the same. They turned the keys and opened the brass cover.

"Take your time. I'll be at my desk when you finish."

Tom put the box on a high narrow table in the center of the room. Lifting the lid, he took out a stack of documents: his parents' marriage certificate signed by Elias, who performed the ceremony, honorable discharge papers for Tom's grandfather who'd served in the army, and Tom's original birth certificate. Beneath these older papers he found a newer unsealed envelope. Scribbled on the front in his father's handwriting was "DTA – 35-89." Tom caught his breath.

He took out a deposit slip and a thin checkbook. Printed across the top of a deposit slip were the words "Designated Trust Account." The meaning of the slip of paper he'd found at the office now made sense: "Designated Trust Account—Safe-Deposit Box." The figure entered at the bottom of the deposit slip caused Tom's mouth to drop open.

It was $1,750,000.

Tom read the number twice. He opened the cover of the checkbook. It was a starter set with one check missing. The check register was blank.

In addition to a general trust account, attorneys could open designated trust accounts that contained funds from a single client, often held for a specific purpose. The file number on the envelope provided circumstantial evidence that Harold Addington was the owner of the funds; however, nothing written on the deposit slip, recorded in the checkbook, or included in the safe-deposit box specifically identified him as the source of the deposit.

Tom held the checkbook up to the light and tried to see if there was an imprint by the pen used to write the missing check that might have completely wiped out the account. Nothing could be seen. Tom put the trust account envelope and its contents in his back pocket.

"Thanks, Mr. Howell," he said when he left the vault.

"Anytime, Tom."

Tom walked directly across the lobby to Clayton Loughton's office. Loughton had been president of the bank for ten years and occupied an office with a glass front at the far end of the main floor. Tom peered through the glass. The banker motioned for him to enter.

"Have a seat, Tom," Loughton said. "Let me show you something."

The banker picked up a golf ball and tossed it to him. Loughton, a brown-haired man in his late forties, routinely finished in the top flight of the local golf tournaments.

"Do you know what that is?"

"It's a golf ball."

"Not just any golf ball." Loughton held up his index finger. "It's a golf ball with a story. Last week I hit an eight iron on number seventeen, you know, the short par three with the water hazard in front of the hole."

Tom nodded. It was the signature hole for the local golf course.

"I didn't hit the ball solid and it was heading for the edge of the pond when all of a sudden . . ." Loughton paused. Tom tried to look interested. "A turtle popped to the surface of the water. My ball hit his shell, skipped onto the green, and stopped a couple of inches from the cup. I tapped in for a birdie."

"That should be in the newspaper."

"It was, but I figured you hadn't heard about it."

Tom returned the ball to Loughton, then reached into his back pocket. "I found something in my father's safe-deposit box and need your help. It's about a designated trust account."

Tom placed the envelope on the banker's desk. Loughton didn't touch it. His jovial face turned serious.

"You're the executor of his estate, right?" the banker asked.

"Yes, I sent a certified copy of the letters from the probate court to Lisa Randolph at the bank about a month ago."

Loughton swiveled around and began typing on his computer keyboard. "Is this the designated trust account your father set up earlier this year?"

"Yes." Tom raised his eyebrows.

"Don't be surprised. We're a small bank. If that much money is deposited, I know about it immediately. And even though the interest on lawyer trust accounts is paid to the state, it's something we keep an eye on."

"Is the money still here?" Tom asked, leaning forward in his chair. "There is a check missing from the checkbook."

Loughton entered numbers into his computer.

"Yes, as of this morning there was $1,750,000 in the account. And if someone tried to present a check now, it would be stale. Too much time has passed since your father's death, and he was the only signatory on the account."

Tom retrieved the envelope from the banker's desk.

"It's my duty to locate the owner. Can you tell me where the funds came from? I have an idea, but I need to confirm it."

"No, I can't," Loughton replied without checking his computer.

"You can't tell me, or you don't know?"

"I can't tell you because I don't know. I've already researched that issue. Your father didn't talk to me when he opened the account. He set it up through the bank officer on duty and made a deposit via a cashier's check with no name listed on the remitter line. I examined the check myself."

"What bank was it drawn on?"

"It came from Barbados."

"Arthur Pelham's bank?"

"No, we're used to seeing transfers from his bank. This came from a different bank, one with connections in the UK."

"What kind of connections?"

"I looked it up online. It was linked to a correspondent bank with offices in London, Liverpool, Newcastle, Glasgow, and a couple of other places I can't remember."

"Newcastle?"

"Yes."

"Did you ever ask my father about the account?"

"No, I thought it probably had to do with a real estate closing.

When the funds were still there after his death, I knew it would be up to you as his executor to sort it out. Do the records at his law office identify the owner of the funds?"

"There's a reference to a file number, but that's not enough. Dealing with this much money, I don't want to make a mistake."

"Of course not."

Loughton's phone buzzed.

"Mr. Albright on line 2," a female voice said. "He says it's important."

"I've been waiting for this call," Loughton said, placing his finger on the Response button. "I hope you get the ownership of the account sorted out."

"Thanks for your help."

Tom returned to the office. He put the deposit slip and starter checkbook in the middle drawer of his father's desk and locked it shut. He tapped the top of the desk with his pen. Neither Esther nor Rose Addington seemed to know about the money or the account. He needed to take his investigation to another level.

Tom took out his cell phone, scrolled down to Arthur Pelham's cell phone number, and pressed the Send button.

"Hello, Tom, what can I do for you?" Arthur answered.

"I know you're busy, but it's something I'd rather talk about in person. I promise not to take too long."

"Tom, I'm here for you. Don't talk to me like one of my managers who's afraid of my shadow. What's this about?"

"Harold Addington. I've found something and need to ask you about it."

Arthur was silent for a moment. "I'm in between meetings if you'd like to come by," the older man said.

"I'm on my way."

The Parker-Baldwin house was two minutes away on Oakdale Street. Tom left the deposit slip and checkbook locked in his father's desk. If he didn't have something with him, he couldn't show it. He parked in front of the antebellum white-columned house. It had been impeccably restored and meticulously maintained. The gardeners responsible for upkeep of the property didn't allow a dead leaf to spend more than twenty-four hours on the ground before scooping it up. The lawn was lush, green, and devoid of weeds. Tom approached the house on a sidewalk of brick pavers laid in an intricate geometric design. Parked beside the house were Arthur's sports car and a large sedan with dark windows. A husky man standing beside the car nodded when Tom approached. Arthur Pelham had reached the unfortunate status in life that he required 24/7 personal security. Tom wondered where the bodyguards had been concealed when they ate supper at Rick and Tiffany's house.

He rang the doorbell. Arthur opened it. The older man was wearing an expertly tailored gray suit.

"Come in," Arthur said. "I've been in meetings all day and walked in the door a few minutes before you called."

To the left of the foyer was a large formal living room. On the right was a much smaller parlor. Beyond the small parlor was a sunroom. Arthur led the way into the parlor. Like the entire house, it was furnished with period antiques.

"No cigars in this house," Arthur said affably. "I can't risk smoke getting into the fabric of these chairs. Have a seat."

Tom gingerly sat down in a side chair.

"It'll hold you," Arthur replied with a smile. "It just looks fragile."

"If Rick and I had been turned loose in this house when we were eleven years old, we would have torn it up and caused a huge spike in your insurance premiums."

"Those were good days, much simpler and more carefree than life now." Arthur put his hands together in front of him. "Tell me, what have you found?"

Tom cleared his throat. "You mentioned at Rick's house that you were disappointed in Addington as an employee. Would you be willing to tell me why?"

"Personnel matters aren't subject to public discussion, and even though you're a close friend of the family, I can't discuss something like that outside the company."

"I would never do or say anything that might have a negative impact on you, your family, or your company."

"And I believe you," Arthur replied. "But you're going to have to go first with this conversation."

Tom took a deep breath and decided to get straight to the point.

"Did Harold Addington misappropriate Pelham funds prior to his death?"

A muscle in Arthur's right cheek twitched. "If that occurred, do you have an idea where those funds might be located?"

"Maybe."

They sat for a few moments in awkward silence.

"You're a smart lawyer, Tom," Arthur said, a smile returning to his face. "If you can help me deal in a discreet way with a matter I'd prefer not become public knowledge, it will be greatly appreciated. That would be the case with Harold Addington or anyone else."

"Yes, sir."

"And your assistance would not go unnoticed or unrewarded. If you decide to return to Atlanta, I'm confident you'll eventually join a quality law firm and land Pelham Financial as one of your clients.

If you take Rick's advice and open a practice in Bethel, I'll make sure you have a steady flow of business in your area of expertise that can serve as a financial foundation for your future."

"I really appreciate that."

"So, can I count on you to follow through with anything related to Harold Addington in a professional manner?"

"Yes, sir."

"Excellent." Arthur clapped his hands together. "Keep me current on further developments. I'm leaving town tomorrow, but you know how to reach me at any time. Let's talk next week. In the meantime, I'll make a few phone calls."

"Okay."

Tom felt relieved that he could pass some of his responsibility off to Arthur. The older man checked his watch.

"Look, I'm glad you called. I have a meeting in fifteen minutes at the country club and need to get going."

Arthur walked Tom to the door. "Have you decided whether you're going white-water rafting with Rick this weekend?" he asked.

"Not yet."

"I hope you'll spend time with him. You're a good influence."

"Hopefully better than when we were kids."

"I'm sure of that." Arthur patted Tom on the shoulder. "Rick could use a healthy dose of your drive and ambition."

As Tom left the Parker-Baldwin house he was certain of one thing. Harold Addington stole at least $1,750,000 from Pelham Financial, and Arthur Pelham wanted to get the money back in a way that would avoid negative publicity for his company.

Returning to the office, Tom took out a legal pad and diagrammed what he suspected had taken place. Addington hatched a scheme in which he would use the confidential nature of the designated trust account as a means to launder the money to buy a tangible asset like real estate or purchase rare stamps. Tom knew his father was gullible, especially when it came to someone who liked to fish and enjoyed talking about religion. The thought that Addington may have manipulated John Crane made Tom mad.

The office phone rang. Instead of letting it go to the message machine, Tom decided to answer it.

"Is this Mr. Crane?"

"I'm Tom Crane, his son. My father passed away a few months ago—"

"You're the one I'm supposed to talk to. This is Junior Jackson. I cut Rick Pelham's grass. He told me to give you a call."

"Sure. Just a second. Let me get the file I need to ask you about."

Tom retrieved *Freiburger v. Harrelson.*

"I know this is a long shot," Tom said, picking up the phone, "but did you witness an accident involving a car hitting a pedestrian several months ago?"

"At Poplar and Westover?"

Tom checked the accident report.

"Yes."

"Saw the whole thing. I was on my way to the elementary school to pick up my least young'un from school. She was sick, and my wife couldn't get off work to get her. I wish I'd grabbed her up a few minutes later, 'cause as soon as she got in the truck she hurled all over the front seat. That stuff runs down in every crack and cranny and you can't get the smell out for nothing. It's an old truck, but I try to keep it nice and—"

"You say you saw the accident. Does that mean you can tell me where the pedestrian was standing when the car hit him?"

"Shoot, yeah. He was standing at the edge of the curb waiting to cross. The guy in the car was probably dialing on his cell phone or sending a text message and jumped the curb. His front bumper sent the man flying like a rag doll. I thought the fellow might be dead, but he sat up right quick. I rolled down my window to make sure he was okay, then headed on to the school."

"Where did the man land?"

"In the street. It didn't look nothing like what you see in the movies. You know, a stuntman makes things like that look—"

"Why do you think the driver of the car was using his cell phone?" Tom interrupted. "Did you see him holding it?"

"Nah, but he probably was. Why else would he run off the road and up on the curb?"

"What kind of car was he driving?"

"Lincoln or Buick, something."

"Do you remember the color of his car?"

"Uh, silver, I think."

Tom glanced at the accident report. The car was a silver Lincoln sedan, a rental vehicle.

"Did you notice a pothole in the road?"

"There's potholes all up and down that road. Most of them opened up after the snow and ice we had last winter. Do you remember when it stayed in the teens for over a week? I used to work for the county road department, and when that happens the asphalt around here turns to chalk. As soon as you plug a hole it pops open worse than before. That whole street needs to be repaved, but I think it's a state highway. If that's so, the state has to be the one to do the work. We used to get calls all the time from folks complaining that—"

"If you're asked under oath, would you testify that the silver car left the roadway and hit the pedestrian standing on the curb?"

"I'd have to. That's what happened."

"But you can't swear to the cell phone business or whether a pothole could have caused the car to swerve off the road?"

"Is the driver claiming he hit a pothole?"

"I haven't talked to him."

"I didn't see no huge pothole. If you ask my opinion, the man in the silver car is lucky the fellow he hit didn't bust his head open like a ripe watermelon. How bad was he hurt?"

"It messed up his leg, and he had to have surgery."

"Sorry to hear that. I should have hung around. My uncle has a bum knee. People don't know it, but that sort of thing can be aggravating."

"He's had to miss work while he goes to physical therapy."

"And you're his lawyer?"

"My father was. I'm trying to help him find another one."

"Just out of curiosity, who was a-driving the silver car? I saw his face but didn't know him."

"His name is Harrelson. I think he lives in New York, but he was here on business." Tom hesitated but knew he needed to ask a follow-up question. "If Harrelson is an executive with Pelham Financial, would that be a problem for you testifying about what happened if this case goes to court?"

"You mean 'cause I work for Rick?"

"Yes."

"Nah. Rick don't care about that sort of stuff. He's a good ole boy. This Harrelson fellow needs to take his New York driving back where it belongs. If he lives up there he ought to know how to drive around a pothole. I hear New York City is one big pothole."

"What's your address and phone number in case someone needs to contact you?"

Tom wrote down Jackson's personal information.

"I can't promise to always answer that cell phone number," Jackson said. "If I'm up to my armpits in mud or something worse out at the horse barn, I ain't going to touch that phone."

"I understand. Thanks for calling."

"No problem. Rick says you might be out here on the property sometime. Holler at me. It'll give me an excuse to take a break."

Tom ended the call and completed his notes. Junior Jackson was the kind of witness who could be an insurance defense lawyer's nightmare. Truth in the mouth of a common man was harder to twist than forged steel.

Tom closed the file folder. It would be fun trying *Freiburger v. Harrelson* before an Etowah County jury. But taking the case would not be in Tom's future if his biggest client was Pelham Financial.

chapter
THIRTEEN

I fed Rover," Elias said when Tom got home. "He got anxious about an hour ago."

"That's okay, but he always tries to push up suppertime. Just don't give him more than two large scoops of food, no matter how forlorn he looks."

The microwave beeped. Tom took out one plate and put in another. He poured two glasses of water. When the second plate was ready, he placed it on the table in front of Elias. They sat down. Tom automatically bowed his head and closed his eyes. Elias was quiet for a moment, then prayed a simple, familiar prayer. But this time was different. God's presence enveloped Tom. He gripped the edge of the table with his hands.

"Amen," Elias said.

Tom kept his head bowed for a few extra seconds. When he looked up, Elias was staring at him.

"What's going on?" the old man asked.

"I should make you guess, but I won't." Tom smiled. "God met with me at the office this morning."

Elias's eyes widened. "I'm listening."

Tom began with Psalm 78:72. After listening to a few sentences, Elias pushed his plate away and began pacing back and forth across the kitchen.

"If you don't sit down and eat, I'm going to stop," Tom said.

"Hearing you is meat to my soul and drink to my spirit," the old man replied. "I'm doing my best not to shout."

Tom continued.

"God is good," Elias said when Tom finished. "It's an honor being the first to hear your testimony."

"Actually, you're not the first person I've talked to about this. I ran into Rose Addington at the Chickamauga Diner and somehow it came out. She was excited too, but I'm glad she didn't get up and run around the restaurant."

Elias rubbed his chin. "I thought the two of you would like each other."

Tom stared at Elias. "You wanted to hook me up with Rose Addington?"

"I'm not sure what you mean by 'hook up,' but the first time I met Rose I thought the two of you might be a good match. Remember, I introduced your father to your mother."

"I saw the marriage certificate in the safe-deposit box this afternoon, but that doesn't qualify you to serve as a matchmaker, especially involving a woman you don't know very well."

"I can't turn off my discernment."

"Discernment? Of what?"

"People."

"Then you should have pointed your discernment gun at Harold Addington instead of his daughter. Within the next few days it's going to be very painful for Rose Addington to be around me."

Elias gave Tom a puzzled look. "What do you mean about Harold—"

"I can't go there," Tom interrupted. "And don't try to make me."

Elias grunted but kept quiet.

After the meal, Tom took Rover outside for a walk. With the end of daylight savings time approaching, he wanted to enjoy one of the last opportunities of the fall for post-supper sunlight.

The dead plants in the soybean fields behind the house were cut low to the ground. Tom's boots crunched the dried stalks. Rover wandered to the end of the leash. The clouds in the sky were a splotchy gray as the last rays of the sun retreated beyond the horizon. It was quiet except for the chirping of the few remaining crickets whose songs would soon end after the first hard frost.

When Tom was a boy, he captured a fall cricket and put it in a glass jar. It was an enormous creature that had survived every threat from birds, animals, weather, and people looking for fish bait. Tom borrowed a magnifying glass from his mother's sewing kit and held it close to the jar. The cricket crouched in the strands of straw that covered the bottom of the jar and peered stoically at Tom without any sign of fear. When Tom shook the jar, the cricket didn't hop. Instead, he waited patiently for the man-made earthquake to stop. Tom was so impressed by the cricket that the following day he took the jar outside and released the cricket close to the spot where he'd captured it. The noble insect deserved to live out its days in its natural home.

As he tromped across the field, Tom thought about his life. Relying on himself and doing what he wanted to do had left him with no job, no inheritance, no girlfriend, an uncertain future, and stubborn issues to sort out in shutting down his father's practice. But for the first time in his life, he was under an influence greater than his circumstances—an inner peace based on a reality outside himself.

Standing in the field with a thankful heart, Tom looked up at the darkening sky, closed his eyes, and let the invisible presence wash over him, sending chills across his body. What lay ahead was unknown. However, the inner calm didn't desert him. He tugged on Rover's leash.

"Come on," he said to the dog. "Let's go back a different way."

Tom lived the next two days wrapped in a comfortable spiritual cocoon. Beatrice's back problems proved stubborn, so Tom spent more time at the office reading the Bible and writing down prayers than he did reviewing his father's legal files. He was turning into a hermit and enjoying it. Thursday afternoon the bell on the front door rang. Tom scooted his chair to the side to get a clear view of the person entering the office.

It was Rose Addington.

"Hallo," she said when she caught his eye. "I hope I'm not disturbing you."

"No, come in."

"I was in town again and thought I'd drop by to see how you're doing," Rose continued. "I've thought quite a bit about our chat at lunch the other day. I told Mum about it too. We were wondering if you were going to be at the church again on Sunday. If so, we'd like to invite you and your uncle over for a bite to eat after the service."

"Thanks, but I may be out of town on a white-water rafting trip."

"But your plans aren't set?"

"Almost. A close friend invited me. I'm going to call him today and let him know that I've decided to go on the trip."

"Maybe we can do it another time." Rose peered past Tom into the office. "Is that where you met with the Lord the other morning?"

"Yes."

"Do you mind if I have a look?"

Rose brushed past him before he could answer. Tom caught a whiff of her perfume.

"I see you've been at it again," she said, pointing at the open Bible on the desk.

"Yeah. I've spent more time reading the Bible and writing down my thoughts the past two days than sorting through my father's affairs."

Rose glanced around the room, then up at the ceiling. "That's because this is a thin place."

Tom looked up at the ceiling. All he saw were a few spots where the white paint was beginning to crack.

"A thin place?" he asked.

"It's what the ancients called a place where there's less separation between heaven and earth. It allows easier communion between the Lord and his people. Have you ever heard of Iona or Lindisfarne?"

"No."

"Those are thin places in Scotland and northern England where the early Christians established places of prayer and worship. The old saints didn't have our technology, but they knew how to lay hold of God."

Tom wasn't sure how to respond.

"Do I sound like a mystic to you, Tom?" Rose turned her head toward him with a smile.

"I'm not sure exactly what that means either."

"Now, I'm surprised at that."

"Why?"

"Your uncle Elias, of course. Mum and I spent time with him at his house one afternoon before you arrived. He showed me his study and told me what he did there. He's quite an intercessor."

"Which means he prays a lot?"

"Yes."

"He took you into his study? That's rare. He's very private about that part of his life. When I was a child the study was off-limits."

"The three of us had a season of prayer there together."

"Is it a thin place too?"

"I think so."

Tom laughed.

"What's funny?"

"You and Elias are on thin ice with this thin place stuff."

"But it's not a new idea."

"It is to me." Tom stepped out of the office as a signal to Rose that the conversation was over. "Thanks for stopping by."

Rose didn't move. "I'm not finished," she said. "Have you found out anything else about the professional relationship between our fathers?"

"I'm still working on it."

"Has anything else come to light? I especially wondered if you'd made any sense of the sticky note you found in the bank ledger for, what was the term you used? Trust account?"

Tom licked his lips. "Yes, that's the legal term for the account. The ethical rules require me to make a diligent effort to account for every dollar of client money. That's what I'm doing now."

"Have you located a sum of money for which there is a question about its ownership?"

At that moment Tom decided Rose Addington had more discernment than Elias and would make a better lawyer than some of the new associates hired by Barnes, McGraw, and Crowther. He shifted into lawyer mode.

"There are questions about the money in one of the trust accounts," he replied slowly. "That's what I'm investigating. I'll let you know as soon as I determine if there is a definite connection to your father."

"Do you suspect there might be a link?"

"Get to the point," he said. "What do you suspect that you're not telling me? It might save me a lot of time and wasted energy."

Rose pursed her lips together for a second before answering. "If Papa hired your father and paid him money, would that money go into a trust account and stay there until your father did the work?"

"That's one way to do it."

Rose lowered her gaze for a moment before looking up at Tom. "You told me your father owed money to the government. Mum and I don't want to cause you any embarrassment, but if he wrote himself a check out of the trust account so he could pay his tax debt without doing any work for Papa, we won't be taking any action against his estate or make any public fuss. All we want to know is how much he took and whether there's any money left to be refunded."

Tom's mouth dropped open. "You have this all wrong," he managed. "My father didn't make any wrongful withdrawals from his trust account. He owed money to the government for back taxes, but I'm certain he didn't misappropriate client funds."

"How can you be so sure he didn't take out money before he earned it? You just told me you're still trying to figure out whose money is left in the trust account."

"That's true."

Rose gave him a puzzled look. "I'm confused. Are you saying Papa didn't pay your father money that was placed in a trust account?"

Tom made a split-second decision. "Do you have any evidence that he did?"

"That's not the kind of answer I would have expected from you," she said, her jaw set. "When you're ready to be honest, give me a call. You have a lot to learn about what it means to walk with God."

Rose stepped past him toward the door.

"Just a minute," Tom called after her.

Rose reached Bernice's desk before she turned and faced him. Her face was flushed. "What?"

"Uh, if you locate any checks written to this office by your father, please let me know," Tom said.

"Will you do the same?"

Tom didn't answer. Rose rolled her eyes and spun around. The bell clanged as she jerked the door open and left. Tom returned to the desk. He looked down at the open Bible and closed it. The help he needed to unravel the questions about the designated trust account couldn't be found in the pages of Scripture.

He took out his cell phone and scrolled down to Rick Pelham's phone number. Rick answered on the second ring.

"Are you in for the trip?" Rick asked.

"Yeah," Tom answered without enthusiasm.

"Great. We'll get on the road about six Sunday morning. That's not too early for you, is it?"

"No. Staying with Elias, nothing happens on Saturday night to keep me up late."

"We can take care of that—"

"I wasn't trying to suggest anything."

"Okay, but let me know if you want a change of scenery. Tiffany asked me twice this week if I thought I could talk you into dividing your time between Elias's place and here."

"Maybe in a week or so."

"That will give her some hope. Oh, and there's no need to bring anything for the trip. I have all the gear, including extra wet suits. The water will be cold this time of year. You'll need to have an extra layer of artificial blubber to stay comfortable in the spray."

"And if I fall in, are you going to drag me out?"

"Yeah, unless we both get stuck under the same rock. It's supposed to rain in the mountains Saturday night, which should make for a wild ride on Sunday."

After he hung up, Tom laid his cell phone on the desk. He unlocked the middle drawer and took out the checkbook for the designated trust account. Flipping it open, he stared again at the place where a single check had been ripped out. Rose Addington, for all her knowledge about ancient holy places, was wrong about one thing. John Crane didn't illegally write a check to himself from a trust account.

———

Later that afternoon Tom heard the bell jingle as someone entered. Dreading another clash with Rose Addington, he cautiously peered around the door of the office. It was Lamar Sponcler.

The white-haired lawyer was wearing gray pants, a yellow tie, and a starched shirt that had become wrinkled after a long day.

"Am I interrupting anything?" Sponcler asked.

"No, I was going to leave in a few minutes, but I'm not in a hurry. Come in and have a seat."

Sponcler ran his hand along one of the bookcases. "Your father was a unique man. Very old school in the way he practiced law, but he had a way with people. They trusted him." Sponcler pointed to the boxes of files. "Are those his open files?"

"Some of them. Bernice took care of a lot of the cases before I arrived. These are the ones left for me to deal with. I'm filing motions to withdraw and trying to locate lawyers to assume representation in the others."

"Have some of the clients asked you to take over?"

"Yes."

"That's not surprising." The older lawyer nodded. "Have you thought any more about our conversation at the courthouse?"

Tom hesitated.

"That's okay." Sponcler smiled. "You've had a lot on your mind. But I'd be very interested in discussing an arrangement for you to work with me."

"That's very generous of you," Tom answered sincerely. "However, all my experience has been with complex financial litigation. The further I get from law school, the less I remember about plaintiff's work. That's why you saw me at the courthouse the other day doing research."

"You were researching, not assuming. That's a good thing. And you're not afraid of the courtroom."

"No, I'm not," Tom admitted. "When I was a kid playing baseball, I loved coming up to bat in a pressure situation. Getting ready to try a case gives me the same feeling. I want to do it."

"Listening to you makes me want to get back into the fight." Sponcler laughed. "Not every lawyer who passes the bar has what it takes to go to war for a client in court. Ability can be improved, but it has to be built on something already inside."

Tom put his fingers together in front of his face. "If we joined forces, would I be able to accept cases like the ones I've handled in the past?"

Sponcler wrinkled his nose. "From Arthur Pelham?"

"Maybe."

"Arthur talked with you." Sponcler nodded his head. "I'm not surprised. Pelham Financial has been a big boost to the local economy, but representing them doesn't fit with my practice. Having two hundred little clients is better than representing two big ones. If I lose a client, I can keep on going. If a firm with two clients loses one, fifty percent of the business is gone." Sponcler pointed to the boxes. "Your father knew that. Think some more about my modest proposal."

The following morning Tom called Bernice as soon as he arrived at the office.

"I'm slowly getting better," she said. "I sat up in a regular chair for a couple of hours yesterday working on a jigsaw puzzle and wasn't too stiff when I got up. I hate that I haven't been there to help you."

Bernice loved putting together jigsaw puzzles.

"Take your time coming back. Without a job to go back to, I'm not working very hard." Tom glanced down at the notes he'd made about the designated trust account. "I do have one business question. Do you know anything about a designated trust account opened about six months ago at Bethel Commercial Bank & Trust?"

There was a brief silence on the other end of the line before Bernice spoke. "I remember your daddy started getting an extra envelope from the bank each month."

"Any idea where he kept the monthly statements for that account?"

"I'm not sure, but I know he took at least one out of the office.

I remember because he had the envelope in his hand when he was about to leave early one afternoon and I asked him about it."

"What did he say?"

"He said he had a meeting with a client."

"Which client?"

"He didn't say."

"Could it have been one of the afternoons he went fishing with Harold Addington?"

"Maybe. I don't know. They went fishing a lot once the weather started warming up, and Addington called the office regularly. It was easy to recognize his voice because of the accent." Bernice paused. "But he always sounded on edge to me, especially for someone who was calling about a fishing trip. He spoke fast and demanded that he talk to your daddy right then. And your daddy took the call, even if he was working on something else. I chalked it up to his love of fishing. Was there any money left in the extra trust account?"

"Yes, and I'm trying to figure out who it belongs to."

"How much is it?"

Tom hesitated. "Enough that I don't want there to be any chance of making a mistake about ownership."

"And you think it might belong to the Addington family?"

"It's one option. Addington's daughter thinks Harold paid the firm a retainer, then my father wrote out a fee without doing the work."

"What?!" Bernice exploded. "That's the most ridiculous—"

Tom immediately regretted mentioning Rose's accusation.

"But it's just a misunderstanding on her part. Don't be too hard on her. She just lost her father too."

"Anyone who knew your daddy would never believe he'd do anything dishonest. I hope you straightened her out!"

"Get back to your puzzle."

Bernice wasn't going to be sidetracked. "I can't believe the Addington girl accused your daddy like that. What's her name?"

"Rose, but forget I mentioned it."

"That won't happen," Bernice grunted. "And she won't forget what I'll have to say when I run into her!"

chapter
FOURTEEN

L ater that day Tom leaned back in his father's chair with his feet on the desk. A pile of untouched files were stacked on the floor. He was reading Genesis and reached the part about Jacob's dream of a ladder reaching to heaven with angels ascending and descending on it.

> Then Jacob awoke from his sleep and said, "Surely the LORD is in this place, and I did not know it." And he was afraid and said, "How awesome is this place! This is none other than the house of God, and this is the gate of heaven!"

"A thin place," Tom muttered. "Maybe this is where the people who believe in that stuff got the idea."

> Then Jacob rose early in the morning, and took the stone that he had put at his head, set it up as a pillar, and poured oil on top of it. And he called the name of that place Bethel . . .

Growing up, Tom was familiar with Jacob's ladder from the Sunday school song, but he didn't know the name of his hometown was in the Bible. His cell phone rang. The caller ID showed an unknown number with an Atlanta area code. Tom laid the Bible on the desk and answered.

"Hey, Tom. This is Nate Becker. I hope I'm not calling at a bad time."

Tom took his feet off the desk and sat up straighter. "No, it's fine. I'm at my father's office in Bethel."

"Mark Nelson told me you were going there to close down his practice."

"Yeah. Except for a couple of things to sort out, it's not too complicated."

"There's always something to deal with." Becker put his hand over the receiver and said something Tom couldn't hear. "We've picked up a few new clients over the past six months, and I'm running around like a crazy man. You know Darrin Walker, the CEO of the Advantage Group, don't you?"

Tom had met the head of the investment firm based in San Diego on several occasions. Barnes, McGraw, and Crowther wanted to capture Walker's business when the company expanded to the East Coast.

"Yeah. He's a sharp guy."

"He thinks the same about you. At our initial meeting with him earlier in the week, it came up that you'd left your firm and might be in the market for a new opportunity. Darrin said he'd be interested in letting you work on their business. He mentioned a case in which you represented a codefendant—"

"The Auburndale litigation."

"Yeah, that's it. Apparently, his lawyer at the time rode your coattails to victory."

"We got a good result for everybody."

"Don't be modest. Anyway, the coincidence of all this coming together got my attention, and I brought it up at our partners' meeting. Before you start sending out résumés, we'd like first crack at discussing a position for you with us. I have a ballpark idea about your salary working for Reid McGraw, and I can tell you up front you're looking at a raise with a partner share in a year or two if everyone likes you as much as I'm sure they will."

It was exactly the kind of call Tom had dreamed of receiving. It took the remaining sting out of his termination by the old firm.

"Thanks, Nate. I appreciate you getting in touch with me and not using what happened at Barnes, McGraw, and Crowther as a negotiating point against me."

"I don't know what you're used to, but that's not our style. When Jack Sweet asked me to join him, I'd been canned by the Trimble and Wallace firm. Jack offered me a raise, and we haven't looked back since. It's a good culture over here. We work hard, play hard, and watch each other's backs."

"Would I be in your litigation group?"

"Yes. We handle a broader array of cases than you did at Barnes, McGraw, and Crowther, but we mostly keep to financial and commercial litigation. We also take on an occasional plaintiff's case if we see potential for a recovery. Would you have a problem with that?"

"No."

"Good. Some lawyers get locked into a billable hour mind-set and can't switch sides. We settled a big plaintiff's case a couple of weeks ago. The hourly rate assigned to the lawyers who worked on it was pushing $1,000 an hour. Of course, if we'd tanked, no one would have made a penny."

Tom's eyes opened wide. "With that kind of possible upside, I wouldn't mind taking a risk."

"I didn't think so." Becker covered the receiver with his hand again and spoke to someone else. "Hey, I've got to jump on a conference call. Will you get back to me?"

"Absolutely. Before I talk to anyone else."

"Great. Have a good weekend."

Tom set his phone on the desk. He'd gone from no options to three: continue his father's practice with the added stability of work from Pelham Financial, join forces with Lamar Sponcler and learn at the feet of an accomplished small-town practitioner, or return to Atlanta and slip into familiar work with an excellent firm that already appreciated him. He flipped through the pages of his journal until he found an entry where he'd written Proverbs 3:5-6, followed by a prayer that he would receive a good job offer. He put a red star in the margin.

———

Even though they weren't inviting Esther and Rose Addington to supper, Tom and Elias had decided to cook steaks on the grill Saturday evening. When Tom rolled the grill from the garage, he saw the boxes his father had left stacked against the back wall. Most of them probably contained junk, but Tom suspected there were memories, happy and sad, waiting for him behind the corrugated cardboard walls.

Elias sat in a rocker on the porch while Tom fired up the coals. He lightly seasoned the steaks with a simple rub of salt, pepper, and garlic powder. Rover raised his head and sniffed the air when Tom came out of the house with the steaks on a plate. Placing the plate on the ground, Tom began scraping the rust and debris from the grill with a wire brush.

"How long has it been since you used this?" he called out to Elias.

"Over a year. Your father smoked fish on it one night, and several men from the Mount Pleasant congregation came over to eat with us."

"There are bits of skin stuck to the grill," Tom said. "Didn't you think about cleaning it after you used it?"

Tom had his back to the porch while he scrubbed the grill and turned around just in time to see Rover, his nose in the air, trotting across the yard toward the steak plate. Tom snatched the plate up from the ground.

"Weren't you going to warn me?" he asked Elias. "Rover almost stole our supper."

"Sorry," Elias said, opening his eyes. "I was thinking about that fish. I ate way too much. Your father not only knew how to catch fish, he also knew how to cook them. He could bake it, fry it, sauté it, grill it, smoke it, you name it."

Once the coals were covered in white ash, Tom placed the steaks on the grill, closed the lid, and checked the time on his watch. Rover lay down near the grill. Smoke swirled out the vents.

"How do you want your steak?" he asked Elias. "I like mine medium-rare."

"That's fine. I'm not afraid of red meat so long as we pray over it."

Tom sat on the porch steps. "A lawyer from a good firm in Atlanta called me this afternoon," he said. "He wants to talk to me about coming to work with his group."

"Are you considering it?"

"Yeah."

Tom told Elias about the call from Nate Becker and the conversation with Lamar Sponcler. He didn't mention Arthur Pelham.

"What do you think I should do?" he asked when he finished.

"I'm not sure, so I'm not going to shoot off my mouth about it."

Tom eyed the old man with surprise. "It's not like you to withhold your opinion."

Elias shrugged. "You're learning how to take baby steps with God, and I don't want to mess you up. One of the things an old man like me has to avoid is letting the failures of the past cast doubt on what lies ahead. Right now, your faith is stronger than mine."

"That's impossible."

"No." Elias shook his head. "Childlike faith that hasn't suffered disappointments can be the best kind to have."

Later, while they were eating their steaks, Tom looked over at Elias, who was contentedly chewing a juicy bite.

"Elias, are you a mystic?"

Elias swallowed and eyed Tom for a moment. "No, I'm a carnivore, and every bite of this steak proves it."

Tom chuckled. "Rose Addington claims you're a mystic."

"Really? I thought a mystic was someone who withdraws from the world and spends time having weird spiritual experiences."

"Then she's right," Tom replied with a confident nod. "You are a mystic."

Elias cut another bite of steak. "I'll give you my opinion about one thing," he said, raising his fork to his lips. "When God is moving in your life, you should enjoy the adventure."

Before Tom went to sleep he received a text message from Rick asking him to come a few minutes early. Shortly before dawn, he drove up the long drive to Rick and Tiffany's house. The sun was still below the tree line, the sky streaked with gray. Tom parked in front of the quiet house. Before he got out of the car, the front door opened. He expected to see Rick.

It was Tiffany.

She was wearing jeans, a loose-fitting top, and boots. She was holding two mugs of steaming coffee. She lifted a mug to Tom as he got out of the car.

"Thought you might like a hot one," she said.

"I never turn down a cup of coffee when I have to get up this early in the morning. Where's Rick?" Tom asked, looking past Tiffany. "He sent me a text asking me to come early."

"He's still snoozing. I sent the message. I wanted a few minutes with you alone before you left."

"Alone?"

"Yes, I thought you might want to see the horses. Early in the morning is one of my favorite times to go to the barn. I have a mare filly you have to see."

Tiffany started walking toward the barn. Tom took a sip of coffee and followed. Tiffany's jeans were too tight for horseback riding. The grass was wet with dew, the air chilly. Tiffany hugged herself with her arms.

"I should have brought a jacket. Are you going to wear wet suits on the river?"

"Probably."

Tiffany slowed down so they were walking side by side. When she did, she brushed against him. Tom glanced back at the house.

"I went rafting on a slow section of the river in July," Tiffany said. "It was hot enough to wear a bikini. Did you take any trips to the beach this summer?"

"A couple of times."

"With Clarice?"

"Once," Tom answered.

"What was that crazy girl thinking when she dumped you?" Tiffany asked, shaking her head.

"That she didn't want to deal with my issues."

Tiffany laughed. "You've got it more together than any other man I know."

They reached the barn. The dark wooden structure was a state-of-the-art horse stable. Tiffany pulled back a large door set on rollers. It opened smoothly. There was a broad aisle with stalls on the left and storage rooms on the right.

"How many horses do you have?" Tom asked.

"Seven right now. One is for sale, and I'm interested in buying another one."

"One for each day of the week."

"Not really. It has more to do with why each animal is here."

They stopped in front of the second stall.

"Here's my baby."

A skinny filly whinnied when she saw Tiffany, who held up her hand and waved it in front of the gangly creature's head. The filly stretched out and shook her tail.

"Isn't she a beauty? They stretch or park out like that without being taught. It's bred into them."

"What's her name?"

"She has a fancy registered name, but her barn name is Lizzie. In a few months we'll start training her."

They continued down the row of stalls. Tiffany talked about each horse. The uneasiness Tom felt about her asking him to come with her alone to the barn began to ease. Anyone who loves a hobby wants to share it with others.

"I can see this is your happy place," Tom said when they reached the end of the row.

Tiffany patted the nose of an old gelding that had been a grand champion, then let him nibble a carrot.

"Yes, it is." She sighed as the horse took the last piece of carrot into his mouth. "Do you ever think back to our high school days?"

"Not really."

"I do," Tiffany said, turning so she faced him. "And for the past year I haven't been able to get it out of my mind that I made a huge mistake going to the senior homecoming dance with Rick instead of you."

"That was a long time ago," Tom said with a nervous laugh. "And I didn't ask you."

"You were going to, and Rick stepped in. He's told me the whole story. At the time I was flattered, but life isn't about convincing a lot of guys to like you; it's about finding the right one and not letting him go."

"And who has enough money to finance all this?" Tom gestured with his hand.

"I could walk away from everything and not look back, but I won't have to. You and I both know if I got a divorce based on irreconcilable differences, it would leave me a rich woman. All I'm asking for is a chance to make it work with you."

"Tiffany, don't—"

"Rick will be hurt at first," Tiffany continued. "But he'll find a woman who wants to go four-wheeling with him and be happier in the long run." She stepped closer to Tom, who backed up against the wall. "What woman wants to waste the rest of her life with someone who doesn't have a clue who she is? I'm not talking about an affair. If we can't be together until the divorce is final, I'll have to suffer through the wait. I can endure anything if I know you'll be waiting for me at the end."

Tom slid to the side and out into the aisle.

"We really shouldn't be having this conversation. You made your choice, and Rick is a lifelong friend."

"I've agonized over this speech a thousand times. Do you think it's easy for me to tell you this?"

"I didn't say anything about hard or easy. I just—"

"Please, don't!" Tiffany cut the air with her hand. "Look in your heart, and you'll see the truth I know is there. When you do, I'll be waiting and take all the blame."

Tiffany turned and started walking toward the barn door. Tom followed. They trudged back to the house in silence. When they reached the front steps, Tiffany held out her hand for Tom's coffee cup. He handed it to her. She let her fingers touch his. Her eyes closed for a moment.

"Rick is probably up by now," she said as she took the cup. "I'll let him know you're here."

"I'll wait outside."

The door closed. Tom rubbed his eyes. His head was spinning. He couldn't deny that Tiffany's words contained more than a grain of truth. There had been a unique quality to their high school romance. Tom had experienced deep passionate feelings for Tiffany he'd never duplicated with multiple girlfriends since. Images from their days and nights together crept out of his memory vault. There had been lots of good times, not just of the romantic variety, but also long talks on the phone and walks in the woods. Agitated, Tom started pacing back and forth in front of the house.

His thoughts were interrupted by a car coming up the driveway. When it stopped, Tom didn't recognize the man behind the wheel.

"You must be Tom Crane," the sandy-haired man said, getting out of the car and extending his hand. "Rick told me you'd be joining us."

"Yes."

"I'm Nick Whalen, a horse trainer at a stable near Chattanooga. Riders from my place often compete against Tiffany, and I recently sold her a nice filly."

"Lizzie."

"Right."

"I met Lizzie a few minutes ago when Tiffany and I went to the barn."

Nick looked past Tom. "Where's Tiffany?"

"Inside with Rick."

Each mention of Tiffany's name made Tom's stomach twist in a knot. Glancing at his car, he wondered if he could feign sickness so he could get away from the property.

"I've sold Tiffany a couple of other horses," Nick continued, oblivious to Tom's torment. "She's always in the market for an upgrade."

A shiny red pickup truck rumbled up the driveway. The vehicle had oversize tires on chrome wheels. As it drew closer, the driver gunned the engine, causing the truck to lurch forward.

"Do you know Hal Millsap?" Nick asked.

"No."

The front door of the house opened, and Rick stepped outside. Tiffany wasn't with him.

"Good morning, boys," he said, stretching his arms in the air.

When he saw Rick, Tom replayed in a split second his entire conversation with Tiffany at the barn. He shuddered. Rick slapped him on the back.

"I'm glad you decided to come."

Tom didn't reply. Hal pulled his truck directly in front of the other three men and lowered the window. Rick motioned for him to keep going.

"Move on," Rick said. "I don't want that thing sitting here all day. Someone will think I'm sponsoring a tractor pull."

Hal spit out the window, leaving a small brown stain on the pristine white concrete. Rick swore.

"Hey! I'll have to wash that off before we leave," Rick said. "If Tiffany sees it, she'll have a fit."

Hal parked his truck and got out. He was a tall gangly man with black hair and a goatee. His right cheek bulged. When Tom shook his hand, Hal grinned, revealing specks of tobacco scattered across the front of his teeth.

"Hal works in human resources at Pelham Financial," Rick said to Tom. "He hires and fires all the folks working the customer call center, mailroom, and telephone solicitation departments."

"And I love doing it," Hal responded. "Especially the firing part. There's nothing more satisfying than bringing in a single mom with three or four kids at home and telling her to hit the door and don't look back. Just last week I got to terminate a woman like that. You could hear her screeching in the parking lot. I had to turn up the country music on the CD in my office to drown her out."

"Don't believe a word of that garbage," Rick said. "The people who work for Hal love him, and he needs that oversize truck of his to deliver turkeys at Thanksgiving and toys at Christmas. Hal, tell Tom where you went to college."

Hal rubbed his goatee. "I helped Vanderbilt fill its federally mandated quota of rednecks."

"Where he was Phi Beta Kappa in psychology and human

relations," Rick added. "Tiffany wishes my IQ was half of his. But be careful, Hal, Tom is a brainy guy too."

"I look forward to testing myself against a worthy adversary," Hal said. "I'm sure Rick has packed a portable Trivial Pursuit game we can play while we're on the road."

Tom didn't feel like entering into any joking banter.

"Clean it up," Rick said to Hal, pointing to the nasty brown stain.

"Yes, Mr. Pelham," Hal said. He stepped into the bushes and grabbed a garden hose. He grinned at Tom and Nick. "I've had to do this before."

Hal turned on the water and washed away the small brown stain. "Just like my sins," he said.

"If you didn't chew, you'd have one less thing to repent of," Rick said.

In addition to his pickup truck, Rick owned a shiny new SUV. All the gear for the trip was stowed in the back of the vehicle. Tom started to get in the backseat.

"No, you're up front," Hal said. "Rick told us to treat you like visiting royalty."

Tom got in beside Rick and tried to put his encounter with Tiffany out of his mind. Hal disappeared for a moment and returned without the bulge in his cheek.

"It's in a place she'll never suspect," he said to Rick. "But when next year the grass is extra green over by that forsythia bush, you'll know why."

chapter
FIFTEEN

It was an hour and a half to the Ocoee River. Rick skirted Chattanooga and drove toward the mountains that funneled water into the steep valley where the river flowed. Tom spent most of the time staring out the passenger window. It was too hard to look at Rick.

"In May, Nick and I kayaked the upper part of the river," Rick said. "It made me respect the people who ran the rapids during the Olympics in '96. Turning around and paddling upstream to a specific point is tough. It's hard enough just staying upright in the current."

"Paddling upstream against a strong current describes my love life," Hal said.

"No woman who still has all her teeth wants to kiss someone with tobacco juice drooling out the side of his mouth," Rick said, glancing in the rearview mirror. "Tom can give you pointers on how to impress the ladies. He's not been without a good-looking girl hanging on to him since ninth grade."

Tom clenched his teeth.

"What's your secret?" Hal asked. "I know we've just met, but I let you sit up front even though Rick's driving makes me carsick if I sit in the backseat."

"My secret," Tom responded as he scrambled to come up with an answer that would end the conversation, "is finding a woman who is as afraid of commitment as I am."

"That's profound," Hal said reverentially. "I never learned that in any of my upper-level psychology courses."

The winding two-lane road reached the edge of the river and passed a hydroelectric power station built in the early 1900s. For more than sixty years, a wooden flume diverted the majority of the water from the riverbed to the power station. It wasn't until repairs were required to the flume in 1976 and the normal flow of water was restored that the white-water potential of the river became known. The Tennessee Valley Authority planned for the release of water into the riverbed to be temporary, but the resulting outcry led to a compromise in which the TVA designated about a hundred days a year for water to cascade over and around the rocks.

They reached the upper section of the river. The Olympic course was actually a river within the river. Massive boulders were repositioned to create a narrower channel that intensified the force of the current. Rick pulled off the road and they got out of the vehicle to stretch. Nick pointed across the riverbed to the new channel.

"Those rapids lead to the Edge of the World."

The greenish water foamed in the distance. Hal took a bag of chew from the back pocket of his jeans and popped a wad into his right cheek.

"You can't appreciate it from this far away," Rick said. "When you're sitting in the middle of the current and know there's no turning back, it is a major adrenaline rush."

While they watched, a helmeted kayaker entered the rapids.

"He's about to get to the worst part," Rick said.

At that moment, the kayak surged up in the air and disappeared.

"Wipeout," Nick said. "It happens so fast you don't have a chance to react."

The kayaker reappeared for an instant, then was swept from view.

Hal spit onto a smooth stone. "Tom, are you sure you're up for this? Riding this river looks like total commitment to me."

"You'll be the first one to kiss a rock," Rick replied. "Tom knows how to handle a paddle."

They returned to the SUV and drove downriver to the entry point for the middle Ocoee section. Rafts were piled up on top of colorfully decorated school buses displaying the names of different rafting companies. Rick pulled into a reserved spot for one of the rafting companies.

"Rick, you can't park here," Hal protested. "You'll get towed, and I'll have to hitchhike home with Tom and end up riding with the carload of beautiful, uncommitted women who stop to pick him up."

"Don't worry," Rick said. "I have permission from our guide."

A muscular man in his forties with his head wrapped in a red bandanna approached and greeted Rick.

"This is Gary Wheeler," Rick said. "He owns Ocoee Extreme."

"Welcome," Wheeler said to the assembled group. "We had a big rain last night, so the river is in top form. I think it's going to be one of the best days of the year."

Hal punched Tom and winked.

"The river isn't going to feel like bathwater," the guide continued. "If you fall out, your body temperature can drop faster than the water rushing over the rocks at Hell's Hole."

"I have wet suits for everybody," Rick said, popping open the back of his SUV. "The pink one is for Hal."

"The bathhouse is over there," Wheeler said, pointing to a garishly painted wooden structure.

The men changed into the wet suits. All the suits were black. They strapped on lightweight life jackets.

"This neoprene can't hide my muscles," Hal said, flexing his long arms. "But this one-size-fits-all approach is going to leave my ankles exposed to hypothermia."

"Which is why Wheeler is going to put you in the safest part of the boat," Rick answered. "The rest of us are experienced."

Outside, the guide was standing next to a raft that was narrower and sleeker than the ones piled on top of the converted school buses. It even had a name, Bubba's Boat, stenciled across the front.

"It's named after one of the rapids you'll see today," Wheeler said. "Give me a hand, and we'll take her down to the river."

Each man grabbed the rope that circled the raft, and they carried it to the edge of the water.

"Before we put in, I want to tell you what we're going to do, describe some of the rapids we'll face, and go over safety procedures," Wheeler said.

"Use small words," Hal said. "And remember, I've never done this before."

The guide's description of the river brought back memories for Tom. There'd been summers when he rafted the Ocoee two or three times. He'd even taken girls on rafting trips, but never Tiffany. His most memorable rafting date was a dark-haired young woman named Cynthia who screamed the entire trip in a voice that made the roar of the rapids sound soothing. It was the last time he asked her out.

"We'll try to catch some surf near Dixie Drive," Wheeler said. "And then pass through Torpedo, Table Saw, and Diamond Splitter. We'll hop out for a rest before tackling Hell's Hole, which, as most of you know, is near the power plant. If the river isn't too crowded, we'll try to make our way upstream to repeat some spots if you guys are up to it."

"I just showed them my guns," Hal replied, flexing his right arm again.

"He's talking about biceps, not jaw muscles," Rick replied.

"We're all going to wear helmets and life jackets," Wheeler said, pointing to a pile of both items at his feet. "The last thing you need is to hit your head on a rock or log and lose consciousness. If you should fall out of the boat, turn so you face downstream and let the current take you to a calmer place where you can swim to the side and either wait for us to pick you up or crawl out on the rocks. Your life jacket will keep your head above-water. Don't try to swim against the current. That's impossible."

"What if you go overboard, Captain?" Hal asked.

"I'll do what I'm telling you to do. Rick has been with me many times, and I understand Nick and Tom have experience on the river."

"It's been awhile," Tom replied.

"It's like riding a bike," Rick replied. "It'll all come back to you. The main point is to dig our paddles in the water and keep the boat from getting sideways in the current."

"That's right," Wheeler said. "If I'm not with you, concentrate on getting down the river safely. We'll regroup for another run that includes the extras you paid me for."

"I thought this was free," Hal said.

"Pelham Financial is paying for it," Rick replied.

"Just like everything else in Etowah County," Hal said.

They carried the boat into the shallows. Smooth stones covered the bottom. The river water covered Tom's surf shoes.

"You're right; it's chilly," he said to Wheeler.

"It feels great to me," Hal said. "I take a lot of cold showers, especially before the meetings at work when Rick's father chews me out in front of the rest of the local management team."

Wheeler positioned everyone in the boat. He put Rick and Tom up front with Nick and Hal in the rear. Hal slapped the water with his paddle and sprayed water into the raft.

The middle section of the Ocoee explodes with five miles of almost continuous white water. Empowered by the recent rain, the current was running as strong as Tom had ever seen it. Focusing on what lay ahead in the rapids helped him push aside his encounter with Tiffany. They quickly started moving down the river, bobbing up and down in the water. Hal let out a war whoop.

Rick glanced over his shoulder. "This is nothing."

"Just practicing."

"When we get to the rough stuff, you'll be paddling too hard to yell," Wheeler called out.

They quickly approached the first rapid, Grumpy, a class 4 section of white water. With Wheeler barking out commands, they shot through it. The river felt alive beneath the boat. Cold spray splashed over the sides.

"Paddles in the boat," Wheeler said when they were through.

They coasted through a calmer section. Wheeler guided the boat with an oar he used like a rudder.

"That was fun," Hal said.

Tom licked his lips. Other rapids quickly followed. Because it was late in the season, there weren't many boats on the water. Wheeler kept his promise to let them test their strength by paddling upstream to repeat a couple of sections. Tom dug his paddle in the swirling water and did his part to help the boat conquer the current. He'd forgotten how much he enjoyed the river.

"I love this narrow raft," he called out when they made their way through a rapid named Double Suck for the second time. "It's a lot more maneuverable."

"Don't relax yet," Wheeler replied. "Double Trouble is just ahead."

From his position in the front of the raft Tom could see the rolling rage of the water in front of the boat.

"Dig hard on the right!" Wheeler called out as they entered the rapid.

Rick and Nick thrust their oars into the water. Tom sat poised, waiting for his instructions.

"Quick on the left!" Wheeler yelled.

Tom stuck his oar into the water. He made two firm strokes, but when he prepared for a third, the raft suddenly flipped up like a bucking bull, throwing him into the water. He landed on his back with his legs up in the air. His head went under the water. The wet suit minimized the shock of the cold, but he came up sputtering from a mouthful of the river. A sudden shift in the current spun him around 360 degrees. When he regained his bearings, he could see the raft, with at least two people in it, continuing down the river.

Tom saw an arm flailing in the air. It was Hal Millsap. He was trying to swim across the rushing current to the opposite side of the river.

"No!" Tom yelled. "Go with the river!"

The river spun Hal around so he was facing Tom, who saw terror in Hal's eyes. Tom motioned downriver. Hal nodded and turned around. They swept around a corner. There were fallen trees jutting out into the water on the left bank of the river. Tom saw Hal trying to move in that direction. A thick limb jutted out into the river just ahead of him.

"No!" Tom yelled again.

Just before he reached the limb, Hal disappeared beneath the water. One of his hands, but not his head, broke the surface. Tom leaned to the side and kicked hard with his legs, pushing himself toward the spot where Hal had gone under. When he reached it, Tom felt his legs collide with Hal's body. The submerged man grabbed Tom's waist with his hands, but the slick neoprene suit didn't allow a handhold. Tom reached up with his right arm and grabbed a thick limb as his legs swept forward out of Hal's grasp.

Using the limb as leverage, Tom turned so he was facing the current. A smaller secondary branch of the tree went downward, disappearing into the water near the spot where Hal's hand surfaced. Grabbing the smaller limb with his left hand, Tom jerked as hard as he could. He felt the limb crack. He pulled again, and it broke free. Hal suddenly surfaced directly in front of Tom, striking him hard on the chin with his helmet.

Stunned, Tom lost his hold on the larger limb and was swept downriver by the current.

chapter
SIXTEEN

A splash of cold water washed over Tom's face, and he blinked his eyes. Turing his head to the side, he saw Hal, his face tilted back and his eyes closed, floating about six feet away from him. Tom swam to him.

"Hal!"

There was no response. Hal's lips were slightly blue.

Tom grabbed one of the straps on Hal's life jacket. They came around a bend into a calmer stretch of water. Tom saw that the raft was out of the river and resting on rocks in a shallow area. Rick, Nick, and Wheeler were looking upstream.

"Over here!" Tom shouted.

Wheeler saw them and dived into the water.

"He's unconscious or worse," Tom sputtered when Wheeler reached them. "Got caught in tree limbs and was pulled under."

"Get to shore," Wheeler said. "I'll take him."

Wheeler grabbed Hal in a rescue hold and started pulling him toward the shallows. They continued to move downriver. Rick and Nick ran along the shore. Tom reached the bank slightly ahead of Wheeler and stumbled onto the rocks. Rick came up to him.

"What happened to your face?" he asked.

Tom looked down and saw blood dripping onto his wet suit. He touched his chin. His fingers came away red.

"Hal hit me with his helmet."

Nick was waiting for Wheeler when he reached the shallows. The two men grabbed Hal under his arms and dragged him out of the water. His body was limp. Wheeler laid Hal on his back and started giving him mouth-to-mouth resuscitation.

Tom prayed silently.

With a slight lurch of his chest, Hal gave a choking sound and water drained from his mouth. Wheeler turned Hal's head to the side until it cleared, then continued administering mouth-to-mouth. Hal choked again and coughed up more water. He started breathing on his own, but it was a mixture of gasps and chokes.

"Is he going to be all right?" Rick asked in a subdued voice.

"He's alive," Wheeler said grimly. "The rest depends on how long he was underwater."

Hal's breathing became smoother. The color returned to his lips. He groaned and opened his eyes. Wheeler raised Hal's head and held it in his lap.

"Can you hear me?" Wheeler asked.

Hal nodded slightly. "Where–" he said, then choked violently.

Wheeler held Hal's head higher. He spit out more water, then took a deep breath. Tom, who'd barely been breathing himself, did the same. Hal opened his eyes and looked around. The men clustered around him.

"Wh-what . . . ?" Hal asked groggily.

At the sound of Hal's voice, all the men relaxed. Wheeler glanced over at Tom.

"You need to get some pressure on that cut. Rick, grab the first-aid kit from the raft."

"What happened?" Hal managed.

"You and Tom were knocked out of the raft by a boulder that was a few inches beneath the water. Usually it's visible, and I can steer around it. You'll have to ask Tom about everything after that. I didn't see you again until the two of you floated around the bend. You were unconscious with a quart of river water in your lungs."

Rick returned with the first-aid kit. Wheeler took out a thick piece of gauze and handed it to Tom, who pressed it against his chin. Wheeler then tore the wrapping from a pair of butterfly bandages.

"Let's see if this will do the trick," he said, squatting next to Tom.

Tom tilted up his head. Wheeler removed the bloody gauze from Tom's chin, applied a fresh piece, and stretched two bandages over the wound.

"That should hold until we get out of here. You may need a few stitches." He turned to Hal. "Can you drink something?"

"Yeah. It's weird, but I'm thirsty."

"Can you walk?"

"I think so."

With Wheeler and Nick on opposite sides supporting him, Hal got to his feet and unsteadily made his way across the rocks to the raft.

"What happened in the river?" Rick asked Tom.

Tom didn't answer. They reached the raft. Hal leaned against the inflated side and took a few sips of water. Wheeler handed Tom a bottle of water and an energy bar. The men stood in a silent circle for a few moments. Merely being alive was something worth savoring. Hal ate a small piece of apple that Wheeler cut with his knife.

"Man, this tastes good," he said.

Tom felt slightly queasy. He nibbled on the energy bar.

"I remember my foot getting caught on something and going

under the water," Hal said. "That's it, until I started coughing up water."

"Did you see how he got free?" Wheeler asked Tom.

Tom took another drink of water and bit off more energy bar. The other four men stared at Tom.

"Counselor, you're not going to dodge our questions," Rick said. "Go ahead and give a complete account before I have to get rough with you in your weakened condition."

Tom swallowed the bite and told them what happened. Hal's face turned pale as he listened. Rick shook his head when Tom described his efforts to break off the limb.

"That tree hasn't been down in the water for very long," Wheeler said. "It sounds like Hal's foot got lodged in a tangle of branches, and the current pushed his body forward. That sort of thing can also happen with submerged rocks."

Tom glanced at Hal's right ankle. It was red and scraped. Hal reached down and rubbed it, then looked up at Tom.

"Thanks," he said.

"You should thank him." Tom pointed at Wheeler. "He's the one who brought you back."

"And gave you mouth-to-mouth," Rick said with a short laugh. "That must have been nasty."

Wheeler reached out and patted Hal on the shoulder. "At least you didn't spit up."

The men rested on the rocks, eating snacks and recovering. The sun crested the trees, warmed their bodies, and restored their souls.

"I feel like I've been in a mixed martial arts cage fight," Hal said, standing up to stretch. "Every muscle in my body is aching."

"Both of them?" Rick asked.

"Everything in you was fighting to survive," Wheeler said.

Tom moved his shoulders and raised his arms. His muscles felt fine, but his chin had started to hurt.

"How about you, Tom?" Rick asked.

"I'm okay except for the place where Hal head-butted me."

Wheeler collected the trash from the other men. "Do you want to finish the trip?" he asked them. "If not, I can hike out to the road and come back with a vehicle."

"It's up to Hal," Rick replied. "I don't want to make him get back in the raft if it will cause a problem. He's been through more than enough already."

"I'll be okay if I can sit in the middle of the boat," Hal answered. "I'm not ready to lean over the water with a paddle."

"We can do that," Wheeler said. "There will still be rough spots, but we'll take the safest way through the remaining rapids."

They put the boat in the water. Wheeler placed Nick and Rick up front, with Tom in the rear and Hal in the middle sitting on the floor. There was some paddling required, but Wheeler positioned the boat at the entry point of each stretch of white water and expertly guided it through.

During one lull, Wheeler caught Tom's eye and motioned toward Hal, who was sitting in the bottom of the boat with his knees pulled up to his chest.

"Quick thinking," Wheeler said in a low voice. "I've never lost anyone on this river. Today was as close as it gets."

Tom pointed up.

Wheeler nodded. "Yeah, I was praying too."

The last major stretch of white water was Hell's Hole. Other rafters were off to the side resting for a few minutes before tackling the class 4 rapids, but Wheeler didn't stop. The raft bucked and reared. Tom saw Hal clutching the ropes that ran around the inside of the boat. His knuckles were white.

Then it was over. The water calmed. It was a short paddle ride to the takeout point. When they reached it, a man in his early twenties wearing an Ocoee Adventures T-shirt was waiting for them on the bank.

"What took you so long?" he asked as he grabbed the raft and helped pull it onto the bank.

"We had a close call," Wheeler replied.

"And I'm banned from further rafting trips," Hal added, stepping out of the boat.

"I didn't say that," Wheeler said.

"It's a self-imposed ban," Hal answered. "I don't think I'll be going into the deep end of a swimming pool for a while."

Wheeler and his helper put the raft on top of a van and drove the men upriver. Tom sat behind Wheeler and stared out the window. Other groups in rafts were smiling and laughing as they bobbed up and down in the water. Tom tried to spot the place where they'd fallen out of the raft.

"Is that where we fell in?" he asked, tapping Wheeler on the arm.

"Close, but you can't see it from the road," Wheeler answered. "The next trip I make, I'm going to check the tree where Hal was caught and report it. They may send a crew to clear it away if it's deemed an extreme hazard."

They reached the bathhouse and changed into regular clothes. Gathering outside, they looked like the same group that had started the trip a couple of hours earlier, but a near-death experience has an impact on young men who think they're going to live forever.

"If you ever decide to lift your self-imposed ban," Wheeler said to Hal, "I run a lot of wide-body rafts on the river. It's a different trip, not nearly as close to the edge."

"Thanks, but don't count on me to pay your bills." Hal shook

Wheeler's hand. "Saving my life is another matter. Send me an invoice for that, and I'll gladly pay it."

"Included in the trip."

The men said their good-byes and piled into Rick's SUV. Tom and Hal sat in the backseat. In ten minutes the river was out of sight. Rick put in a CD. The men rode in silence. About halfway home, Hal leaned over to Tom.

"I'm sorry about your dad. I never met him, but Rick says he was a good man."

"Yes, I'd like to think he tried to save the man who drowned with him."

"If there's anything I can ever do for you, let me know," Hal said. "I mean it. Wheeler gave me CPR, but he wouldn't have gotten the chance if you hadn't gotten me untangled from that tree."

"Somehow I just knew I needed to break off the limb."

It was late afternoon when they pulled into Rick's driveway. The farther they got from the river, the less real the danger seemed, and Hal's sense of humor returned. As soon as they stopped, the front door of the house opened and Tiffany came out. She greeted Rick with a kiss on the cheek, but her eyes were on Tom when she did it.

"What happened to your chin?" she asked. "Did you hit it on a rock?"

"Harder than that," Hal responded. "My head."

"Not exactly his head," Rick corrected. "It was Hal's helmet. It cracked Tom on the chin while he was saving Hal's life."

"You're kidding," Tiffany said.

"I wish he was," Hal replied. "Tom and I fell out of the boat. My foot got caught in a branch, and the current pulled me under. Tom broke the branch and set me loose. I had so much water in my lungs the guide had to give me CPR to revive me."

Tiffany reached up and gently touched Tom's chin. He winced and pulled away.

"You should get that checked at the hospital," she said. "Unless you get it stitched up, it might leave a nasty scar."

"Even if you don't get stitches, it's going to be a big plus with the ladies," Rick said. "Every girl who sees it and asks how you got it will find out you're a hero."

"I'm not a hero. I reacted in the moment."

"Sounds like you're a hero to me," Tiffany replied.

Seeing Tiffany caused Tom's head to spin again. He had to get away.

"See you later," he said to the group. "I'm going to the ER."

"Do you want me to go with you?" Tiffany asked.

"No thanks," Tom said quickly.

"Call if you need anything," she said. "Anytime."

Tom checked his chin in the rearview mirror of his car. It was a puffy mess held together by two butterfly strips that were beginning to lose their grip. He drove to the hospital where an ER doctor, who told Tom that his ambition was to become a plastic surgeon, closed the wound with five neat stitches.

_____

Tom woke up sore Monday morning and took a hot shower to relax his muscles. Elias didn't appear for breakfast, and Tom walked quietly down the hall to the old man's bedroom. Rover followed after him and sniffed at the bottom of the closed door. Tom knocked softly. There was no answer. He knocked louder.

"Come in," Elias said in a groggy voice.

Tom opened the door. Elias's bedroom was sparsely furnished with a high poster bed, an antique chest of drawers, and a walnut nightstand. A small rug covered the bare wooden floor to the right of the bed. The old man, his white hair sticking out at odd angles, rubbed his eyes.

"Are you okay?" Tom asked. "I fixed oatmeal with raisins and brown sugar for breakfast."

"Leave it on the stove but turn off the burner. I'll be up later. I didn't sleep much last night. The Lord kept me up for a few hours."

"Were you in the study?"

"Yes."

"I'll let you go back to sleep."

Tom backed out of the room. Rover moaned.

"Can Rover stay in here?" Tom asked. "He'll probably sleep on the rug until you're ready to get up."

"Sure."

Tom left his drooling dog and mystic uncle at the house.

————

When he arrived at the office, Bernice's car was parked out front. The secretary was sitting at her desk, a cane propped up against the wall near her chair.

"Good morning," Tom said. "You didn't have to come in. How are you feeling?"

"I should be asking you that question," Bernice replied, pointing to Tom's chin.

"I had an accident—"

"No need to tell me," Bernice interrupted. "I already heard what happened on the river. Jeanne Tucker called last night before I went to bed and told me you saved Hal Millsap's life."

"How did she find out about it?"

"I think she heard about it from a woman who takes care of Hal's dogs when he's out of town. Of course, Jeanne thought I should know since I work here."

"That makes sense."

Bernice peered through her glasses at Tom's face. "Is the cut on your chin the only injury you have?"

"Yes."

"Sue Ann Margraf phoned after I hung up with Jeanne to ask about you. She saw your car in the parking lot at the ER and heard your ear almost got cut off by a tree limb. It had me worried."

"The hospital isn't supposed to give out information about a patient's care."

"I don't see how it matters." Bernice shrugged. "Sue Ann was obviously wrong. I can see from here that your ears are fine. I'm not sure how her story got started."

The door opened. Tom turned around as a man in a deputy sheriff's uniform entered.

"Are you J. Thomas Crane, executor of the estate of John A. Crane?" the young man asked.

"Yes," Tom replied.

"I have a subpoena for you," the deputy replied, handing Tom an envelope.

The return address on the envelope was the Etowah County District Attorney's Office. The envelope was sealed shut. The deputy left.

"What's that about?" Bernice asked.

Tom loosened the corner of the flap with his index finger. "I don't know."

SEVENTEEN

om removed the subpoena from the envelope. It was
a standard form issued by the DA's office with Judge
Caldwell's signature stamped at the bottom. Because it
was a form, the judge probably didn't know anything about it.

> You are hereby ordered to produce and deliver for inspection any
> and all records related to the representation by the late John A.
> Crane, attorney-at-law, of Harold Addington, deceased, of Etowah
> County, Georgia, of any sort, wherever situated, without exception.
> /s/Nathan Caldwell, Judge of Superior Court

The date and time for compliance was set for Wednesday morning at 9:00 a.m. in front of Judge Caldwell.

"Charlie Williams wants all the records I have related to my
father's representation of Harold Addington," Tom said.

"Addington's crazy daughter is behind this," Bernice said tersely.
"I can't believe Charlie is letting her manipulate him into serving a
subpoena on you."

"Maybe, maybe not."

"What do you mean?"

Tom didn't answer.

"Tell me," Bernice continued. "When it comes to the office, I know how to keep things confidential. Your daddy trusted me, and you can too."

Tom sat down beside Bernice's desk. "It's complicated. Charlie was asking questions about this before I met Rose."

"But I already told you that your daddy didn't do anything except talk to Harold Addington about fishing."

It was a moment of decision for Tom. Should he tell Bernice about the designated trust account and the issues related to it or not? He pressed his lips together.

"I hope you're right," he said. "All I can do is show up in court with an empty folder and hope that satisfies Charlie's curiosity."

"Are you going to let the Addington family know about the subpoena?"

"I have to. They have a right to be there with an attorney representing them."

Bernice stared at Tom. He could tell she suspected something.

"If the Addington girl brings up her silly claim that your daddy charged a fee for work he didn't do, I hope Judge Caldwell holds her in contempt of court," she said with a sniff.

"He's not going to hold her in contempt for asking a question, but the judge will ask for proof, just like I did."

Tom retreated into the office and closed the door. Taking out his cell phone, he called Arthur Pelham. The head of Pelham Financial answered on the second ring.

"Tom, how are you?" Arthur asked. "Rick told me about your close call on the river. Sounds like you were a real hero. I appreciate you saving Hal Millsap. He's doing a fine job for us."

"Nothing stays private in Bethel, does it?"

"No." Arthur laughed. "That's the benefit and the curse of a small town. It keeps you honest."

"Speaking of private information, I received a subpoena this morning from Charlie Williams. He wants all the information I have about my father's dealings with Harold Addington. I have to respond on Wednesday morning. I was waiting to hear from you about Addington."

"I set that process in motion immediately after we talked in Bethel, and I'm still working on that," Arthur answered in a serious tone of voice. "Things are moving faster than I thought. What are you going to give them?"

"Nothing that would cause embarrassment to Pelham Financial; however, once the district attorney gets involved, it's out of my control. Has Charlie Williams been in touch with anyone at your company?"

"Not yet."

"There could be a subpoena on its way to you right now, or Williams may wait to expand his investigation until after I respond."

"Unless I'm forced to get involved, I'm going to rely on you to keep me abreast of any new developments. Are you sure this has to do with what we discussed the other day?"

"What else could it be?"

"I don't know." Arthur cleared his throat. "But if it has to do with the same situation, it means there is a hole in our firm's security system. That concerns me greatly. You're doing what you can, which I appreciate. Will a representative of Harold Addington's estate be in court on Wednesday?"

"I have to notify his family of the hearing. His daughter, Rose, is the executrix of the estate."

"What do you think the judge will do?"

"I hope nothing."

"Good. Once this subpoena is behind us, you can move forward to rectify this wrong in a discreet way. Everything is being put together and should be complete by the end of the week. I know you'd like to close the books on this and move on."

"Yes, sir. I think the judge should sign off on any action taken. Judge Caldwell is serving as interim probate judge."

"He's a good man. Would that create a public record?"

"I could request that the order be sealed because it involves an attorney trust account."

"The money is in your father's trust account?"

"Yes." Tom inwardly kicked himself for slipping up. He'd probably confirmed what Arthur suspected. "Actually, it's a designated trust account opened shortly before his death. That, along with some other factors, raised my suspicions and prompted me to contact you."

"I've always said you were smart," Arthur replied in a relaxed voice. "And I assume you apply the same analytical intuition to the rest of your practice."

"I do my best."

"That's all anyone can ask. Listen, thanks for calling me so promptly. I'll make sure you're notified if we receive a subpoena. Otherwise, I'll wait to hear from you on Wednesday."

"Yes, sir."

Even though Tom wasn't representing Arthur Pelham, it felt like he was.

———

Before calling Rose Addington, Tom turned to Psalm 72:78 and prayed for skill and integrity. Rose didn't answer, and he left a voice mail asking her to return the call. The phone on his desk buzzed.

"Hal Millsap is on the phone," Bernice said.

"Put him through."

"The press is here," Hal said. "And they're clamoring for a glimpse of the hero of the Ocoee."

"The press?"

"Yep. Mr. Grayson Hill of the *Bethel Examiner* is sitting in one of our conference rooms. He's writing an article and wants to add pictures. I think he wants you to play the role of the river guide who gave me mouth-to-mouth resuscitation."

"That's not happening."

"I told him you'd say that, and frankly, it's a relief to me. If you have a few minutes, Grayson would like to ask you a few questions and take a photo of us together."

"Okay. I'll be right over."

Tom stepped into the reception area. "Do you know Grayson Hill, a reporter for the paper?"

"Sonny Hill? He graduated from journalism school this past June. His mother used to work with Carl at the plant. I've known the family for years."

"He's writing an article about what happened on the river."

"Help him out."

"That's what I'm going to do. I'm meeting him at Hal Millsap's office."

It was a five-minute drive to the Pelham Financial executive office building. The primary nerve center of the investment firm was in New York, but there was enough going on in Bethel to justify an impressive brick building surrounded by carefully landscaped grounds with a large marble fountain in front. A white sign with gold letters read "Pelham Financial–Bethel."

Most of the Pelham employees in Bethel worked at a renovated textile mill that had been purchased by Arthur and transformed into a telephone marketing, customer assistance, data entry, mail processing, and bookkeeping center. That, too, was a model facility, which had been featured in newspaper and magazine articles about how a Southern town was brought back from manufacturing death to high-tech life.

Tom parked in a space reserved for visitors. In the far corner of the lot he saw Hal's red truck. A brick walkway led to the main entrance. Inside there was a large open reception area. Two attractive young women sat behind identical desks to the right of the entrance. Tom approached the first desk. A brunette greeted him with a smile. Tom introduced himself.

"I'm here to see Hal Millsap and a reporter from the newspaper."

"The reporter is already here, and I'll let Mr. Millsap know you've arrived," the woman answered with a strong Southern accent.

While the woman typed a message on her computer, Tom looked at the name tag she was wearing: Leanne Henderson.

"Are you related to Scotty Henderson?" Tom asked. "He was a classmate of mine in high school."

"I'm his little sister," the woman answered with a shy smile. "I doubt you remember me, but I went to all the football games and saw you play. I was in the eighth grade when you and Scotty graduated."

Tom recalled a scrawny girl with frizzy dark hair and braces.

"You had braces," he said.

The woman licked her straight white teeth. "Yes."

"Sorry," Tom said, catching himself staring. "Where's Scotty these days?"

"About twenty miles west of Knoxville. He's a veterinarian, married with two kids and a third on the way."

The Henderson family owned a large herd of Black Angus

cattle. The phone on the woman's desk chirped. She picked it up, then scooted back her chair.

"Follow me," she said. "They're in conference room four."

Tom followed Leanne. They passed through a security door and down a hallway lined with conference rooms.

"Why so many conference rooms?" Tom asked.

"For meetings with customers who come in from out of town. Did you see the lodge?"

"No."

"It's only been open a couple of weeks. A hundred people can stay there. The plan is to host financial retreats in Bethel and bring in clients for investment seminars."

Leanne stopped at the door to a rectangular conference room. Hal Millsap, wearing a suit and tie, was sitting at a table with a young man in blue jeans and a T-shirt. A camera bag rested on the table beside a laptop computer.

"Here's the hero!" Hal said, jumping to his feet.

"Hero?" Leanne asked.

"You'll read about it in the paper tomorrow, darling," Hal said.

The reporter had swept-back spiked blond hair that made him appear to be standing in a perpetual wind tunnel.

"I've told Grayson everything that happened," Hal said, "but he has to verify some of the facts with you. I didn't know reporters still did that."

Tom sat down and answered a few questions.

"See?" Hal said to the reporter. "I was telling the truth."

Grayson turned his computer so Tom and Hal could see it. "I've downloaded stock photos of the river that are in the public domain, but I'd like a few shots of the two of you together. That's important for a personal-interest article."

"How about a picture of Tom pulling me out of the fountain in front of the building?" Hal asked.

"Let's do some shots in here first."

Grayson pulled a foam board with a diagram of the river on it from beneath the table. He asked Hal to hold it while Tom pointed to the place near Double Trouble rapids where they were thrown from the boat. Outside, Grayson took multiple photos in front of the fountain.

"How long is the article going to be?" Hal asked. "I'm sure my mother will want a bunch of copies."

"As long as my editor will allow."

Grayson and his wind-tunnel hair left.

"Do you have a minute to come up to my new office?" Hal asked. "I enjoy showing it off. Up until six months ago I was at the old Blackstock mill."

"You got a promotion?"

"Yeah, but I'm at the bottom of the food chain at this place."

Hal's office was on the second floor. It reminded Tom of his work space at Barnes, McGraw, and Crowther. Through a single window Tom could see the lodge Leanne mentioned. It was built of the same brick as the office building and connected by a covered walkway. Hal closed the door. Tom sat down.

"Most of the big bosses are on the first floor," Hal said. "Except Mr. Pelham. He has an office on this floor with its own conference room. It's off-limits to worker bees like me."

"But you're friends with Rick."

"That's personal. His father is always Mr. Pelham to me, and I've never been invited over to the house when Mr. Pelham was there."

Tom glanced around the office. A group photo of employees hung on the wall. Arthur was standing in front.

"Who's in that picture?"

Hal followed Tom's gaze and turned in his chair. "That's the local management team."

"Including Harold Addington?"

"Yes."

Hal walked over to the picture and pointed to a man in the front row close to Arthur.

"There he is," Hal said.

Tom could see the family resemblance between Addington and his daughter.

"Did you know him?" Tom asked.

"Barely."

"What was his job?"

"Mr. Addington was in charge of developing the European market for our products, especially the high-yield certificates of deposit from the bank in Barbados."

"Why was he working from here instead of New York or Boston?"

"I think he got in hot water in Boston, and they brought him to Bethel to rehabilitate him."

"Rehabilitate? I thought you didn't know much about him."

"Because I work in human resources, I hear scuttlebutt about other employees."

"Anything you can share with me?"

Hal lowered his voice. "Mr. Addington had access to highly sensitive proprietary information about Mr. Pelham's investment strategies. The details about that sort of stuff are way above my pay grade, but every financial firm on the planet would like to know what Mr. Pelham is thinking about the markets. Arthur Pelham is a genius. There's no other explanation for his ability to outperform ninety percent of the competition year after year."

"Ninety percent?"

"Maybe I'm off a bit on the number, but the company has been on a phenomenal run, especially over the past fifteen years. Anyway, once someone has been on the inside, upper management tries hard to keep them around. It's great for job security."

"Any idea how Addington messed up?"

Hal shrugged. "The only way he could. He was a salesman who didn't sell up to expectations. I think the problem may have been that Pelham Financial was new to the European market. It takes time to build trust with clients."

"Yeah."

"I can understand why you're interested in the last man to see your father alive. You almost became that person to me."

"I'm glad I wasn't," Tom answered.

"Me too." Hal stepped back and leaned against his desk. "Can I ask your opinion about a personal matter?"

"Sure."

"Do you think the article in the newspaper will help or hurt my chances of convincing Leanne Henderson to go out with me?"

"Help," Tom answered immediately. "You came so close to death that it will make spending time with you seem extra special."

"Are you sure about that?"

"Put it to the test," Tom said. "Give her a copy of the article, ask the name of her favorite restaurant, and offer to take her there this weekend to help you celebrate being alive."

"Wow." Hal nodded. "That's awesome."

"Of course, if she turns you down, it's a strong signal that she wishes you were dead."

Hal picked up a paperweight and cocked his arm as if preparing to throw it at Tom. "You need a knot on your head to go with the cut on your chin."

On his way back to the office, Tom's cell phone rang. He glanced down at the caller ID. It was Rose Addington. He pressed the Receive button.

we acknowledge

not know Bart Can... but that's about all now on... head to me with the car... on our way.

On his way back to the office, Tom's cell phone rang. He glanced down at the caller ID. It was Rose Addington. He pressed the Accept button.

I owe you an apology," Rose said as soon as Tom answered. "Whatever happened between our fathers is no excuse for my going off on a rant directed at you. I'm sorry for the way I acted at your office."

"We both have questions," Tom answered evenly. "And I'm trying to find answers. If it turns out my father owes your family money, then I promise to make it good as soon as I can."

"Mum and I aren't greedy."

"What I said stands because it's the right thing to do."

Tom turned into a parking space in front of the office but stayed in the car. He didn't want Bernice to hear the conversation. He told Rose about the subpoena.

"You may want to have a lawyer in court to represent your father's estate when I respond on Wednesday."

"Do you have any idea why the government's barrister thinks the scant bit of information you have is important?"

"If so, it's not in the subpoena," Tom said, dodging the question.

"Doesn't he have to say what he's looking for? Isn't there something in your Constitution that you can point out to the judge?"

"An accused has the right to face his accusers, but no one is accused of anything. At least, not yet."

"But it sounds to me like this subpoena is a first step to that happening."

Once again, Tom was impressed with Rose's insight. However, the accused in this case was most likely her father, a dead man.

"That would require the DA to either file what is called an accusation or present evidence to a grand jury for an indictment."

"You seem rather calm about this."

"I'm in court all the time, so this is my world. Of course, I'm usually representing someone else. I have no choice but to respond."

"Do you think my mum and I should hire a barrister?"

"Like I said, that would be a good idea."

Tom would much rather deal with a lawyer than Rose.

"Can you recommend someone?"

"No."

Rose was silent for a moment. "Would that be because you and I might not see eye to eye about this matter?"

"Unfortunately, yes."

"It's coming clearer to me now. Thanks for speaking with me."

The call ended. Tom put his phone in his pocket and got out of the car. Rose Addington was right. One way or the other, everything was soon going to become much clearer.

The *Bethel Examiner* was delivered midmorning the following day. The paperboy for the downtown route that included the Crane law office dropped off four extra copies at Bernice's desk. Tom, who was in his father's office with the door closed, heard her call out.

"Tom! Come see yourself!"

Tom opened the door. "You could use the intercom feature on the phone," he said.

"Don't get all professional on me. If I want to tell Carl something important, I use my voice."

Bernice laid out the paper and opened it to the third-page headline: "Local Rafters Survive Close Call on Ocoee River."

"That's original," Tom observed.

"Quit it," Bernice said, shushing him. "Sonny is still a baby. And I'm reading the article. The paperboy dropped off extra copies. Get your own."

Tom turned to the article in another copy and read it. There wasn't much competing news in Bethel, and Grayson's editor had been generous with space.

"That's what happened," he said when he reached the end. "Even the quotes are correct. I didn't realize he was going to talk to Gary Wheeler, the river guide."

"Hush, I'm still reading," Bernice responded. "I can practically feel the freezing water drawing the life out of your bodies. *Hypothermia* is a scary-sounding word."

Tom waited until Bernice finished.

"What is the big award they give to the best journalists each year?" she asked.

"Pulitzer prize?"

"Sonny should get one. And these pictures of the two of you at the Pelham office building are good too."

The phone rang. Bernice answered it. "Yes, he's here," she said, placing the caller on hold.

"You're not going to do anything this afternoon but talk on the phone about this," she said. "If you try to dodge the calls, they'll just try again tomorrow."

"Okay," Tom said, retreating to the office. "Pass them along."

Bernice's prediction about phone calls proved accurate. Tom spent most of the next two hours talking to one person after another, often reconnecting with people from his past. But he didn't just talk about himself and what happened on the river. He asked about their lives too. That felt good. A small step away from selfishness is a long journey for the heart.

———

At noon Bernice left to go home for the rest of the day. Tom turned on the answering machine so he wouldn't be disturbed and went into his father's office. It had been several days since he'd read the Bible and written down his thoughts and prayers. He took out a legal pad that he'd been using as a journal and began to read. Halfway down the page, his mind started to wander. He opened the Bible to Isaiah. After a few verses, the words on the page began to run together. Tom stared across the room.

And thought about Tiffany.

Every logical cell in his being argued that spending half a second mulling over the possibility of life with Tiffany at his side was a waste of time. But other, less logical cells exerted a powerful influence over where his mind went when set free to roam. He couldn't escape her challenge to look into his heart and admit the truth. And when he did, Tom ran directly into the ache of genuine longing he felt for her. He could try to suppress it and he might struggle to ignore it, but it was there.

Tom got up from the chair and began to pace back and forth. He'd kept his distance when he was with Tiffany, but in the safety of the office, he didn't have to put up a false front. Images of future happiness sprang up so fast in his imagination that he couldn't fully enjoy one before another leaped forward and demanded his attention. He saw himself with her in multiple places he'd visited across the country. With her beside him, every venue would be fresh and new.

Tom's entrenched reluctance to commit to a woman evaporated at the prospect of life with Tiffany. Of course, their relationship would have an opportunity to flourish only postdivorce and after a private marriage ceremony a long way from Bethel. The pain of the split for Rick would be intense for both of them, but Tiffany was right. It would pass. Future legal business with Pelham Financial would disappear. But money gained from legal work seemed cheap compared to life with the only woman who'd ever come close to being his soul mate.

Tom sat down at the desk and turned on his computer. Running a search for Tiffany's name, he scored multiple hits that documented her appearance in horse shows. There were online videos of her riding championship horses in places like Louisville, San Diego, and Kansas City. Seeing how much Tiffany enjoyed herself made Tom smile. Happiness should mark every aspect of her life. And while Rick was a good guy, he'd not matured into the kind of man Tiffany deserved. Better to move on now than stagnate in a dead-end relationship.

A new e-mail came into Tom's in-box and interrupted his thoughts with a ping. It was from Nate Becker. Tom clicked it open.

Tom,

The partners of the firm met yesterday and unanimously voted to offer you a position with the firm. Attached is a proposed

employment agreement. Look it over and let me know what you
think. Please keep the terms confidential.
All the best,
Nate

Tom scrolled through the boilerplate language on the first page
of the agreement and reached the specific terms that began on page
two. When he saw the base salary amount, he stopped and read the
figure twice. It was more than he could have reasonably expected
to earn as a junior partner at Barnes, McGraw, and Crowther. The
other benefits were equally impressive. Sweet and Becker didn't hold
to the archaic law firm philosophy of money trickling down from the
senior partners. They turned on the spigot and splashed everyone.

Tom sat back in the chair and smiled. The possibility of staying in Bethel to practice law had been an entertaining diversion,
but his desire was to fight in the legal arenas where the best attorneys crossed swords. Sweet and Becker could make that happen. He
quickly typed a reply to Nate Becker.

Nate,
Thanks so much for the offer. Everything looks great. I'm moving as fast as I can to close out my responsibilities in Bethel and
will be in touch with you soon.
Tom

That evening Tom couldn't suppress his excitement about the
job offer. He caught himself smiling for no apparent reason.

"What's on your mind?" Elias asked after they finished cleaning
the supper dishes. "You seem happy tonight."

"I am," Tom replied.

Elias sat in his chair with Rover at his feet while Tom told him about the e-mail from Nate Becker. "I can't tell you any details, but it's a very generous offer with loads of opportunity down the road. I can practice law in the niche I'm familiar with and develop an even greater level of expertise. Sweet and Becker's office is closer to my apartment than the old firm."

"Sounds good," Elias said.

"Better than good. It's the best news I've gotten since coming to Bethel."

Elias didn't reply. Rover moaned and rolled onto his side.

Before going to bed, Tom spent a few minutes writing down a prayer of thanks. He was a different person from the one who'd driven from Atlanta to Bethel after the farewell lunch at the cheap sushi restaurant. When he returned to the big city, he'd take the new and improved version of himself with him.

Just before he dozed off, his thoughts returned to Tiffany. He rolled onto his back and stared at the ceiling. Living in Atlanta would create the distance needed for the situation to sort out without his direct involvement. If Tiffany ended the marriage, Tom could consider a relationship with a clear conscience. He fell asleep to pleasant thoughts of a happier future.

———

Wednesday morning Tom put on his blue suit, straightened his yellow tie, and went downstairs. Elias was in the front room with Rover.

"Going to court?" the old man asked.

"Yes."

"Your daddy would be proud of you. I'm not sure how and when the great cloud of witnesses is allowed to peer over the edge of heaven, but if your daddy has a front-row seat, he's enjoying the view."

At 8:55 a.m., Tom clicked shut his briefcase. All it contained was the empty folder. He'd not heard from Arthur about service of a subpoena on Pelham Financial. No lawyer had contacted him on behalf of Esther and Rose Addington. Bernice glanced up when Tom came out into the reception area.

"What's in the briefcase?" she asked.

"An empty folder."

The morning was overcast, with dark clouds moving across the sky. Tom entered the courthouse and walked upstairs to the main courtroom. Inside, Charlie Williams was talking to Rose Addington. No other lawyers were in sight. Rose, a serious expression on her face, stepped away from Williams and sat in the front row of the spectator area. A court reporter was setting up her machine. Tom shook Williams's hand.

"Why a court reporter?" he asked.

"To record the proceedings."

"I know that," Tom replied curtly.

Judge Caldwell, wearing his judicial robe, came in through a side door and sat down. The judge nodded to the court reporter, who raised a gray voice mask to her face.

"Proceed," the judge said.

"Your Honor," Williams said, "we're here pursuant to a subpoena served upon Thomas Crane as executor of the estate of John Crane. The subpoena required Mr. Crane to produce any and all information related to John Crane's legal representation of Harold Addington, also deceased."

Tom opened his briefcase, took out the empty file folder, and showed it to the judge.

"This is all I've located in response to the subpoena," Tom said. "I don't know why it's empty. I've not been able to locate any correspondence between my father and Mr. Addington, and there's no record of payment of any attorney fees. Perhaps Mr. Williams can inform both of us why he issued the subpoena."

"Mr. Williams?" the judge asked, handing the empty folder to the DA.

"Your Honor, shortly after Mr. Crane and Mr. Addington drowned, it came to my attention that there may have been criminal activity involved."

Tom spun around and saw that Rose Addington, her eyes wide, had her hand over her mouth.

"What kind of criminal activity?" the judge asked.

"Related to the cause of death."

"You mean someone may have murdered them?" Tom asked.

"No." Williams shook his head and looked directly at Tom. "As far as I know, there were no third parties involved."

"Harold Addington drowned my father?"

"It's not clear who may have been the perpetrator."

It took Tom a split second to process the implication of the DA's statement. "That's crazy!" Tom raised his voice.

"Did your father have serious financial problems?" Williams asked.

"You know he owed money to the IRS, but he'd made arrangements for a repayment plan."

Williams glanced over his shoulder at Rose. "And I have reason to believe that Harold Addington hired your father and paid him a substantial sum of money as a deposit. If that money isn't accounted for, it would be important to the investigation."

"What evidence for that do you have?" Tom asked sharply.

Williams looked at the judge. "Your Honor, based on prosecutorial privilege, I'm not going to answer that question. It's part of an ongoing investigation."

"Mr. Williams," the judge said, his face stern, "you have a duty to fulfill your oath of office, but I'm very concerned that you act in a responsible manner before impugning the reputation of a man like John Crane. I never met Mr. Addington, but the same standard should apply to him as well."

"I'm not trying to impugn anyone," Williams replied. "No one in the media was notified about this hearing by my office. It was my intention to keep this a closed hearing. Ms. Rose Addington, the executrix of Harold Addington's estate, is here because Mr. Crane contacted her. I can understand Mr. Crane's reluctance to turn over any embarrassing information—"

"Are you accusing me of lying?" Tom interrupted.

"Enough!" Judge Caldwell called out, striking the bench with his gavel. "Mr. Crane, do you have anything else to produce in response to the subpoena?"

Tom had second thoughts about withholding information about the designated trust account, but he vigorously pushed them aside. He wasn't going to be bullied by Williams's insinuations.

"No, sir."

The judge turned to the court reporter. "I'm instructing you not to transcribe this hearing until further notice and to keep what you heard here confidential."

"Yes, sir," the court reporter said, lowering her mask.

"Court is adjourned."

The judge, his face visibly flushed, left the courtroom. The court reporter followed him. Tom turned angrily toward Williams.

"Don't say anything you'll regret, Tom," Williams said and held up his hand. "I'm not going to indict a dead man, but if you want this to go away, you need to give me a reason to drop it."

"And prosecutorial privilege doesn't protect you from a civil suit for reckless slander."

"You're on my turf," Williams said, handing the empty folder back to Tom. "If you find out anything, let me know."

Williams picked up his briefcase and left the courtroom. Tom faced Rose from the other side of the bar that separated the gallery from the lawyer's area. Rose, her eyes sad, remained seated.

"Well?" Tom asked. "Are you spreading lies to destroy my father's reputation?"

"You should know the answer to that. This was as much a shock to me as it was to you. I don't want to believe either of our fathers—" She stopped. "I can't even bring myself to say it."

Tears rolled from Rose's eyes down her cheeks. Tom's jaw loosened. He opened the low gate in the bar that separated the two areas and stood in front of Rose. She took a tissue from her purse and dabbed her eyes.

"This is worse than anything I could have imagined." She sniffled. "I had no idea what was going to happen here this morning, and I'm not sure what to think about it now. All my mum and I wanted to do was find out why my papa hired your father as a solicitor. I don't know what Mr. Williams was talking about. When I came into the courtroom, he told me what I was about to hear would be painful. I had no idea—" Rose stopped again.

Tom stared at Rose for a moment. He couldn't see anything false or feigned about her response.

"Let's go to my father's office," he said.

"What?"

"It will only take a few minutes. I want to show you something that I didn't bring to court because I didn't believe I had to and wasn't sure I should."

Rose gave Tom a puzzled look.

"Or you can go home," Tom said with a shrug. "It's up to you. But I don't want you to be blindsided the way I was this morning."

Rose put her tissue in her purse and stood up. "I'll come."

They walked silently from the courthouse and down the hill to the office. Tom held the door open for Rose.

"Bernice, this is Rose Addington," he said.

"What is she doing here?"

"I asked her to come."

"I don't think that's a good idea," Bernice said. "After what—"

"Don't start," Tom interrupted. "Please hold all my phone calls."

Tom escorted Rose into the office and closed the door.

"Why is she so mad at me?" Rose asked.

"She's upset about the questions you asked me the other day about my father. I'll take care of it later. I have something more important to show you."

Tom unlocked the middle drawer of his father's desk and took out the deposit slip, envelope, starter checkbook, and sticky note from the trust account check register. He came over to Rose's side of the desk and handed her the sticky note.

"You already know about this. But the rest of it is new. I didn't turn it over to the district attorney because I'm not sure that it falls within the scope of the subpoena."

Tom told Rose about his discovery of the designated trust account. He handed her the deposit slip; her mouth dropped open when she saw the amount.

"Is this my papa's money?"

"That's my question to you."

Tom waited. Rose shook her head. "No, he would have told my mum about something this large."

"Are you sure she didn't know about it?"

"Positive. I've gone over all the financial records and reconciled everything since his passing. Papa made generous provision for my mum, but she's not going to be a rich woman. Part of his estate is going to fund a charitable trust."

"A charitable trust?"

"Yes."

Tom wasn't moved by that information. Giving could be motivated by guilt—an effort by Harold Addington to buy his way into heaven.

"I think the money in this designated trust account may be connected to Pelham Financial," Tom said, shifting in his chair. "The bank president said the check opening the account came from a bank in Barbados with connections in London and Newcastle."

"Newcastle?"

"Yes." Tom took a deep breath and exhaled. "Rose, I've confirmed from more than one source that your father was in hot water at his job. Your mother said as much when we met the other day. I know it's hard for you to hear this, but the path the money took through Newcastle and Barbados raises the possibility that the designated trust account contains funds misappropriated from Pelham Financial. If that's true, the money has to be returned to the company. If it's not, I have to find out who it belongs to."

Rose looked puzzled for moment. "Are you saying my father embezzled money from Pelham and gave it to your father to put in a special account?"

Tom looked into Rose's eyes. His resolve wavered. "Maybe."

He waited for her to explode. Instead, she stared past him at the bookcase over his left shoulder.

"Something's not clear about this money you found," she said slowly. "We can agree on that. But I'm not sure you have the right idea in mind. I never knew your father, nor you mine. For many years Papa pursued money and success, but five years ago he had a major change in his life. Since then he's lived as a good, honest Christian man. And everything I hear about your father indicates he was the same way."

"For a much longer time."

"It's impossible for us to imagine them stealing or murdering or doing anything illegal. Even hearing the words from my mouth sounds absurd."

"What's your explanation?"

Rose shook her head. "I don't know, but I think it's best to start over, and for the time being assume what we believe about our fathers is true until proven otherwise."

Tom thought about Arthur Pelham's promise to provide evidence of Harold Addington's embezzlement by the end of the week. Better to wait until proof existed than to hypothesize in its absence.

"All right," he replied. "Now that you know what I've found, maybe you can look for additional information. What your mother found in the nightstand doesn't answer these questions, and I've run out of rocks to turn over."

"Have you gone through all your father's personal effects and belongings?" Rose asked.

"There are boxes of stuff in Elias's garage," Tom admitted, "but most of it came from the sale of my parents' home several years ago. Anything relevant to what we're looking for is going to be recent."

"Is that how you investigate a case? By ignoring obvious places to look?"

"No, I just don't want to sort through a bunch of junk."

"That's what I'm going to do."

Tom doubted any junk pile at the Addington residence was comparable to the boxes stacked in Elias's garage, but he didn't see any use in arguing.

"I'll get started this evening."

"And what will you be looking for?" Rose asked.

"Uh, anything that pertains to our fathers."

"Especially what was in the empty folder you brought to court this morning." Rose pointed to the manila file. "It makes no sense to me that a solicitor would open a matter and not have a scrap of paper about it."

Tom couldn't disagree. And the lack of documentation concerning the designated trust account was even more troubling.

"Are you going to tell anyone what Williams said in court?" he asked.

"Not even my mum. It would devastate her."

"Okay. We'll keep this between us and talk in the next few days."

Rose stood up. Tom held the door open for her. He heard Bernice huff as Rose passed by. As soon as the door closed behind her, Bernice spun around in her chair.

"What's going on?" she demanded.

Tom told her about the hearing in front of Judge Caldwell. The anger Bernice felt toward Rose was instantly redirected.

"That's total nonsense. We have enough crime in Etowah County that Charlie Williams has better things to do than make a ridiculous claim about your father killing Harold Addington. Now, if it was the other way around—"

"Don't go there," Tom interrupted. "There are other issues involving Harold Addington."

Bernice raised her eyebrows.

"And I'm still sorting them out."

chapter
NINETEEN

Tom left work early so he could begin sorting through the boxes in Elias's garage. The old man joined him outside, not to help but to watch from a chair. Rover sat at Elias's feet.

"You keep surprising me," Elias said as Tom carried out a box and set it on the ground.

"How's that?"

"I never thought you'd tackle those boxes. Are you sure you don't want me to call the Burk girl?"

"I need to do this myself."

Tom sat opposite Elias. He placed a box between them and opened it. It contained cookbooks from a small antique bookcase that used to sit in his mother's kitchen. Little strips of paper extended from the sides of the volumes. Tom opened one to a pork loin recipe his mother often prepared when guests came for dinner. He saw her faded handwriting on a slip protruding from another book. When he pulled it out, it read "Tom's Favorite Cookies." He didn't have to open the cookbook to know it contained a recipe for chocolate chip cookies with chopped pecans and a hint of brown sugar. His mother would cut the cookies thin and cook them crisp so they could withstand a dousing in milk and still deliver a sharp crunch.

"This makes me hungry," Tom said, showing the slip to Elias and telling him about the cookies.

"I remember those," Elias said. "She used to put them in a jar in the cabinet above the stove so you couldn't get to them."

"And she kept putting them there after I could."

Tom gently shut the book. "How can I throw this away?"

"You don't have to."

Tom set the cookie recipe book aside and repacked the box. He'd intended on flying through the boxes, but sitting in the warm afternoon sun, it was more pleasant to slow down and reminisce. Unfortunately, pleasant memories from the past couldn't completely dispel Charlie Williams's harsh accusation from the morning. Tom resisted the urge to tell Elias about the DA's suspicions. As with Esther Addington, the old man would be horribly upset by the news, and sharing the information wouldn't relieve Tom's hurt. He looked through a box that contained high school yearbooks for both his parents and himself and set it aside to keep. When he opened the next box he caught his breath.

It contained legal-size file folders.

He pulled out the first one. Written on the tab was "Creswell Estate." But to his surprise, it didn't contain records from the probate court. Instead, there were extensive notes by his father that included Bible references. As he read the correspondence he realized it was a case in which his father helped Christians try to resolve a dispute without going to court.

"Did you know he did this?" Tom asked Elias, holding out a Settlement Agreement form that contained Bible verses about forgiveness.

Elias squinted at the papers for a minute. "Oh, yes. I'm the one who told Billy Creswell to call your father. After Billy's father died, his two sisters who lived in Florida came up to claim an equal share of the estate. It upset Billy because he and his wife had cared for Billy's parents without help from the sisters for years."

Tom turned to the back page of the agreement to see what happened. "They gave Billy an extra $20,000 for eight years of care? That's not much extra from an estate worth over $500,000."

"Yeah, but Billy got a chance to say a few things to his sisters. I guess the repentance on their part was a bit shallow."

"Especially if you measure that sort of thing by actions."

"Which is a good test," the old man agreed.

Tom continued checking the files in the box. Each one had to do with Christians and churches.

"I wonder why he didn't keep these files at the office," Tom said.

"Maybe because most of the meetings took place in the evenings."

Tom pulled out the last folder in the box. This one was different. The case involved a rural church pastor who'd stolen money for years from the cash offerings received on Sunday morning.

"Do you know Rev. Dennis Mullin?" Tom asked.

"No." Elias shook his head.

Tom turned over another sheet of paper. "He lived in Floyd County. Reverend Mullin was pilfering money from the offering plates on Sunday. The owner of a local department store became suspicious and started marking the bills he gave at church. The next week, the minister's wife would use the money to buy fancy shoes or expensive clothes. Instead of seeking a criminal warrant, the leaders of the church tried the peacemaking thing."

Tom kept reading. "But it didn't work out. Mullin denied any wrongdoing and resigned." Tom glanced up at Elias. "How can a man who claims to be a Christian do something so obviously wrong that anyone with half a conscience would say it's a sin?"

"He divides his mind," Elias said, raising his hand to his forehead. "One part preaches the gospel and prays for the sick. The other part steals money and justifies it by convincing himself that he's underpaid for his work as a minister. The same thing happens for other kinds of sins. Many preachers live isolated lives. They hunker down and don't let anyone get close enough to see what they're really like. Then when temptation comes along, they don't have anyone to call on for help or keep them accountable."

"What kept you honest?"

"A mixture of love and fear. I both loved God and feared him."

Tom thought about Harold Addington. "You say this happens a lot?"

"Unfortunately, yes."

"And it's not limited to ministers?"

"Any Christian can fall into this trap."

Tom worked his way through ten boxes. The Addington name didn't appear. Tom stood and stretched.

"Most of this stuff can go to the Burk family and be put in a yard sale," Tom said. "Where should I put it?"

"Back in the garage but in a different place."

Elias used his hands and arms to help himself up from the chair. "Watching you work has made me hungry. Let's eat."

The following morning Tom was drinking a cup of coffee at the office and talking to Bernice when the phone rang. She listened for a moment and put the caller on hold.

"Owen Harrelson is on the phone. Remember him? He's the one who hit Randall Freiburger. He must have found out about you investigating the case. Do you want to talk to him?"

"Yes," Tom responded quickly. "I'll take it in the office."

Tom quickly found the file. Getting a statement from the defendant before his insurance company started stonewalling would be a coup for the lawyer who eventually represented Freiburger.

"This is Tom Crane," he said.

"Arthur Pelham asked me to give you a call about the Addington matter," Harrelson said. "It's a sensitive situation, but Mr. Pelham assures me I can speak frankly and confidentially with you about it."

"Uh, sure." Tom quickly had to reorient himself. "My interest in the matter isn't as an attorney but as the executor of my father's estate. I have to make sure trust account funds are returned to the proper party."

"A duty I fully appreciate in my role as internal affairs officer for Pelham Financial."

At a company like Pelham Financial, an internal affairs officer was a cross between an auditor and a CIA operative.

"As I'm sure you know," Harrelson continued, "my job is to minimize the opportunities for employee embezzlement and investigate it when it occurs. Petty thefts can't be totally avoided, but we've never suffered any major misappropriation of client funds. The Addington matter falls in the middle."

"The middle?"

"Yes, everything is relative when you're talking about a company that manages over $35 billion. All Pelham employees with access to client accounts are bonded, and I was about to turn the loss over to our insurer when Arthur stopped by my office and said you might be able to help us recover the funds off the record. That would allow us to dodge an embarrassing blip in publicity and a negative entry on our balance sheet. It would also remove the need for the insurer on the bond to recover the funds from Addington's estate. It's my understanding he had a very valuable stamp collection, so I feel certain we'd recover the money, one way or the other."

Tom was impressed with Harrelson's research. "What can you send me to support Pelham's ownership of the funds?"

"I've reconstructed the transfers. Addington sold certificates of deposit for our bank in Barbados to legitimate buyers but didn't report the transactions. Instead, he generated CDs to a shell company in the UK. He held the CDs for a monthly cycle, redeemed them, deposited the money in the Newcastle branch of a British bank, then transferred the funds out of the UK back to Barbados, where they ended up in an account for another dummy company he controlled."

Tom quickly scribbled notes on a legal pad as Harrelson talked. He reviewed the arrows and boxes he'd drawn to illustrate the transactions.

"What did he give the real purchasers of the CDs to make them think their money was in the Barbados bank?"

"Phony certificates that looked legitimate. Because Addington was the only person who knew about the investments, there wouldn't be any communication from the home office with the customers at the time of purchase. Monthly transfers to Pelham's bank in Barbados for new CD accounts were averaging ten to twenty million euros a month, so everything looked legit. I'm not sure about Addington's long-range plans, but he only diverted funds from people and companies that expressed an interest in keeping the money on deposit for longer than a year. It was probably the beginnings of a Ponzi scheme in which he paid interest on existing accounts from funds collected on new ones. It would be impossible for one of our advisers working in the US market to pull something like this off because the deposit information passes through multiple hands; however, Addington was on a corporate island by himself developing a new market. Selling CDs was his job, and he was very good at it. Of course, it helped that we pay among the best rates for bank CDs on the planet. As soon as he died, there was an automatic audit of his accounts, and the embezzlement was discovered."

"Sounds like a breakdown in organizational structure."

Harrelson was silent for a moment. "That would be one way to put it. There are safeguards in place to prevent something like this from happening in the future."

"How did you find out about the phony companies in the UK and Barbados? Wouldn't that information be protected by privacy laws?"

Harrelson coughed. "We have a close working relationship with the bank regulators in Barbados. Discreet inquiries are allowed if we provide reasonable grounds for obtaining information."

"It's a more informal financial world than here."

"And in some ways more efficient. Hopefully, this is the background information you need. How do you want me to send you the data? I can send hard copies via overnight courier or scan it as an e-mail attachment to a secure server. It's about twenty pages in all."

"E-mail is fine." Tom gave him the address. "Did Arthur mention that I'd like to obtain probate court approval before I turn over the money? I can ask the judge to seal the order after it's entered. That would also protect me if the state bar association ever makes an inquiry."

"What would trigger an inquiry?"

"Nothing, unless someone complains. In this situation the only person who might do that would be a member of Addington's family. Are you going to notify them about the embezzlement?"

"We'd hoped that wouldn't be necessary. Harold Addington is dead, so he's not subject to prosecution. Return of the money will satisfy our interests. The only loss to the company is the interest we'll have to pay to the legitimate holders of CDs whose money never made it into their accounts. If Addington's widow and children never know what happened, it's fine with us."

"That's generous, but I may have to tell Rose Addington, the executrix of Harold Addington's estate."

"Why?"

"She's persistent."

"About what?"

Tom suddenly felt nervous. At that moment, he couldn't remember why he'd decided to show Rose the bank account information and deeply regretted that he had.

"The relationship between her father and mine," he said, choosing his words carefully. "Ms. Addington believes my father was representing her father, which was probably true since the money ended up in a designated trust account."

"Why did Addington hire your father?"

"Based on what you've told me, I believe he intended to use my father's trust account to launder the money. It's the only explanation that makes sense."

"That's what I concluded too."

"You did?"

"Yes. Does Ms. Addington know about the designated trust account?"

Tom licked his lips. "Yes, I told her."

"Why did you do that?" Harrelson raised his voice.

"Because I had to respond to a subpoena. Ms. Addington showed up in court, then we had a meeting in my father's office."

"That's not a reason to tell her about the money."

"It was a mistake." Tom saw no way to wiggle out of an admission.

"Obviously, and because of it you'll have to tell her about the theft. Arthur was willing to spare Addington's family the pain of disclosure, but that's no longer possible. Can I trust you to handle it?"

Tom felt like a guilty schoolboy. "Yes, sir."

"And will you be able to obtain a sealed order from the probate judge without generating any publicity?"

"Yes."

"I hope so. The supporting data will be in your in-box within thirty minutes."

"Should I communicate in the future with you or Arthur?"

"Me. You'll have my contact information in the e-mail."

The call ended. Tom felt stupid for telling Rose Addington, but as executor of the estate he'd not done anything wrong. His error came in making the powerful men at Pelham Financial uncomfortable about his actions.

A few minutes later he received an e-mail from Harrelson's administrative assistant. Tom printed out the information. It was the type of clear-cut evidence he loved to receive in cases at Barnes, McGraw, and Crowther. Harrelson's staff had done their homework. The dates, documents, and amounts matched. The identity of the European investors was blacked out to protect their privacy, but Harold Addington's name appeared at every crucial juncture.

It felt odd reading confidential bank records released without any judicial action or notification to the owner of the accounts. Money poured into Addington's Barbados account over a two-week period from the Newcastle bank and was withdrawn five days before John

Crane opened the designated trust account. Harrelson was right
when he said the lax island ways were more efficient when it came
to catching bad guys. Of course, the same attitude also made being
a bad guy easier. Tom put the information in the empty Addington
file and placed the folder in the bottom drawer of the desk.

That evening Tom didn't look through any more boxes in
Elias's garage. Nothing could trump the information that streamed
through cyberspace.

After supper, he and Elias sat on the front porch in a pair of
weathered wooden rockers. It was cool but comfortable. Rover
ambled off the porch and sniffed around the yard.

"He won't wander off, will he?" Elias asked. "When I've gone for
walks with him, I always put on his leash."

"It's okay. He considers this home now."

"How about you?"

"You keep bringing that up. Are you trying to forget about the
great job offer I received in Atlanta?"

"Have you accepted it yet?"

"No, but I will."

They rocked back and forth in silence for a few minutes.

"I wish I didn't have the pressure of shutting down my father's
office," Tom said. "A few weeks of vacation sitting on this porch in
the evenings would be nice right now."

"What kind of pressure? I thought you were just calling clients
and helping them find other lawyers."

"That part is easy. The pressure has to do with Harold
Addington. I can't tell you the details, but it's a serious situation, and
I'm about to be at odds with Rose."

"You need someone like your father to step in and be a
peacemaker."

"I don't have a problem with Rose. The wrongs are in the past, and she didn't do them. But I'm going to have to tell her some very hard things that are going to hurt her and devastate the rest of the Addington family if she chooses to let them know."

Elias stopped rocking. "That's why you asked me the other day how a serious Christian could commit an obvious sin. You were thinking about Harold Addington."

"Yeah," Tom admitted, "but please don't ask me any details."

"I'm too old to be curious, but I'll pray for you to have wisdom."

"And that Rose will be able to accept the truth."

chapter
TWENTY

The next day Tom decided it would be best to call Rose as soon as he reached the office. There was no use putting off the inevitable. He took out the Addington folder and stared at the number for a few seconds with a heavy heart before picking up the phone. Rose was a nice young woman who loved her father. To permanently soil his memory with a stain that couldn't be removed was sobering. Tom could only hope Elias's prayers proved potent. He placed the call.

"Hello," Rose said.

"It's Tom Crane. I have some information to go over with you."

"Me too," Rose responded. "When can we get together?"

"Uh, any time today."

Tom doubted anything Rose had found would prove relevant.

"I'll be down to see you in a couple of hours. Mum isn't feeling too well, and I have some things to do around here first."

"Okay."

After the call ended Bernice arrived at the office. Tom saw that she still moved slower than normal. Leaving the Addington file on his desk, he stepped into the reception area.

"Did your back flare up again?" he asked. "I thought it was getting better."

"I raked a few leaves yesterday, which was a big mistake. It will loosen up."

"You can go home early if you need to. Rose Addington is coming in to meet with me in a few hours."

Bernice eased herself into her chair. "I won't go home until she leaves. My back may hurt, but I'm more uncomfortable with the idea of leaving you alone with her. She's a clever thing, and when she starts flapping her eyelashes at you and jabbering away in that accent of hers, you're likely to buy whatever she's selling."

Tom sat on the edge of Bernice's desk. "I appreciate the offer of protection, but this is going to be a very painful conversation that should be handled privately. I have information that confirms some bad financial dealings by her father. My guess is that I'm going to need a box of tissues, not a witness to a meltdown."

"At least leave the door cracked open. I can position my chair—"

"Nope," Tom interrupted, then stood up and eyed Bernice suspiciously. "Did you ever do that when my father was meeting with a client?"

The older woman hesitated. "There were a few times."

"This won't be one of them."

Tom spent part of the next two hours getting ready for the meeting with Rose. He prepared a PowerPoint presentation based on the information he'd received from Owen Harrelson and made extra copies of the documents. His phone buzzed.

"Ms. Addington is here," Bernice announced in an official-sounding voice.

"I'll be right out."

Rose was standing in the middle of the reception area with a slender leather pouch in her right hand. She was wearing a tartan skirt and a light blue sweater. Tom noticed that Rose did, in fact, have beautiful eyelashes.

"You're not Scottish, are you?" Tom asked.

"Not a bit, but that doesn't keep me from liking the colors."

Tom saw Bernice roll her eyes.

"Come into the office," Tom said.

"Would you like me to join you?" Bernice asked.

"It's fine with me if she does," Rose said.

"That won't be necessary," Tom said, holding his hand out to stop Bernice, who was sliding back her chair.

Tom firmly closed the door. Rose sat in one of the side chairs. Tom positioned the computer screen so she could see it. Before he could start his presentation, Rose reached into the leather pouch and took out a sheet of paper.

"I found this in my father's office at the house," she said. "Mum and I cleaned out all the valuable stamps and important papers in the home safe weeks ago, but I'd not gone through everything in his desk. Most of it wasn't important, but he had a memo to your father in a bottom drawer."

Rose handed a single sheet of paper to Tom. It was dated three days before the designated trust account was opened.

To: John Crane, Esq.
From: Harold Addington

John,
This will confirm our conversation this past Wednesday at Gilbert Lake. I have no confidence in PF's willingness to address its issues in an appropriate way. Once the funds are received

by you, please deposit them in a designated trust account and notify me.

Your legal assistance and personal friendship during this difficult time are greatly appreciated.

Tom read the memo three times.

"What does this mean?" he asked. "It's vague."

"It seems clear enough to me. Papa was aware of problems at Pelham and hired your father to advise him. The money in the trust account has something to do with Papa's plans to correct the situation."

"That's a stretch. It might make sense if he'd told your mother about the problem and what he intended to do about it."

"What could she do but worry? Obviously, your father was his confidant." Rose pointed to the memo. "And attorney."

Tom placed the sheet of paper on the front of his desk. "My father didn't have a copy of this memo in his file. How can I know it was delivered?"

"Why would you have any doubt?" Rose asked with a puzzled expression. "Wasn't the money deposited into your father's trust account a few days after the date of this memo?"

"Yes, three days."

"Would that be what is called circumstantial evidence?"

"Maybe." Tom paused. "But since we talked I've seen direct, not circumstantial, evidence about the origin of the money."

"You found your father's file?"

"No, something more complete than anything he could have prepared. I've organized the information for you on my computer."

Tom hit the space bar on his computer, and the first PowerPoint slide appeared. Rose listened attentively and looked at each sheet of paper as he handed it to her. At first she didn't seem to grasp the significance of what she was seeing, but after he explained how her father sold CDs to European customers without forwarding the money to an account in the name of the person or company buying the CD, her face suddenly turned red, and she snatched the paper from his hand.

"This is a lie!"

Tom stopped. Rose's lower lip quivered, and he slid the box of tissues on the edge of the desk closer to her. She didn't grab one.

"Do you believe this nonsense?" she asked.

"I don't want to. But it's clear what happened."

"But why would my father ask your father for help?" She pointed to the memo. "If he was stealing money, he'd keep it secret."

"I'm getting to that. Do you want to see what I have or not?"

Rose bit her lower lip. "Go ahead."

The multiple instances of Harold Addington's signature on documents related to the formation of the dummy companies and again on the forms used to open the account at the non-Pelham bank in Barbados were overwhelming evidence that Addington had engaged in a well-thought-out scheme. Tom clicked on the last slide, which gave possible reasons why Harold Addington asked John Crane to open the designated trust account.

"Most likely, the bank account was a way to launder the money," Tom said. "A lawyer's trust account is confidential, and my father would have been prohibited by the rules of professional responsibility from revealing its owner in the absence of proof that the money was connected to the commission of a crime."

"Maybe he did."

"What?"

"Knew the money was connected to the commission of a crime."

"Nothing supports that," Tom answered. "The memo from your father indicates he sought legal advice from my father to correct a wrong, not commit one."

"So, you believe the memo when it's convenient?"

"No," Tom protested.

Rose pointed at the papers on the edge of the desk. "If my father was right about Pelham, I have no doubt the company could fabricate a bunch of fake documents to make him look like a criminal. Where are the names of the people who supposedly gave Papa money that he never transferred to Barbados?"

"The names were blacked out. That's private information."

"Which means there's no way to prove it happened."

Tom didn't say anything.

"And you're sitting here swallowing everything somebody at Pelham told you. Who did you talk to? I'd like to call him myself."

"I'm not sure that's a good idea."

"Why? Because it will make Arthur Pelham mad at you?"

"Hold on," Tom said angrily. "What gives you the right to come in here and lecture me?"

"You're the one who prepared the fancy presentation," Rose shot back. "It would have been a lot simpler to show me what you were given without dressing it up. I'm not a lawyer or an accountant, but I have a dose of business sense. I can understand this sort of thing and have enough spiritual discernment to know there's more to this than some bogus papers Arthur Pelham sent you."

"Arthur Pelham didn't provide this information."

"But one of his people did, right?"

Tom didn't answer.

Rose ran both her hands through her hair. "Tom, we've been coming at this from opposite directions since the first time we talked about it, and I don't see much chance of resolving it. My mum and I don't know where the money in the trust account came from. My father was a frugal man, but he didn't squirrel away millions of dollars in secret bank accounts. If you want to write a check to Pelham Financial for every penny you have in the trust account, go ahead and do it. But don't ask our family to agree that my father stole it. That will never happen."

Tom thought about Elias's comment that a Christian like Harold Addington could compartmentalize his mind, reserving a dark corner for a secret sin that even a heathen person would see as wrong. Addington projected an image of honesty. His family was totally unaware of the darkness that crouched out of sight, and the opportunity for Harold to confess his deceit died with him. However, Rose's last comment opened a door that might enable Tom to resolve the current impasse.

"Would you be willing to sign an affidavit releasing my father's estate from any claims you and your family might have against the money in the designated trust account?" he asked.

"Yes, as long as that's all it said," Rose said with a sigh. "But before you draw up any papers, I want you to pray and ask God if that's the right thing to do."

"Pray about it?"

"Yes."

"Okay." Tom shrugged.

Rose stood to leave. "When will I hear from you?"

Tom was tempted to tell her five minutes. "Soon," he replied.

Rose put her hand on the knob and turned around. "Until proven otherwise, I'm going to believe there's enough of the Lord in you to admit you're wrong."

Rose may have meant the remark as a compliment, but it stung like an insult. Tom didn't answer. She opened the office door and closed it behind her. Tom counted to fifteen before checking to see if she'd left the building. He cracked open the door. Bernice was sitting at her desk. The reception area was empty.

"Did she say anything on her way out?" Tom asked the secretary.

"No. How did she take the news?"

"Denial. She's a decent person who doesn't want to think her father was a crook. Who can blame her for that?"

"You're sounding more and more like your father." Bernice sniffed. "He always tried to see the good part of a bad apple."

Returning to the office, Tom stared at the memo from Harold Addington to his father. Rose had created a new problem. Should Tom give a copy of the memo to Charlie Williams? There was no doubt it was covered by the scope of the subpoena. Tom slowly opened the top drawer of the desk and slid the memo inside.

Bernice left the office around 3:00 p.m. Alone, Tom decided he should give at least token service to Rose Addington's request that he pray about the situation with Pelham Financial. Grabbing a Bible, he positioned a blank legal pad close at hand on the desk. After a couple of minutes of sterile silence, his mind drifted to Tiffany. He pushed that thought aside and glanced down at the Bible in an effort to refocus. It was opened to the book of Ephesians. He began to read. When he reached chapter 5, he read verses 11 through 14, then read them again:

> Have nothing to do with the fruitless deeds of darkness, but rather expose them. For it is shameful even to mention what the disobedient do in secret. But everything exposed by the light becomes visible, for it is light that makes everything visible.

That was it. Tom knew what he had to do. He wrote the reference on his legal pad. Regardless of the reaction by Rose or anyone else, he had to expose the deeds of darkness perpetrated by Harold Addington. Tom turned on his computer and typed out a simple affidavit for Rose to sign as executrix of her father's estate and sent it to her as an e-mail attachment. Within a few minutes, he received a reply.

I'll sign the affidavit and return to you as soon as possible.
Rose

Tom called Owen Harrelson with the good news. "I met with Rose Addington, and she's not going to oppose release of the funds to Pelham Financial. All I'm waiting for is an affidavit confirming her agreement."

"Excellent. Did she admit the embezzlement?"

"No, she vehemently denied it, even in the face of the evidence I showed her. But I assured her no one had any interest in embarrassing her or her family."

"That's one hundred percent true. What's the next step?"

"Once I receive the affidavit, I can schedule a hearing in front of Judge Caldwell. I'll show him the information you sent me and ask him to sign an order authorizing me to disperse the funds to Pelham."

"Do I need to come to the hearing?"

"Isn't there someone in Bethel who can verify the business records?"

"Not at this time. The need-to-know loop within the company about this situation is small, and Arthur is the only person with the authority to expand it. He's out of the office until early next week, but I'm sure he wants this taken care of as soon as possible."

"I do too."

"You have my cell phone number. Call me, and I'll fly down the next day."

Later, as Tom was checking his e-mail, a message from Tiffany popped up. A tingle ran through him as he opened it. It was short but filled with meaning.

Hi, Tom,
I've been thinking about you. Have you been thinking about me?
Tiffany

Tom stared at the screen. The safest thing to do would be to ignore the e-mail, return to Atlanta, and wait to see what happened between Tiffany and Rick. However, that's not what he wanted to do. He hit the Reply button and typed one word:

Yes

Seconds later a reply came:

Say no more. I understand. I am deleting both these e-mails before logging off the computer. You do the same. Sweet daydreams.

Tom closed his eyes and rubbed his temples with his fingers. How did Tiffany know his thoughts drifted back to her several times a day? The bond between them ignored space and distance. The question in Tom's mind was not if, but when they could be together. Coming back to Bethel, he'd discovered a lot more than he expected.

Saturday afternoon Tom decided to take Rover for a walk to the top of a ridge that skirted the north boundary of Etowah County. He invited Elias to come along.

"Walking on flat ground for half a mile to Austin's Pond is my

limit," Elias replied. "And are you sure Rover is going to enjoy climb-
ing up to the ridgeline? That's a steep hike."

"If I bring enough water for both of us, and he doesn't trip over
his tongue, I think he should be fine."

Elias's concern about Rover proved accurate. The dog used his
nose as an excuse to lag behind and lingered to sniff fallen logs before
moving on. Tom sharply pulled on the leash a few times, then gave up.
It would be easier to wait for Rover than drag him up the mountain.

Most of the leaves had fallen from the trees, and the few that
remained clung stubbornly to the branches like brittle brown fingers. It was a cool day, but even the slow pace of their climb kept
Tom warm. He stuffed his lightweight jacket into a small backpack.
Taking out a plastic bottle of water, he took a long drink, then poured
the rest into a plastic bowl for Rover. The sight of the water caused
Rover to trot up the hill for a drink. Tom watched as the dog noisily
lapped up the water until the bowl was dry.

"That's it until we reach the top," Tom said.

On the crest of the hill was an oblong exposed rock. The rock was
multicolored, the result of countless layers of paint. A fresh area of yellow paint was emblazoned with a marriage proposal from Michael to
Janine. Whether Janine accepted or not wasn't recorded. Other parts of
the rock announced birthdays, the scores of high school football games,
crude artworks akin to prehistoric cave etchings, and the names of
people who'd climbed the rock and wanted to prove it by signing the
massive open-air guest book. Somewhere beneath the layers of paint on
the east side of the rock Tom had once written, with high school ardor,
"Tom + Tiffany." Beside their names they'd made handprints that over-
lapped. They'd walked to the top of the rock one summer evening and
stayed until the moon came up. The memory made Tom's heart ache.

Leaving Rover tied to a tree at the base of the rock, Tom

scrambled to the top. He could see Bethel to the south, Lookout Mountain to the northeast, and Rover stretched out in a sunny spot below him.

Tom had brought a small Bible with him. Pulling it from the backpack, he held it in his hand while he enjoyed the vista. He'd read so much during the past few days that parts of the book were becoming familiar. Recently the gospel of John had been a favorite destination. Not stopping at the mind, it spoke to the heart. Tom opened the Bible to John 17. He'd always assumed the only prayer of Jesus recorded in the Scriptures was the Lord's Prayer. Then he discovered John 17, an entire chapter devoted to Jesus' praying. Tom read the chapter out loud. The words on the page echoed through the centuries. On top of the rock he felt close to both God and Tiffany.

Walking down the trail, he didn't have to drag Rover along. The dog knew he was heading toward a car ride.

"How was your walk?" Elias asked when they sat at the supper table.

Tom nudged Rover with his toe. The dog, whose stomach was comfortably full after a big meal, groaned slightly.

"You were right about Rover," Tom said. "He's not a candidate to hike the Appalachian Trail."

The following morning Elias wanted to return to the Rocky River Church. Tom hesitated. He didn't want to run into Rose and Esther Addington.

"I think I'll stay here," he said. "Or I might go fishing. The disciples spent as much time hanging out with Jesus at the lake as they did going to meetings at the synagogue."

"Every fisherman in the churches I've pastored reached the same conclusion. Often, that also meant buying an expensive bass boat. They believed you could get to Jesus a lot faster if you had a 200-horsepower outboard pushing you forward."

"There's no bass boat in my future." Tom smiled. "But I may go back to Austin's Pond."

"Take an extra handkerchief."

"I'm not going to cry."

"Maybe, maybe not. If I remember, you didn't have a lot of control over that the other day."

After Elias left, Tom went to the garage. His father's fishing poles rested neatly in a vertical row on hooks on the back wall. Multiple tackle boxes were lined up on a wooden table beneath the poles. John Crane loved to fish. Although he enjoyed fishing as a boy, Tom never developed an adult passion for the sport.

Each fishing pole had a specific function. There were fly-casting rods for mountain trout, stiffer poles for largemouth bass, long poles for crappie, slender ones for bream, and thick ones for surf casting at the beach. Tom selected one of the bass poles. The next task was finding the right tackle box. There were five to choose from, each stocked with lures, line, sinkers, and appropriate accessories. Tom checked a couple of boxes before finding the one that contained the combination of artificial minnows and plastic worms used for largemouth bass. The bass box didn't contain a pair of the special pliers used to extract a hook from a fish's throat. Tom leaned the pole against the bench and opened another one.

It didn't contain a pair of pliers. In fact, it didn't hold any fishing tackle at all.

Inside the tackle box he found a bundle of folded papers. Taking them out, he opened the one on top. It was the original memo from Harold Addington to his father. Even though he knew what it said, Tom read it again. The presence of the memo in the tackle box certainly answered the question he'd raised with Rose about whether his father received the information. Tom took out the next sheet of paper. It contained columns of dates and figures going back five years. The numbers ranged from 500,000 to 2,000,000. The last entry caught Tom's attention. It was 1,750,000, dated less than a week before that of the memo. He opened another sheet on which his father had written across the top "Harold Addington—Notes from Fishing Trip on Gilbert Lake."

Tom quickly scanned the notes. There was no doubt about the subject. It had to do with Pelham Financial's bank in Barbados. Beside the words "Island Properties" his father had written "grossly overvalued on financial statement." Names of resorts and developments followed. Beside the names were numbers, some as high as 80,000,000. Next to the large numbers his father had written much smaller ones, often no more than ten percent of the larger amounts.

The next paragraph began "Certificates of deposit—insider loans." The next line read "Interest on CDs not paid by earnings but from new deposits. Bribes to regulator in Barbados."

Another sheet of paper contained notes of his father's legal research. All the references were familiar to Tom, who had used the well-known provisions of the federal security laws as either a sword or a shield, depending on the case. At the bottom of the page, his father had scribbled several phone numbers, including the number for Tom's office at Barnes, McGraw, and Crowther and Arthur Pelham's cell phone number.

Finally a crumpled paper listed the fish John Crane caught and released over the last four months of his life. He recorded the name of the pond or lake, the date, the weight of the fish, its girth, length, and the type of lure used to catch it. He also noted the weather and temperature. On a trip to Austin's Pond a month before the fatal accident, John Crane caught a six-pound-four-ounce largemouth bass named "Spud" that had a distinctive nick in its tail. It had been caught on several previous occasions. Tom returned the fishing pole to its place on the wall and closed the tackle box. He wasn't going fishing. He took the information he'd discovered into the house and spread the papers out on the kitchen table.

By the time Elias returned from church and opened the front door, Tom had thoroughly studied the information. He hurriedly folded up the papers as Elias came into the kitchen.

"A homemade apple pie," Elias announced, holding up a pie pan. "Betsy Case brought several to church and gave one to me. She has a small orchard on her property and an early variety ripened last week. They're too tart to eat raw but taste great in a pie."

Elias placed the pie on the table. It gave off a sweet pungent fragrance.

"Look at that crust," Elias continued enthusiastically. "She sprinkles brown sugar and melted butter on top before she bakes it. I don't care what we eat for lunch, but let's make it quick so we can cut into this pie. Oh, you should have come with me. Esther and Rose Addington weren't there, but I saw Tiffany Pelham as I was leaving."

"Was Rick with her?"

"No."

"Did you talk to her?"

"Just for a second. She said you encouraged her to visit the church and was disappointed you didn't come. Lane preached a good message. I started to take notes but didn't have any paper stuck in my Bible." Elias stopped. "Did you go fishing?"

"No, while I was getting all the gear together I realized I wasn't in the mood."

"Did you find something in the garage that upset you?"

"What do you mean?"

"I think he had an old fishing pole that belonged to you when you were a boy out there. Something like that might make you feel blue."

"No, I didn't see one."

Tom spent the rest of the day in upheaval. Harold Addington had obviously presented himself to John Crane as a whistle-blower with information that could destroy Pelham Financial. But if Addington was lying, it could have been a subterfuge to convince John Crane to help him launder the money in the designated trust account. Gaining his father's trust and spinning a tall tale would be one way to do that.

———

Tom was still unsettled when he drove to town in the morning. The information from the tackle box was on the seat beside him. When he reached the office, he reviewed the Pelham documents, searching for a piece that might solve the contradiction. He heard the front door open.

"Good morning!" he called out to Bernice.

Bernice didn't answer. When he looked up, Rose Addington was standing in front of him.

"Sorry, I thought you were Bernice," he said. "Have a seat."

"It's not necessary," Rose replied. "I brought the affidavit. I signed it on Friday in front of a notary public at the bank, but you'd left the office by the time I stopped by."

Rose handed him the affidavit. Tom could tell at a glance that everything was in order but pretended to study it while furiously debating what to do. He coughed and cleared his throat.

"Is that all you need?" Rose asked. "If so, I'll be on my way."

"Did you make a copy of the affidavit for yourself?"

"Yes."

"How is your mother doing?"

Rose gave him a puzzled look. "In what way?"

"Uh, about this."

"I didn't tell her, but all this is a small loss compared to my papa's death. I hope she'll be able to sell the house soon and go back to Newcastle."

"Do you think there might be any other records in your father's papers?"

Rose pointed to Tom's computer. "You have everything you need to make up your mind."

"But as you said the other day, it's important to be thorough."

Rose smiled wryly. "And there's a time to shake the dust from your feet and walk away from a bad situation."

Tom placed the affidavit on top of the information he'd found in the tackle box. "You're right. This has placed a lot of extra stress on your family during a time you didn't need it. I'm sorry for being the source for much of it."

"You had a job to do." Rose shrugged. "And you'll have to live with the way you went about it." She paused for a moment. "Oh, one thing I would like to know. How did the Lord let you know what you should do?"

"A couple of Bible verses."

Rose waited. Tom didn't speak.

"Which you're not going to tell me?"

Tom looked down at the desk and debated what to do. When he glanced up, he saw Rose Addington walking quickly toward the front door. A few moments later the door opened. This time it was Bernice.

"What was she doing here so early?" Bernice asked with a flick of her head.

"She dropped by an affidavit that will let me close the estate without worrying about any loose ends related to her father."

"And she won't be coming back?"

"No."

"Then it's been a good day already."

Tom didn't call Owen Harrelson to let him know Rose had signed the affidavit. Instead, he started working on the last unopened box of files in his father's office. When he found an unmarked folder, he had a momentary sense of dread that it might contain information that would further complicate the Addington situation. To his relief, it was a research file for an unrelated case. Close to noon he checked with Bernice.

"How's it going?"

"I'm almost finished organizing the records for the closed files that need to be sent off-site," she said. "Are you going to keep the mini-warehouse?"

"Yes. If I wanted to destroy the files, I'd have to make an effort to contact the clients first. It will be easier to keep the mini-warehouse space and let some time pass."

"How much time?"

"Seven years."

"What will happen if a client wants an old file and you're in Atlanta?"

"You'll meet them at the mini-warehouse and send me a bill for driving over there to give it to them. Will you promise to let me know when that happens?"

Bernice hesitated.

"It will give me an excuse to send a little something so you and Carl can go out to eat."

"Okay."

"You'd better. Is Bob Gray still managing the mini-warehouses?"

"Yes."

"I'll tell Bob to let me know if he sees you snooping around over there."

Tom checked his watch. "I'm going to eat lunch at the Chickamauga. How long are you going to stay?"

"A few more minutes. If it's okay, I won't come back until tomorrow morning."

"Yes. I'm definitely winding down."

Tom sat alone at the counter of the restaurant. No one tried to talk to him. An older couple was sitting at the table where he had eaten with Rose. They bowed their heads, and the man prayed a blessing. Tom thought about his conversation with Rose the day he first encountered the Lord. If not for the problems associated with Harold Addington, Tom could see himself enjoying a friendship with the attractive young British woman. After he finished eating, he stepped onto the sidewalk and almost bumped into Charlie Williams.

"I called your father's office, and Bernice told me you'd come over here for lunch," Williams said. "Do you have a few minutes? I need to talk to you."

The DA's attitude didn't seem aggressive.

"Okay, I'm heading back to the office."

"I'll walk with you," Williams said.

The two men crossed the street.

"Have you given any more thought to staying in Bethel?" Williams asked.

"Yeah, but I don't think that's likely."

"Any job offers in Atlanta?"

"I've been contacted by a good firm."

"I knew you wouldn't have any trouble landing a job," Williams said. "All things considered, it might be best for you to leave here."

Tom glanced at Williams. Nothing about the DA's expression gave away a secondary meaning for his comment. They reached the office. Bernice was gone. Tom unlocked the door.

"It's been awhile since I was here," Williams said. "Your father didn't handle many criminal cases, and we always met at the courthouse."

Tom thought about the memo in the top drawer of the desk. His heart started to beat faster. He vainly tried to make it slow down.

"What's on your mind?" he asked, trying to sound casual.

"First, I want to apologize for the way I came across in front of Judge Caldwell," Williams said. "The judge was right. I should have shown more respect for your father than to throw out serious accusations without any confirmed evidence of wrongdoing."

"I appreciate you saying that." Tom relaxed a little bit. "And it means a lot hearing it from you in person."

"However, I still have some unanswered questions," Williams continued. "And I wanted to come to you informally about them."

"What kind of questions?"

The DA reached into the coat pocket of his jacket and took out something that he didn't show Tom.

"Did you get a copy of the coroner's report on your father?"

"Yes, he gave the cause of death as asphyxiation due to water in his lungs."

"That's right; however, the results for Harold Addington were more ambivalent."

"In what way?"

"There was water in his lungs, but it wasn't clear that he drowned."

Tom shifted in his chair. "Then how did he die?"

"There were abrasions around Addington's neck. A forensic pathologist from Atlanta examined the body and concluded the marks were most likely caused by some type of rope. He harvested a few strands of fiber from Addington's skin. The only ropelike item at the scene was a red-and-white fish stringer floating on the surface of the pond. The fibers from Addington's neck were analyzed and came back as a match to the stringer."

Tom's mouth went dry. "How long have you known this?"

"I had everything except the lab results on the fibers before I served you with the subpoena. It's been an ongoing investigation, but because both men were dead, it didn't receive high priority at the lab in Atlanta."

"What were you looking for when you served me with the subpoena?" Tom asked as he frantically tried to figure out any connection between what he'd found and Williams's investigation.

"An answer to this." Williams laid a clear plastic bag on the desk.

Tom picked it up. Inside was a crumpled piece of greenish paper.

"It got wet and faded, but you can still make it out," Williams said.

Tom turned the bag sideways. It was a check. There was no name and address printed on the top, but on the payee line it read in faded ink, "John Crane." The amount was $250,000. In the memo section someone had written "Deposit." The signature was washed out. The handwriting could have been his father's, but he wasn't sure. Part of the bank routing and account information printed across the bottom of the check had been torn off; however, several numbers were still clear.

"Do you have any idea why your father would have a $250,000 check payable to himself in his pocket when he went fishing with Harold Addington?" Williams asked.

"No."

"Did he have $250,000 in his business or personal bank accounts?"

"No."

"Then whose account is it?"

Tom opened the middle drawer of the desk and took out the starter checkbook for the designated trust account but left the memo from Addington to his father in the drawer. Tom compared the numbers on the check in the plastic bag with the account information in the checkbook. It was a match.

"It's from a trust account," he said.

"That contained money belonging to Harold Addington?" Williams leaned forward as if about to pounce.

"No." Tom picked up a folder with his right hand. "In here is an affidavit from Rose Addington confirming that her father's estate has no claim to any trust account funds."

Tom handed the affidavit to Williams, who silently read it.

"Why did you get this affidavit from Ms. Addington?"

"To remove any question that the trust account contained funds belonging to Harold Addington. It's embarrassing to admit, but my father's record keeping wasn't the best. There was confusion that I've had to sort out."

"Why would he write a check for such a large amount to himself from the trust account?"

"I don't know."

"He didn't have an open file with Addington that gives you an idea what was going on?"

Tom hesitated. "Based on the affidavit, the money in the trust account didn't belong to Addington anyway."

It wasn't a lie, but it wasn't the whole truth. The existence of the $250,000 check shook every assumption Tom had about his father. John Crane was more than Harold Addington's confidant; he may have been a coconspirator.

"Whose money was it?" Williams asked.

"That's confidential, but it didn't belong to Harold Addington."

Williams put his large hands together in front of him. Tom's mouth went dry.

"Tom, I can't ignore the physical evidence from the scene that raises the possibility of criminal activity playing a role in Harold Addington's death. And nothing you've told me today gives me reason to close the case."

Tom licked his lips. "Are you going to talk to Addington's widow and daughter about this?"

"I went on my own fishing expedition to their house several weeks ago. They knew less than nothing, and I don't see the point in causing them additional anguish based on unconfirmed speculation." Williams looked directly into Tom's eyes. "But if something comes to light, I'll do what I have to do."

"I understand," Tom replied, hoping his voice didn't tremble. "Will you let me make a copy of the check?"

Williams handed the plastic bag to Tom. "Leave it in the bag. It's fragile."

Tom took the bag to the copy machine and made a copy of both sides of the check. He rested his hands on the machine and took several deep breaths. The back of the check was blank. His father never endorsed it. He returned the bag to Williams.

"What are you going to do next?" Tom asked.

It was the DA's turn to dodge a question. "Pick a jury in an aggravated battery case next week. I intend to send a man who beat up his girlfriend and her fifteen-year-old daughter to prison for at least fifteen years."

After Williams left, Tom locked the door again and returned to the office. He sat in his father's chair and stared across the room. All he could think about was an overturned boat, a fish stringer floating on the water, and a crumpled check in a clear plastic bag.

chapter
TWENTY-THREE

Tom couldn't concentrate on work. He took out the legal pad he'd been using to journal his thoughts and prayers and opened the Bible. But it was no use. The Scriptures made sense to a spiritual man only when he was capable of being spiritually minded. Tom's thoughts were trapped in the murky waters of Austin's Pond. Nothing he read in the Bible could make that water clear. He closed the book and left the office.

As soon as he pulled into Elias's dirt driveway, he knew he couldn't stay there either. The turmoil inside his chest was not going to allow him to remain physically still. He parked the car under the massive oak tree. When he went inside, Elias was napping in his chair with his mouth slightly open. Rover lay at the older man's feet. Both man and dog were snoring slightly. They were perfect bookends. If he'd not been upset, Tom would have smiled.

Rover raised his head and barked when Tom walked across the room. Elias stirred in his chair and opened his eyes.

"Is it suppertime already?" the old man asked. "It seems like I just finished eating a sandwich for lunch."

"I came home early," Tom replied. "Sorry I interrupted your nap. I'll be out in the garage for a while."

"All right." Elias nodded and closed his eyes.

Rover stayed with Elias.

Tom began with the fishing tackle. He searched through every tackle box and inspected every piece of fishing equipment for any connection between his father and Harold Addington. He found several fish stringers. Some were blue and white, others were red and white. He picked up a red-and-white one, ran his fingers along the smooth surface of the thin nylon rope, and shuddered at the thought of a stringer wrapped around a human being's throat and twisted tight. He moved from the fishing gear to the camping equipment but found nothing except musty sleeping bags, old-fashioned tents, and antiquated outdoor cooking equipment.

He turned to the boxes. He'd looked at less than a fourth of them with Elias. This time he didn't stop to reminisce and squelched any hint of nostalgia. He opened each box with purpose, taking only enough time to make sure he didn't miss something. It took more than two and a half hours to inspect every box. Three cartons of files slowed him down as he flipped through every folder. None of them contained information about Harold Addington. One of the last boxes he opened was filled with financial records from the office. Why and how the information ended up in Elias's garage was a mystery. Tom sifted through every bit of it, but the records related to the general operating account, not a trust account. Tom put that box in his car so he could return it to the office.

He peeked in the front door of the house. Elias was still asleep in his chair. Still agitated, Tom decided to go to Austin's Pond. He drove past the parking area where he and Elias began their walk and opened the gate to a dirt road that led to the barn. When he reached the end of the road, an older model pickup truck with faded green paint was parked in the middle of the road. Tom pulled his car onto the grass beside the truck. He walked cautiously around the truck until he could see the pond. A solitary fisherman, wearing blue overalls and a brown cap pulled low over his face, was standing on the bank at the far end of the pond. He was casting into the area where the large bass hid in the brushy bottom. The man looked up at Tom and continued fishing. Tom walked over to the picnic table and sat down.

Tom didn't know what he expected to find at the pond. Only the water knew what happened the day John Crane and Harold Addington died. Its dark surface revealed nothing. Tom considered looking for clues but knew in his heart there weren't any. Instead, he stayed at the table and faced again what Charlie Williams told him at the office.

Before meeting with the DA, Tom was convinced Harold Addington was the man who'd compartmentalized his life, separating the moral from the criminal. Now he had to admit that John Crane, for some insane reason, might have been the one who ignored the line between right and wrong. Continuing to stare across the pond, Tom focused his attention on the area where the two men would have been in the boat. He tried to visualize their last moments.

Then it came to him.

Whatever his father did, he did in self-defense. While the two men were in the boat the truth came out. John Crane realized what Harold Addington was attempting to do with the money in the designated trust. They argued. That led to a physical confrontation. For two older men who were inexperienced fighters it would have been an awkward, quickly exhausting battle. In the midst of the conflict, John Crane wrapped the stringer cord around Addington's neck, but it didn't stop the attack. He fell overboard and drowned. Addington, whose breathing was severely impaired, also fell out of the boat. Fully clothed and weakened, both men died. It was a plausible scenario. Tom played it through again, then realized it had one big fatal flaw.

It didn't explain the check in the plastic bag.

People might write checks under duress. But not to themselves. Tom looked down at the ground. Bud Austin had cut the grass around the edge of the pond to lessen the chance of a surprise encounter with a snake. Tom rubbed the grass with the toe of his shoe. Even though he'd not walked around the pond, his mind had come full circle. The pond wasn't going to give up its secrets. Tom could not escape the possibility that his father might have caused another man's death. As he walked to his car, Tom glanced toward the end of the pond. The man who'd been fishing wasn't in sight.

When Tom reached his car, the man in the overalls was putting his fishing pole in the back of the pickup truck. He looked to be in his late twenties with dark hair, brown eyes, and unshaven face.

"Didn't bring your pole?" the man asked.

"Not today. Did you catch anything?"

"Yeah, but I always throw 'em back. The big ones are too pretty to keep."

"That's what my father did. He fished this pond a lot."

"Who's your daddy?"

"John Crane, the lawyer who drowned here a few months ago."

The man took off his cap. "I was sorry to hear about his passing. He was a good fisherman, showed me where that brush pile is under the water at the far end of the pond. I've lost a lot of lures that got tangled in the branches, but it's the best place to catch big fish."

"Yeah. What's your name?"

"Barry Fortenberry. I've been coming here since I was a kid."

"Tom Crane."

The two men shook hands. Fortenberry had the strong grip of a man who worked with his hands for a living. The fisherman got in his truck.

"I'll pull down close to the pond so you can turn around easier," he said.

Tom got in his car. The truck rumbled forward toward the water. Tom turned around and drove away. He didn't see Fortenberry's truck in his rearview mirror.

"Where have you been?" Elias asked when Tom walked through the front door. "I didn't know whether to wait until you came back to eat supper or not. I warmed up some meat loaf with mashed potatoes and green beans."

"I'm not hungry. Did you feed Rover?"

"Yes. Are you sure you don't want anything? I saved you a plate."

"No."

Tom started to walk up the stairs.

"Where did you say you went?" Elias asked again.

"I was in the garage for a while, then drove over to Austin's Pond."

Tom didn't wait for Elias to ask another question. He continued up to the blue bedroom.

The following morning, a split second passed before Tom remembered his conversation with Charlie Williams. It was the only moment of peace he had as he prepared to go to the office. Elias fixed breakfast. After not eating any supper, Tom was hungry. They ate in silence.

"Do you want to tell me what's troubling you?" Elias asked after Tom finished eating a plate of three pancakes topped with peaches.

"Just something I'm going to have to work through," Tom mumbled.

"I'm sorry. If I can help, let me know."

Tom glanced over at the old man. If he'd not wanted to burden Elias about the subpoena, he definitely didn't want to tell him about the new revelations.

"Just keep your integrity," Tom said. "It helps to know there's someone who's consistent like you in the world."

The thought of sitting behind his father's desk had suddenly become abhorrent. As soon as he arrived at the office, Tom called and left a message for Owen Harrelson. He then logged on to the Internet and started reading about Pelham Financial. He typed in key words he'd found in the notes taken from the tackle box: "island properties" and "Barbados bank regulators." Generic articles led to more obscure ones, including a few online rants by people whose investments didn't live up to expectations. That kind of complaint was common in the financial industry. For every negative post there were ten positive ones from customers satisfied with steady, predictable, and above-market returns they'd received from Pelham.

Tom confirmed that Barbados bank regulators, like many others in the Caribbean region, had a laid-back attitude toward financial oversight. He accessed Pelham's most recent annual financial statement. As a private company, Pelham Financial wasn't required to disclose the same detailed information as a publicly owned corporation. Thus the annual statement read more like an advertisement than an analysis of the company's financial viability. Tom found references to "island properties" as part of the company's portfolio but nothing about "insider loans." Arthur Pelham owned a controlling interest in the company, which made him a very rich man. Tom remembered Tiffany's words that she'd be a wealthy divorcée.

Bernice arrived.

"My back is feeling a lot better," she said as she sat down behind her desk. "I wasn't stiff at all when I woke up this morning. Most women my age can't make that claim."

"Good." Tom pointed to the box of financial records he'd found in the garage. "Look what I found at Elias's house. They're bank records for the regular operating account from a couple of years ago. I want to make sure there isn't anything in there that needs my attention."

"So that's where they were," Bernice replied, leaning over and taking out a few pages. "I asked your daddy about that stuff for months, and he denied knowing where they might be. He must have taken them home by mistake."

"How did you balance the checkbook?" Tom asked, then stopped and held up his hand. "No need to answer."

Tom's cell phone chirped. It was Owen Harrelson.

"I'll take this in the office. Glad you're feeling better."

Tom closed the door.

"Did you get the affidavit?" Harrelson asked.

"Yes. Rose Addington brought it by yesterday morning."

"Good. Do you have a date for the hearing in front of the judge? Early this week is better for me."

"Not yet."

"But she brought the affidavit by yesterday morning. Didn't you call the judge's office?"

Tom didn't like the demanding tone of Harrelson's voice. "No," he answered testily.

"What have you been doing? Do you have anything more important going on than this?"

"I'll contact the judge today and let you know immediately."

"See that you do."

The call ended. Tom laid the phone on the desk. He'd obviously caught Harrelson before the Pelham executive had his second cup of coffee. It was a few minutes before he could call Judge Caldwell's secretary.

Tom's computer screen was still on the Pelham website. He returned to the search box and typed in "Owen Harrelson." A bio popped up. The internal affairs officer looked a lot like Olson Crowther. He had a military haircut and a no-nonsense expression on his face. Harrelson was an executive vice president and a member of the senior management committee, which meant he probably had as much access to Arthur Pelham as anyone else in the company. If he was upset, Arthur might be upset. One of Harrelson's previous jobs was with a bank in the UK. The name of the bank seemed vaguely familiar. Tom tapped his finger against the desk for a moment, then looked at the documents Harrelson sent outlining Harold Addington's embezzlement scheme. The name of the bank was on the second page. It was the same bank Addington used to transfer the funds from Newcastle to Barbados. Harrelson worked there for eight years.

Going back to the Pelham website, Tom typed in Harold Addington's name. There were no matches. The Brit had been purged. Tom then typed Addington's name into a general search engine. There were multiple hits about his professional life in the financial industry and hobby as a philatelist. Addington's work history was divided between marketing and internal oversight, the latter job similar to Owen Harrelson's position at Pelham.

The courthouse was now open, and Tom called Judge Caldwell's office. The judge didn't have an available spot on his calendar until the end of the week. Tom didn't want to tell Harrelson on the phone that it would be several days before they could see the judge, so he sent him an e-mail notifying him of the date and time of the hearing. There wasn't an immediate reply. Maybe Harrelson was in a break room drinking a desperately needed second cup of coffee. Tom took a few minutes to prepare a simple motion and order authorizing him, as executor of his father's estate, to turn over the balance in the designated trust account to Pelham Financial.

Working on the Addington/Pelham matter helped get Tom's mind off his father. But now that he'd done all he could before the hearing, the specter of what happened at the pond returned. He fidgeted in the office for a few minutes, then walked into the reception area. Bernice had the bank records from the garage spread out on her desk.

"Making any progress?" he asked.

"What you see is progress. It looks like everything is here except for a few statements shredded by mice looking for something to line their nest."

"I hope there isn't a mouse hiding in the bottom of the box."

"I already checked, and if I'd found one, you would have heard me scream on Main Street."

"I'm going out for a while," Tom said.

"When will you be back?"

"Uh, a couple of hours or so."

Bernice gave him a puzzled look. "Where are you going?"

Tom hesitated. It would be odd to tell her that he didn't have any destination in mind. "Uh, I'm going to the Rocky River Church and see if Lane Conner has time to talk with me. Elias and I heard him speak a couple of weeks ago, and he said he wanted to get together before I left town."

"Do you want me to call the church and find out if he's available?"

"No, it's a nice day for a drive."

Bernice shrugged and returned to stacking checks.

Driving through town with the car windows down and the breeze blowing against his face, Tom felt a little bit better. The road to the church was one of the more scenic in the area. He passed Henderson's cattle farm with its lush green grass and contented cattle grazing in the morning sun, then crossed the bubbling creek that gave the Rocky River Church its name. There were a couple of cars parked near a small sign that read "Church Office." Tom didn't feel comfortable barging in without making an appointment but hoped the minister wouldn't mind. He opened the door. A young woman with blond hair was sitting behind a desk.

"I'm Tom Crane. I was wondering if Reverend Conner was in. I don't have an appointment, so it's okay if—"

The woman picked up a phone, pressed a button, and announced Tom's presence.

"Have a seat. He'll be right out," she said.

Tom sat on an upholstered sofa.

"I've known your uncle Elias since I was little girl," the woman said. "He baptized my mama and daddy in the creek on the other side of the church. I'm sorry about your daddy. I never met him, but of course I've heard a lot of good things about him."

"Thanks," Tom managed.

Lane Conner came into the room. He was wearing a flannel shirt, blue jeans, and cowboy boots.

"That's how we dressed where I grew up in south Georgia," the minister said in response to Tom's look. "My kinfolk have been farmers for generations. Come into the office."

Tom followed the minister into a large office lined with bookshelves.

"Have you read all those books?" Tom asked as they sat down.

"Parts of most of them," Conner replied with a smile. "I'm not the first man to read the Bible, and I want to benefit from the wisdom of those who've studied it before me. Computer research for pastors hasn't caught up to what's available in the legal field, probably because there isn't as much money to be made."

"That may be true, but you're a better speaker than most of the lawyers I listen to."

"Coming from you, that's a high compliment."

Tom shifted in his seat. "Like I said, I don't want to take up too much of your time."

"Don't worry about it. What brought you by?"

Tom suddenly realized what Conner would be interested in hearing about. "Some things have happened in my life since I met you a few weeks ago."

Telling Lane Conner what God had been doing in his life made it seem more official. Tom started with his first prayer based on Psalm 78:72 and went from there.

"I guess you hear stories like this a lot," he said at one point.

"Not as often as I'd like." Conner tapped his finger on his desk. "What you mentioned about 1 Corinthians is very true. You might also want to read the book of 1 John. It says there that the Holy Spirit is a better teacher than any author on these shelves."

When Tom finished, Conner stared at him for a few seconds as if he were about to quiz Tom on his Bible knowledge.

"Did you know Harold Addington?" Conner asked.

"Uh, no. I never met him. How about you?"

"He came to the church on a regular basis, and we spent quite a bit of one-on-one time together in this office. I delivered the eulogy at his funeral. Harold Addington was a man who was willing to make hard choices to do the right thing even if it might cause negative consequences for himself."

"Are you sure about that?"

"Yes."

"What kind of choices?"

"I can't answer that specifically because what he told me was shared in confidence. But he said he talked to your father about it."

Tom's eyes opened wide. "My father?"

"Yes."

Tom paused. "Did you talk to my father about these choices, whatever they might be?"

"No."

"Do Esther and Rose Addington know what you're talking about?"

"Now you're sounding like a lawyer," Conner replied. "But the answer is no."

"How serious was the situation you talked to Harold Addington about?"

"Serious enough to affect a lot of people. Harold Addington was a moral, upright man. I'm sorry he died prematurely."

"Do you suspect any foul play?"

"No, no. Good people die in accidents leaving the rest of us to wonder why it happened. Most of those questions are unanswerable this side of heaven. But it doesn't keep me from having regrets." Conner took a deep breath. "May I ask you a question?"

Tom nodded.

"If we're talking about the same serious situation, what are you going to do about it now that Harold and your father are gone?"

"What do you think I should do?"

"Finish it," Conner replied as emphatically as he spoke when preaching a sermon. "Accidents happen, but I don't think it's an accident that you, like your father, are a lawyer. And from what I've heard, you have much more expertise in these areas than he did. The fact that you came here today so we could talk about Harold was an answer to prayer."

"How?"

"I've been praying for you about this ever since we met at the church."

Tom was momentarily speechless. "Have you talked to anyone else? Especially Charlie Williams, the DA, or anyone else who works for the government?"

"No, just Harold. That's what he requested, and I honored it while he was alive and hope I still am. The fact that I know he confided in your father is the reason I brought it up to you at all. My guess is you know more than I do."

Tom stood up. "Thanks for taking time to meet with me."

"Come back any time," Conner said, his voice more casual. "It was great hearing what God is doing in your life."

Tom drove slowly back to the office. His mind, on the other hand, was racing.

chapter
TWENTY-FOUR

Bernice greeted him with a question: "Did Owen Harrelson get in touch with you?"

"No."

Tom took out his cell phone to see if he'd missed a call and realized he'd turned the phone off before he went into Lane Conner's office.

"What did he want?"

"To talk to you. He called three times while you were gone. Said it was important. Do you need his number?"

"No, I have it."

Tom went into the office and closed the door. Each conversation with Harrelson was more contentious than the last. He placed the call.

"Harrelson here," the executive growled.

"It's Tom Crane."

"I got your e-mail. I see you were too scared to call me directly. I told you to schedule the hearing toward the beginning of the week."

Tom kept his voice level. "I took the first available slot on the judge's calendar. If this week doesn't work for you, we can try to reschedule early next week."

"Do that. Arranging a trip to Bethel toward the end of this week will create a scheduling nightmare."

"Okay, I'll contact the judge's office and let you know."

Since Harrelson was already mad at him, Tom decided to ask a question that had been bugging him since he made his PowerPoint presentation to Rose Addington.

"Now that we have a couple of extra days, I'd like to supplement my file in case the judge has any reluctance in signing the order."

"What would you add?"

"The identities and contact information for the European investors who dealt with Harold Addington. The names are blacked out in the information you sent me."

"Of course I removed the names. Our client lists are confidential."

"And it would remain confidential with me. All I want to do is confirm the dates the customers thought they were buying CDs in the Barbados bank. It won't be necessary to tell them their money was diverted."

"I already gave you the dates."

"But I have no way to cross-check the amounts," Tom persisted. "This would provide independent, corroborating evidence from a source outside Pelham."

The phone was silent for a moment. "Are you questioning the truth of the information I provided to you?"

Tom had engaged in conversations like this before. Usually it happened when he was taking the deposition of an opposing party in a lawsuit.

"No, but it might be important to the judge. One of the things I have to do is anticipate what he may want, and I don't want you to waste a trip."

"You're not getting the names of our clients. Drop it."

Tom wasn't going to be put off. "What about additional records from the bank Addington used in the UK? I understand you used to work there. Do you have a contact who could provide specific deposit records from Addington that will match up with the amounts given to him by the depositors? That would be another way to provide independent verification of what occurred."

"No, and I think you've played lawyer long enough." Harrelson raised his voice. "Your job is to get an order signed by the judge and put an end to this attempt to embezzle money. That's what you need to be thinking about. I'm about to go into an important meeting. This conversation is over."

The phone clicked off. Tom stared at his cell phone. He wasn't used to someone hanging up on him. He glanced again at the papers in the folder. Harrelson was hiding something. The Pelham executive had been very defensive about his security measures. Most likely it was a serious slipup by his department. But his adamant refusal to supplement the information furnished to Tom raised another possibility—Harrelson might be guilty of a wrong beyond negligent financial safeguards.

Tom took out a legal pad and started making notes. He outlined three possible scenarios: Harrelson could be an incompetent employee, a knowing participant in an embezzlement scheme as Addington's partner, or the person Harold Addington was trying to expose with John Crane's help. Caught in the middle of Tom's theories were the rope burns around Harold Addington's neck and the faded check in the plastic bag. Tom tore off the sheets of paper on which he'd written his notes and slipped them into the growing Addington file.

Tom and Bernice left the office together. He stopped to lock the front door.

"You've been awfully quiet the past few days," Bernice said.

"I've had a lot on my mind."

"And I'm here to help. I appreciate the paycheck, but I've never worked here primarily for the money."

"I know. You're doing a lot already."

That night Tom couldn't sleep. His conversations with Lane Conner and Owen Harrelson kept playing in his mind. Slipping out of bed, he went downstairs to the kitchen and ate a piece of apple pie. He checked to see if light was shining beneath the door to Elias's study. All was dark. Glancing down the hall in the direction of the old man's bedroom, Tom opened the study door.

The pine-paneled room had a faded oval rug on the floor. To the left was a rolltop desk. Several books were stacked on the desk. Above the desk was a crude painting of the Crane family homeplace. Tom vaguely remembered the aunt who did it. In the middle of the room was a straight-backed chair with a decorative pillow on the floor in front of it. An open Bible rested on the seat of the chair. On the walls were several cross-stitched Bible verses in small frames. One verse caught Tom's eye:

Now it came to pass in those days that He went out to the mountain to pray, and continued all night in prayer to God.

–Luke 6:12

Tom picked up the Bible from the chair and read the passage. It was a night of decision for Jesus. The following morning he selected the twelve apostles. Tom, too, had some big decisions to make. He had to expose the deeds of darkness but wasn't sure where to shine the light.

He nudged the pillow with his foot. Elias probably used the pillow while he knelt in front of the chair to pray. Tom hadn't knelt to pray since he was a little boy repeating a rote prayer before going to bed. Slipping out of the chair, he placed the Bible on the seat, dropped to his knees on the pillow, bowed his head, and closed his eyes.

Praying in the quiet of the night without pen and paper or a computer screen was new. Tom expected to be distracted. To his surprise, his mind cleared and calm flowed over him like a soothing balm. For the first time since he'd talked to Charlie Williams, he felt inner peace. What happened at Austin's Pond was deeply troubling, but there was a place in the presence of God where that problem didn't reign supreme. That was because the study was a thin place. He opened his eyes.

Another verse on the wall read:

My times are in your hands. –Psalm 31:15

Tom suspected Elias didn't stay in the room for a set amount of time but left when he knew he was finished. Tom bowed his head again. As he prayed about some of the thorny challenges in his path, he realized that what happened in the world outside the study didn't trump what took place within it. When he finally stood up, he didn't know all the future held, but he knew his next step.

———

The following morning he phoned Rose Addington as soon as he got to the office. Her mother answered the phone.

"What do you want?" Esther asked curtly.

"To speak to Rose. There's something I need to clear up with her."

"Just a minute. I'll see if she's available."

While he waited Tom had a change in strategy. He'd intended to talk to Rose on the phone.

"Hello?" Rose said in a questioning voice.

"I guess you didn't expect to hear from me again."

"No, I didn't."

"Well, I've continued to pray about the situation we discussed, and I'd like to get together if you're willing to."

"If it's about the money, that's not necessary. I signed the affidavit and won't be changing my mind."

"I'm not trying to change your mind; I'd like to talk to you about the changes in mine."

"Hold on a bit."

The phone was silent for a moment. Tom could hear a muffled discussion.

"All right. I've got to book a flight back to Europe and make a few international calls this morning related to the adoption agency. I can be at your office around noon."

"Let's meet at the Chickamauga Diner." Tom paused. "And please don't schedule a flight until after we talk."

"Why not?"

"That's part of the discussion."

"Uh, okay."

When Tom came out of the office, Bernice had arrived.

"You look better today," she said after inspecting him for a moment.

"I should. I'm going to have lunch with Rose Addington."

Bernice's face fell. "Boy, that woman has bewitched you. I'll be glad when she's on a plane back to wherever she came from, with a big ocean separating the two of you."

"And I asked her not to book a flight until after we talked," Tom said with a mischievous grin. "Did you know she likes collard greens with vinegar?"

Bernice huffed and didn't respond.

Tom arrived at the diner before Rose. In his hand was the folder containing the information from the tackle box. The table where he and Rose had eaten their meal together was available, and he sat down to wait for her. Noon came and went. Five minutes passed. Tom finished a glass of tea and asked for a refill. Ten minutes passed. At that point Tom realized Rose might have changed her mind. He couldn't blame her. At 12:15 Tom called the waitress over and asked for the check so he could pay for his drink. He left a generous tip for taking up a table during prime time and walked up to the cash register. After paying, he turned toward the door. Rose Addington was hurriedly coming inside.

"Sorry I'm late," she said, flustered. "I had to finish a long telephone call and didn't get away when I planned to. But I see you're running a bit behind as well."

Tom motioned to Alex Giles, who gave him a puzzled look and pointed toward the table Tom had just left. Tom led Rose to the rear of the restaurant.

"I must say your call caught my mum and me off guard," she said.

"That's understandable. As I told you on the phone, I've continued to pray and realized last night I've approached this situation with assumptions instead of an open mind seeking the truth. Every lawyer knows that's a mistake. I tried to make everything else fit what I thought."

262

"What does that mean at this point?" Rose asked. "I thought this was over."

The waitress came to take their orders. Once again, Rose included collard greens as one of her vegetables.

"Before I answer, I need to show you something I found in one of my father's tackle boxes in Elias's garage. I had this information the other day when you brought the affidavit to the office but didn't mention it. That was wrong, and you have a right to see it."

Tom handed her the sheets and watched her face as she read them. Her eyes widened.

"I knew Papa didn't embezzle any money," she said when he finished. "Why did you hide this from me?"

"For the reasons I gave you a minute ago, and because these are just notes of a conversation, not evidence that proves anything. I still think it's likely the money in the designated trust account belongs to Pelham Financial, but it's also possible your father didn't intend to keep it for himself. He may have been trying to prevent someone else from getting it. If he and my father had some sort of plan in place to do that, we need to figure out what it was and whether there's anything we can do to finish it."

"We?"

"Yes, that's why I asked you not to buy an airplane ticket."

Tom told her about his conversation with Lane Conner. "That was the wake-up call that made me realize I may have misjudged your father."

"I didn't misjudge your father."

Tom winced. He didn't know how Rose would react if she knew the details about the cause of her father's death. The waitress arrived with their food.

"I'll ask the blessing this time," Tom said.

Rose bowed her head and closed her eyes. Tom kept his open and leaned forward. He said a short prayer of thanks for the food.

"And help us do what's right about all this confusing information," Rose continued. "May you expose the deeds of darkness. Amen."

Tom raised his eyebrows. "I read that verse in the Bible the other day when I was wondering what to do."

"Ephesians chapter 5."

"Yeah, that's it."

"Good. We already agree about one thing."

While they ate, Tom explained the different theories he'd come up with about where the money came from and why it had ended up in the designated trust account. He quickly dismissed the idea that Harold Addington and Owen Harrelson were working together to embezzle funds. Rose ate and listened.

"You need to eat," she said when Tom paused. "Your fried chicken is going to get cold. Let me think about what you've said while we finish."

Tom bit into a crunchy piece of chicken. They ate in silence for several minutes. Rose Addington was very deliberate in all her actions, even the way she approached a plate of food. She ate a final bite and placed her fork and knife in the middle of the plate.

"Who do you trust at Pelham Financial?" she asked. "And I mean trust without question."

Tom knew acquaintances from the past and recent contacts like Hal Millsap, but only one person had been around Tom since he was a little boy.

"Arthur Pelham," he answered.

"Are you sure?" Rose asked doubtfully. "Didn't he believe my father embezzled money?"

"During our conversation at the Parker-Baldwin house, we didn't talk specifics. I believe Arthur formed a wrong opinion based on bad information given to him by Owen Harrelson." Tom remembered a detail he'd left out earlier. "Mr. Pelham's cell phone number was written beside my phone number at the bottom of the page of notes I found. That would indicate my father intended at some point to talk to him. That would make sense because Arthur has the authority to deal with any wrong that occurred."

"Maybe." Rose nodded. "There's a simple way to find out how he'll react."

Tom thought for a moment. "Tell him now. Show him what we've found and ask him what he's going to do about it."

"Exactly. If he gets defensive like Harrelson did when you asked for more information, then the rottenness may go to the core."

In his heart Tom didn't believe that was likely. Arthur Pelham was a brilliant man. He didn't need to do anything illegal to be fabulously wealthy and successful.

"I need to talk to Arthur before the hearing next week in front of Judge Caldwell, but I don't know where he is. He could be out of the country."

"All you can do is try."

After Tom paid for the meal, they stood on the sidewalk outside the restaurant.

"I want you to be in the room when I talk on the phone to Arthur," he said.

"Why?"

"Because even though I trust Arthur, I don't trust myself. I'm so close to him and his family that it might affect how I interpret what he says."

"Would you tell him I was listening?"

"No, because he might not be willing to open up. He hasn't had a chance to get to know you like I have."

Rose gave Tom a puzzled look. "Is that a compliment?"

"Yes."

"All right. Just let me know when."

"Tom!" a female voice called out.

Tom turned and saw Tiffany on the other side of the street. She was alone with a shopping bag in her hand.

"That's Tiffany Pelham," Tom said to Rose. "Rick Pelham's wife."

Tiffany crossed the street. She was wearing casual slacks and a light-blue top. She came up to Tom and gave him a quick kiss on the right check that came within a fraction of an inch of his lips.

"What are you up to?" she asked.

"Uh, finishing lunch," Tom answered. "Tiffany, this is Rose Addington. Harold Addington was her father."

Tiffany turned to Rose. "Oh, I'm sorry about your dad. How is your mother doing?"

"Getting by."

Tiffany redirected her attention to Tom. "You're going to have to come out for dinner again."

Tom licked his lips, and his tongue touched the place where Tiffany kissed him. "I'd like that."

"Are you available Friday night?"

"Uh, who would be there?"

"You, me, and Rick, of course. Unless you'd like to bring someone else."

"Would you join us?" Tom asked Rose. "They have a beautiful home, and Tiffany raises horses that she'll be glad to show off for you."

"I'd love to have you come," Tiffany chimed in. "Rick has his guy friends over all the time. I need a woman to keep me company."

Rose hesitated.

"Do you have other plans?" Tom asked.

"No," she said.

"Then I'll pick you up."

"Okay."

"Come around 6:00 p.m.," Tiffany said. "You know the filly I showed you the other day? She's starting to trot around in the field and has the most beautiful natural gait. I'll have to show you what she can do."

"I'd like that." Tom paused. "Oh, do you have any idea where Arthur is this week?"

"He and Larina have been in Barbados for a few days, but I think they're coming back to New York today. Why?"

"I need to talk to him."

"Business?" Tiffany asked, raising her eyebrows.

"Yeah. We need to finish a conversation we started when he was in Bethel."

Tom could tell Tiffany wanted to say something else, but she glanced at Rose and kept quiet.

"See you two tomorrow," she said lightly.

Tiffany turned away and crossed the street. Tom watched her leave. When Tiffany kissed him, he felt like a twelve-year-old boy who'd just received his first meaningful peck on the cheek. Even contact with her on a street corner was charged with energy.

"Where are you parked?" he asked Rose.

"Over there," she said, pointing down the street. "Are you going to follow up with Mr. Pelham?"

"Yes, but I won't call his cell phone. I'll do it through his office so I can set a specific time for our conversation. That way you can be part of it."

"Will it be before or after the dinner party?"

"Does it make a difference?"

"I'm not sure, but Mr. Pelham's response could have a huge impact on your relationship, not only with him, but also with his son and daughter-in-law. You seem very close to them."

"We've been friends for many years."

They waited for a car to pass by before crossing the street together.

"Are you going to send Mr. Pelham copies of the memo from my dad and the notes made by your father before we talk to him?" Rose asked.

"Do you think I should?"

"I believe he should see them before we talk. Otherwise, he'll want to take time to look everything over before letting you know what he thinks. Of course, if he trots down the hall to Owen Harrelson's office, then it might be a very brief conversation. Are you ready for that?"

"No," Tom replied honestly, "but if I wanted to avoid that possibility, I wouldn't have called you. I know this is what I'm supposed to do regardless of the consequences. I just hope Arthur will be glad I contacted him."

"You've counted the cost," Rose said. "Let me know if you set up a call with Mr. Pelham for tomorrow. I'm spending most of the day with my mum, so I'm available."

"Okay, thanks again for agreeing to meet with me."

"As you said, it's the right thing to do."

chapter
TWENTY-FIVE

R ose and I had a good time at lunch," Tom said to Bernice
when he returned to the office.

"You're getting mean," Bernice replied. "You may laugh
at my concern, but your hanging around that woman is making me
so tense it's causing my back to hurt again."

"It is?"

"No, but you deserve to think so."

Tom leaned against the corner of Bernice's desk. "Don't worry.
This is something I've prayed about and believe is the right thing
to do."

"Since I don't know what you're talking about, I can't offer an
opinion. But I hope your prayers are on target. I've been praying you
won't get mixed up with the wrong woman."

"There's nothing like that between us. It takes more than long
eyelashes and a cool accent to get my attention."

"Humph," Bernice snorted. "There's more to her than that, and
a hundred prayers don't stop you from being a man."

Tom let Bernice have the last word. He went into the office
to decide the best way to approach Arthur Pelham. Rose had

recommended full disclosure. He called Arthur's office in New York and was transferred to his administrative assistant.

"This is Tom Crane," he began. "I'm a lawyer from Bethel—"

"No need to introduce yourself, Mr. Crane," an efficient-sounding woman responded. "Mr. Pelham told me you might be calling. How may I help you?"

"I want to send some information to Mr. Pelham for his review. It's my understanding he's returning to New York later today, but I didn't know if he would be coming into the office or checking a secure e-mail account."

"He's already in New York and working from home."

"Then I'd like to send him some documents only he will see."

"Certainly." There was a brief pause. "Give me your e-mail address, and I'll send instructions to you."

Tom gave her his contact information.

"The protocol for this account allows only Mr. Pelham to access it. Even I won't see what you forward."

After the call ended, Tom stuck his head in the reception area. "Where can I buy a scanner?"

Bernice thought for a moment. "If you plan on speeding, stay away from Highway 201. The curve near the Holcomb place is where the deputies like to hang out. The straight stretch beyond Elias's house is as good as any to go fast. But if you still want a scanner, I think they sell them at Hobart's Pawnshop."

"Not a police scanner," Tom said patiently. "I want to scan some documents and send them as an e-mail attachment."

Bernice gave him a blank look for a second. "Oh. You might want to try Lee Office Supply, but I don't know how to work one of those things."

Fifteen minutes later Tom returned with an inexpensive

scanner and set it up in his office. He scanned all the information about the designated trust account, then added the documents Owen Harrelson sent. He also included the notes from Harold Addington's nightstand and the memo to John Crane that Tom found in the tackle box. Finally he composed a long e-mail outlining what had happened.

Before sending the e-mail, Tom waited fifteen minutes and read it again to make sure it said what he wanted and didn't contain any typos or grammatical errors. There was something else he needed to do but couldn't put his finger on what it might be. Then he did something he'd never done before. He closed his eyes and prayed that God would bless the e-mail. He said amen and pressed the Send button.

The rest of the afternoon he kept checking his computer for a response. Each time there was nothing. Bernice left the office, and Tom was about to follow her out the door when he looked one more time. A message from Arthur's private e-mail popped up. Tom's heart started pounding. He opened the e-mail.

> Received. I'll call you tomorrow morning at 10:00 a.m. to discuss.
> Can you videoconference a call?
> Arthur

Arthur's answer revealed nothing about the CEO's opinion. Tom quickly wrote Arthur, then phoned Rose and read the e-mail to her.

"What time do you want me there?" she asked.

"Maybe ten or fifteen minutes early. I'll send you a copy of the e-mail I sent him."

"What about the camera?"

"You'll stay out of sight."

"Are you sure about this?"

Tom remembered his prayer time in Elias's study. "Yes."

The following morning Tom came out of his father's office shortly before 10:00 a.m. and stood beside Bernice's desk. While they talked, he kept checking his watch and straightening his tie.

"Are you expecting someone?" she asked.

Tom nodded.

"Not Rose Addington?" Bernice asked ominously.

"And here she is," Tom replied as Rose opened the door.

Rose entered and greeted Bernice, who mumbled in reply.

"We'll be in here for a while," Tom said as he ushered Rose into the office. "No interruptions, please."

"I wouldn't think of it."

Tom closed the door. His computer was on the desk with the relevant papers organized around it.

"I thought you could sit over there," he said, pointing to a chair he'd moved close to one of the bookcases. "You can hear but not be seen."

"I hope I don't have to sneeze."

"If that happens, I'll be watching and make it look like I did it."

"I'm not sure about this." Rose shook her head. "It seems deceitful."

Tom positioned himself in front of the computer's miniature camera.

"You have a right to hear what Arthur has to say," he said.

The signal for the videophone call came through. In a few seconds Tom was staring at Arthur's face on the screen. Arthur was wearing a suit and tie, which made Tom glad he'd dressed for a formal business meeting. Arthur looked tense and tired.

"You kept me up most of the night," Arthur began. "That was quite a bombshell you dropped on me."

"Yes, sir."

"And I'll ask the most important question first. Does Owen Harrelson know about the information you found in your father's records?"

"No, sir."

Even with the slightly fuzzy resolution on the screen, Tom could see Arthur relax. The older man sighed.

"I'd hoped to finish out my career without having to deal with a situation like this, but now that it's here, I have no choice but to face it. Have you talked to anyone else about this?"

"Rose and Esther Addington are aware of the memos and notes from Harold Addington. Most of my conversations have been with Rose because she's the executrix of the estate. I had to show her the information Harrelson sent in order to persuade her to sign the affidavit renouncing any claim to the money in the designated trust account."

"Does she know we're going to talk?"

Tom glanced at Rose in the corner of the room. "Yes."

"I suppose that couldn't be avoided. Has anyone else seen what you sent me?"

"No."

"Are you sure?"

"Yes."

Arthur ran his fingers across his white hair. "Is our conversation protected from further disclosure by the attorney-client privilege?"

"My role in this is as executor of my father's estate, not as a lawyer, which means I can't represent Pelham Financial's interests in this matter."

"But can I trust you as a friend of our family to keep it confidential?"

"Yes, sir."

A door opened, and Arthur glanced over his shoulder. Tom couldn't see who entered.

"I don't care how important he says it is," Arthur said. "Tell him to wait."

The door closed. Arthur looked directly at Tom. "My concern is much greater than the amount of money in your father's trust account. That larger fear is what kept me awake last night. If the information in your father's records is correct, Owen, either acting alone or with others, may have embezzled a significant amount of money."

"That's the conclusion I reached."

"And if that information becomes public knowledge, it will destroy the company. Ever since the Madoff scandal, public and governmental tolerance for any breach of fiduciary duty is nil. If Pelham Financial goes under, over a thousand people, including hundreds in Bethel, will lose their jobs. I'm not even going to mention what this would do to my family. But in a situation like this, personal interest has to take a backseat to the greater good."

Tom's respect for Arthur Pelham jumped a couple of notches up the ladder.

"As soon as I received your e-mail, I brought in one of the top men in our auditing department. He has no intraoffice connection with Owen and reports directly to me. He's trying to determine how broad and deep the problem runs. My hope is that I can get to the bottom of this and take care of it without destroying the company or jeopardizing the money that clients have entrusted to us. If I have to make up losses personally, I'll do it to the extent my resources will allow."

"What about the fidelity bonds?"

"You know how those contracts are written. Smaller amounts are paid to keep a client's business. Larger claims result in litigation over whether coverage exists at all with a view toward forcing a settlement for a fraction of the amount involved."

Tom knew Arthur was right.

"When do you expect to receive a preliminary report from your auditor?" Tom asked.

"Later today. Of course, his investigation may continue to implicate Harold Addington. Nothing you sent exonerates him. Addington could have been manipulating your father as part of a broader scheme."

"That thought crossed my mind," Tom said, avoiding eye contact with Rose. "But if that's true, it makes no sense that he would have told my father about illegal insider loans and bribery of bank regulators in Barbados. When are you going to talk to Harrelson? He's scheduled to come to Bethel early next week for a court hearing to approve the release of the money in the designated trust account to Pelham. If it turns out he's implicated in something illegal, that trip needs to be canceled."

"I'm not going to discuss anything with anyone until the internal investigation is complete. I canceled an executive committee meeting set for this afternoon because I can't stomach the possibility of being in the same room with Owen. If the scope of this problem is as broad as I fear, the next person Owen talks to will be wearing a badge."

"Yes, sir."

Arthur sighed. "You know, I left Bethel for Yale thinking I was sophisticated and smart enough to handle whatever life threw at me.

Years of success reinforced my pride. Now, at a time when I was looking forward to slowing down a bit, something like this jumps up and threatens to destroy all I've worked so hard to build. The worst part is thinking about all the people who are going to be hurt if this can't be handled privately and confidentially."

"I'm sorry too."

"I know. And I can't tell you how much I appreciate what you've done," Arthur said with obvious sincerity. "I'll be in touch. Let me know if anything else surfaces on your end."

"Yes, sir."

The screen went blank. Tom closed his computer.

"What did you think?" he asked Rose.

"He sounded sincere, almost broken. His concern for others was touching, but do you think he'll have the courage to deal with a problem this large in an honest way regardless of the outcome?"

"If anyone can, Arthur will. You couldn't see his face. He looked sad but resolute."

"Is this the end for us? It seems the next steps are up to Mr. Pelham. There's nothing for you to do if he assumes responsibility to deal with the problem."

"True," Tom said with a sense of relief. "I want to stop carrying this burden."

"I'm sure you do."

Rose moved toward the door.

"What are you going to tell your mother?" Tom asked.

"The gist of it with as few details as possible. We know Papa didn't do anything wrong, but it stings to think others might have a different opinion. I won't be telling her what Mr. Pelham mentioned on that point."

"I agree. Thanks for coming."

Tom walked around to the front of the desk and held the door open for Rose. Neither of them spoke in Bernice's hearing.

"Did you have a fight?" Bernice asked as soon as the front door closed behind Rose.

"Is that a wish or a question?"

"Just curious. She seemed to be giving you the silent treatment."

"No, we're in perfect agreement."

"Someday, will you tell me what's going on between the two of you?"

"No, but I can tell you this part of it is over."

Bernice shook her head. "I've heard that before."

Tom spent the rest of the day working his way through the last box of his father's files and following up with clients who'd been hard to reach. Bernice finished going through the financial records Tom found in Elias's garage. Fortunately, there were no unpleasant surprises.

Late in the afternoon Tom phoned Lane Conner. The minister wasn't available, but Tom left a voice mail thanking him for his advice and letting him know that he'd followed it. After he hung up the phone, Tom thought about Tiffany. If the situation at Pelham Financial deteriorated to the place where the company failed, taking Arthur and his millions with it, Tiffany's glib confidence that she would walk away from her marriage a wealthy woman might prove unfounded. Government authorities and irate investors would sue Arthur and Rick, and no matter how many trees Rick harvested, he couldn't support Tiffany and her horse habit by selling wood chips.

After supper Tom and Elias sat on the front porch as the last rays of the sun crept below the low hills in the distance. Rover's bond with Elias had strengthened to the point that he preferred lying at the old man's feet to being close to Tom. However, Tom wasn't jealous. If the dog could bring the joy of canine companionship to Elias, it was a good thing. The difficult day would be when Tom left Bethel and took Rover with him to Atlanta. Tonight, separation wasn't a topic of conversation. Instead, Tom told Elias about his meeting with Lane Conner. He left out the discussion about Harold Addington.

"I'm glad you went to see him," Elias said when Tom finished. "After you told him what God has done in your life, did he ask you when you were going to get baptized?"

"No." Tom turned his head in surprise.

"It would be a good thing to do it while you're here. A heated baptismal pool in a church is fine, but the creek beside the Rocky River Church has a fine spot. It would be chilly this time of year, but you're young enough to handle it. If you went swimming in the Ocoee, you can handle a dunking at the church."

"It wasn't a swim. I was wearing a wet suit after I fell out of a raft."

"Lane would probably wear waders when he baptizes you," Elias continued. "I know it's old-fashioned to get baptized in a creek, but there's something about flowing water that shows the symbolism of washing away sins in a powerful way."

Tom couldn't imagine himself wading into a creek wearing a flimsy white gown.

"I'm not sure I want to do that."

"Pray about it. Did you know Nathan Caldwell was baptized in the creek near the old church on Polk Road? The church burned down years ago and wasn't rebuilt, but that's where his family went. He was about sixteen at the time."

"I've never discussed baptism with Judge Caldwell."

"You should." Elias smiled. "And it would be a good idea to invite him to come when you get baptized. It's important that people you know hear your testimony."

"Testimony?"

"A short version of what you told Lane. You'll be surprised how much bolder you'll be about sharing your faith after you've spoken about it in public." Elias paused. "Another person you should invite is Rick Pelham. You've been friends for so long it might have a big impact on him."

Elias's words about Rick pierced Tom's heart in a sudden, unintended way. He was glad the darkening shadows hid the expression on his face. He got up from the chair and leaned against one of the supporting posts on the porch. Rick Pelham had never done anything to hurt Tom. He'd been a loyal, lifelong friend.

In the cool of the evening Tom mentally stepped back from the hot fantasy he'd been entertaining about Tiffany. He looked down at the floor of the porch and lightly kicked the wooden post with his shoe. The post hadn't moved since the porch was built. Rick Pelham had always been just as solid in his support for Tom.

"It's getting dark," Elias said, slowly rising from the rocking chair. "I'm ready to go inside and eat a piece of coconut pie. Do you want one?"

"Not right now. I'm going to stay out here and sort a few things out."

Elias opened the screen door. "You could also invite Arthur Pelham to your baptism," the old man said. "There was a time when

Arthur showed an interest in spiritual things, but then I think he decided he was smarter than God."

Tom grunted.

"I think he'd come if you asked him."

Tom didn't answer. Instead, he thought about Rick and Tiffany and shook his head at his selfish stupidity. He wasn't any better than the minister who stole money from the offering plate so his wife could buy expensive shoes. In fact, Tom's wrong was worse. In the house of his mind, he'd constructed a false vision of the future inhabited by a grotesque distortion of what was right. He'd deceived himself and believed the lies of his own making.

In the honesty of the moment, he had to admit that nurturing a secret hope Rick and Tiffany's marriage would split apart so he could step in was completely at odds with the changes Jesus Christ had been bringing to his life. Tom thought about the times he'd spent with God in his father's office and felt anger mixed with shame—anger at himself for tacitly encouraging Tiffany's feelings for him, shame that he'd been so stupid not to see his thoughts and actions as a sin.

Tom put his hands on the railing that surrounded the porch. There really wasn't much for him to sort out. He bowed his head and asked God to forgive him. He wasn't sure if a short prayer was enough, but he knew it was a start. The tougher questions had to do with Tiffany—what he would say, when he should say it, and how she would react.

chapter
TWENTY-SIX

T he following day Tom sat in his office waiting to hear from Arthur. The longer it took the Pelham CEO to contact him, the greater Tom sensed the problems at the company might be. Tom pitied the older man's no-win predicament. Shortly before noon, he received a message from Arthur's private e-mail account.

> Please let me know a good time to call for a face-to-face conference.
> Arthur

Tom immediately responded.

> I'm available at your convenience.
> Tom

Less than a minute after he sent his reply, a video call came through on his computer. Tom buzzed Bernice and asked her not to disturb him. Arthur's face appeared on the screen. He looked more tired than he had the previous day. He managed a weak smile as he greeted Tom.

"Rick says you're going to have dinner with him and Tiffany tonight," Arthur said.

"Yes, sir."

"You won't mention our discussions, will you?"

"Of course not."

"Did you talk to Harold Addington's daughter?"

"Yes, she knows about our call."

"What was her response?"

"The same as mine. We've turned this matter over to you and trust you to handle it the best way possible."

"Are you sure that's how she feels?"

"Yes, sir."

"Good." Arthur nodded. "Our internal investigation took longer than expected because I didn't want to increase the number of people working on it. It's reasonably clear what happened. Owen Harrelson and a man he knows in the UK hatched a scheme to embezzle money shortly after we began doing business in Europe. The plan was simple. In fact, if you substitute Owen's name for Addington's, it outlines exactly what happened. The transactions were set up so Addington would get the blame if something went wrong. Most of the information in the memo to your father related to future activity, not something that had already occurred."

"That's good news."

"No," Arthur corrected, "it's great news. The auditor interviewed several of our European clients who purchased CDs issued by our bank in Barbados and then followed leads furnished by them."

"Harrelson didn't want me to talk to the clients."

"And I know why. The investors whose money was diverted

had contact with both Addington's and Owen's UK connection, a man named George Nettles. He's employed by the UK bank where Owen worked before joining us. Nettles held himself out to investors as a Pelham employee. He's the one who furnished the customers with the phony CDs and set up the bank transfers to make it look like Addington was behind the scheme. At some point, Addington figured out there was something wrong with several of his accounts. I suspect it had to do with information he received from a client about Nettles. Addington did some investigation and discovered he'd been linked to illegal transactions. He stepped in and diverted the money before Owen, Nettles, and whoever else was working with them could withdraw it. When Addington died, Owen had no choice but to make it look like Addington was at fault. That's when he reported the missing money to me. We didn't know where the funds were located until after I met with you at the Parker-Baldwin house."

"Why would Addington want to put money in my father's trust account?"

"The way the scheme was structured, he had to be concerned that he would be blamed if it was exposed. He must have trusted your father, which is easy for me to believe, and hid the money in your father's account."

"What was Addington going to do next?"

"I'm not sure. We may never know."

"What is Harrelson's status?"

"On hold."

"Why?"

"I could fire him immediately, but the current facts only establish criminal activity by Nettles in the UK. I've talked to the white-collar-crime office at the US Attorney's Office here in New

York City, and they'd like evidence that will justify an indictment against Owen. I want to give it to them."

"What kind of evidence?"

Arthur cleared his throat. "The kind you may be able to get for me."

"Me?" Tom asked in surprise.

"Yes. You don't have to agree to do anything, but are you at least willing to hear my proposal?"

"Okay," Tom answered slowly.

"For the time being, Owen will be kept in the dark." Arthur picked up a sheet of paper and referred to it while he talked. "You would tell him that although you realize you can't talk to customers, you'd like to speak with the person who discovered the accounts Addington set up with the bank in the UK. Owen will protest and say it isn't necessary. You'll refuse to back down and tell him you're going to delay a decision about turning over the money until he agrees. You might also threaten to go directly to me about it. I'm confident Owen desperately wants to get this matter closed to avoid further scrutiny. Whether he ultimately agrees to let you talk to Nettles or not isn't the key point. The lawyer who's working the case at the US Attorney's Office believes Owen will contact Nettles because you're putting pressure on him. She's seeking a court order authorizing covert surveillance of Owen so they can listen in on his conversation with Nettles and record something incriminating. If they don't talk, the British authorities can arrest Nettles and hope he'll turn on Owen and testify against him."

Tom made notes while Arthur talked. "What if I actually talk to Nettles?"

"Treat it as you would if you were investigating a case. Just remember that everything you say is being recorded." Arthur paused. "You're not recording our conversation, are you?"

"No, there's an ethical prohibition against a lawyer recording a conversation with a client absent permission. Technically you're not a client, but I'm taking notes, not recording us. Anyway, I don't have that capability in this office."

"I'll be a client someday whether you agree to give this a try or not." Arthur put down the paper he'd been holding. "My biggest relief is that the scope of the criminal activity is small. They'd barely gotten started. I'm sorry Harold Addington died, but his death stopped Owen's scheme better than anything he could have done if he'd lived. The company will weather this storm. Our employees won't lose their jobs. Our customers won't lose any money. Are you willing to help with the investigation?"

"Yes," Tom said immediately. "When should I contact Harrelson?"

"Wait until the US Attorney's Office confirms that the surveillance order has been signed."

"Should I contact the attorney directly?"

"If you want to, but she's going to let me know when to proceed. I told her I was going to discuss the situation with you today. It was her idea to approach Harrelson about Nettles."

"What's the prosecutor's name?"

"It's almost unpronounceable. I think it's Slavic. Good English names like Pelham and Crane aren't as common in New York City as they are in Etowah County. I'll send you her contact information later."

"Nettles and Harrelson are good English names too."

"But not all Englishmen are honorable. Thanks for doing this."

"You're welcome. And speaking of honorable, it's the right thing for me to finish what my father wanted to do for Harold Addington."

"Yes, it is." Arthur glanced at his watch. "Are you going to tell his widow and daughter about this?"

"I'd like to tell Rose the part about her father being exonerated and nothing more. That would obviously be very important to the family."

"Let's keep it to that. They'll find out soon enough what's going on. I don't want any media attention at this stage. Once the indictments are issued, that won't be possible. The publicity will be bad, but I believe we'll weather the storm."

Late that afternoon Tom pulled up to the Addington house to pick up Rose for dinner. He parked in front of the lions that guarded the door. The surveillance cameras caught him from every angle. A few seconds after he rang the chime, Rose opened the door. Tom's eyes widened. He'd seen Rose at church but never wearing evening clothes. She had on a sleek dark-blue dress. Her auburn hair was styled, and she'd added an extra touch of makeup that made her eyes glisten.

"You look great," he said. "But it's not going to be a dressy dinner. Rick may show up in a T-shirt and blue jeans."

"No, he won't," Rose replied, smiling. "I called Tiffany, and we decided to make it a fancy occasion."

Tom looked down at himself. He was wearing khaki pants and an open-collared shirt. "Should we go back to Elias's house so I can change?"

"No, Tiffany said there was no way Rick would wear a sport coat and tie. You're fine."

Tom held the car door open for Rose.

"Did you hear from Arthur Pelham?" she asked as soon as he was seated.

"Yes, and the internal investigation completely cleared your father of any wrongdoing."

Rose closed her eyes and leaned her head back against the seat for a moment.

"Thank you, Lord," she said. "And you. This wouldn't have happened if you hadn't insisted on continuing to dig through the information. Let me call my mum and let her know."

Tom listened as Rose relayed the information to her mother.

"I won't be too late." Rose ended the call and returned her phone to her purse. "What else did he say?"

Tom knew he had to give Rose at least a tidbit more. "Circumstantial evidence implicates Owen Harrelson, which makes sense. As internal affairs officer for the company, he was the fox guarding the henhouse."

"Is he going to be arrested?"

"Not yet, the government is still investigating the case."

Rose seemed satisfied. They left the neighborhood and turned toward Bethel. Rick and Tiffany's house was on the other side of town. Rose settled back in the seat.

"Tell me about Rick and Tiffany. Being the fourth person with a group of three people who've known each other for a long time can be awkward. Not that I mind. I'm sure I'll enjoy listening to you reminisce. It will give me another window into America."

"I'm not sure you'll glean much sociological insight from listening to Rick and me talk. He's a country boy at heart who'd rather be tramping through the woods than sitting around a dinner table."

"What about Tiffany?"

Rose's question made Tom feel anxious. "Uh, I've not known her as long as I have Rick. We met when we were in high school."

They rode in silence for a few minutes.

"Did you date Tiffany?"

"Yeah, for a few months. But we've both changed a lot. I mean, she married Rick, and I—" Tom stopped.

"Never married?" Rose completed his sentence.

"No. I was going to say that I've had a few girlfriends, none of whom ever seemed like the right one to marry. What about you?" Tom asked, trying to divert the conversation away from Tiffany and him. "Why haven't you met the right guy?"

"I did meet him. We were engaged, and he was killed in an auto accident in Devonshire. Hit by a drunken driver."

"I'm sorry."

"It happened five years ago last month."

As they drew closer to Rick and Tiffany's driveway, the embarrassment and shame Tom had felt the previous night on the porch returned. What lay ahead at the top of the hill was unknown. He took a deep breath and sighed. Rose didn't seem to notice.

"Impressive place," she said as they drove up the driveway.

"There's the horse barn," Tom said as he pointed. "I'm not sure Tiffany will want to take you there if she's wearing a nice dress and shoes."

They parked in front of the house. Bosco was lying down near the door. He hopped up when Tom stopped the car and trotted over with a soggy yellow tennis ball in his mouth.

"Tell your master to buy you a new ball," Tom said as he hurled the ball across the yard and down the hill.

The dog took off. Tom rang the doorbell with the hand that hadn't handled the tennis ball. Tiffany opened the door. She looked stunning in a low-cut dress with an expensive-looking necklace around her neck.

"I'm so glad you're here," she said.

Tiffany threw her arms around Tom's neck and pressed herself against him. He held his hand that was wet with dog slobber away from her body. Tiffany released him and gave Rose a quick hug.

"Come in," she said. "Rick is upstairs getting ready. He wasn't excited when I told him we were going to dress up, but he came around in the end. Tom, do you want a cigar?"

"Not now," he answered. "Maybe after supper."

Tiffany took Rose by the arm. "You look beautiful. I'm surprised Tom didn't drive past the house so he could spend more time alone with you. Let me show you around." Tiffany glanced over her shoulder. "Tom, you might want to wait for Rick in the den."

Tiffany's voice faded as she and Rose continued down the hallway. The resolve Tom had on the porch wavered when he saw Tiffany in person. He went into a downstairs bathroom to wash his hands. As he looked in the mirror, his eyes accused him of cowardice. He closed his eyes and asked for help. Coming out of the bathroom, he ran into Rick, who was wearing gray slacks and a starched shirt.

"Rick. Is that you?" he asked.

"Shut up," Rick answered.

"The voice is familiar, but I didn't recognize you underneath all that starch."

Rick ran his fingers down the front of his shirt. "I feel like a little kid whose big sister made him play dressup with her."

They entered the den.

"Tiffany said you were bringing Harold Addington's daughter. Are you dating her?"

"No, we've spent time together wrapping up a business matter that had to do with my father's estate. Soon she'll go back to Europe, and I'll be heading down to Atlanta."

"I'm not giving up on keeping you in Bethel. If you hadn't been with us on the rafting trip, Hal Millsap wouldn't be doing his part to support the chewing tobacco industry."

Tiffany and Rose returned from their tour of the house.

"We're going to save the barn for another time," Tiffany said. "And I'm not going to say another word all night. I could listen to Rose talk in that accent of hers for hours."

Tom introduced Rose to Rick.

"Please say Tom's name," Rick said to Rose.

"Tom Crane."

"Actually, it's Joshua Thomas Crane," Rick said.

Rose looked at Tom. "That's a name with significance. Joshua Thomas Crane, Esquire."

"And that's a very sexy accent," Rick said to Rose.

"Brits like to hear your accent," Rose replied. "The slurring of words in the Southern drawl is pleasant to our ears."

"Well, I'm your man," Rick replied, reaching out and offering Rose his arm. "Let me say the alphabet for you."

Tiffany hooked her arm around Tom's. They followed Rick and Rose down the hall. Tiffany squeezed Tom's arm several times during the short walk to the dining room. Tom felt torn in two as desire battled his will.

"Since this is such a momentous occasion, I thought we would eat in here," Tiffany said, releasing Tom after one last squeeze.

Shiny plates and gold-plated utensils glistened on the table.

"What's the occasion?" Rose asked.

"Any time Tom comes for dinner," Tiffany said.

Tom smiled awkwardly. He and Rose sat across from each other, with Rick and Tiffany at opposite ends of the long table.

"I feel like I'm in an old English manor house," Rose said as she glanced to either side. "You need a cell phone to talk to each other."

"We've been married so long, we can read each other's thoughts," Rick replied.

"Not all the time," Tiffany answered with a smile and nod toward Tom.

Marie brought in the first course, an artichoke soup whipped into a smooth puree. Tom didn't like artichokes, but the soup was delicious. It was nice to get the meal started so he could focus on something besides Tiffany. A small salad with fresh fruit and homemade dressing followed. The main course was a medium-rare tenderloin steak seasoned with wine and mushrooms. While they ate, Tiffany and Rick both asked Rose questions about her family and work with orphans. Tiffany seemed genuinely interested. Tom enjoyed learning more about Rose too.

"Rick, we need to send money to Rose's ministry," Tiffany said at one point.

Rick nodded his head. "As soon as Tom leaves the ranks of the unemployed, he and I could sponsor several kids on our own."

"You're unemployed?" Rose asked Tom.

"I lost my job a few days before I came back to Bethel," Tom said, swallowing a bite of steak.

"Sorry, buddy," Rick said sheepishly. "I wasn't trying to embarrass you."

"It's going to work out for the best. I have an excellent offer from another Atlanta law firm that I intend to accept in a few days."

"Is that for certain?" Tiffany asked.

"Yes."

"I'm sure everything will work out just fine," Tiffany replied, then turned to Rose. "You may have been in the dark about Tom's job status, but tell us something interesting you've learned about him during the past few weeks."

"That's easy," Rose answered. "Tom has been going through the most marvelous spiritual transformation, and I've been privileged to have a ringside seat. He's encountered God's personal love in such a sweet way. I know he's been spending hours and hours at the office reading the Bible and jotting down his thoughts and prayers. What else? Oh, he's learning how to hear the voice of the Lord in areas where he needs practical guidance. For me, it's been wonderful hearing about it all. It's so fresh and new."

Rick's and Tiffany's faces showed a mixture of shock and disbelief. Tiffany held her fork in midair.

"Is this true?" Rick asked Tom after he regained his bearings. "I mean, are we talking something beyond going to church?"

"Yeah," Tom replied. "Everything she said and then some. Rose and I have had some great talks. She knows so much more than I do about what it means to be a genuine Christian. Of course, Elias has been a great help too. He's so excited that he wants to go to heaven right away and tell my father about it."

Tiffany's face looked pale. Tom realized he'd stumbled onto the best way to communicate what she needed to know.

"I met with Lane Conner the other day," he continued. "I may ask him to baptize me in the creek that runs by the church before I go back to Atlanta. If I can set it up, I'd like both of you to come. I'll be sharing my testimony."

"Are you talking about putting on a flimsy robe and wading into the water to be dunked?" Rick asked.

"Don't worry. I'll wear swim trunks underneath. And I'm going to invite your father to come if he's in town."

"Do you send written invitations to something like that?" Tiffany asked.

"I'll just give everyone a call. It won't be a mob scene." Tom looked at Rose. "I hope you'll still be in town."

"I hope so too," Rose replied with a smile. "I wouldn't want to miss it. The water might be a bit chilly. It's hard to give a testimony when your teeth are chattering."

"The creek near the church won't be any colder than the Ocoee." Tom turned to Rick. "I could always wear a wet suit. Could I borrow one from you?"

"Uh, sure."

The conversation turned to more mundane matters as they ate peach melba for dessert, but Tom knew Rick's and Tiffany's minds were stuck in place. As for him, the inner turmoil associated with Tiffany had fled. For now.

After supper they remained at the table. Rick and Tom talked about old times. Rose seemed content to listen. Tiffany participated some in the conversation but mostly kept quiet. When Tom and Rose got up to leave, Tiffany touched Tom's arm and held him back in the dining room as Rick and Rose moved into the hallway.

"What does this mean to *us*?" she asked in a low but intense voice.

Tom looked directly in her eyes. "It means I'm going to pray your marriage to Rick gets better, not wish that it would end."

Tiffany looked down. Tom saw her bite her lip. After a moment passed, she started walking rapidly after Rick and Rose. Tom followed.

"Thank you so much," Rose said to Tiffany when they reached the front door. "It was a wonderful meal. I needed a time like this."

Tiffany gave her a quick hug. She stood in front of Tom and folded her arms across her chest. Rick shook Tom's hand.

"Next time you see me I won't be wearing a starched shirt," Rick said. "I'll call you next week. Deer season starts soon, and I want to show you a spot I've picked out."

"Can I bring Rover?"

"Absolutely."

Outside, Tom held the door open for Rose. When he glanced over his shoulder, Tiffany was still standing in the open door, a blank stare on her face. Tom drove slowly down the driveway.

"May I say something personal to you?" Rose asked when they reached the bottom of the hill. "It has to do with Tiffany."

"Yes."

"She still has feelings for you."

"I know," Tom replied. "But something happened when you started talking about God that changed everything. Before we left the house I told Tiffany I was going to pray for her marriage to succeed, not hope it would fall apart."

"What did she say?"

"Nothing."

As they passed through Bethel, Tom looked sideways at Rose. "How long are you going to stay with your mother in Bethel?"

"I'm not sure. I still haven't booked my airplane ticket."

"Would you consider staying a few extra days?"

"Why?"

"To come to my baptism." Tom paused. "And because I'd like to get to know you better. We've spent most of our time focusing on the money issue. I mean, you didn't even know I'd lost my job."

"Do you have other dark secrets?"

Tom remembered his meeting with Charlie Williams.

"Yes," he admitted. "But I'd rather talk about good things, not bad."

"Yes, there's enough darkness in the world. I like being positive." Rose touched him lightly on the arm. "It's kind of you to ask me to stay. And I meant every word I said tonight that it's been a delight watching the Lord work in your life."

"Then stay in Bethel until I'm baptized."

"Maybe," Rose replied with a smile.

After he dropped off Rose, Tom didn't think about Tiffany Pelham while he drove to Elias's house. Between the Pelhams' front porch and their dining room table, her spell over him was broken.

The pleasant scent left by Rose Addington, however, lingered in his car.

The following Monday morning at 10:00 a.m. Tom received a call on his cell phone from Arthur's assistant.

"Mr. Pelham had to go to Washington, DC, and asked me to let you know everything is in place so that you can proceed."

"Was he more specific?"

"No. He said you'd understand what he meant."

Tom recalled Arthur's statement that the Harrelson investigation was being transferred to the federal authorities in Washington.

"Do you know why he went to Washington?"

"No, sir."

"Did he leave you the name and phone number of an assistant US attorney in New York?"

"No, he left early this morning on the corporate jet and told me he'd be unavailable for the rest of the day."

"Okay."

Tom logged on to the website for the US Attorney's Office in New York City. There were scores of assistant attorneys, several with names that might be Slavic. Cold-calling government attorneys to ask for information about an ongoing criminal investigation would be a waste of time. And Tom didn't need someone to hold his hand when he talked to Owen Harrelson.

Before making the call he wrote down a list of questions as if preparing for a deposition. Because the conversation was going to be recorded, Tom didn't want to sound unprepared. And he didn't want it to veer offtrack. As he placed the call to Harrelson's cell phone, Tom secretly wished the internal affairs officer wouldn't cooperate. If that happened, it would painlessly end Tom's involvement in the matter.

Harrelson didn't answer, and the call went to voice mail. Relieved, Tom left a message.

Fifteen minutes later his phone beeped and signaled a call from an unavailable number. He pressed the Receive button.

"Hello."

"Owen Harrelson here," the familiar voice said. "Sorry I missed your call. Is everything set for the hearing next week?"

Tom looked down at his questions. "Almost. The only thing I need is corroborating evidence supporting the relationship between Addington and the British bank account used to funnel the money from the European customers to Barbados. I have the data from Barbados but not the specific information from the UK."

"Crane, you have what you need," Harrelson responded bluntly. "Quit dragging your feet. Arthur and I want this taken care of as soon as possible."

Tom was ready. "I understand the reason why you don't want to disclose client names, but blanket refusal of access to the bank records in the UK doesn't make sense."

"That's not going to happen," Harrelson said, his voice getting louder. "And I've already consulted our legal department about taking action against you if you don't turn over the money in the trust account."

"I'd do the same if I was in your position."

Harrelson was silent for a moment. "Since you still want to argue about this, do I need to bring Arthur into this conversation?"

"Is he available?"

"No, he's in Washington, but your stalling has gone on long enough. If you won't cooperate, the three of us can get on a conference call when he gets back. I can assure you it won't be a pleasant conversation."

"I think that's a good idea. I'm available any time."

Tom was now enjoying making Harrelson squirm.

"Look, Arthur's primary desire is to get this over with," Harrelson said in a more subdued voice. "And I'd rather tell him it's taken care of than accuse you of failing to cooperate."

"I'm not asking for much. All I want to do is speak with a contact at the UK bank."

"What kind of confirmation will satisfy you so we can move forward?"

"The information from Barbados is detailed. The data from the UK is not. I'd like proof Addington controlled the British account."

"I'm not sure I can get a written record, but I might be able to arrange a phone call for you with an officer at the bank who can verbally confirm Addington's relationship to the accounts."

Tom swallowed. "What's his name?"

"I'm not going to tell you until I find out if he's willing to help. We worked together in the past, and he, of course, knows about Addington's scheme. If the embezzlement had resulted in a criminal prosecution, my contact would have been a primary source of information for the UK prosecutors. His job at the bank is similar to mine here at Pelham. That's why we worked together in the past. But before I go to the trouble of seeing if I can set this up, I have to know from you that it won't lead to more questions and more delays. I've humored you because of your personal relationship with Arthur, but that leniency ends now. Are we clear on that?"

"Yes. If your friend can do what you say, that will be sufficient."

"He's not a friend; he's a former business associate. I'll give him a call shortly. He should be at the office."

"Thanks for your—"

Harrelson ended the call in the middle of Tom's thank-you. Tom slowly lowered the cell phone from his ear and laid it on the desk.

Shortly after he passed the bar exam, Tom observed the trial of a former client of Barnes, McGraw, and Crowther who was charged with embezzlement. The prosecution's case included a recorded phone conversation in which the defendant talked to a coconspirator who was secretly cooperating with the authorities. Tom never imagined he could find himself in a similar situation. Someday he might have to sit on a witness stand, face Harrelson across a courtroom, and confirm the date and time they talked.

Tom waited. His next phone call should be from someone with the US Attorney's Office in New York or Washington. There was a knock on the door. He jumped.

"Come in," he said.

"What are you doing all closed up in here?" Bernice asked. "You've been spending so much time with the door shut you've hurt my feelings."

"I don't mean to hurt your feelings," Tom replied, "but I've kept you in the dark more to protect you from a hassle than to deny you information. I promise that as soon as possible, I'll fill you in on as many details as I can."

Bernice pressed her lips together. Tom could tell she wasn't satisfied. His cell phone beeped. It was an unavailable number again.

"Uh, I've got to take this in private, Bernice," he said. "Please shut the door."

Bernice turned around and slammed the door. Tom raised the phone to his ear. "Hello."

It wasn't anyone with the US Attorney's Office. It was Owen Harrelson.

"I'm going to conference you in," Harrelson said. "You're going to be talking to George Nettles."

Tom's heart started beating faster. "Okay," Tom said.

"Are you there, George?" Harrelson asked.

"I'm here," a man with a deep voice replied.

"We're on the line with Tom Crane. As you know, the money Addington misappropriated ended up in his father's trust account."

"Is he the man whose father died in the boating accident with Addington?" Nettles asked.

"Yes," Harrelson answered.

"Right," Nettles responded. "Sorry to hear about that, although it caused this unfortunate financial situation to come to light."

Tom chafed at such a callous reference to his father.

"I sent you copies of what I furnished Tom last week," Harrelson continued. "But he has other questions. Have you pulled up information about the account Addington set up with the bank?"

"Yes, it's in front of me."

"Tom, go ahead and ask your questions," Harrelson said.

Tom suddenly felt tongue-tied. He quickly referred to his notes. "Uh, what is the account number and when was it opened?"

Nettles rattled off a series of numbers and dates.

"And who were authorized signatories on the account?" Tom asked.

"Harold Addington, but it wasn't a personal account. The name listed was Bellevue, Ltd."

"Is that a British company?"

"Yes, the documents furnished by Addington indicated that he registered it himself in the UK."

"Why isn't the Bellevue name listed on the check transferring the money to the bank in Barbados?"

"We issue a few checks to a customer when an account is opened. The printed checks are sent by post at a later time. That never happened with this account. Apparently he didn't anticipate much activity."

"Okay. What are the dates and amounts of deposits Addington made to the account?"

As Nettles spoke, Tom wrote down the information, all of which matched the amounts entrusted to Addington by investors who thought they were buying CDs in the Pelham bank in Barbados.

"Do you have anything with Addington's signature on it completed when he opened the account?" Tom asked, backtracking for a moment.

"Yes."

"Can you furnish it to me?"

"I'm not supposed to release that information, but given the circumstances I can send you copies of disclosure forms he signed. What is your fax number?"

"I don't have a fax machine at this office. Can you scan and send to me?"

"No, that would create a record of the transfer of information here at the bank. If you want this information, I'm going to have to furnish it outside normal channels."

Tom's mind raced. He glanced down at the desk and saw a letter from Lamar Sponcler's office.

"Send the documents to this number," he said, giving Nettles the fax number on Sponcler's letterhead. "It's a law firm around the corner from me."

"I can't do that unless you'll be there to receive it."

"I'll go as soon as we hang up."

"Owen, this is highly irregular," Nettles said.

"I know," Harrelson said. "I promise this is the last you'll hear from me about this."

"Mr. Crane, may I have your word that you will shred the documents as soon as you review them?" Nettles asked.

"Yes," Tom answered.

Tom knew the documents were meaningless. Establishing the connection between Harrelson and Nettles was the important thing.

"I'll load the information into the machine within the next five minutes," Nettles said. "Good day to you both."

"Thanks, George," Harrelson said. "That's all."

Nettles clicked off.

"And I don't want to hear any other objections from you," Harrelson added to Tom. "I'll see you next week in Bethel. Make sure there won't be any holdups." Tom chuckled at Harrelson's choice of words. The call ended, and he slipped his phone into his pocket.

"I'm going to Lamar Sponcler's office to pick up a fax," he said to Bernice as he left the office.

Tom walked around the corner and down two blocks to a building with a large sign on the front that read "Lamar Sponcler, Trial Lawyer." Tom pushed open the door. Betty Sosebee, Sponcler's long-time secretary, was talking on the phone. The gray-haired woman saw Tom and motioned for him to sit down. Behind Betty's desk Tom saw a fax machine. As he watched, it began to slowly spit out a sheet of paper. Betty hung up the phone.

"Hey, Tom," she said. "Lamar is at a hearing in Catoosa County, but I expect him back soon. Do you want me to have him give you a buzz?"

"No thanks. I came over to pick up a fax. My father didn't have a machine so I gave someone your number. I hope it was okay."

Betty spun around in her chair. "This may be it right now."

As she picked up the top sheet of paper, Tom quickly walked over to the machine and took it from her hand. "This is it," he said.

"Top secret?" Betty smiled.

"Sorry, but in a way it is."

The cover page was followed by three forms, all with Harold Addington's signature on the bottom. Tom folded them in two.

"Thanks, Betty," he said. "I didn't mean to be rude."

"Don't worry about it. When Lamar gets focused on something he can be a pain to deal with. Let me know if I can help in the future."

Outside on the sidewalk, Tom looked at Addington's signature and decided to add a step of his own to verifying Harrelson's scheme. He walked down the street to the courthouse and into the probate court office. A young female clerk was on duty. Tom introduced himself.

"Where's Sara Jo?" Tom asked, referring to the usual clerk on duty.

"Out of town with her daughter who's having a baby. May I help you?"

"I'd like to see the file for Harold Addington's estate."

"Sure." The clerk got up from her desk and walked over to a filing cabinet.

The clerk pulled a folder from the cabinet and handed it to Tom. "Do you want to take it from the office?"

"No. I can check it here."

There was a shelf built into the wall opposite the clerk's desk. Tom placed the file on the shelf and turned to Addington's will. Flipping to the last page, he compared the dead man's signature on the will to the signatures on the forms sent by Nettles. There was no doubt. The signatures were identical. Most likely Harrelson and Nettles transferred the signature by obtaining it in an electronic format from another source and inserting it onto the bank forms. Whatever their method, the result was impeccable. If he'd not talked to Arthur, Tom's suspicions of Harold Addington would have resurfaced. He handed the file to the clerk.

"Thanks," he said. "That's all I needed."

"You're welcome. Come back anytime. I'll be filling in for two more weeks, then it's back to the county commissioner's office. I like it a lot better over here. It's so quiet and peaceful. Over there all I ever hear is complaints about sewer problems."

"That stinks."

The woman laughed. Tom smiled crookedly at his unintended pun.

There wasn't a shredder at his father's office, so Tom went down the hall to the clerk of court, who let him run the sheets through her machine. With a sense of finality, Tom returned to the office. The rest of Tom's day was as quiet as the probate court office. Late in the afternoon he thought about Rose Addington and called her.

"Is everything okay?" she asked quickly.

"Yeah. Why?"

"I've just been agitated all day."

"Maybe it would do you good to get out of the house for a while. Could I come by and take you for a drive?"

"Where would we go?"

"Anywhere you like."

Rose was silent for a moment. "This may sound strange, but I'd like to go to the pond where the accident happened. Before I leave Bethel I need to get some closure. Would you be willing to take me there?"

"Absolutely. What you're saying makes perfect sense to me."

———

The afternoon was cool, and Rose was wearing a sweater and jeans. During the drive to Austin's Pond, Tom told her what happened when he went there with Elias.

"That's powerful," Rose said. "I need to get into the river of grief and follow the tributary God has for me."

They turned onto the access road for the pond. "Do you want to walk to the pond or drive directly to it?"

"A walk would be good."

Tom parked near the pasture gate. "We can take this old road-bed. It's less than half a mile to the water."

At one point they had to cross a narrow ditch. Tom held out his hand to help Rose over. Their fingers lingered together for a moment. When they reached the clearing for the pond, a breeze stirred Rose's hair. She brushed it from her face.

"Tell me what you know," she said.

Unlike his time with Elias, Tom wasn't irritated by Rose's questions. He pointed out the place where the overturned boat was found floating in the water. Rose bit her lower lip.

"Where were the bodies?"

"Between the boat and the shore."

Rose shook her head. "It doesn't seem that far to the land."

"Was your father a good swimmer?"

"Decent enough. And yours?"

"Very good, but they were fully clothed, and once their clothes got wet they went down."

Rose sighed. "My father had issues with his heart. He was on medication. It makes me wonder if he had a heart attack. Mum and I didn't request a copy of the report by the medical examiner. Did you?"

Tom licked his lips. "Yes."

Rose touched a partially buried rock with her toe. "I should do that too."

"The important thing is they're both in heaven," Tom replied quickly.

"Yes." Rose pointed to the opposite end of the pond. "Is that the bench where you had your cry?"

"Yes."

"I'd like to spend a bit of time there alone."

Rose walked slowly around the pond to the concrete picnic table. Tom sat down on the grass and tossed a twig into the water. The wind pushed it away from the bank. Rose sat on the table and let her legs swing beneath her. Tom couldn't see her face. The phone in Tom's pocket beeped, and he took it out. It was Arthur Pelham.

"Hello," he said.

"It's Arthur. I have an update—"

Service was poor at the pond, and Arthur's voice cut in and out. Tom kept talking as he quickly walked up the slight hill that led down to the pond.

"—according to the US Attorney's Office in Washington," Arthur said and stopped.

"I only heard that last part," Tom said. "I'm at Austin's Pond and service is lousy."

"Why are you there?" Arthur asked.

"Rose Addington wanted to come. It has to do with saying good-bye to her father."

"Can she hear you now?"

"No, she's at the other end of the pond. I'm standing on top of a little hill nearby."

"Did you understand anything I said?"

"Not really, you were cutting in and out."

"I'll start over. Nice work with Harrelson and Nettles. The US Attorney's Office called and told me they were able to record everything. There's no doubt the two of them have been working together this whole time."

"Good. Who's handling the investigation? You never sent me the name of the government lawyer you spoke to in New York."

"She was taken off the case once it went to Washington. Anyway, your part is finished. The last step is to transfer the money from the trust account. I'm going to give you the wiring instructions for our bank in Barbados. Confirmation for receipt of the wire will be delivered to your e-mail address. Here's the number."

Before Tom could tell Arthur that he didn't have anything to write on, the older man rattled off a long number.

"Send me an e-mail with the wiring instructions," Tom said. "I don't have anything to write on."

"Do you have a pen?"

Tom felt in his pocket. "Yes."

"Then write it on your hand if you have to. I'm in a limo on my way to the airport where I'm getting on a plane to Japan and won't be back for six days. I want to know this is taken care of before I get in the air."

"Okay, but please give it to me slowly."

Tom carefully wrote the numbers on the palm of his left hand, then read them back to Arthur.

"That's it," Arthur said. "I had to use a different corresponding bank than normal because the money is in the local bank in Bethel. We stopped using Bethel Commercial Bank & Trust years ago. If you wire the money first thing in the morning, the deposit should be confirmed by the time I'm on the ground in Japan."

"I'd still like to get an order from Judge Caldwell authorizing transfer of the funds."

"Is that really necessary at this point?" Arthur asked. "Everyone except Harrelson agrees the money belongs to our investors, and I want those funds properly credited to our clients' accounts as soon as possible. We'll have to make up the lost interest, but that's a pittance in the overall scheme of things."

Tom couldn't come up with a good argument for a court order except it had been part of his plan before he found out what really happened. Arthur had a legitimate reason to set things right as soon as possible, and Tom had the information he needed for the estate file.

"All right. I guess there's no one left to complain except Harrelson."

"From what I've been told, he'll be taken into custody this weekend. The British authorities can deal with Nettles at the same time." There was a brief pause. "I'm at the airport. Thanks again for all you've done. When I get back, we'll sit down and see what I can do to help you professionally."

The call ended. Tom returned to the pond. Harrelson and the saga of designated trust account were history.

It was time to concentrate on Rose Addington.

chapter
TWENTY-EIGHT

om stepped into the clearing and glanced toward the picnic table. Rose wasn't there. He quickly looked around the pond but didn't see her.

"Rose!" he called out.

There was no answer. He started jogging around the pond toward the picnic table. He stopped and called out again.

"Rose!"

"Over here," a faint voice replied.

He turned in the direction of the sound. "Where are you?" he called out.

"The road!"

Tom continued around the pond and saw Rose walking down the roadway behind the barn toward him.

"Why did you leave?" he asked, slightly out of breath.

"Just walking. I looked up, and you were gone. What were you doing?"

"Arthur called and gave me instructions for returning the money in the designated trust account to Pelham Financial. I couldn't get a clear signal until I walked up the hill." Tom held out his hand. "These wiring numbers are worth almost two million dollars."

"Then make sure you don't wash your hand."

Tom motioned toward the picnic table. "How was your time alone?"

"A bit empty. I'm not sure what I expected, but there isn't much for me here, at least not now. Today isn't my day."

"I'm sorry."

Rose smiled. "We British have to maintain our reputation for a stiff upper lip and pressing on with dogged determination in the face of hardship."

"What does pressing on mean for you now?"

Rose didn't hesitate. "Following the call of the Lord to serve the children I can help."

It was the kind of unselfish answer Tom had never heard from another human being his age before he met Rose Addington. He looked down at her, not sure if he wanted to kiss her stiff upper lip or applaud her fortitude.

"Are you ready to leave?" she asked.

"Yes."

When they reached the car, Tom copied the wiring instructions from his hand onto a slip of paper.

"What else did Mr. Pelham say?" Rose asked.

"The federal government has taken over the case. With all the investor fraud that's happened during the past few years, things like this get immediate attention. By the first of the week, we'll be reading about Owen Harrelson in the newspaper and on the Internet."

"That's sad."

"How can you say that after he set up your father as the fall guy if his scheme went bad?" Tom asked in surprise.

"Do you think our fathers are looking down from heaven wishing ill toward any person?"

Tom didn't reply, but he wouldn't mind knocking Owen Harrelson to the ground, so long as it didn't break Tom's hand. The arrogant executive could have killed Randall Freiburger and attempted to embezzle $1,750,000. They drove back to Esther's house.

"When will I see you again?" Tom asked as he walked Rose to the door.

"I'm available," she replied with a smile. "Within reason, of course. You have my number."

"Give me a reason."

Rose paused. "I've heard about a scenic overlook near a big rock where people paint messages—"

"I can take you there," Tom cut in.

"You wouldn't mind? I feel like I'm asking you to be my personal tour guide."

"One who loves his new job. How about Saturday?"

"So long as it's in the morning. Mum and I have plans for the afternoon."

"Morning is great. I'll pick you up about seven thirty. Wear comfortable shoes."

———

Tom found Elias sitting in the front room.

"How was your time with Rose Addington?" the old man asked.

"Good. She's different from any other woman I've met."

"And that's a good thing?"

"Your matchmaking days are over. Just be glad God answered your prayers for my soul."

"What I pray isn't up to you. Oh, Lane Conner called while you were out."

"Did he leave a message?"

"No, he just asked me to have you call him back."

Tom checked his watch. "I'll try to connect with him on Sunday. I need to schedule my baptism before the creek gets clogged with ice."

"Yes!" Elias clapped his hands together so loudly that Rover's head popped up from the floor.

———

The following morning Tom went to Bethel Commercial Bank & Trust. Charles Loughton wasn't available, so a young bank officer helped him complete the wire transfer. The young man didn't seem interested in asking questions, which suited Tom. Fifteen minutes later Tom walked out of the bank, looked up at the sky, and took a deep breath. He was a free man.

Back at his father's office, he turned on his computer. There was an e-mail in his in-box from Owen Harrelson, sent the previous evening and asking Tom to call. He ignored it. After lunch he told Bernice she could go home. There wasn't much left for her, or him, to do.

By the end of the day, Tom had finished going through the few remaining files in his father's office. He typed a few letters and stuck them in envelopes. It would take a day to dispose of the outdated library and pack up his father's personal belongings. There wasn't even enough money left in the operating account to pay Bernice's wages. Tom's own bank account was shrinking rapidly. It was time for action.

He called Nate Becker to accept the job and set a start date, but the Atlanta lawyer was out of the office until the following week. Tom hesitated for moment, then left a short message to return the call. He didn't want to communicate something as important as acceptance of a job via voice mail.

He and Elias had a quiet supper.

"What are you going to do when I'm gone and no one is bringing you food?" Tom asked.

"Eat a good breakfast. That's easier for me to cook. After that, I'll eat sandwiches and fruit. Before you came I wasn't taking good care of myself, so anything will be an improvement."

Elias ate a bite of corn casserole.

"Did you talk to Lane Conner?" the old man asked.

"No, remember, I'm going to get with him on Sunday."

"That's right," Elias said. "I forgot. How are things at the office?"

"About done. I sent Bernice home early today. Tomorrow morning Rose Addington and I are going to hike up to look at the painted rock."

"With or without Rover?"

Tom looked at the dog, who was curled up near his water bowl in the corner of the kitchen.

"I don't think he had a very good time the other day. He'll be happier napping at your feet in the living room."

That night at 3:00 a.m. Tom came downstairs. No light shone from beneath the study door, so he went inside and knelt in front of the straight-backed chair and thanked God for resolving the problem of the designated trust account. As Rose told Rick and Tiffany, seeking God's help to get through a practical problem had been a new experience for Tom. Although the situation worked out in the end, he'd felt like a metal ball in a pinball machine as he bounced from one perspective to another. He prayed that the next time he faced a challenge he would be able to hear more accurately and see more clearly. Following the Lord in a straight line would be much more efficient.

Saturday dawned cool and clear. Tom could see his breath as he walked across the yard to his car. He threw a small backpack and a couple of bottles of water in the car.

Before he could ring the doorbell at the Addington house, Rose came outside. She was wearing a green sweater, hiking pants, and lightweight boots. She'd tied her hair in a ponytail. Her auburn hair looked great against the green sweater.

"Mum's still resting, and I didn't want the bell to wake her," Rose said.

"You look like you've done this before," Tom replied.

"I like to tramp through meadow and moorland. And the weather is finally getting to a comfortable spot."

"You'll only see a meadow if we pass one in the car, and I hope we don't get stuck in the moorland. But it's a perfect day for a walk up the ridge."

Tom held the door open for Rose. It felt comfortable having her slip into the front seat of the car. When they reached the highway, he turned onto the main road and accelerated rapidly.

"Feeling frisky?" Rose asked as the sudden increase in speed pushed them against the seats.

They came around a curve as a sheriff's department car passed them going in the opposite direction. Tom took his foot off the gas and let the car slow down. He glanced in the rearview mirror to see if the officer was turning around. The patrol car passed from sight.

"I don't need to attract the attention of the police. I haven't had a speeding ticket in three years, and my car insurance premium is about to drop to a more reasonable level."

They arrived at the parking lot for the trail. It was empty.

"The high school crowd comes on Friday and Saturday nights and fills this space up," Tom said. "That's when the kids walk to the top with cans of spray paint and beer."

"Did you do that when you were in school?"

"Yes, and I'm glad some of the writings I left on the rock are covered with multiple layers of paint."

Tom slipped his arms through the backpack. It was still cool enough that they could see their breath.

"Ready?" he asked Rose.

"Yes," she replied, looking up at the ridge. "Let's take an easy pace, okay?"

"Sure. My buddies and I would race to the top, but that's not what I'm interested in today."

Rose smiled. "'My heart's in the Highlands.'"

"Robert Burns."

"Yes."

"The trail to the highlands starts over here." Tom pointed to a narrow gap in the trees.

Tom led the way through the switchbacks cut into the side of the hill. Rose's breathing remained steady, proof she was in good shape. When he'd climbed with Rover it took thirty minutes to reach the top. With Rose walking steadily beside him they reached the summit in twenty minutes. The visibility was good, and they could see the higher hills that were stepping stones to the Great Smoky

Mountains. This morning the Smokies weren't shrouded with the haze that gave them their name.

"The exposed rock is over this little rise," Tom said as he continued on the path that ran along the top of the ridge.

They reached the rock. It bore fresh paint memorializing the score of the previous night's high school football game in which Etowah County defeated a team from Rossville. The numbers of the players who made outstanding plays for the Etowah team were listed beside the score. Tom explained everything to Rose.

"Was your number ever painted on the rock?" she asked.

"Several times, but it would take an archaeologist to uncover it."

"What happens if the local team loses?"

"Sometimes the winning team sneaks up here and paints the score on the rock as a way to rub it in."

"I'd like to see an American football game while I'm here."

"A high school game?"

"Yes."

"That's easy enough. There's another home game next Friday night. It will be a perfect chance for you to see what it's all about."

They scrambled up to the top of the rock. The day was getting warmer, but a cool breeze blew across the top of the hill. Rose sat close to Tom without touching him. He nudged closer until they made contact. She didn't move away. They surveyed the surrounding countryside without speaking for a few minutes.

"Does it remind you of any place in Britain?" he asked.

"A bit. You have more trees in the States, which is a nice touch."

"And these forests are a shadow of what it was like when the first settlers arrived. Back then, trees twenty feet in diameter and large enough to live in were common."

"Live in? Like a tree house?"

"Not exactly. Elias has an old photograph of a family standing inside a tulip poplar tree that had been cut down and hollowed out as a temporary shelter."

Tom handed Rose a bottle of water and opened the other for himself. They drank in silence. Rose screwed the top onto her bottle and set it on the rock beside her.

"Mum and I are meeting with a real estate agent this afternoon to talk about selling the house."

"Who is it?"

"Anita Bishop."

"She sells a lot of houses." Tom nodded.

"What sort of questions should I ask her?"

Tom gave Rose a basic real estate primer.

"That helps," Rose said when he finished. "It's handy having a free solicitor."

Tom then asked Rose about her siblings and their families. It was the most talkative he'd found her on any subject. She showed him photos stored on her phone. Tom tried to keep the names of the nieces and nephews straight in his mind.

"I can't wait to see them again," Rose said, closing her phone. "But I know it will be sad without Papa around. It especially hurts that the grandchildren won't have the chance to spend time with him."

Rose then asked Tom what he had been reading in the Bible. They talked about Isaiah and John.

"It'll take me awhile to catch up with you," Tom said after she quoted a verse.

"I'm sure there are laws and court cases you've memorized because they come up so often."

Rose wanted to know about his legal career. As Tom described his journey, he realized how focused he'd been on getting ahead with minimal attention left for the people around him. He'd had a good working relationship with Mark Nelson, but too often Tom was curt and abrupt with support staff. He determined then and there that he would turn over a new leaf at Sweet and Becker. When he explained to Rose about his termination from Barnes, McGraw, and Crowther, she shook her head.

"That must have been very tough for you."

"Yeah, but it helped a lot when I received that great job offer from another law firm."

"Did you consider staying in Bethel?"

"I was encouraged by several people I respect to give it a try, but I don't think it's the thing to do." Tom paused. "And not only for business reasons. It wouldn't be good for Rick and Tiffany's marriage if I stayed. If I'm in town, it will be tougher for her."

Tom stared across the hills toward the mountains. "Elias says people are like houses. Most of the rooms may be filled with light, but there can still be a dark corner."

"Yes." Rose nodded. "I've experienced that."

Tom waited.

"My papa was like that years ago," Rose said, then looked up at Tom. "Before God changed his life."

"So what I said makes sense to you?"

"Yes. It would be hard for me to trust a man who didn't realize how deceitful the human heart can be."

"Do you trust me?"

"I'm beginning to."

Rose leaned into Tom for a moment, then stood to her feet and stretched. Tom didn't want to move.

"I'd best get going," Rose said. "I'll need to help my mum get ready."

Tom got up. When he did, he faced Rose, put his hands on her shoulders, and kissed her. She didn't pull away.

"Was it okay to do that?" he asked when their lips parted.

"If it wasn't, I wouldn't have let you do it."

Tom dipped in for another kiss, but Rose turned her head to the side.

"That's all the trust and encouragement I'm comfortable with for the time being."

Tom straightened up. "Why?"

"This is going to be different for you, Tom. You're not the same man who dated scores of women since you turned sixteen."

"Scores of women? Who told you that?"

"Tiffany. She says you've had a commitment problem."

"When did that come up?"

"She phoned me after we had dinner the other night. She was still trying to understand what's happened to you and wanted to ask me more about it. It was a great opportunity to talk to her."

"What did you tell her?"

"More of the same. That you've had a genuine change and were in the midst of discovering what that meant for every area of your life."

It was an accurate assessment.

"What did she say?" he asked.

"She listened. I'm not sure what she really thought, but you should be careful. Dark corners have a way of creeping back. And Tiffany might try to change in an effort to win you, not because God is moving on her heart."

"Do you think that really might happen?"

"Yes. Her feelings for you run deep."

"How about your feelings?"

"Deep enough to let you kiss me."

Looking into Rose's eyes, Tom soaked up her beauty—part physical, part inner—radiating out. He leaned forward again. Rose kept him at bay with a finger to his chest.

"Let's get going," she said.

"Okay," Tom said, taking a deep breath. "Thinking and acting differently are going to take some getting used to."

They scrambled down from the rock. When they reached the parking area, a sheriff's department car was parked behind Tom's vehicle. Tom's stomach twisted in a knot. He turned to Rose.

"I guess he recorded my speed and tracked me down."

A deputy sheriff got out as Tom approached. Another sheriff's department car, its blue lights flashing, pulled into the parking area. Tom reached behind his back to get his wallet.

"Keep your hands where I can see them!" the deputy called out.

Puzzled, Tom held his hands out in front of him.

"Ma'am, step to the side and put your hands behind your head," the deputy ordered Rose.

Tom glanced at Rose, whose face was pale. She clasped her fingers behind her head and moved away from Tom.

"Are you Joshua Thomas Crane?" the deputy asked.

"Yes, what's going on here?"

"You're under arrest. Put your hands on the roof of my car and spread your feet apart."

chapter
TWENTY-NINE

After he frisked Tom, the deputy told him to take off his backpack and empty his pockets. A female deputy got out of the second car. She searched Rose. Tom couldn't hear their conversation.

"Look, I couldn't have been going more than fifteen miles over the speed limit," Tom protested. "There's no need to turn this into a major event. And the woman with me was a passenger."

"Please get in the backseat of the patrol car," the deputy replied.

"Why?"

"So I can transport you to the jail."

"What about her?" Tom motioned to Rose.

"Is that Rose Addington?"

"Yes."

"She'll go in the other car."

Tom didn't budge. "I'm not going anywhere until you tell me why I'm being arrested."

"Mr. Crane, if you don't cooperate, I'll handcuff you," the deputy replied evenly.

Out of the corner of his eye, Tom saw the female officer putting Rose in the back of the other car.

"What about my vehicle?" Tom asked.

"You'll be able to turn over your personal possessions, including your car keys, to a friend or relative after you're processed at the jail."

Tom could not believe what he was hearing. "Are you going to read me my Miranda rights?" he asked.

"No, because I'm not going to ask you any questions. Anything you say will be voluntary. Now, please get in the car."

Tom lowered his head and got in the backseat of the car. The deputy closed the door. The vehicle containing Rose pulled out of the lot first. The officers turned on the sirens and flashing lights and drove at a high rate of speed toward town. Several times Tom started to ask the deputy another question but realized it was futile. The man was a uniformed transport driver, nothing more.

The Etowah County jail was behind the courthouse. The older part of the jail, built in the 1920s, had been converted to offices after a new cell block, complete with electric doors, was constructed in the 1970s. The two cars pulled into a secure space where prisoners could be taken directly into a holding area. Tom had never seen the inside of the new jail. The officer kept him in the car while the female deputy took Rose inside.

"I want to talk to Ms. Addington," Tom said to the deputy in the front seat.

"Our instructions were to keep you separate," the deputy replied.

"But I'm her lawyer."

The deputy looked in the rearview mirror. "If that's so, you'll need to register as her attorney at the front desk. Then you can meet with her."

"Take me to the front desk."

"You have to be processed yourself."

When Rose was no longer visible, the deputy opened the door for Tom.

"Have you been to the booking area before?" the deputy asked.

"No, I've never represented any criminal defendants in Etowah County."

"Come with me."

The deputy led Tom to a metal door and pushed a button. A few seconds later the door buzzed and the deputy pulled it open. "Straight ahead," he said.

Tom and the deputy walked down a short hallway and beyond another metal door that buzzed as they approached it. They entered a room where another officer sat at a desk with a pile of paperwork in front of him. Through a glass partition Tom could see Rose sitting with her back to him.

"Rose!" he called out.

"She can't hear you in the women's section," the deputy said. "This is Officer Johnson. He'll take over from here."

Johnson motioned for Tom to sit down.

"Are you going to tell me why I've been arrested?" Tom asked.

"Your full name," Johnson replied.

"Not until you answer my question."

The officer looked Tom in the eye. "As soon as I complete my paperwork, someone is going to meet with you. If you cooperate, that will happen sooner; if you don't, it will take longer. The choice is yours."

"Joshua Thomas Crane."

The officer asked a series of basic questions. He fingerprinted Tom and made him stand for a mug shot photo. As he waited for the camera to flash, Tom thought about Rose being submitted to the same indignity. He started getting angry.

"This way," Johnson said.

"What's going on?" Tom asked sharply. "Tell me. Right now."

Ignoring him, Johnson led Tom from the booking area and down a hallway to a metal door marked "Interview 2."

"In there," the officer said, holding open the door.

Tom entered the room. Seated behind a plain metal desk was Charlie Williams. The DA motioned for the officer to leave. Williams nudged a chair away from the table with his foot.

"Have a seat," he said.

"What's this about, Charlie?" Tom demanded, continuing to stand.

"Before I answer, I need to inform you of your Miranda rights."

Tom stood mute as the DA repeated the familiar litany.

"Are you going to stand or sit?" Williams asked.

"Stand. And I'm formally notifying you that no one has a right to question Rose Addington until I have a chance to talk to her."

"You're not in a position to make demands."

"I'm still a lawyer, and as her attorney, I'm notifying you that she is not to be questioned."

"Have you filed a notice of representation?"

"No, but I'm telling you as an officer of the court and hope you'll comply with my request."

"Duly noted."

Tom stared at Williams. "Charlie, quit sparring and tell me what's going on."

Williams opened a folder on the table in front of him and took out a sheet of paper. He held it in a way that Tom couldn't read it.

"This is an indictment returned yesterday afternoon by the

Etowah County grand jury charging you and Rose Addington with felony theft by deception and conspiracy to commit theft by deception."

"What?"

"The indictment was based upon credible information that you and Ms. Addington conspired to embezzle a large sum of money from Pelham Financial by depositing $1,750,000 in an offshore bank account."

"Who at Pelham provided the information?"

"Owen Harrelson, the chief internal affairs officer, was the primary witness. He flew down yesterday and testified in front of the grand jury."

Tom stared at Williams for a moment, then sat down in the seat. Suddenly everything made sense.

"Embezzlement occurred," Tom said, his voice calmer. "But the perpetrators were Harrelson and a man named George Nettles, who works for a bank in the UK. Arthur Pelham will confirm everything. I've been cooperating for several days with Mr. Pelham and lawyers from the US Attorney's Office in New York and Washington. What you have in your folder is a last-ditch attempt by Harrelson to avoid prosecution himself."

"Do you want to explain that to me?"

"Yes."

While Tom talked, Williams made notes on a legal pad. When Tom mentioned that Harrelson sent him documents implicating Harold Addington in an embezzlement scheme, the DA slipped some papers from his folder.

"Do you recognize these?" he asked, sliding them across the table to Tom.

Tom flipped through the familiar documents. "Yes, this is exactly what he sent me."

Tom continued to lay out the sequence of events.

"Why didn't you tell me about the designated trust account?" Williams interrupted at one point. "I asked you several times for information about your father and Harold Addington and even served you with a subpoena."

"My knowledge didn't come all at once. It took time for me to unravel the connections. The documents I found in Elias's garage didn't surface until after we had the hearing in front of Judge Caldwell. Eventually Arthur Pelham took over. All I did toward the end was follow his orders based on instructions received from the federal prosecutors. The last step was wiring the money to Pelham's bank in Barbados. I did that a couple of days ago."

"What was Rose Addington's role in this?"

"Nothing except as executrix of her father's estate. At first I believed what Harrelson told me about Harold Addington and confronted her with the alleged facts. She didn't like it, of course, and part of the reason I kept digging was to satisfy her."

"Are you romantically involved with her?"

Tom raised his eyebrows. "Is that relevant?"

"Maybe, maybe not, but you'd ask the same question if you were sitting in my chair."

"Yes, but her plans are to return to Europe in the near future."

"And your plans?"

"I'm going to accept a job with Sweet and Becker, an Atlanta law firm that specializes in financial and commercial litigation. I'd considered staying in Bethel and hanging out a shingle, but I need to be in a big city to practice in the area of the law where I have real expertise."

"In the course of your law practice, have you seen different kinds of schemes people put together to misappropriate funds?" Williams asked.

"A few. Most securities litigation has to do with finger-pointing after deals fail, not outright theft."

"And you're pointing the finger at Owen Harrelson and this man named Nettles?"

"Only because it's the truth. Arthur Pelham is in Japan, but you can confirm everything I've told you in a fifteen-minute conversation with him."

"That might not be necessary." Williams reached for the papers he'd shown Tom. "If the US Attorney's Office is about to issue a warrant for Harrelson, his credibility as a witness in front of our grand jury will be shot."

"Arthur said that would most likely happen today. Is Harrelson still in Bethel?"

"I'm not sure, but I have his contact information. He testified early yesterday morning. He expressed concern that Ms. Addington might flee the country and wanted to get an indictment issued quickly. Who were you talking with at the US Attorney's Office?"

"Arthur never gave me a name."

"Okay." Williams nodded. "How can I get copies of the notes your father took and the memos prepared by Harold Addington?"

"They're in the desk in my father's office along with copies of the documents Harrelson gave you. The e-mail he sent me is stored in my laptop. There are other e-mails from Arthur but nothing that gives the kind of detail I'm providing now."

"Does Bernice Lawson know about this?"

"Not really. My father didn't mention it to her when he was working with Harold Addington and neither did I."

"She didn't know about the trust account?"

"No, she'll admit her bookkeeping skills aren't the best. My father always oversaw his trust accounts. When I found the empty folder with Addington's name on it shortly after I arrived in Bethel, I asked Bernice about it, and she couldn't help me."

Williams pressed his lips together for a moment. "Would you be willing to ride over to your father's office with me so I could see what you have?"

"Does that mean I can't stay at the jail?"

"Yeah." Williams smiled slightly.

"What about Rose? She didn't know I was contacting Harrelson and Nettles on behalf of the Feds to obtain additional information. She's got to be frantic."

"We'll sort that out as soon as we can. For now, I want to confirm what you're telling me."

"Okay."

"Wait here for a minute."

Williams left the interview room. Tom stared at the bare walls for a few moments, then closed his eyes. The initial shock had worn off as he talked. Looking back, it wasn't surprising that Harrelson would make a desperate move to escape prosecution. However, his gambit was too late. Tom's greatest concern was that Rose was alone in a jail cell unaware of what was going on.

Several minutes passed. Williams didn't return. Tom glanced down to check the time on his watch, but it had been confiscated in the booking area along with his other personal possessions. He rubbed the black ink that still smudged his fingertips. Once this was over, he would have a story to tell that would rival what had happened on the Ocoee. He began to pace back and forth in the windowless room. He tried to crack open the door, but a locking mechanism had triggered as soon as Williams left. Solitary confinement had a sharp psychological component. After less than an hour, he could feel its edge. He sat down, put his head on the desk, and began to pray. He mouthed a few words. Finally, the door opened and Williams returned.

"What took so long?" he asked.

"I had to make a few phone calls and decided it would be best to spend a few minutes with Ms. Addington," the DA said.

"How is she?" Tom asked quickly.

"Unlike you, she didn't have much to say. She refused to discuss anything without the presence of a barrister, as she calls it."

"She's got to be terrified."

"Actually, she didn't seem too surprised that we caught her."

"What?" Tom asked in shock.

"Just an impression." Williams shrugged his shoulders. "I also spoke with Noah Keller. He's in the process of executing a search warrant at your father's law office. I mentioned the documents in the desk and on your laptop. He went through everything in the desk and found the copy you made of the check taken from your father's pocket after he drowned and the deposit slip for the designated trust account."

"What about the memos from Harold Addington to my father?"

"Are you sure that's where you put them?"

"Yes, in the bottom drawer on the right."

"Noah didn't find anything," Williams replied, looking directly into Tom's eyes. "Also, there wasn't a laptop in sight. Are you sure you didn't put it in your car or take it to Elias's house?"

Tom jumped up from his seat. "There's been a burglary—"

"Hold it," Williams replied, motioning with his hand for Tom to sit down. "You gave a very convincing presentation, but there are incontrovertible facts that do not support your story. Everything I've uncovered indicates that you and Ms. Addington stole $1,750,000 from Pelham Financial and transferred it to an account in Barbados set up by her late father."

"Arthur Pelham will verify—"

"No, he won't," Williams interrupted him. "And Arthur Pelham isn't in Japan. He testified in front of the grand jury yesterday and verified everything Owen Harrelson said."

Tom's mouth dropped open. He slumped down in the chair. "Arthur gave me the wiring instructions for the money," he said numbly.

"What proof do you have of that?"

Tom held up his left hand. "He called me on his way to the airport in Washington, DC, and I wrote the wiring instructions on my hand because I didn't have anything else available."

Williams looked at Tom with pity. "That's quick thinking but not very probative. The grand jury had evidence that the money was deposited two days ago in an account set up by Harold Addington a few months before his death. I received confirmation from Clayton Loughton that you personally handed the wiring instructions to a bank officer. Once the money left the designated trust account, the embezzlement was complete."

Tom rubbed his temples. His head was starting to hurt. Williams put his hands on the table and leaned forward.

"Tom, you know I can't make a specific promise of leniency, but it looks to me like Ms. Addington tricked you into completing what her father started. She kept her distance so the evidence against her is circumstantial, not direct. In my view, you shouldn't take the lion's share of the blame and punishment for this. I've known and respected your family as long as I've been in Etowah County, but there's no way I can keep you from going to prison. However, if you help me get substantial jail time for Ms. Addington, it won't hurt your chances of getting out while you still have the ability to go for walks in the woods."

Tom couldn't believe what he was hearing. His head was pounding. "How would I connect Rose to this?"

Williams put his beefy hands together. "You plead guilty, then testify for the State when her case comes to trial. I'm sure the two of you had conversations that furthered the conspiracy. You already said she pushed you along. If she gave you any information that advanced the conspiracy, it would be sufficient to meet the requirements of the statute."

"All she had were the notes her father made about Pelham. I made a copy of those and kept them at the office. But now you say they're gone. Beyond that, this was my doing based on what Arthur told me. He lied to me from the first time we talked at the Parker-Baldwin house until our last phone conversation when he gave me the wiring instructions for transfer of the money."

"Is that your defense? Your word against Arthur Pelham's? How do you think that's going to play in front of an Etowah County jury?"

Tom set his jaw. "I guess we're going to have to find out."

"I'm not going to take that as a final answer," Williams said, standing up.

The DA picked up the folder, walked to the door, then stopped and turned around. "One last thing. I think your father figured out what Addington was doing and confronted him about it at Austin's Pond. I realize the way the two of them died casts suspicion on your father, but I don't believe that's the whole story."

Tom didn't respond. Williams opened the door.

"Officer Weldon!" the DA called out.

A middle-aged man with graying hair came into the interview room.

"Please show Mr. Crane where he can change clothes and take

him to the disciplinary cell. Because he's a lawyer, I don't want him mixing with the rest of the jail population. Segregate him during meals but provide extra exercise time outside and in the gym. He's not a high-security risk."

The DA left. Tom followed Weldon back to the booking area where he was handed an orange jumpsuit with "Etowah County Correctional Center" stenciled on the back. The officer handed him an orange plastic bag.

"Put your street clothes and shoes in here."

Tom slipped into the jumpsuit and stared at himself in the mirror. The ramifications of his arrest began to hit him in waves. There would be a front-page newspaper article in Bethel; the news would be picked up by the *Atlanta Journal-Constitution*; reporters from TV stations in Chattanooga and Atlanta would descend on the Etowah County jail; there would be a lot of false misinformation spewed across the Internet. He would be disbarred. There was a knock on the bathroom door.

"Let's go," the officer said.

Tom followed Weldon down a short hallway and through a solid metal door to another hallway.

"Is there an outside window in the disciplinary cell?" Tom asked.

"No, but you can see the guard station through the little opening in the door, not that there's much to watch. Smith spends most of his time staring at the monitors."

They reached the cell. The window in the door was a narrow slit. The officer entered a code on a number pad beside the door, and it clicked open.

"Lunch is in forty-five minutes," Weldon said. "Then you can go outside for an hour in the exercise yard."

"When can I make a phone call?"

"After you eat. There is a pay phone in the hallway near the booking area."

Not thinking of anything else that would prolong the conversation, Tom stepped into the cell. The door clicked behind him. There was a cot with a thin mattress on it to the right, a toilet without a seat against the rear wall, and a chair in front of a small bare table to the left. Tom sat down on the bed, which bowed beneath his weight. Places like this cell existed in countless communities across the country, but Tom never thought about the people who inhabited them. Now he was one of them.

He put his hurting head in his hands. One part of his brain was still trying to digest the magnitude of Arthur Pelham's betrayal. The other part was worried about Rose. Each problem towered over Tom like a high, unassailable wall. His analytical ability was worthless. He had no crevice of information that could provide a toehold toward escape from the abyss into which he'd fallen.

The cell door opened, and Officer Weldon handed him a tray of food and a paper cup that contained a dark-brown liquid.

"I'll be back for the tray in fifteen minutes," Weldon said, then closed the door.

Tom took a bite of a chicken salad sandwich. It tasted like rubber. He nibbled a few stale potato chips. Dessert was a dingy white pudding. Tom wasn't hungry. He sipped the drink. It was unsweetened tea. He was thirsty and drained the cup. The final swallow was bitter, and when he looked down, he saw bits of tea leaves.

Weldon returned, and Tom handed him the tray.

"You can make a phone call now."

They returned to the hallway near the booking area. An old-fashioned pay phone hung on the concrete wall. Scribbled on the wall beside the phone were phone numbers for two bail-bond companies and the number for Lamar Sponcler's office. If it hadn't been Saturday afternoon, Tom might have phoned the lawyer. Instead, he dialed Elias's number. The phone rang and rang. Elias didn't have an answering machine so Tom waited. Finally, the familiar voice answered.

"Hello."

"Elias, I'm at the jail. I've been arrested."

"I know. A couple of men from the sheriff's department left a few minutes ago," the old man said, his voice shaky. "They had a search warrant and wanted to go through the whole house. I got dizzy and had to lie down."

The ripples of agony had already begun.

chapter
THIRTY

T his doesn't make any sense," the old man said when Tom paused for a moment. "Everybody knows you wouldn't steal any money. There's got to be a misunderstanding."

"There is. And it started when I believed Arthur Pelham. It's a complicated story that I can't get into right now, but I need you to call Esther Addington. If they showed up with a search warrant at your house, the same thing probably happened at hers. Please let her know you talked to me, and I'm going to take care of it. Can you do that?"

"Yes, but what are you going to do?"

"I don't know." Tom rested his head against the wall for a moment. "Contact one of the local magistrates and find out if I can make bond. I was so upset after my arrest that I didn't ask Charlie Williams about it."

"Gary Abernathy is still the chief magistrate. I've known him for years."

"And he liked my father. He won't mind if you call him at home. The amount of the bond may be high. I don't have much in my checking account—"

"You can have all I have," Elias interrupted. "And I can put up this place as a property bond."

"I know you mean that," Tom replied softly. "But it's likely going to be more than we can pay. Also ask Abernathy about the amount of Rose's bond. Her mother should have the assets to get her out."

"How will I let you know?"

Tom hadn't thought about that simple but difficult logistical issue. "Uh, I'm sure they have visiting hours at some point today. You could drive to the jail and see me."

"I'll get on it as soon as my head clears."

"Thanks, Elias." Tom paused. "When you were praying in the night, did you ever suspect I might be in danger?"

"Yes, but it had to do with the Pelham family. My concern was with Tiffany."

Tom grunted. "You were half right."

"I'm sorry," Elias said. "I should have—"

"No," Tom interrupted. "That won't do any good."

Elias mumbled something Tom couldn't understand. All he caught was the old man saying, "Bye."

Tom hung up the phone. Officer Weldon was talking to Officer Johnson.

"Can I go to the exercise yard?" Tom asked.

"I'll take him," Johnson said. "The other prisoners have finished and are back in the cell blocks."

Johnson led Tom through a series of doors. The last one opened onto a rectangular 200-by-300-foot space. It was surrounded by a ten-foot fence topped with coiled razor wire. There was a basketball goal with a metal net at the far end of the yard.

"There he is!" called out a man in a group of a dozen or so standing outside the fence.

Several people raised cameras and began taking photos. Tom quickly stepped back into the hallway. "Take me back to my cell. I'm not going to perform like an animal in a cage."

"Suit yourself," Johnson replied. "Reporters have been swarming all over the place. I've never seen anything like it."

In his cell, Tom lay on his back in the bunk. The flimsy mattress sagged beneath him. He stared at the gray ceiling and mentally reviewed all that had happened since he discovered the existence of the designated trust account. He replayed his conversations with Owen Harrelson, Arthur Pelham, and Charlie Williams.

Looking back, he could see how skillfully Harrelson and Arthur played him. Because he trusted Arthur, he'd been at a terrible disadvantage. Now he saw no avenue of escape. He had no tape-recorded phone conversations, no incriminating e-mails, and no documents that would create doubt about the twisted lies presented to the grand jury. Every time he thought about Arthur Pelham, he remembered the older man offering to step in as a substitute father. Arthur's depraved hypocrisy knew no limits. How could someone he'd known and trusted his whole life do this to him?

Tom knew that the answer lay in the massive scope of fraud and corruption within the Pelham Financial empire. Tom's alleged embezzlement of $1,750,000 was a paltry sum. References in Harold Addington's memo to "island properties" and "insider loans" weren't future plans but present realities. Tom had ignored Addington's warnings. Now both he and Rose were suffering for it.

Tom thought about the photographers lurking outside the exercise yard. His life of normal, comfortable obscurity was gone forever. He began to pace back and forth in the cell. The flip-flops on his feet slapped against the cement floor. It was four strides from the back wall to the door and three from one side of the room to the other.

Tom tried to pray, but how could he expect that to work when someone as experienced as Elias had failed? The door buzzed. The sound echoed in the silence, and he spun around with a wide-eyed look on his face. It was Weldon.

"You have a visitor," he said. "Follow me."

Tom followed the guard into a room that contained three cubicles where prisoners could talk via phone to someone on the other side of a glass partition. Elias, wearing a coat and tie, was sitting in the nearest cubicle. Tom sat down. Elias, with great sadness in his eyes, looked like he'd aged five years in a single day. Tom clenched his jaw and picked up the phone. Elias did the same.

"Did you talk to Esther Addington?" Tom asked.

"Yes," Elias said in a tremulous voice. "Detectives from the sheriff's department searched her house."

"Do you know if they found anything?"

"She didn't say."

"Did they take anything from your house?"

"No. They went through every room."

"Including your study?"

"Yes."

"What about the garage?"

"I know two men went out there, but they couldn't have gone through everything. They were back in less than thirty minutes."

"Okay. Did you contact Gary Abernathy?"

"Yes, he didn't issue the arrest warrant for you and Rose, but he knew all about it." Elias glanced over his shoulder. "There are TV crews outside the jail and reporters in the lobby."

"Did anyone try to talk to you?"

"No."

"What did Abernathy tell you?"

"Your bond has been set at $1 million."

Tom's eyes widened. "What about Rose?"

"They're not going to set a bond because she's not a US citizen. Abernathy said Charlie Williams is afraid she'll leave the country and go someplace where they can't bring her back."

"Does Esther know that?"

"No, I didn't call her back."

Tom stared past Elias at the blank beige wall behind him. "I'm not sure any bondsman in Etowah County would vouch for a $1 million bond," Tom said. "And even if he could, it would cost at least $100,000 to get it. I guess I'm stuck here until I'm brought over for arraignment in front of Judge Caldwell."

He dreaded the look he knew would be on Judge Caldwell's face when Tom was escorted into the courtroom wearing handcuffs.

"What can I do to help you?" Elias asked, his eyes filling with tears.

"Take care of Rover," Tom said, forcing a slight smile. "And don't be so hard—"

The door behind Tom opened, and Johnson stepped inside. "Come with me," the officer said to Tom.

"But we're not finished," Tom protested.

"Yes, you are."

Elias had a bewildered look on his face as Tom left the room. Johnson took him to the booking area and told him to sit down. The officer reached under his desk and handed Tom an orange plastic bag. It contained Tom's personal belongings.

"You can change in there." The officer motioned to the nearby bathroom.

"Why do I need to put on my regular clothes?"

"You've been bonded out."

Tom stared at the guard for a moment without moving.

"Someone posted your bond," the guard repeated.

"The bond was $1 million," Tom replied in shock.

"I know," Johnson replied, shaking his head. "I've been working for the sheriff's department twenty-one years. It's the largest one I've ever seen anyone make. You must have some rich friends who care a lot about you."

After Tom dressed, Johnson took him down a different hallway. They passed through a pair of secure doors and entered the area for the administrative offices. Since it was Saturday, only a couple of people were working. They stared at Tom as he walked past.

"This is as far as I go," Johnson said, motioning to a regular door. "They're in there."

Tom entered a small room that contained a rectangular table and three plastic chairs. Standing by the table was an unfamiliar man in a rumpled suit with a briefcase in his hand. Beside him was Hal Millsap, who stepped forward and grabbed Tom's hand.

"Tom, this is Ken Grant. He's a bail bondsman from Chattanooga. I've made arrangements for him to sign your bond."

"Who paid the bond fee?"

"Several people chipped in, and I called Mr. Grant," Hal replied. "He agreed to come down immediately."

"Who chipped in?" Tom persisted.

"We'll discuss that later."

The bondsman put his briefcase on the table. "Mr. Crane, I have some papers for you to sign. Since you're a lawyer, I'm sure there's no need to explain them to you."

Tom sat down at the table.

"Sign here," Grant said, pushing several sheets of paper in front of Tom. "You're agreeing to be jointly liable on the bond and understand the consequences should you fail to appear in court and a bench warrant for your arrest be issued by the judge. Do you have any questions?"

"No," Tom said as he quickly scanned the paperwork.

"Your arraignment is set for next Friday at 9:00 a.m. in front of Judge Caldwell. Have you contacted an attorney to represent you?"

"Not yet."

Tom signed the papers and Grant scooped them up and returned them to his briefcase. "Thanks for the business. I'll be on my way."

Grant left Tom and Hal alone in the room.

As soon as the door closed, Hal spoke. "Don't try to cross-examine me. I've been running around like a crazy man since I found out you were arrested, and I'm sworn not to reveal the names of the people who contributed money to get you out."

Tom looked at his watch. It had been eight hours since he'd been brought to the jail.

"How did you get all this put together on a Saturday?"

"I'll answer that because it's a mundane question, but there are quite a few people who don't want to see you spend the night in jail. Once Mr. Grant knew I had the money, he was thrilled to drive to Bethel to get it."

"The bond fee would be at least $100,000. That money is gone."

"True, but if you hadn't jerked me out of the river, I would be permanently on vacation from planet Earth. Organizing the effort to get you out was the least I could do."

"You've got to—"

Hal held up his hand. "Please, I'm not answering that kind of question."

"You know the charges against me?"

"Yes, you allegedly stole money from Pelham Financial, but there are people who don't believe that's possible."

"When word gets around that you've helped me get out, you'll lose your job."

Hal gave him a grim smile. "When I used to go to Sunday school, I remember the teacher saying something about counting the cost before building a house. That's what I did, and it's too late to back out now. If I lose my job, I'll have to find another one. I've already answered more questions than I intended to." Hal pointed toward the door. "There are reporters outside hoping for a crack at you. Unless you want to wade through a sea of microphones and cameras, I made arrangements for you to sneak out a different way."

"I don't have anything to say to the media."

"Then follow me."

Hal led the way into the hallway Tom had just left.

"I was meeting with Elias in the visitation room when a guard pulled me out and brought me here," Tom said. "If he's still here, he could give me a ride. I need to pick up my car. It's at the parking lot for the trail up to the painted rock."

"Let Elias leave without you. I was outside when he arrived, and no one seemed to notice him. They'll figure out soon enough that you've been staying with him. For now, let me get you away from here. I can take you to your car. From there, you're on your own."

Hal stuck his head in a doorway. "Bobby, we'd like to go out the back way."

A young deputy sheriff joined them and unlocked a metal door with a key. It opened into a deserted kitchen area. They walked through the kitchen to a double door that the deputy unlocked with another key. Beyond the door was a loading dock. Hal's truck was backed up to the dock.

"Thanks," Hal said to the deputy. "I'll get you four tickets to the Georgia-Auburn game."

"Thanks, Hal. My father-in-law won't believe it when I tell him we can go."

The deputy closed the doors behind Hal and Tom.

"The tint on these windows is so thick it's barely legal," Hal said, "but you should probably sit on the floor until we're away from here."

Tom pulled up his knees so he could squeeze into the floorboard space. Hal drove away from the dock.

"Let's see," he said after he made a right-hand turn. "I'll describe the scene for you. There are three TV trucks with their antennas sticking up in the air. It looks like the evening news is going to have to run without a live shot of the accused."

"The sheriff's department will release my mug shot," Tom replied from his hiding place. "Or they'll use a photo of when I stuck my head out the door into the exercise yard for a few seconds."

"I'd recommend one of the pictures from the newspaper article about you saving my life," Hal replied. "I'm sure the reporters will get statements from Charlie Williams and someone at Pelham to spice it up."

"Williams told me Arthur Pelham and Owen Harrelson are in town."

"Maybe. I'm not on the distribution list for Mr. Pelham's daily itinerary, and nobody wants to see Harrelson coming. He only pays a visit when someone is in trouble."

The truck stopped.

"We're at the stoplight at the intersection of Cornwell and Dantszler Streets," Hal said. "In a couple of blocks, I think it will be safe for you to sit up. I'd hate to get stopped by the police and get a ticket because you're not wearing a seat belt."

The truck moved forward.

"How can I thank the people who contributed toward my bond if I don't know who they are?" Tom asked.

"I'll do that for you."

They drove a bit farther.

"Okay," Hal said, "the coast is clear."

Tom hoisted himself onto the passenger seat of the truck. They were on the outskirts of town. They passed a house with a light on in the kitchen. Inside, Tom could see a family preparing to sit down for supper. He was struck by how normal everything looked outside the truck's windows. Hal turned onto the highway, and the truck picked up speed. Tom suddenly felt very tired. He leaned his head back until it touched the headrest and closed his eyes. He felt the truck go around several corners.

"Here we are," Hal said as he turned into the gravel parking lot. "Your car is still here."

Tom opened his eyes. In the fading light he could see a layer of dust covering his vehicle. "I don't have words to tell you—"

"Then don't mess up by trying."

"But I appreciate you believing in me."

"I'm not sure what happened and what didn't, but I couldn't stand the thought of you sitting in a jail cell."

"Somehow I'll pay back the bond fee."

"That would be nice, but it's not what you need to be thinking about. Let me know if there's anything I can do for you."

Tom shook Hal's hand and got out of the truck. By the time Tom unlocked the door of his car, Hal had left the parking area in a cloud of red dust. Tom followed at a slower pace. He wasn't sure exactly where he should go. Fatigue beckoned him toward Elias's house, but he was worried he might encounter reporters lurking at the end of the driveway.

Instead of going home, Tom retraced the route to Bethel.

He drove to his father's office. The parking spaces in front of the building were empty. Yellow police tape was stretched across the front door. Tom drove around the corner and parked at the back of the building. He put on the camouflage cap Elias gave him and pulled it down over his eyes. Walking around the corner to the office, he slipped under the police tape and inspected the lock on the door. There was no sign of forced entry. He went inside but didn't turn on the light in the reception area. Going directly into his father's office, he closed the door and turned on the lights.

Other than the missing laptop computer, everything seemed to be in its place; however, when he opened the desk drawers all the information and documents related to the designated trust account were missing. The burglars knew what they were after. The thought that someone had violated the privacy of the office made his skin crawl. Not sure if he'd locked the front door behind him, Tom turned out the light, returned to the reception area, and flipped the lock shut. He put his hand to the glass door and peered outside.

It was dark. The street was deserted. Tom went back into his father's office and sat behind the desk. The Bible he'd been reading rested on top of a legal pad on which he'd written his thoughts and prayers. There was no indication anyone had disturbed them. Neither did Tom. If he went to prison, he'd have plenty of time to read the Bible—if he wanted to.

A loud banging noise startled him, and he spun around. A face was pressed against the glass door.

chapter
THIRTY-ONE

It was Noah Keller.

The dark-haired detective held up his badge and motioned for Tom to open the door. Tom unlocked the door and cracked it open.

"You can't be in here," the detective said. "This is a crime scene."

"And it's my office," Tom replied.

"Is your name on the lease?"

"No, but I'm here as executor of my father's estate. There was a burglary, and I have a right to find out what was taken."

Keller scowled. "I'm not going to argue with you, Mr. Crane. Either leave now or I'm going to take you back to the jail."

Tom stepped outside and locked the door.

"And I'll take that key," Keller said.

All fight drained out of him, Tom placed the key in the detective's hand.

"This will be tagged and placed in the evidence locker at the jail. You'll receive a receipt in the mail within the next five to seven business days."

346

Tom walked around the corner to his car. When he drove past the office, Keller was snooping around in the reception area.

The exhaustion Tom felt earlier returned, and by the time he reached the end of Elias's driveway his eyelids were heavy. Fortunately, no posse of reporters was camped out near the mailbox. He parked beneath the large oak tree and trudged up the steps onto the porch. The front door was locked, a sure sign Elias had been bothered by news seekers. Tom unlocked the door and went inside. Rover was lying on his side in the front room. Elias wasn't in sight. The dog woofed in greeting and trotted over to Tom. A glob of drool fell out of the dog's mouth onto the floor. The sight made Tom long for the days when cleaning up Rover's slobber was one of the bigger hassles he faced. The light was on in Elias's study. The door opened, and the old man came out. He narrowed his eyes and gave Tom a strange look.

"Are you Tom's angel?" he asked.

"Uh, no."

Elias brushed his hand across his eyes and stared at Tom again. "How did you get out of jail?"

"Hal Millsap and an unknown group of friends put together the money to pay a bondsman in Chattanooga. I've been out since shortly after you came to visit."

"Where have you been?"

Tom told Elias about his encounter with Noah Keller.

"I have a spare key to the office," Elias said. "It's on the hook in the kitchen."

"That's not necessary. I'm not sure what I expected to find, but I don't want to go back and risk getting thrown back in jail."

"When you left the visitation room, I had no idea what was going to happen to you, so I came home to pray," Elias said.

"We're past the point of that doing any good."

Elias didn't argue.

"Did any reporters try to talk to you?" Tom asked.

"Around suppertime a young man and a young woman knocked on the door and said they were from Atlanta."

"What did they ask you?" he asked.

"Not much after I quoted a few verses for them about how the Lord detests it when the innocent are deprived of justice and the guilty go free. There are several passages like that in Proverbs."

"Did they take any pictures?"

"Not of me. The young man had a camera and took photographs of the house. After they left, I locked the door so I wouldn't be bothered."

"I'm sorry for the embarrassment this is causing you—" Tom began.

"My reputation means nothing." Elias sighed. "All that matters is what the Lord has done in your life, and I refuse to let the devil steal that happiness from me. The troubles of this life are temporary; the joy that awaits will never end. Please don't—"

"Not now, Elias," Tom said. "After what's happened I can't hear that kind of talk. I'm going to bed."

Upstairs, Tom took a shower to wash away the smell of the jail that lingered in his nostrils, brushed his teeth, and lay down to sleep.

He woke up at 3:00 a.m. and sat up straight in bed. The events of the day crashed down on him. Slipping out of bed, he went downstairs to the kitchen. There was no light shining from beneath the study door. Tom was glad that Elias had decided to go to sleep. He drank a glass of water. He thought about the nasty tea served at the jail. The sweet well water had never tasted so good.

When he came out of the kitchen, Tom rested his hand on the stair railing for a moment. A loud cry made him jump.

"You can't have him!" Elias called out from the study.

Tom walked softly over to the study. The light was still off.

"You can't have him!" the old man cried out again. "I'm striking six times against the ground! It is the arrow of the Lord's victory!"

Tom heard Elias sharply clap his hands together six times. A couple of minutes passed in silence. Tom turned away. As he crept up the stairs, the skin on the back of his neck tingled. He stopped at the top of the stairs and listened again. Nothing.

———

Tom woke to the smell of bacon. As soon as he entered the kitchen, Elias handed him a cup of coffee. Thick pieces of homemade bread were soaking in an egg batter. Elias turned on the burner beneath an iron skillet.

"How does French toast sound?" he asked.

"A lot better than the breakfast they're probably serving at the jail."

Tom sat at the kitchen table and took a sip of coffee. Elias dropped a pat of butter into the skillet.

"What were you doing last night?" Tom asked.

"Did I wake you up?" Elias didn't turn around.

"No, I heard you when I came downstairs to drink a glass of water."

"Trying to do my part."

"The thing about the arrows. What's that all about?"

"It's in the Bible," Elias responded with his back still turned to Tom. "If you want to find it you can."

Surprised by Elias's reluctance to talk about religion, Tom took another sip of coffee. After a good night's sleep he felt more like fighting.

"I need to speak with Esther Addington," he said.

Elias pointed to a phone number stuck to the refrigerator with a magnet that advertised a used-car lot. "She gave me a private number when we talked yesterday. She's not answering the house phone. Her other children will be coming in as soon as they can make arrangements to fly over from Britain."

"If Esther hires me as Rose's lawyer, I can use that as an excuse to meet with her at the jail."

"Is that possible?"

"Yes, but I'm not sure Charlie Williams will let me do it without a court order."

Elias flipped over a piece of toast and dropped another pat of butter in the skillet. "But would you actually represent her?"

"No, she'll need a lawyer when we go to court, but it would be a way to talk to her now. Rose doesn't know I was following Arthur Pelham's instructions and needs the background information. Williams wanted me to testify against Rose and make it look like she was the instigator of the theft." Tom paused. "He'll probably try the same approach with her and try to get Rose to testify against me."

Elias finished cooking the French toast and bacon. He placed a little pitcher of heated maple syrup and a stick of softened butter on the table. Rover walked over to the table with his nose in the air.

"He smells the bacon," Elias said.

"Sit," Tom said to the dog, who flopped down on the floor.

Elias prayed a blessing over the food and added a few sentences of request that God would direct Tom's path. Tom appreciated Elias's sincerity but doubted the words reached further than the smell of the bacon.

"Who's going to be your lawyer?" Elias asked.

"I thought about that when I was sitting in the jail cell. I'm not sure what to do. No local defense lawyer is sophisticated enough to take on this type of case, and it will cost $200,000 to hire a good white-collar-crime lawyer in Atlanta."

"Two hundred thousand dollars?" Elias shook his head.

Tom ate the last bite of French toast. "I can't solve that today. In an hour or so I'm going to call Esther and start there."

"And I'm going to Rocky River Church," Elias said.

"Are you sure you want to face all the stares and questions?" Tom asked in surprise.

"Rather from people I know than strangers. Some of the church folks will pray for you."

Tom didn't respond.

Tom went upstairs after breakfast and turned on his cell phone. There were more than fifty new messages. Most of them were from people he knew in Atlanta who learned about his arrest from a brief TV news report. The callers sounded understandably awkward. There was also a succinct call from Nate Becker withdrawing the job offer for "reasons I'm sure you understand." It was another blow that underlined the unrelenting horror of what was happening.

Two reporters offered a "fair chance to present his side" if he granted "exclusive access." Tom wondered how they got his number and deleted those calls. Toward the end of the messages a familiar, slightly shrill voice came on the line. It was Clarice, who'd obviously been crying. He listened to her message twice.

"Tom, no matter what I read in the paper or see on TV, I'll never believe you've done anything dishonest," she said. "I'm very, very sorry this has happened. You're a good man and don't deserve this. If you ever need to talk to someone, call me. I mean it."

Clarice's message broke down the spartan defenses Tom had built to help him survive the previous twenty-four hours. A tear stung the corner of his eye as he pressed the button to save her message. A few minutes later he phoned Esther Addington.

"May I come over?" he asked.

"Yes."

"Are there any reporters there?"

"Not since last night. They really wanted to see Rose, but she's–" Esther stopped.

"I'm on my way," Tom said.

The street in front of the Addington home was Sunday morning quiet. Tom rang the doorbell and waited. It took a couple of minutes to open. Esther Addington looked very feeble.

"Come in," she said.

She led the way into the living room. The house was quiet and deserted. She sat on a sofa. Tom sat in a side chair. He put his hands together in front of him.

"Let me tell you everything I know," he said.

Esther listened impassively while he laid out the events of the past weeks except for the autopsy information. Esther shook her head.

"That sounds like Harold," she said.

"Why?"

"About five years ago he got caught up in a scandal at a bank where he was working as a consultant. His main contact at the bank was a man whose wife also had MS and wanted to take her overseas for experimental treatment not covered by the government health plan. The man came up with a scheme to borrow money on a supposedly temporary basis. When the man was caught he said Harold was in on it too. Eventually Harold was cleared; however, his contract with the bank was terminated. It was a stressful time, but God used it to bring Harold back to faith."

"Rose told me that last part, but I didn't know the background. What was the name of the bank?"

Esther repeated the name of the bank in the UK where George Nettles worked.

"Did you have any accounts there?" Tom asked.

"Yes."

Tom nodded. "That's why Nettles and Harrelson would have documents with Harold's signature on them."

"Yes, we closed the accounts when Harold came to work for Pelham Financial." Esther paused. "Late last year Harold received a phone call one night from the man whose wife was sick. He'd gotten out of prison and wanted Harold to know it."

"What was his name?"

"Brigham was his last name. I can't remember his first name."

"Did he threaten your husband?"

"If he did, Harold didn't tell me."

"Did you ask?"

Esther managed a wan smile. "You never met Harold. We didn't have a marriage in which the husband tells everything to the wife. When I saw that closed look on his face, I knew it was pointless to try to break through."

"Have you tried to visit Rose at the jail?"

"I was going to go today."

"Let me take you."

"Why would you want to go back?"

Tom leaned forward. "I need to talk to Rose and tell her what I've shared with you. The best way to do that would be for you to hire me as her lawyer. It would just be temporary, of course, but it would give me the right to talk to her without being overheard and fill her in on information she doesn't know. After that I can give you the names of some good lawyers who could actually represent her."

Tom watched while Esther considered his proposal.

"All right." Esther sighed. "I don't see how that would hurt anything. It will take me a few minutes to get ready."

Tom waited in the living room. At least the Addington family had enough money to hire Rose a competent attorney, and without his cooperation it would be hard to prove she was a coconspirator in a crime. The phony evidence prepared by Owen Harrelson implicated Harold, not her, and contrary to Charlie Williams's blustering, she hadn't done anything that would constitute acts in furtherance of a conspiracy. Tom wired the money into a bank account to which she had no access. But right now, he knew none of that would comfort Esther Addington, and he wasn't sure how Rose would receive it.

Esther returned to the room. "I'm ready."

They passed several downtown churches on the way to the jail. The continuation of ordinary life by the citizens of Etowah County seemed surreal to Tom.

"I wish Rose and I were going to church this morning," Esther said, staring out the window as people walked up the sidewalk to the entrance of a redbrick church with a tall white steeple.

They arrived at the jail. There were no TV trucks in the parking lot.

"Identify yourself to the officer on duty and tell him you've hired me to represent Rose. I'll do the rest."

Esther nodded. They entered the lobby. A young female deputy was sitting behind a glass partition reading a book. When she looked up and saw Tom, her mouth dropped open.

"What are you doing here?" she asked.

Tom nudged Esther.

"I'm Esther Addington, and I've hired Mr. Crane to represent my daughter."

Tom slid one of his business cards from Barnes, McGraw, and Crowther beneath an opening in the glass.

"And I'd like to see my client," he said. "Please have her brought up to one of the interview rooms."

"Just a minute," the deputy responded, staring at Tom's card. "I'll have to check on that."

The woman disappeared through a door. Tom calculated the chance of receiving a favorable response to his request at less than twenty-five percent.

"What's going to happen now?" Esther asked.

"It depends on who she talks to."

Several minutes passed. When the deputy returned, she was accompanied by an officer about Tom's age. He opened the door for the cubicle and came into the lobby. His name badge read "David Galloway, Assistant Chief Deputy." Galloway and Tom had played together on the same high school football team.

"Tom," Galloway said, extending his hand. "I'm sorry about what's happened. Between you and me, there are folks in the sheriff's department who don't like the way this has been handled. Everybody knows your family, and this just doesn't add up."

"They're right."

Tom introduced Galloway to Esther.

"I know you're a lawyer," Galloway continued, "but under the circumstances you're going to have to tell me a way I can let you meet with Rose Addington without getting into a lot of trouble."

Tom thought for a moment. "Call Judge Caldwell and ask him."

Galloway's eyes opened wide. "Are you serious? Call the judge at home on a Sunday morning?"

"He's the one who will eventually decide if I can talk to Rose. I may as well find out now."

"I don't have his cell phone number."

"I do."

Tom took out his phone, found the number, and showed it to the officer. Galloway pressed his lips together.

"He's probably at church," Tom continued. "But it would mean a lot to me if you'd try."

"The worst thing he can do is yell at me." Galloway shrugged. "And if I were in your shoes, I'd want an old teammate to help if he could."

Galloway left. On an issue like this, without any specific rules that applied, Nathan Caldwell was the kind of judge who didn't need to hear from the lawyers. He would do what he wanted to do. When Galloway returned, the officer's face was impassive. Tom's heart sank.

"You can meet with her," Galloway said.

"You talked to the judge?" Tom asked.

"Yes. I told him what you wanted to do. He said if anyone asked me about it to have them contact him on Monday."

"Thanks." Tom turned to Esther. "Wait here. I'll ask the guard on duty to take Rose to the visitation area as soon as we're finished."

Tom followed Galloway through a metal door. They turned

right into the much smaller women's area of the jail. There was a single interview room.

"Wait here, and I'll have her brought up," Galloway said. "One of the guards will take you back to the front when you're finished."

Tom's heart beat faster as he waited. Rose entered the hallway wearing a smaller version of the orange jumpsuit. She looked at him with a steely gaze. The female guard left them facing each other.

"We can talk in here," Tom said, motioning toward the interview room.

"About what?" Rose asked, not moving.

"Everything. After we've talked, you can see your mother in the visitation room. I gave her a ride to the jail."

"I want to see her now. I have nothing to say to you."

"But I have plenty to say to you. Please, let's go in here so we can talk in private."

Rose slowly walked into the interview room while Tom held the door for her.

"Why aren't you in jail?" she asked as she sat down.

"Someone posted my bond, and I got out last night."

"I don't have a bond."

"I know. It's because you're considered a greater flight risk as a non-US citizen."

"How did you get in here to talk to me?"

"Your mother hired me to be your lawyer. It's a—"

"What?!" Rose exploded. "That's the most outrageous—"

"It's just a way for me to meet with you," Tom said, holding his hands out in front of him. "I'm going to help your mother find a lawyer who can actually represent you. I need to tell you why we were arrested."

Rose sat with her jaw clenched. Tom quickly explained what had happened with Owen Harrelson and Arthur Pelham.

"I got trapped, and you had nothing to do with any of this. That's what I'll tell your lawyer, and I'll work with him any way I can to get you out of this."

"Is there anything else you need to tell me?" Rose asked.

"About what?"

"Our fathers and how they died."

Tom swallowed. "I'm not sure what you mean."

"I think you know exactly what I mean."

"The autopsy?"

Rose's eyes filled with tears that she angrily wiped away. She stood to her feet. "How could you deceive me about that?"

"I didn't deceive you. Charlie Williams wasn't sure what to make of–"

"That's not what he told me," Rose said, cutting him off. "I saw the autopsy results. My papa was trying to expose a multimillion-dollar theft by people at Pelham and trusted your father with the information. The money–"

"I know how it looks, but–"

"Don't interrupt me! The money transferred to your father's trust account was going to prove what was going on, but once your father got control of it, he decided to kill my father and keep it for himself."

"That's not true."

"Stop lying to me! Williams showed me the check your father wrote to himself!"

"Let me explain. That check doesn't mean–" Tom protested.

"No," she replied, spinning around. "Listening to you is one mistake I'm never going to make again! Leave now and stay away from my mother."

Rose jerked open the door. "I don't want to talk to this man anymore!" she shouted down the hallway. "Get him out of here. He's not my barrister!"

chapter
THIRTY-TWO

Rose ran down the hallway toward a female guard, who opened a metal door. The door slammed shut. Tom stared down the hallway for a moment, then slowly walked away. A guard in the booking area for the female prisoners pressed a button so he could leave. Esther Addington was waiting for him in the lobby.

"How is Rose?" she asked anxiously.

"Upset with me. She doesn't want me to have any contact with you."

"Why?"

There was no use keeping silent. Tom told Esther about the results of the autopsy. The older woman's face, already pale, became more ashen.

"I know how it looks," he said, "but there has to be an explanation."

"Rose is right," Esther replied in a trembling voice. "I'll make other arrangements to get home."

"There's a taxi service on Oakdale Street. Someone from the jail can call and—"

"I'm quite capable of taking care of myself."

Tom nodded glumly and left the jail. Getting in his car, he leaned his head against the back of the seat. The encounter with Rose had drained every bit of fight from him. He closed his eyes and tried to imagine his life twenty-four hours earlier. It wasn't possible. He was being pulled apart on a rack, and his future would be nothing except humiliation and ever-increasing pain. Then an idea he'd never thought would cross his mind appeared with a sudden and surprising appeal.

Tom could leave this life for the next. It would be better for him. Better for everyone.

There was an old deer rifle in a gun case beneath the bed in the bedroom where his father slept when he moved in with Elias. The rifle fired bullets that were powerful enough to kill a buck two hundred yards away. From close range, it would be an instantaneous and painless death. Tom saw himself kneeling in Elias's study for a final prayer, then taking the gun outside to a spot behind the garage. He could sit down, lean against the wall, place the barrel of the rifle beneath his chin, and pull the trigger. The key to the gun case was in a small envelope in his father's desk at the office.

He started the car's engine and drove to the office. On the way he passed two downtown churches that were now disgorging the morning's worshippers. No one seemed to recognize his car. Adjacent to the church his parents attended was the cemetery where they were buried along with more than a score of Crane relatives. Elias owned a couple of plots in the cemetery. His uncle only needed one for himself and would certainly allow Tom's body to be buried in the other.

Tom didn't bother trying to hide his car. He parked directly in front of the office, got out, ripped off the police tape, and fumbled for his key. It wasn't there. He'd not replaced the key confiscated by Detective Keller.

Tom calmly returned to his car, opened the trunk, and took out the lug wrench. Glancing around to make sure the side street was empty, he carefully aimed the wrench at a spot near the lock and smashed the glass. He reached inside and flipped the lock. He went straight to the desk. The key for the gun case was still in the envelope in the bottom left drawer of the desk. He slipped it into his pocket and left. Now the police couldn't deny there had been a break-in.

A strange peace descended on Tom as he drove to Elias's house. He'd passed into the eye of the storm, a place of calm where he could act dispassionately before the swirling insanity of everything else that was going on around him returned on Monday morning. Elias's car was gone. Tom parked beneath the large oak tree and went into the house. Rover was lying on his side in the front room. He raised his head when Tom passed, then rolled over. The dog would be happier with Elias than he had been with Tom.

Tom headed down the hallway to his father's old bedroom. He pulled the gun case out from beneath the bed and turned the key in the lock. The gun lay nestled in gray foam padding along with two boxes of ammunition. Tom took five bullets from an ammunition box and loaded one of them in the rifle. He slipped the other bullets in his pocket. The smooth wood of the rifle felt cool against his hands. He ignored Rover as he passed through the front room but then stopped at the front door. When he'd played out this scenario in his car outside the jail, he'd spent a few moments in Elias's study.

Tom checked his watch. There was plenty of time before Elias might return from church. He went into the study and leaned the rifle against the wall. Kneeling in front of the chair, he bowed his head and quickly asked God to forgive him for all the stupid mistakes he'd made in his life. Suicide was probably a sin too; however, the overwhelming problems he would experience if he continued to live, and the difficulties he would bring to others, made putting an end to life a reasonable option. Once gone, he could do no more wrong. Elias's Bible was lying on the seat of the chair. Turning to the concordance in the back, Tom looked up the word *death*. A portion of a verse in 1 Corinthians 15 caught his eye: "O death, where is your sting?" He closed the Bible. That was it. Death no longer had the ability to hurt him. Its sting was gone. He had nothing to fear.

Grabbing the gun, Tom resolutely left the house. It was a slightly overcast day. He glanced up at the sky and wondered what it would look like from heaven's perspective. Behind the garage Elias had parked a rusty utility trailer. The tires on the trailer were flat and rotting off the rims. Tom sat on the ground next to the trailer. He raised the gun to his shoulder and pointed it across the open field. He flipped off the safety, aimed at a stump about fifty yards away, and pulled the trigger. A tiny cloud of dust sprouted beside the stump. The gun worked. And unlike the stump, Tom wouldn't miss his next target. He inserted another bullet into the chamber and positioned the gun so the muzzle rested against the bottom of his chin. He had to fully extend his arms to press his thumb against the trigger yet keep the gun steady. He closed his eyes for a final prayer.

"Tom!" a female voice called out. "Are you in there?"

Tom opened his eyes, lowered the gun, and crawled a few feet so he could peek around the corner.

It was Tiffany Pelham.

She was standing on the front porch looking in the windows of the house. Tom leaned back against the garage and repositioned the gun. He hesitated. If he pulled the trigger now, Tiffany would be the one to find him. The high-powered rifle would be effective but messy. Leaning the rifle against the back of the garage, Tom walked around the corner of the building.

"I'm over here!" he called out.

Tiffany saw him and ran down the front steps and across the yard. She didn't stop until she reached him, threw her arms around him, buried her head in his shoulder, and cried. Tom, his arms hanging limply at his sides, stared past her head toward the driveway.

"What are you doing here?" he asked when her sobs stopped for a moment.

Tiffany's crying continued without an answer. There was nothing to do but wait. Finally she pulled back, sniffled, and rubbed her eyes.

"Where can we talk?" she asked.

"Uh, right here."

Tiffany glanced over her shoulder. "No, it has to be someplace private."

"There's no place more private than this. Elias is at church."

"No, but I don't want Elias walking in on us while I'm talking."

"Where do you want to go?"

Tiffany looked in Tom's eyes. "Austin's Pond."

"Austin's Pond? Why there?"

"Can we go there?" Tiffany ignored his question. "We'll both need to drive. I can't leave my car here."

"Okay," Tom replied reluctantly.

Leaving the gun behind the garage, Tom went into the house to get his car keys and wallet. As he walked, he quickly checked his commitment to carry through with his plan to kill himself. Freeing Tiffany from her attachment to him would be another reason to cut his ties with Earth. When he returned to the front yard, Tiffany was already in her car. She lowered the window.

"You lead. I'll follow."

On the way to the pond, Tom kept a close eye on Tiffany in the rearview mirror. That she still loved him despite the criminal charges showed the depth of her fantasy. He would have to be as harsh as possible with her at the pond. Her final memory of him, if not bloody, needed to end any chance that she could imagine them living happily ever after. He turned onto the dirt road that led directly to the pond. He reached the barn and let the car slowly roll to a stop. Tiffany pulled in beside him.

"Let's sit at the picnic table," Tiffany said.

They walked toward the concrete table.

"It'll be better if I say a few things first," Tom began. "There's no way—"

"Wait. Not yet."

They reached the table. Tom sat on the bench in the spot where he'd wept over the loss of his parents. Tiffany stood in front of him, her lower lip quivering.

"Tiffany, this is going to be hard enough without you saying things that are going to embarrass you after you hear from me. You've got to realize—"

"Stop!" Tiffany put her fist to her lips for a second, then pointed toward the far end of the pond.

"What?" Tom asked, mystified.

"Arthur had your father and Harold Addington killed!" Tiffany buried her face in her hands.

A sick, sour feeling hit Tom in his stomach.

"I heard him talking about it two nights ago at the barn. He didn't know I was checking on a horse in one of the stalls, and he came in with two of his security guys. He told them he'd testified earlier in the day in front of the grand jury, and that you and Rose Addington were going to be arrested. However, if going to jail didn't take care of the problem, it would be necessary to do to you what they did to your father and Harold Addington. One of the men argued with Arthur and told him two more deaths would bring down too much suspicion from the police. Arthur got mad and told him there might not be any other option. At that point they walked away from the stall. I didn't hear anything else that was said."

Stunned, Tom didn't respond.

"Rick and I have suspected something wasn't right with Arthur's business for years," Tiffany said, "but I had no idea it involved murder."

"Does Rick know about this conversation?" Tom managed.

"No."

"And you're sure about what you heard?"

"Yes." Tiffany covered her face with her hands again for a moment. "What are you going to do? I can't stand the thought of you getting locked up in jail."

Tom eyed her suspiciously. He'd been deceived so many times the past few weeks he wasn't sure who and what to believe. Tiffany might be exaggerating something she heard in an effort to drive him toward her. But why she would still want him made no sense at all.

"If what you're saying is true, you'll have to tell it to the police," he said.

"If?" Tiffany asked sharply. "Do you think I'm making this up?"

Tom spoke slowly. "What Arthur is doing makes me believe anything is possible."

"And if Arthur finds out I overheard—" She stopped.

Tom closed his eyes and rubbed his temples. He was completely confused. A moment later he felt Tiffany's fingers gently touching the back of his neck and jerked his head up. Tiffany pulled away.

"What are you doing?" he asked.

"I feel so terrible for you."

"That won't help. Do you know the names of the bodyguards?"

"Jeff Scarboro and Mitt Crusan. Scarboro is over all the other security guys, but Crusan is the one who scares me the most."

Tom couldn't shake the thought that something about Tiffany's story didn't add up.

"Trying to prove something like this is very tough," he said, shaking his head.

"I heard the words with my own ears. What else is needed?"

"There aren't any details."

"I don't have any doubts." Tiffany wrung her hands. "How am I going to stand being in the same room with Arthur? He's going to know something is wrong."

Tom didn't answer. Tiffany stepped closer.

"What if we got in the car and never came back?" she said. "I've got loads of money in an overseas bank account. All we have to do is get out of the country. There are still places that don't send Americans back to the US. Isn't Venezuela one of them?"

"No," Tom said, standing up. "We'd be caught and you'd end up in prison too."

"Being separated from you is going to be worse than prison." Tiffany grabbed his arm.

Tom jerked his arm free. "We need to get out of here before anyone knows you came to see me."

Tom started jogging toward his car. Tiffany struggled to keep up.

"What are you going to do?" she asked.

"I'm not sure, but you need to forget about me. Forever."

"I can't help how I feel," she called after him.

Tom reached his car first and got in without saying anything else. Tiffany mouthed words outside his window and pleaded with her hands as he put the car in reverse. He spun the tires in the dirt as he turned around and drove away.

Tom had no doubt that Arthur Pelham was a thief, and the financier might be a murderer, but Tom couldn't rely on Tiffany to prove anything. Her story could easily be part of a plan to get him to run away with her. But more important, nothing Tiffany said convinced Tom that he should continue to live.

When he reached Elias's house, the old man's car was in its usual spot beside the garage. Tom got out, quietly shut the car door, and returned to the spot where he'd left the deer rifle.

It was gone.

Looking up at the sky in despair, he slowly walked toward the house and up the front steps. Elias was sitting in the front room with the rifle across his lap.

"How did you find that?" Tom pointed at the rifle.

"I took Rover out for a walk when I got home from church, and he went directly to the last place you'd been. Tom, killing yourself is not an answer to your problems."

Tom flopped down on the sofa. "What is the answer?"

"Cry out to God for help."

"Do you realize how hollow that sounds to me? My life went into the toilet after I came back to Bethel and started talking to God."

"I can't disagree with you."

"Then give me that rifle."

Elias didn't move. Tom could see that the old man was gripping the rifle so tightly that his knuckles were white.

"I've had more failures than successes in life," Elias said. "But I'm not going to quit because of a mountain of disappointments. What you're facing is beyond me. All I know to do is call for help."

"What did you do with the bullets?"

"Put them someplace where you won't find them. And that includes the other two boxes in the gun case."

Before Tom said anything else there was a loud knock at the front door.

"You stay here," Tom said. "I'll see who it is."

T om opened the door. Standing on the front porch was an unshaven man in his late twenties wearing overalls and a faded baseball cap.

"Barry Fortenberry," the man said. "Did I just see your car leaving Austin's Pond?"

"Yes."

"I tried to flag you down, but you didn't see me. I meant to come by the other day to give you something."

Fortenberry reached in the front pocket of his overalls and took out a brownish lump with a metal chain attached to it.

"I was fishing at the far end of the pond a week ago and saw this in the shallow water. I thought you might want to have it."

He handed the misshapen lump to Tom. It was a long rectangular wallet. Tom opened it and saw his father's fishing license.

"Where was it again?" Tom asked.

"Stuck in the mud about two feet from the edge of the water. Your daddy kept notes stuck inside where he wrote down information about how to fish different places. I saw him pull it out many times. He always put it in his back pocket, then chained it to the belt loop on his pants."

Tom pulled several sodden pieces of paper from the wallet. The writing on the pages was washed away. The steel chain hung down a foot from the edge of the wallet. Tom felt the chain.

"Would the wallet float with this chain on it?"

"Nah," Fortenberry answered. "The wallet might do pretty good, but the chain has more heft to it than you'd think. It would take it straight to the bottom."

"I appreciate you bringing this by," Tom said, looking up at the fisherman. "It means a lot that you'd go to the trouble."

"No problem. Like I told you the other day, your daddy was always good to me. It made me sad when I realized what I'd found."

Fortenberry stepped off the front porch and returned to his truck. Tom went inside the house. Elias was in the kitchen. There was no sign of the rifle.

"Where's the gun?" Tom asked.

"A safe place. And don't ask any more questions about it. Who was at the door?"

Tom put the wallet on the table. "Do you recognize that?"

"It's your daddy's."

"Right. A fisherman found it at the edge of the pond." Tom paused. "That's odd since the boat turned over at least thirty yards from the shore."

Elias shook his head. Suddenly Tom sat up straighter.

"Do you have the clothes my father was wearing when he died?"

"Uh, they gave me his things in a plastic bag at the funeral home," Elias responded. "I may have thrown the bag away, but if not, it would be in the closet in his bedroom."

Tom bolted out of his chair and down the hallway. The gun case was still on the floor beside the bed. He stepped over it and pushed back the sliding door for the closet. On the floor in the right-hand corner of the closet was a black plastic bag. Tom grabbed it and ripped it open. On top was a shirt he didn't recognize. Beneath the shirt was another, smaller bag containing shoes. In the bottom was a pair of brown crumpled pants, the durable kind preferred by sportsmen. Tom held up the pants and ran his hand along the seam that held the thick belt loops. On the left-hand side of the pants, he felt something metal. It was the ring that attached the wallet to the pants. The chain had been ripped from its connection to the belt loop, leaving a single ring that was partially pried open. He carried the pants out to the kitchen.

"Look," he said to Elias. "The chain on the wallet was broken off at the link where it connected to his pants. It took some force to do that."

"What are you saying?" Elias asked.

"There was some kind of fight."

"Fight?"

"Yes, near the shore. My father didn't drown because the boat tipped over."

Elias's face went pale. He swayed unsteadily in his chair. Tom put his hand on the old man's shoulder.

"I feel light-headed," Elias said.

Elias tried to get up but immediately slumped toward the floor. Tom tried to catch him, but he hit the floor with a thud. Elias's eyes rolled back in his head. Rover came over and nuzzled the older man's face. Tom ran over to the sink, moistened a washcloth, and put it on Elias's forehead. The old man groaned.

"Elias, can you hear me?"

Elias groaned again. Tom picked him up and carried him out of the house. As they walked down the front steps, Elias opened his eyes.

"Where?" he muttered.

"To the hospital."

Elias nodded slightly and closed his eyes. Tom put him in the passenger seat, then raced around to the driver's side. The sports car left a boiling cloud of dust as it sped down the driveway and onto the highway. Less than ten minutes later Tom squealed into the hospital parking lot. He stopped in front of the doors where the ambulances brought patients and ran inside. A pair of orderlies scrambled out, put Elias on a gurney, and rolled him inside. Tom moved his car to a regular parking spot and went inside where an intake nurse asked him a series of preliminary questions. After writing down Elias's name, she asked Tom his relationship to the old man.

"Great-nephew."

"And your name."

"Tom Crane."

The nurse's eyes narrowed, and Tom saw her glance toward the security guard on duty in the ER.

"You can wait in there," the nurse said curtly and pointed to the general waiting area.

Tom sat down. No one else seemed to be paying any attention to him. He flipped the pages of a magazine, but the words and pictures were a blur. He was worried about Elias. The old man had been under so much stress, all of it Tom's fault. He closed his eyes. A moment later he felt a tap on the shoulder.

"Mr. Crane?"

"Yes." Tom opened his eyes.

It was the same doctor who'd stitched up Tom's chin.

"We're admitting your uncle to the hospital and sending him upstairs for additional testing. He appears to have suffered a heart attack, and I want the cardiologist on call to assess the damage."

"Is he going to be all right?"

"He's stable now, and we're going to watch him closely while continuing our evaluation." The doctor cleared his throat. "How is your chin doing?"

Tom touched the slightly raised line of skin. If he'd pulled the trigger on the rifle, it would have obliterated the doctor's careful work.

"Better every day."

The doctor looked around the waiting area. Everyone in the room was staring at them. Several members of the hospital staff were eyeing Tom from across the room.

"Would you consider going someplace else to wait for news?" the doctor asked in a low voice. "Your presence is a distraction, and there's nothing you can do for your uncle. If you give me your phone number, I promise to notify you as soon as we receive the results of any tests. Once your uncle is in a room, you can stay with him."

"Nobody was paying attention to me a few minutes ago."

"Word gets out fast, and I don't want you to be bothered."

Tom gave the doctor his cell phone number. As he left the ER, he felt multiple sets of eyes boring holes in his back. He got in his car and started the motor but didn't have any place to go. He drove slowly down several residential streets, then past the courthouse, the Chickamauga Diner, and his father's office. It was starting to get dark, and the broken shards of glass on the sidewalk glittered when the headlights of his car hit them. He drove out of town, past Rocky River Church and the country club. Turning back he passed the corporate headquarters of Pelham Financial. The brick building was beautifully lit up. Inside the city limits, he passed a row of older homes. At a stop sign, he looked to the left and saw the Parker-Baldwin house. Rick Pelham's truck was parked out front.

At the sight of Arthur Pelham's residence, anger boiled up inside

Tom. He drove slowly past the historic home and glared. When he passed Rick's truck, he had a view of the sunroom on the east side of the house. Through the windows he could see Arthur and Rick sitting in chairs and talking. Tom pulled his car to the curb and turned off the headlights. He wanted to confront Arthur but knew he'd never get inside the front door if he knocked or make it past the guards lurking unseen outside the house.

Getting out of the car, he walked quietly through the yard of the adjacent lot until he was even with the Parker-Baldwin house. A hedgerow separated the two homes. He continued down the hedge, which abruptly ended and a wooden privacy fence began. There was a gate in the fence. Tom pressed the latch. The gate clicked open, and he slipped through.

He was now behind the Parker-Baldwin house. There was no sign of Arthur's security men. He could see the back of Arthur's head above a chair in the sunroom. Rick was to his father's right and had a serious expression on his face as he was gesturing with his hands. There was an exterior door to the sunroom on the back of the house. Tom crept up to the door and turned the knob. When the door clicked, he threw it open and stepped inside.

"What?" Arthur blurted out as he turned around in his chair.

"Tom," Rick said.

Arthur jumped up from his seat. "Scarboro!" he called out as he took a step toward the door for the main part of the house.

Before Arthur could take another step, Rick was on his feet blocking his father's way.

"Sit down," Rick said. "I'm glad Tom is here."

"You don't know what you're talking about," Arthur answered, trying to push Rick out of the way.

"Yes, I do," Rick replied.

Rick's strong arm continued to block his father's way. Tom stepped forward into the room.

"Move!" Arthur shouted. "This is dangerous."

"Dangerous?" Tom asked in as calm a voice as he could muster. "As dangerous as the lies you told to the grand jury about Rose Addington and me?"

"You're the one who's going to prison for embezzlement! And it was your lies that will send you there."

"As dangerous as what you did to my father and Harold Addington at Austin's Pond?" Tom continued.

"I don't know what you're talking about. Addington was a thief who dragged your father into his scheme."

"So you had both of them killed?"

"That's ridiculous. The truth will come out in court."

Arthur tried again to push past Rick, who grabbed his father with both hands and shoved him down into his chair.

"No," Rick replied. "This is what's going to come out in court."

He took a folded sheet of paper from his pocket and dropped it into Arthur's lap. The older man opened it. His eyes widened.

"Who gave you this?" he asked.

Rick, a sad expression on his face, turned to Tom. "My father and several executives at the company have been inflating the value of assets on the company's books, siphoning off money in loans they never intended to repay, and paying interest on CDs in the Barbados bank with money from new investors."

"A Ponzi scheme?" Tom asked.

"Nonsense," Arthur cut in. "Our books are audited every year."

"Did you tell the auditors the history of Biscayne Key in Saint Croix?" Rick asked.

"An island property?" Tom asked.

"And a legitimate resort development," Arthur said.

"No," Rick replied grimly. "Biscayne Key is valued on the books at $550 million, but that's because it's been sold five times in the past ten years with each sale to a Pelham-controlled shell company that inflated the purchase price. That property isn't worth more than the $50 million originally paid for it. But based on the inflated value, you've borrowed $350 million against it. Of course, the loan isn't in your name. What company is it? Global Resources?"

Arthur's face went pale.

"And that's not all." Rick jerked the sheet from Arthur's fingers and handed it to Tom. "It's only one of dozens of similar deals."

Tom glanced down at the paper that was a blur of names, dates, and numbers with a lot of zeros.

"You would destroy your own family?" Arthur asked numbly.

"No." Rick shook his head. "You're the one who's destroyed this family."

Arthur suddenly jumped out of the chair and bolted for the exit. Rick stuck out his arm, but the older man got past him and banged into the door leading from the sunroom to the main part of the house. He jerked open the door.

"Scarboro!" Arthur called out.

Rick grabbed Arthur and pulled him back into the room. "We're not finished yet."

Seconds later a large man in dark pants and a white golf shirt burst into the room.

"It's Crane," Arthur said, pointing at Tom.

Scarboro stepped toward Tom. When he did, Rick hit him in the side of the head with his fist. The blow knocked the security guard off balance. Scarboro turned toward Rick, who punched him directly in the nose. Blood spurted out as the guard stumbled backward.

"Stop it!" Arthur yelled, stepping between Rick and Scarboro.

Scarboro reached behind his back, and Tom saw he had a gun tucked in his pants. Tom launched himself across the room and tackled the security guard from behind. The gun hit the floor and slid toward Arthur. Rick grabbed a metal lamp and hit Scarboro in the back of the head. The man went limp. Arthur picked up the gun and pointed it at Tom. Rick took a step toward his father, who then aimed the gun at him.

"Sit down," Arthur said to Rick. "We can straighten out our misunderstanding later."

Rick didn't answer but stepped sideways so he was standing between Arthur and Tom.

"Move!" Arthur commanded.

Rick took a step closer to his father. "Are you going to shoot me?"

"Out of the way!"

Rick took another step. Tom could see Arthur's hand was shaking slightly. The old man put both hands on the pistol and raised it so it was chest high. Tom watched Arthur's hand tense as he squeezed the trigger.

"No!" Tom cried out.

Rick calmly stepped forward and snatched the pistol from Arthur's hand. He held the gun up in Arthur's face. "You would have shot me?"

Arthur, his shoulders slumped, didn't respond.

"But you couldn't, because the safety was on." Rick fingered a small lever on the side of the pistol. "I guess what I've learned about guns turned out to be important."

He turned to Tom. "I think we should call the police. And first thing in the morning I'll be talking to an investigator who works for the Securities and Exchange Commission. I've been cooperating with a government investigation of the company for over a year. My father and the other members of the board of directors of Pelham Financial ignored me, but I don't want to be held responsible for something I didn't do. You know what that feels like."

"No one will believe you," Arthur spit out.

"You're wrong," Rick replied.

He pointed at Scarboro's body on the floor. The security guard moved slightly and groaned.

"The other night Tiffany heard you in the barn talking with Scarboro and Crusan about killing Tom's father and Harold Addington."

Arthur opened his mouth, then closed it without saying anything. Rick took out his cell phone and dialed 911.

THIRY-FOUR

Noah Keller spent over three hours at the Parker-Baldwin house. At first it looked like Tom was going directly back to jail, but after separately interviewing the four men who'd been in the sunroom, Keller announced the investigation would continue the following day when Charlie Williams returned from an out-of-town trip.

"I want something done about this tonight," Arthur demanded. "Crane broke in here and—"

"That's in my notes, Mr. Pelham," Keller responded. "In the meantime, I'm telling all of you to stay in the Bethel area until after DA Williams contacts you tomorrow."

"I have an important meeting in New York at 10:00 a.m.," Arthur replied. "There's no reason for me to stay."

"Sir, your meeting will have to be rescheduled. I'm going to call the airport and tell them not to allow your plane to take off, and order a couple of deputies to remain on duty outside the house for the rest of the night. They will also make sure your son and Mr. Crane don't come back. I don't know who acted in self-defense here, but I'm not going to let anything else happen tonight."

"Detective, I hope you realize the gravity of your actions," Arthur sputtered.

"That's exactly what I'm trying to do. Otherwise, I'd take all of you to the jail for the night."

Arthur's face flushed again. Tom thought about the isolation cell.

"May I leave now?" Tom asked the detective.

"Only if you agree not to leave Etowah County."

"Yes."

Tom and Rick walked out of the house together. It was much colder. Tom rubbed his hands together. "Did Tiffany know you were coming here tonight?" he asked.

"Yes, there are no secrets between us."

Tom glanced sideways, but Rick was facing forward. They reached Rick's truck. A sheriff's department's car was parked behind it.

"I'm sorry about all this," Rick said, shaking his head. "That's a weak thing to say, but it's all I've got."

"You did more than apologize." Tom tilted his head toward the house. "You saved my life as much as I did Hal Millsap's when I broke off the limb that was holding him underwater."

"We'll see about that." Rick got in his truck, started the engine, and lowered the window. "I hope Elias gets better. Let me know."

Rick pulled forward and drove slowly down the street. Tom watched the taillights of the truck until he turned a corner. The pool of sorrow caused by Arthur Pelham's sin would continue to grow. Tom and the Addington family had suffered the ultimate loss. Rick, even though he was cooperating with the government, would receive scars of shame and disgrace that would never go away. And if Pelham Financial failed, the impact would be felt by virtually every family in Bethel. Life was complicated.

Tom returned to the hospital. It seemed like he'd been gone for days, not hours. At the front desk, he learned that Elias was in an ICU room on the second floor. Tom went upstairs to the waiting area and asked about Elias's condition. The face of the woman on duty hardened when Tom identified himself.

"Just a minute," she said curtly.

Tom lingered by the desk, but the woman motioned for him to sit down. He watched as she made a couple of phone calls, all the time keeping a close eye on him. She put down the phone and called him forward.

"Dr. Thomas, the cardiologist, is at the nurse's station. He'll see you now."

The ICU at Pelham General Hospital was laid out like a donut with the nurse's station in the middle. Dr. Ken Thomas, a middle-aged physician with salt-and-pepper hair, was flipping through a medical chart.

Tom introduced himself. "We met a few years ago at a benefit golf tournament at the country club."

"Right," the doctor replied without emotion. "Your uncle has been asking for you."

"How is he?"

"He's suffered a mild heart attack that doesn't appear to have caused serious damage. Of course, at his age, something like this can become critical very quickly."

"May I see him?"

"Yes," the doctor said and pointed to a room behind him. "He's in there. Don't stay more than five minutes."

Tom went into the room. Elias was lying on the bed with an IV in his arm and several wires that snaked their way to monitoring devices. His eyes were closed. Tom approached the bed. The old man looked frail and weak. If he was asleep it would be better to let him rest. As he watched Elias breathe slowly but regularly, Tom had a sense the old man's work behind the scenes in his study played a key part in Tom's vindication. Gratitude welled up in his heart.

"Thank you," he said softly.

"You're welcome," Elias replied, his eyes still closed.

Startled, Tom waited for the old man to continue, but Elias didn't stir. Tom slipped from the room.

"Any idea how long he'll be here?" he asked the doctor.

"Several days at least."

Tom left the hospital. Now that he knew Elias was stable, all he could think about was getting to Rose. Returning to the jail was out of the question. It was too late, and Rose had made it clear to the jail personnel that Tom wasn't her "barrister." There was nothing to do but wait.

As he turned into the driveway leading to Elias's house, Tom felt a sense of foreboding. The old house was dark. He parked beneath the large oak tree and turned off the lights of the car so his eyes could adjust to the shadows.

As long as Arthur Pelham was free, Tom felt vulnerable. He got out and slowly walked around the outside of the house. Seeing nothing out of the ordinary, he climbed the steps. He hadn't locked the door behind him when he carried Elias to the car. He turned the knob and pushed the door open. The house was quiet as only an isolated rural home can be. He squinted slightly as he stepped into the front room.

Suddenly, something crashed to the floor. Tom jumped back and threw up his hands to fend off an attacker. Hearing a moan, he turned on the overhead light and saw Rover lying on the floor with an electric cord wrapped around his right-rear leg and a shattered ceramic lamp behind him. The dog gave Tom his most forlorn look. Tom knelt down and unwrapped the cord.

"How did you get tangled up in that?" he asked.

Rover's tongue was hanging out the side of his mouth as he panted. Once free, he got up and shook himself.

"Is anybody here that shouldn't be?" Tom asked.

Rover trotted into the kitchen. Tom followed and found the dog pawing his empty water dish. Tom filled the dish with fresh water from the sink and set it on the floor. Rover buried his nose in the water and lapped noisily. Tom went through the rest of the house, making sure it really was deserted, then locked and bolted the front door. Taking off his shoes but not getting undressed, he propped up in bed and stared into the darkness. Every sense was on high alert.

———

The next thing he knew, Tom opened his eyes as the sun peeked through a gap in the window curtain. The previous night's fears had fled. Tom swung his feet over the edge of the bed. Rover was lying on his side in his customary spot. Tom stretched his arms over his head and checked the clock. It was thirty minutes later than he usually got up. Physical and emotional exhaustion had taken their toll.

While the coffee brewed, Tom cleaned up the mess from the broken lamp. He was caught between hope and apprehension. He wanted to believe that events set in motion the previous night would clear his name, but like a check in the mail, he couldn't be sure until the funds hit his account. Thinking about that analogy brought an ironic smile to his face.

A woman who knew Elias had brought over a loaf of home-made bread that made the store-bought variety seem as tasteless as cardboard. Tom was finishing his second piece of toast made from the slightly nutty loaf when he heard a knock on the door. Through the window he could see a sheriff's department's car parked in the front yard. His heart sank.

Charlie Williams and Noah Keller were standing on the front porch. The DA was wearing an open-collared shirt and casual pants. Keller had on the same clothes from the previous night. Tom cracked open the door.

"Can we come in?" Williams asked. "We have some questions for you."

Tom sighed. "Do you want any coffee?"

"I've had too many cups of coffee already," Williams replied.

Williams and Keller sat on the sofa. Tom sat in Elias's chair.

"Sorry to hear about Elias," Williams began. "What happened?"

"He collapsed when I told him my father's death may not have been an accident."

Williams and Keller exchanged a look.

"It's more than a probability," Keller said. "Mitt Crusan, one of the men on Arthur Pelham's security detail, came in last night and implicated Mr. Pelham and Jeff Scarboro in the deaths of your father and Harold Addington. That, along with a statement from Tiffany Pelham, justifies opening a formal investigation."

"You talked to Tiffany?"

"At 2:00 a.m. She partially confirmed Crusan's story."

"What details did Crusan give?"

"That's part of an ongoing investigation—" Keller responded.

"But in my opinion you're entitled to know part of it," Williams interrupted. "Arthur Pelham, his two security guards, your father, and Harold Addington were at Austin's Pond. Your father tried to leave. He and Arthur tussled briefly, and Arthur pushed him into the water. According to Crusan, Arthur then ordered Scarboro to hold your father underwater until he drowned."

"Why was my father there at all?" Tom asked numbly.

"Crusan claims Addington brought him on the pretext of fishing but knew there was going to be a meeting with Arthur. After your father was killed, Arthur and Addington argued, and Scarboro strangled Addington. Then they made the deaths look like a boating accident."

"Addington may have been part of the embezzlement scheme after all?" Tom asked.

"Crusan's statement is just the beginning. He's talking to try to save himself. For all we know, he could have done what he claims Scarboro did. Before it's over, they may all be pointing fingers at one another."

"What about the $250,000 check?"

"My guess, it was either a forgery by Arthur or something Addington did. There may have been two break-ins at your father's office: one shortly after his death, the other while you were in jail."

"That's why the Addington folder was empty."

"Yes, and the check could have been stolen at that time. But that's speculation." Williams checked his watch. "I talked with an investigator at the Securities and Exchange Commission in Washington during the drive to see you. He confirmed what Rick Pelham told Noah last night. Arthur has been the target of a federal investigation for over two years."

Tom sat back in the chair. "What are you going to do about the charges against me?"

"Nothing for now," Williams replied.

"What?" Tom sat upright.

"You heard me," Williams answered. "I shared the information about your father out of respect for him, but prosecutorial discretion is based on careful deliberation. Right now, the investigation is expanding."

"What about Rose?"

"There are serious questions about her father but less about her. I'm going to recommend that the magistrate set a bond for Ms. Addington with two conditions: surrender of her passport and an agreement not to leave Etowah County while charges are still pending."

"What sort of bond? Not a million dollars?"

"No, I was considering $100,000. Her mother has enough property in the county to make that."

"That's not exactly what I wanted to hear."

"It's different from what the two of you were facing yesterday."

"What about Arthur's passport?" Tom asked. "Are you going to confiscate it and make him stay in Etowah County?"

"That will be up to me," Williams said.

"Will you keep me informed?"

"Why do you think I drove out here at this time of the day with all that's going on?"

"Yes, and I appreciate it. When will Rose know she can post bond and get out?"

"Sometime this morning."

The two men left. Tom finished a second cup of coffee, then showered and put on clean clothes. He considered staying at home, but feeling restless he decided to go into town. When he arrived at the office there were still broken shards of glass on the sidewalk where he'd shattered the door. He was cleaning up the glass when Bernice arrived. She got out of the car with tears streaming down her face.

"I can't believe this is happening!" she wailed. She came over and threw her arms around Tom's neck. "I've not been able to sleep since Hal Millsap called me."

Tom held her until she calmed down. "Come inside," he said. "There are good things that you don't know about."

"Good things?" Bernice wiped her eyes. "Tell me now."

"I will, I will."

Tom held the door open.

"What happened to the door?" Bernice asked as if suddenly noticing it.

"I didn't have a key and had to get in," Tom replied. "Who should we get to fix it?"

"I don't know. And I can't believe you're thinking about that at a time like this."

Tom took Bernice into his father's office and brought her up to date. "And I'm sorry now that I didn't talk to you sooner," he said. "You have a good sense about people, except for Rose Addington."

"I was suspicious because I didn't know her."

"There's something else you should know," Tom said, taking a deep breath. "And it's very bad."

"What?" The look of alarm returned to Bernice's face.

"I believe my father was murdered."

Bernice's face grew pale, then tears started to stream down her face. She buried her face in her hands. Seeing Bernice cry made tears come to Tom's eyes.

"Your daddy was such a good man," Bernice managed through her sobs. "I can't believe someone would want to hurt him."

Tears continued to roll down both their cheeks. Tom looked around the office with blurred vision. Every inch of the space spoke of his father's presence. It was almost more than his heart could bear.

He'd grieved at Austin's Pond for his mother. He mourned the loss of his father sitting in John Crane's chair.

"Do you know what happened?" Bernice asked after several minutes passed.

"Arthur Pelham was involved." Tom cleared his throat. "I'm sure more details will come out, but it just hurts that he's gone."

Bernice, her eyes red and swollen, nodded.

"You should go home," Tom said.

"I came in to protect you. I didn't know what you'd face if you were here."

Another wave of sorrow washed over both of them. Tom got up and wiped his eyes.

"This is too painful. I'm going to the lumberyard and buy a piece of plywood to cover the hole in the door."

Bernice nodded. "I need a few minutes alone in here."

Tom drove to a local building supply store and bought a piece of plywood that he screwed onto the door frame of the office. He wrote "Office Closed" on a sheet of paper and taped it to the wood. Working with his hands helped him not feel the pain in his heart. When he finished, Bernice was sitting at her desk. She had a slight smile on her face.

"You know," she said, "while you were boarding up the door, I remembered something your daddy gave me after your mama died."

She opened the top drawer of her desk, took out a slip of paper, and handed it to Tom. In now-faded handwriting, his father had written:

> The righteous perish, and no one ponders it in his heart; devout men are taken away, and no one understands that the righteous are taken away to be spared from evil. Those who walk uprightly enter into peace; they find rest as they lie in death. (Isaiah 57:1–2)

Tom looked up. Bernice spoke. "I was sitting here thinking that your mama and daddy are at rest, forever together in a place without evil or pain. Someday we'll be with them. And none of our memories will hurt us again."

Tom closed his eyes. The same presence he'd experienced in his father's office enveloped him standing in the reception room. The air smelled fresher. His heart felt lighter.

"This helps," Tom said, handing the slip of paper back to Bernice.

"Good. It made me feel close to your daddy even though he's gone."

A banging on the door interrupted the moment.

An unfamiliar voice called out, "Is anybody in there?"

"Don't answer it," Bernice whispered.

"I'm looking for Tom Crane."

"Who is it?" Tom asked.

"Christopher Olney. I work for the Securities and Exchange Commission."

Tom looked at Bernice and shrugged. "I'd better let him in. We're not in heaven with my parents yet."

Tom opened the door. Olney looked about the same age as Tom. He was wearing a suit and tie and carried a black briefcase in his hand.

"I'm Tom Crane."

Olney stepped forward and extended his hand. "Rick Pelham gave me your address and said I might find you here. I'm with the investigative unit. Is there someplace we can talk privately?"

"In there," Tom said and stepped aside so Olney could enter the office. Tom turned to Bernice. "No interruptions, please."

"Any exceptions?"

Tom thought for a moment. "Rose Addington."

Tom closed the door and offered Olney a seat.

"I'll get right to it," Olney said. "This morning FBI and SEC agents are raiding the offices of Pelham Financial in New York, Boston, Los Angeles, Washington, DC, and here in Bethel. We're going to seize paper and electronic records and conduct preliminary interviews with employees willing to make statements. All the assets of the company have been frozen by order of Susan Fielder, a federal judge in the Southern District of New York. Within the next few days, she'll appoint a receiver to oversee the administration and distribution of the Pelham assets. Parallel action is being taken by the authorities in the UK."

Tom thought about the people at the local Pelham office. "What about Arthur Pelham and Owen Harrelson?"

"They're currently designated as 'persons of interest,' but that's a preliminary step to formal indictment of those implicated by the ongoing investigation."

"And me?" Tom asked.

"You're also a person of interest."

Tom swallowed. So far, nobody viewed him as a gullible-but-innocent by-product of a wide-ranging embezzlement scheme carried out by others. "I'm sorry to hear that."

"My bosses would like to review the sequence of events leading up to your arrest by the local authorities, and I'm here to ask if you'll voluntarily cooperate with that investigation."

"What do you mean by cooperate?"

"It's simple. Tell us what you know and show us what you have. It's likely duplicative of what we already know; however, we want to be thorough."

"Already know? Do you mean you were watching me this whole time?"

"We were aware of the transfer of money by Addington to a

designated trust account administered by your father. The uncertainty lay in whether your father and Addington were low-level participants in the embezzlement scheme or had another agenda. That couldn't be determined prior to their deaths."

"Were you aware they were murdered?"

"Not until someone from our office talked to Rick Pelham early this morning. That obviously lies outside our jurisdiction and doesn't answer the questions we have about the financial transactions."

The sterile, clinical way in which Olney discussed the deaths of Tom's father and Harold Addington hurt. Tom looked away for a moment. "What specifically do you want from me?" he asked with a sigh.

"Tell me what happened and why you acted as you did. Until you transferred the money from the designated trust account to the bank in Barbados, you weren't under suspicion for illegal activity."

"But now I am?"

Olney tilted his head to the side. "That's for you to explain, if you're willing to. As a lawyer, you know that anything you say to me can, and will, be used against you if criminal charges are filed."

Tom's efforts to lay everything on the table for Charlie Williams hadn't ended well. He wondered if he had a better chance with Olney. The SEC investigator sat waiting for a response. Olney was just doing his job. Eventually Tom's story was going to come out. He offered a silent prayer for guidance, then spoke.

"I can't corroborate some of what happened because my laptop and hard copies of documents were stolen two days ago from this office, but I'll verbally tell you what happened."

"I understand."

390

Olney placed his briefcase in his lap and clicked it open. He took out a sheet of paper and handed it to Tom. "This is a waiver of your right to remain silent."

Tom didn't need to read the document to know what it said, but he did anyway. After Tom signed it, Olney took out a digital recorder. "May I record our conversation?"

Tom opened the top drawer of the desk and took out a smaller unit. "Only if I can."

It was the investigator's turn to hesitate. "Agreed," he said. "Let's get to it."

Two hours later Olney reached up and turned off his recorder.

"Are you finished?" Tom asked.

"Yes, that's all." Olney waited while Tom turned off his recorder. "Based on our interview, it will be my recommendation that you be included in our list of potential witnesses. And not be indicted unless something else turns up."

Tom felt relief but no joy. "What about Rose Addington?"

"She never was a direct target of our investigation. Her father's role remains ambiguous. There are indications he may have intended to participate in the scheme but no evidence that he was successful."

"You don't believe he was a decoy or fall guy being set up by Pelham, Harrelson, and Nettles?"

"That's your theory, which is new to us. I'll include it in my report."

"Are you going to talk to Rose Addington or her mother? They've been through so much, and I don't want them to face renewed accusations against Harold."

"That's not my call. I was sent here to meet with you."

Tom wanted to protect Rose but realized he had no control over what happened.

"Will you be in touch with our local DA? That should have an impact on the state charges against Rose and me."

"He'll be briefed within the next couple of days by an attorney from the Department of Justice."

Olney stood up, signaling an end to the meeting. "And I'm sorry about your father," the agent said. "Usually these types of scams don't involve murder. If that happened here, I hope justice is done."

Tom opened the door for the investigator. Bernice was in the lobby talking to a man holding a microphone in front of her face. A woman stood behind the man with a TV camera on her shoulder.

"There he is," the man said, suddenly ignoring Bernice. The camera turned toward Tom. "Mr. Crane, what do you think about the FBI action taken against Pelham Financial this morning?"

"He knows more about it than I do," Tom said, motioning toward Olney.

The reporter ignored the agent.

"Is it true there was a fight at Arthur Pelham's home last night when you threatened to expose his embezzlement?"

"I'm not going to comment on that," Tom said.

"Does this mean the criminal charges against you and Ms. Addington are going to be dismissed?" the reporter persisted.

"That will be decided by Mr. Williams, the district attorney, or Judge Nathan Caldwell, the superior court judge."

Tom stepped back into the office and closed the door before the reporter launched another question. He sat down and called ICU at the hospital. Once he reached the proper person, the woman immediately transferred him to the nurse's station.

"Your uncle is stable and resting," the nurse on duty informed him. "Dr. Thomas has already been by to see him this morning and will be back this afternoon."

"When should I be there if I want to talk to the doctor?"

"Around 4:00 p.m."

"Is my uncle conscious?"

"Yes, he was watching the news on TV earlier."

"About Pelham Financial?"

"Yes, they ran a live feed from the headquarters for half an hour. Did you know this was going to happen?"

Tom didn't respond. "Thanks for the update on my uncle."

It was going to be impossible to hide from scrutiny, but Tom wanted to stay as far from the spotlight as possible. He walked quietly over to the door and listened. Not hearing anything, he opened it. Bernice was sitting at her desk. The reception room was empty.

"I'm not answering the phone," Bernice said as she brushed back a stray strand of hair. "Everything is going to the answering machine. And I didn't really want to talk to that reporter, but he was nice enough, very polite when he asked to come in. He mostly wanted to know about you."

"What did you tell him?"

"Nothing much, just that I'd known you and your daddy for years and what a wonderful man he was and how smart you are."

"I haven't felt very smart."

"Don't be too hard on yourself." Bernice sighed. "But I'd like to go home. I'm completely drained."

"Sure," Tom said.

Shortly after Bernice left, Tom's cell phone rang, and he took it from his pocket. It was Rose Addington.

"Where are you?" he asked before Rose could say anything.

"At home with my mum. And you?"

"Leaving my father's office. When did you get out of jail?"

"Just before noon. I've been home for a couple of hours."

"When can I see you?"

"Come now if you'd like. That's why I phoned. Have you been watching the news reports?"

"No."

"It's a bit hard to take it all in."

"I'm on my way."

As he drove through town, Tom saw a TV truck set up near the courthouse. A camera crew was shooting a street scene near the Chickamauga Diner, probably as background about Bethel.

Turning onto Rose's street, Tom saw two unfamiliar cars parked in front of the Addington residence. When Tom drove past and slowed down, a man in one of the cars took his picture. Three other people got out of the other car when he pulled up to the Addington house.

"Will you answer a few questions?" a blond-haired woman called out.

Tom held up his hand and shook his head. He rang the front doorbell. A moment later he saw Rose peeking through the leaded-glass sidelight.

"Come in," she said, opening the door just far enough to let him inside.

"Did you talk to any reporters?" Tom asked, motioning toward the street.

"No. I don't know enough to answer any questions."

Tom looked down at Rose, his face serious. "Will you ever be able to forgive me for dragging you into this?" he asked.

"I don't think I have a choice."

"I mean in your heart." Tom put his hand to his chest.

Rose closed her eyes for a moment. "Yes, that's already happened. Come in and sit down."

"Where's your mother?"

"Resting upstairs. As soon as I can, I'm going to get her away from Bethel. My sister is on her way and should be here tomorrow. Come into the kitchen. I have a teapot on."

A copper kettle was rattling on the stove. Tom sat at the kitchen table while Rose poured two cups of tea.

"How are you doing?" Tom asked when she placed the tea in front of him.

"Still in shock. Do you have any idea what's going to happen next?"

"How much do you know?"

"Nothing except what I've heard on the news."

As Tom talked, he inwardly debated whether to let Rose know that her father was still under suspicion. He paused when he reached the part about Williams and Keller coming to Elias's house.

"What?" Rose asked. "Are you going to edit what you tell me?"

"No," Tom said, making up his mind. "I'm never going to do that again."

Rose took the news about her father without breaking down.

"I don't buy that part of Crusan's story about your papa luring my father to the pond and believe the federal investigation will clear him of any financial wrongdoing," Tom said. "In the end—"

"The truth may or may not come out," Rose cut in. "I'm convinced Papa was trying to do the right thing. I just wish"—a tear rolled down her cheek and she wiped it away—"none of this had happened."

Rose sipped her tea. When she lowered her cup, Tom saw another tear roll down her cheek. This one she left alone. Rose looked at him and smiled. "But in the midst of all this tragedy, God touched your heart, didn't he?"

"Yes," Tom answered.

"Evil's opportunity will end. But what God has done in your life will last forever."

They finished the tea, then did something Tom had never done with a woman. They held hands and prayed. Rose went first, and as she spoke, Tom felt the slime of the past weeks fall away from his spirit. Rose's confident words emboldened him, and he prayed for her and her family without holding anything back.

When they finished, their hardships no longer reigned supreme.

epilogue

The brown colors of a north Georgia winter have a unique
beauty when bare trees stand like sentinels along the
ridges and the views from the hilltops are unrestricted
by green leaves. The crisp clear days are a time for vision to expand.
Sound carries farther. The cool air makes every sense keener.

When Tom got up to make Sunday morning coffee, a thick frost
covered the broken soybean stalks in the fields near Elias's house.
By afternoon, the sun had banished the frost, but the water in the
creek that flowed by Rocky River Church hadn't forgotten the chill
of night.

Tom stood near the creek with Rev. Lane Conner beside him. A
small crowd of people watched from the bank. Elias, a pair of stents
helping the blood flow more easily through his heart, leaned on a
cane. Next to him stood Bernice and her husband, Carl. Bernice
already had a tissue in her hand. When Tom told Bernice he'd
decided to stay in Bethel and reopen his father's office, her eyes lit
up, and she declared the news made her feel ten years younger.

Behind Bernice, Tom saw Judge Nathan Caldwell, Lamar
Sponcler, Charlie Williams, and a few other members of the local

legal community. Sponcler was making good on his promise to help if Tom chose to remain in Bethel. The older lawyer had referred two good cases to Tom and brought him in as associate counsel on four others. And as news of Tom's decision to stay in Etowah County spread, the phone volume at the Crane law office began picking up.

Two weeks earlier Charlie Williams confirmed that all charges against Rose and Tom had been dropped. The DA had recently asked the local grand jury to indict Arthur Pelham and Owen Harrelson on state criminal charges. The men, along with four other Pelham executives, had already been arrested by federal authorities. George Nettles was in custody in Britain.

Next to Williams were Reverend England and Sister Tamara from the Ebenezer Church. Their enthusiastic faces lit up the crowd. Tom and Reverend England were going to have lunch the following week. He wanted to talk to Tom about another Christian mediation opportunity.

Standing off by themselves were Rick and Tiffany Pelham. Tiffany looked sad but wiser. The wrath of the local community against Arthur was great, and even though Rick hadn't done anything wrong, his last name was an irritant to some. As Tom watched, Hal Millsap moved over and put his hand on Rick's shoulder. Hal had finally admitted to Tom that Rick put up $90,000 of the $100,000 bond fee and would have paid it all except Hal insisted others wanted to play a part as well. Because of his cooperation with the authorities, Rick would be able to keep enough of his property to grow a few trees; Tiffany could keep a couple of horses. And they would have a chance to resurrect their marriage.

Hal, like everyone else who worked for Pelham Financial, lost his job, but he'd received an offer from a small company in Chattanooga. It was less money than he made at Pelham, but the owner liked to give away turkeys to needy families at Thanksgiving and shared Hal's fondness for chewing tobacco.

Tom's eyes returned to the front of the group. He looked at Rose. Each day brought them closer together. There was a small smile on her face, and the joy within her exploded with light that reflected the glory of God himself.

Lane Conner held up his hand to get everyone's attention.

"Tom would like to say a few words before we go into the water."

Speaking before people wasn't one of Tom's phobias, but more than any other time in his life, he wanted to say the right thing. He'd rehearsed a brief speech and received Elias's blessing, but the beginning line of his prepared message suddenly left his mind.

And he thought about his mother and father.

Tears stung the corners of Tom's eyes. He pressed his lips together to keep them from trembling. He wiped away the tears with the back of his hand and cleared his throat. His voice shook slightly as he spoke.

"I just thought about how happy my parents would be to see this day," he said. "Elias tells me they may get to watch from heaven. If that's true, I want to welcome and thank them for all the good things they poured into my life."

Bernice had tissues pressed against both eyes.

"And I want to thank all of you," Tom said, his voice getting stronger. "I'm learning that God placed me in this world, not so other people can serve me, but so I can serve them. Only when we focus our attention on others can we become who we're intended to be ourselves. Many of you did that for me, and I want to follow in your footsteps."

Tom opened the Bible. "The other day I was taking my dog Rover for a walk in the fields near the house. I'd brought a Bible along and sat down on a tree stump to read for a few minutes. Turning to Jeremiah 6:16, I read this: 'Stand at the crossroads and look; ask for the ancient paths, ask where the good way is, and walk in it, and you will find rest for your souls.'"

Tom closed the book and looked up. "That's what's happened to me. I came to Bethel to shut down my father's law practice as fast as possible so I could return to Atlanta. Instead, I found myself at a crossroads, with a chance to encounter Jesus Christ. At that crossroads, I took the ancient path. I've stumbled some, but I've found rest for my soul."

Tom paused to make eye contact with as many people as he could. Every fiber in his being especially wanted to reach out to Rick and Tiffany. Rick's face was serious; Tiffany was teary-eyed.

"If you're at a crossroads, will you consider the ancient path?" he asked. "It's an opportunity not to be wasted or ignored. Only on that path will you find forgiveness and freedom."

Tom turned to Lane Conner and nodded. The minister led him into the cold water. They turned around when it was waist deep. Conner lifted his hand in the air. "Joshua Thomas Crane, I baptize you in the name of the Father, Son, and Holy Spirit."

The minister laid him back in the water. Tom came up sputtering. Sister Tamara shouted. Conner gave Tom a soggy hug and patted him on the back. The two men waded out of the water. Rose, her face still beaming, handed Tom a towel. He kissed her on the cheek, then leaned over and hugged Elias.

"Don't hug me, Tom!" Hal called out. "I'm afraid of cold water!"

At the end of a brief reception in the church fellowship hall, Hal offered to give Elias a ride home from the church.

"I want to ask him a few questions," Hal said. "And he doesn't scare me as much as you do."

Tom chuckled. "That's because you don't know him yet."

After everyone left, Tom and Rose stood in front of the church beside his car. They faced each other. Tom took both her hands in his. "This was a good day, wasn't it?" Tom asked.

"Yes."

"And we've had a wonderful time together while confined to Etowah County by order of Judge Caldwell."

"Yes, we have," she said softly.

"And we'd like to continue to spend a lot of time together in the future."

"Absolutely."

"Would you say we're at a crossroads in our relationship?"

"Yes."

Without a doubt, Rose Addington was the most beautiful woman, inside and out, he'd ever met. Tom leaned over and their lips met. When they parted, Tom looked down at Rose and smiled. "Are you going to say yes to any question I ask?"

Rose, her eyes sparkling, looked deep into his. "You'll find out on the journey we take together."

reading group guide

1. After Tom loses his job and his girlfriend at the beginning of the book, Elias responds to Tom with, "God is good." What did you think of Tom's response? Have you ever experienced a huge, unexpected change in your life, and someone spoke similar words to you? How did that make you feel? Encouraged? Angry? Confused?

2. Though for years Tom held himself back from truly grieving his mother's death, upon returning home he is overcome with emotion while visiting Austin's Pond. Why do you think Tom held those tears back for so long? How did his mother's death forever affect Tom and his father's relationship? Have you ever stored up grieving and then had it triggered by an unrelated incident?

3. Why do you think Elias wanted Tom to read the Bible story of Balaam and his donkey?

4. Elias points out that Tom's first name is Joshua, which means "God rescues" or "Jehovah is salvation." How does the meaning of Tom's name enter into his story?

5. Many people in Bethel urge Tom to stay and continue his father's work. What do you think Tom believes about the kind of man his father was? About the kind of attorney he was? Do you think he considers himself a chip off the old block?

6. Elias is a man of prayer and intercession. Have you ever known someone who was a prayer warrior? How has his or her intercession affected your life and the lives of others?

7. Psalm 78:72 says, "So he shepherded them according to the integrity of his heart, and guided them by the skillfulness of his hands." Why do you think this was one of John Crane's favorite verses? How did reading this verse open Tom's eyes and heart?

8. Rose is convinced that there are "thin places" in this world—physical places where one can better hear from God. Do you believe in thin places? Have you ever experienced a thin place?

9. Do you agree with Elias that Christians can sometimes have "divided hearts"—that they can know the love of God, yet still live with dark secrets and deceptions? Elias says that "people are like houses. Most of the rooms may be filled with light, but there can still be a dark corner." Which characters fit this description? Have you experienced this duality in your own heart? Do we sometimes compartmentalize our lives so that we can legitimize our vices?

10. Have you, like Tom, ever felt that you were caught in a situation where you weren't sure who, if anyone, you could trust? What did you do? Where did you turn?

11. After his arrest, Tom's world crashes down on him, and he feels that he has nowhere to turn. He doesn't trust that God

can resolve his situation, and he is ready to take his own life. How can desperation skew our perceptions of our situations? How does God step in and assure Tom that he is present and in control?

12. What do you think about the verse John Crane wrote down after his wife's death: "The righteous perish, and no one ponders it in his heart; devout men are taken away, and no one understands that the righteous are taken away to be spared from evil. Those who walk uprightly enter into peace; they find rest as they lie in death" (Isaiah 57:1-2). Have you lost someone important in your world? How does this verse affect the way you feel about his or her passing?

13. At his baptism Tom looks around at his friends and supporters and says, "I'm learning that God placed me in this world, not so other people can serve me, but so I can serve them. Only when we focus our attention on others can we become who we're intended to be ourselves." What value do you place on community? Do you serve, and allow yourself to be served by, others who care about you?

14. In the epilogue, Tom claims the verse Jeremiah 6:16: "Stand at the crossroads and look; ask for the ancient paths, ask where the good way is, and walk in it, and you will find rest for your souls." How does the wisdom of this verse affect Tom's decisions about moving forward with his life? Are you at a crossroads in your life? How does this verse speak to you?

acknowledgments

Many thanks to those who advised and inspired me. My wife, Kathy. Allen Arnold, Natalie Hanemann, and Deborah Wiseman, my publishing partners at Thomas Nelson. And my sister, Annette Davis.

A poignant tale of
innocence and courage
in the tradition of
Huckleberry Finn and
To Kill a Mockingbird.
Experience *Jimmy,*
a story that will leave you
forever changed.

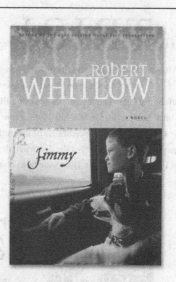

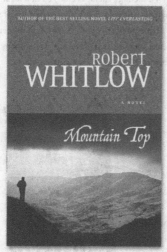

Can he trust his client's
dreams and
visions—even if
they threaten to destroy
his future?

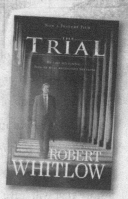
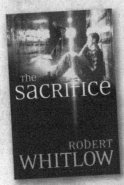

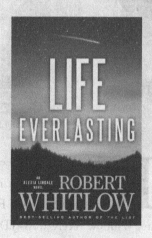

Photo by Stephen Dey

Robert Whitlow is the best-selling author of legal dramas set in the South and winner of the prestigious Christy Award for Contemporary Fiction. A Furman University graduate, Whitlow received his J.D. with honors from the University of Georgia School of Law where he served on the staff of the Georgia Law Review. A practicing attorney, Whitlow and his wife, Kathy, have four adult children. They make their home in North Carolina.

Mount Laurel Library
100 Walt Whitman Avenue
Mount Laurel, NJ 08054-9539
856-234-7319
www.mountlaurellibrary.org

CPSIA information can be obtained
at www.ICGtesting.com
Printed in the USA
LVHW040041080222
710482LV00015B/761

9 781595 544513